CASCADIA FALLEN

TAHOMA'S HAMMER

AUSTIN CHAMBERS

COPYRIGHT

CASCADIA FALLEN: TAHOMA'S HAMMER

EDITOR – Emily Rollen

COVER – Fusion Creative Works, Poulsbo, WA

ISBN – 978-1-7339593-0-8 [Soft cover]

Published by Crossed Cannons Publishing, LLC
P.O. Box 334
Seabeck, WA 98380-0334

Dedicated to my best friend Dorothy,
who has stuck by and supported me for 28 years,
despite myself.

Cascadia Fallen
Tahoma's Hammer

PROLOGUE

"Fear is a Reaction. Courage is a Decision." – Sir Winston Churchill

THE MIDDLE-AGED MAN WAS ADJUSTING THE RADIO ON THE OLDER model truck, a white Ram from the days when they were still made by Dodge. He and the morning country station DJs played a game every day. He hoped they would play country music, but they would fill the airwaves with synthesized pop music. They would also pass time with silly games and lovelorn phone-calls which always drove him to the AM stations. The fifty-two-year-old was in the middle of tuning in his favorite political talk show when he heard the siren.

He was waiting in the first spot at a red light at the east end of a major overpass. Three different flows of traffic shared the three-hundred-foot-long bridge, one direction at a time. The eastbound and westbound flows of local Highway 808 stopped at their respective ends when the southbound traffic from State Highway 5 needed to transition to that road. He was waiting patiently for his turn to go west across the bridge to the highway's southbound on-ramp. He turned the volume knob down and rolled down his driver's window. *Coming off the highway, maybe?* he thought. He scanned his windows and mirrors but couldn't see anything. The flow of traffic from the west was just starting its turn, half headed for the north-bound on-ramp and half headed east. *More drivers that think they're more important than ambulances,* he thought cynically.

Definitely from the north, he surmised as the noise grew in intensity. Suddenly an older white passenger van flew into view on the other end of the overpass as it exited the off-ramp from the north. It was trying and failing to make a desperate, much too fast left turn. The old van slid sideways, plowing its right side into an Acura and shoving that car into a Chevy pick-up. *Oooohhh, CRAP!*

Much earlier in life the man had spent twelve years in the Marines before a severe back injury had forced him out. He had plenty of trauma-care training. He was unbuckled and reaching for the handle when a white Washington State Patrol SUV came sliding into view, stopping about 170 feet in front of his truck. He saw the trooper get out and draw his pistol. He could hear orders being barked as the trooper exited the protection of his car door to approach the van.

The man finished getting out of his truck, drawing his pistol from its holster on his right hip. As fate would have it, he happened to be the manager and lead instructor at the largest gun-club on Washington State's Slaughter Peninsula. He was always armed, usually with a concealed 9mm Glock 19. He kept his position behind his truck door as he scanned the action ahead of him. He knew to stay put and let the cops do their job lest he be perceived as a threat. He could hear more sirens in the distance. His objective in that moment was to protect his fellow drivers if things went sideways.

He watched in horror as the tinted glass from the van's rear driver side window exploded in noise. *KA-KROWWW!* The trooper dropped where he stood, ambushed by an unseen enemy. The man observing had been a firearms instructor for most of his life and a *former* Marine since he was thirty. Like many people who train in the martial arts, he'd made the decision to fight not at that moment but years earlier. He was a sheepdog, and sheepdogs were wired to protect the flock—or the other sheepdogs.

Without thought, he left the safety of his truck door and started sprinting up the warm asphalt toward the action. He could see the trooper on all four limbs, trying to turn and drag himself toward his cruiser but unable to stand. A driver exited the grungy van wearing a tactical vest and balaclava-style hood. He went to the vehicle's front to look at damage, too focused on figuring out the escape plan to notice the bystander running toward him.

The man saw another tactically-clad scumbag come out from around the van holding an AK-47. Then two more. The last two had rifles slung onto their backs and were dragging very large duffle bags. The man's mind couldn't comprehend this as a real event. He felt like he was watching a movie. He saw the lead rifleman start to raise his AK at the retreating trooper's back from a distance of four feet.

The former Marine hit the brakes. At twenty-five yards, he couldn't afford to miss. He had shot practical-shooting competitions for over twenty-five years. He'd probably nailed this shot 5,000 times, but none of those shots seemed to matter anymore. He tightened his grip while leveling the sites to his eyes. Prepping the trigger to the Glock's well-known "breaking-point," he focused on the front site and squeezed, letting the shot surprise him as it exploded. *POP!* Scumbag One's head spewed blood from the near side as the 115-grain hollow-point bullet penetrated his right ear. *POP!* Just under one quarter of a second later the second round hit him in the right side of the pectoral area. It was too late. *KA-KROWWW!* Scumbag One just managed to get a shot off directly into the top of the trooper's back, above the protective plate in his vest. The trooper went limp.

The man started his combat glide, speed walking in a *heel-toe-heel-toe* fashion towards the van driver, trying to keep his muzzle from bouncing. Scumbag Two had frozen for a moment and was drawing his own pistol while trying to dive around the front of the van. *POP-POP!* The man knew he'd hit Scumbag Two in his back or butt with at least one shot but also knew that Two was still a threat. Remembering he was out in the open he sprinted once again for the trooper.

By this time Scumbags Three and Four had dropped their bags and were splitting up. Three took cover behind the trooper's engine block while Four raced for the cars piled-up west of the scene. *POP-POP-POP!* The Sheepdog threw three quick shots into the spot where the SUV's hood and fender met, not really expecting to hit Three but hoping to keep his head down. He kept his gun in his right hand as he reached the trooper. *He's a big boy,* the would-be hero realized. He wanted to drag him but knew instantly the trooper was too heavy. He flipped the trooper over and sat him up. There was blood squirting from the two pair of entry and exit wounds in his torso. Somewhere deep in his mind, the former Marine knew it was too late for the patrolman. *Gotta keep moving!*

He squatted behind the trooper, wrapping his left arm around the man's torso and standing as best as he could. He looked right just as Three was sticking his head over the cruiser's fender. The man scrambled backwards and—*POP!*—squeezed off a rapid shot toward his right that missed left of Three. *KA-KA-KA-KA-KROW!* He kept driving his legs backwards as AK rounds started to fly past him. *Dang it!* He was trying his best to force himself to breathe as the reality that he was about to die in the next minute set in. His body was so fused with adrenaline that automatic breath control had abandoned him much earlier.

He made it past the open car door unscathed. He set the trooper down behind the rear wheel. He squatted there and pulled his one spare mag out of its holder on his left hip. He performed a quick reload and slammed the partial magazine into his coat pocket. He kept scanning throughout the process, something that teaching for many years had allowed him to perfect.

Staying crouched, he decided to go around the rear of the car. Three had started to come around his side of the rear at the same moment. *POP! POP!* He threw two quick shots into his adversary's skull when it appeared behind a rifle barrel. He didn't even look at the mess as he got to it and knelt. *Damn it!* he screamed in his head as the stress mounted.

Four was actively trying to get into cars about twenty yards away, as screaming people panicked. Some drivers had the presence of mind to try backing up, but the unfortunate consequence was a further mess of smashed vehicles as other drivers were frozen in fear. The sirens were louder—he could tell from light reflections that the cavalry would be there in just a few moments. Fearing Four would shoot the lady who was refusing to open her door, he made the mistake of running out from behind his cover.

Four had been scanning towards the Sheepdog every two seconds and caught the movement of him trying to advance. Four caught the man out in the open and opened fire as he turned in that direction. The former Marine raised his pistol, firing back. He felt the heat of the sun as a 7.62 millimeter round shattered his left leg about seven inches below the kneecap. He went down to his other knee, screaming in intense pain as he did. Four had been emboldened by this and had proceeded to make the same mistake. He came out to finish off the Sheepdog, who lined up his sites. *POP! POP! POP! POP!* He performed a "stitch-pattern," hitting the scumbag in the center of his torso with the first shot. The next three shots each hit about two inches higher than the previous. Scumbag Four dropped his rifle and clutched at his chest. Blood loss caused him to pass out and fall forward a few seconds later.

He looked left to reacquire Two but couldn't see him. *He must still be behind the van.* The pain fought its way past the adrenaline, and suddenly it was the foremost thought in his mind. He looked down and was surprised by just how much blood there was. *Wow.* He was also surprised at his own nonchalant reaction. *Dude must've gotten me right in the artery...* Shock took over. Still sitting up on the unwounded knee, he rolled backwards and landed on his butt. Lightheadedness started to creep in. He set the Glock on the ground as instinct told him to put both hands on the gushing wound. *Just need to lay down...*

From the lying position, the world around him started to get surreal. A shadowy figure loomed over him. His eyes were losing focus. He could hear screaming, sirens, and commotion all over the place. The noise seemed like it was being played through a body of water. *Death? No. A deputy. Hey, I know you!*

Slaughter County Deputy Charlie Reeves was kneeling next to his friend, Phillip Edward Walker. Several other deputies and troopers had arrived as well, and they were continuing to clear the scene.

"Hang in there, Phil!" Charlie grabbed his personal tourniquet from his gun belt and applied just below Phil's left knee, trying to keep the life in his friend.

"Cha-Charlie?" Phil asked as hypovolemic shock was setting in. "I... I guess I shoulda ducked, huh?" he asked, passing out.

1

Wake Up!

THE DAY THAT THE WORLD CHANGED FOREVER STARTED LIKE ANY normal, drizzly October day in the Pacific Northwest. Phil Walker, fifty-five, had just finished taking a water jug delivery at the West Sound Sportsmen's Club, the gun club he managed. It was a Tuesday and typically gray. People who weren't from the "Pacific North-Wet" thought it rained all the time. While it *did* rain heavily —and usually slammed everyone for a month or so once or twice per year—it was normally just an annoying drizzle. That's how the day started, which was a welcome break from getting an inch per day like they had for the prior week. The cloud cover normally did a good job of keeping the temperature in the mid-forties to mid-fifties —cold for people from the south but fairly warm for anyone else.

Phil had made the usual small talk with Tony, the delivery driver, who was swapping out the normal six jugs. Tony made deliveries every other Tuesday, usually arriving around nine in the morning.

The gun range was his first stop on the day's route. Its location in the western part of Slaughter County made it an ideal starting point, allowing Tony to continue north and east into the central county from his starting point in Bartlett.

Phil liked Tony. Like himself, the big, jovial delivery driver was a veteran, though a Navy one, which the former Marine tried not to hold against him. Tony was always good for a joke and a smile. While Phil was not much of a comedian, his twelve years in the Corps had taught him the value of having comedians around. Morale was always better—as long as you could keep them working—and they were always smarter than they let on.

The ginger-haired manager had just sat down at his desk. Dakota, his Australian cattle-dog, was snoozing behind the counter after her morning run chasing Canadian geese off the rifle range. He was starting to review the roster for the class he was teaching the coming weekend, "Rifle Tactics II." He planned to double check the Range Officer schedule after that. Knowing weekday mornings were slow and he had a good vantage of incoming people, he was just about to drop his pants and pull off his prosthetic leg and pad to let his skin breathe for a bit.

"Sorry, brother," Tony chuckled as he entered the office. "I forgot to get your signature. You know, I am still waiting for Azul-Aqua to join the 21st century an' upgrade from carbon-triplicate to e-tablets."

"Hmmm," Phil surmised, signing the form. "You think that'll happen soon?"

"Prob'ly about the start of the 22nd century! Gotta run. Peace. See ya' in two weeks." Tony gathered his clipboard and headed out of the office.

"Later." Phil returned to schedules, contemplating switching to crutches for the day. Dakota sat up and just stared at him. "What," he said. "You shouldn't need to go piss or poop for a while yet."

About twenty seconds later—at 9:17 A.M.—the room came alive with shaking, as if a sci-fi creature were digging its way out of the earth under the office. Phil sat in disbelief for the first five or six seconds. *What the…why the hell is my chair wobbling?*

Boxes of ammo started to fall off of shelves. *THUMP!* Other pieces of equipment and merchandise were rocking in their cases and cabinets as if they were in the front row of a rock concert. The spilling of fifty 45-caliber rounds out of a torn open box was the event that had finally spoken to Phil—*Earthquake!*

He dragged himself under the desk. Dakota tried to beat him under there, and he held her close to comfort her whimpering, waiting until the rocking stopped. Fifty-eight seconds after it started, the thunderous shaking ceased. Phil waited a few seconds to make sure nothing else fell off the shelf over the office's desk and peeked out. *Glad I don't have to put the leg back-on…*

He climbed out to see a day's worth of clean-up. *Well, dang.* He remembered he had two customers and a range officer on the pistol line that morning. *This sucks,* he thought as he and Dakota headed out to go check on everyone.

DOWN AT WASHINGTON State Naval Shipyard in Bartlett, Phil's son, Crane, was working steadily and generally enjoying life as a ship-wright. WSNS was by far the largest employer in the county. The twenty-four-year-old was one of the shipyard's newest journeyman mechanics, having just graduated from his apprenticeship. At 5' 9" tall, Crane was a couple inches shorter than his dad. Unlike Phil's auburn-red short hair, Crane's hair was somewhat medium-length and more stylish, a browner shade of orange. People could always tell they were father and son, though, as they had the same muscu-lar, stout build. Crane was well-liked by everyone, considered easy-going and hardworking by peers and supervisors alike.

"I don't know, man, the Rams have Jaxson Marson—their 'D' is looking pretty tough this year." Crane was jawing football with Billy Soren as they finished a small modification to a scaffold under the aircraft-carrier USS Ronald Reagan. It was sitting in the only dry-dock on the west coast the Navy would trust to put it in—Dry-dock F. "I mean…I love the 'Hawks, too. But they need to shore up their offensive line, just like every year."

"That statement is *offensive*," Billy emphasized on purpose. "Two more. That should be it," he yelled down to Tracy Hillard, the trades-helper assigned to work with Crane and Billy on this job. Yelling in the dry-docks usually didn't indicate anger—it was a sign that production work was loud. Even when the immediate job site didn't require earplugs, there was just a general hum in a full dry-dock that made passing information up and down a scaffold difficult. Throughout the 1,200-foot-long pit were machines for blasting paint, applying paint, welding, and moving material or workers. It all made a combined noise that tended to bounce off the hull and walls and funnel in on wherever a person was trying to speak. And there was a ton of work going on in this dock, trying to get another "bird-farm" back to the fleet.

Tracy acknowledged the order with a thumbs up and started making her way 180-feet north to the closest rack that had the exact pipe they needed.

"You say something just like that every week no matter who we're playing," Billy mused, adding himself to the Seahawks roster for the argument. "Sometimes I think you're not a fan—you're just screwing with me."

"That's most likely true!" Crane replied gleefully, knowing it would annoy Billy.

Crane liked working with Billy. He learned something new on almost every job. Scaffold-building comprised about ninety percent of what the shipwrights did on a day-to-day basis. The rest of their work usually involved other jobs using the scaffold and framing skill sets, such as installing guardrails, stairs, decks, and heavy equipment platforms. The vast majority of what they did was not to work on the ship itself but to make it safe for others to go to work. To a much smaller extent, they built the dock-settings and performed other jobs that required transits and levels. The shipwrights shared a camaraderie with each other similar to what cops, firefighters, and veterans do, a by-product of doing a job that can kill a person—a job in which co-workers must earn each other's trust that the other won't do something stupid and hurt them both. That camaraderie was the key difference between being a shipwright and doing most other jobs in the shipyard.

The two friends continued to trade barbs. When Tracy tied the needed material to a rope and canvas bag they had hung from the scaffold, Billy pulled it up and handed the pieces to Crane one at a time. This was the senior mechanic's prerogative—make the youngsters do the labor when his own fifty-something-year-old body was hurting. Crane and Billy were simply adding a small section outwards onto a larger existing scaffold. Small modifications were a common request, in this case a little higher and farther out towards one of the carrier's shafting-struts. The propellers and shafts were all removed, getting resurfaced in the machine shop. The struts were large arms that helped keep the shafts straight between the points where they exited the ship and the propellers.

Crane attached his fall protection gear to the framework above him and hopped out onto the small jut-out they had just built. The scaffold started wiggling, which was what scaffolds did when the ground under them turned into jelly. Like many others that day, it took Crane far longer than it should have to realize what was happening. Disbelief was born out of a series of thoughts in which the rational mind told a person a lie—that the thing that was happening to them was something other than what it actually was. When the scaffold Crane was working on started to shake, his first thought was to see what dummy had just bumped it with a forklift. It wasn't until his feet were weightless and he was slamming into the leg straps of his safety harness that he realized something was way out of control.

Gravity worked faster than reaction time—something the fall protection instructors had tried to warn him would happen. Crane only fell about two feet, thanks to the modern shock-absorbing systems built into the lanyard. The back of his legs slammed into the plank he had just been standing on, and since he had not yet turned their lock-tabs, the planks flipped back. They clattered to the dry-dock floor about fifteen feet below a short second later. He came to a stop, suspended against the outer side of the guardrails separating him and Billy.

"What the *HELL*!" Crane yelled, glaring at Billy—not so much thinking that he'd done something but because the sudden adrenal dump needed a target.

Billy had woken up to the truth. "Earthquake! We need to get outta here!" He had the presence of mind to hook up to the pipe above him when he clambered with one leg up and over the upper guardrail while standing on the lower one. He grabbed Crane by the front of the safety harness and spun him around so his partner could step onto the guardrails himself. Like hornets in a freshly-kicked nest, they climbed over, unhooked, and ran to the scaffold's stairs. They flew down two flights, barely touching the steps, and found Tracy looking like a deer in headlights at the bottom.

Billy had been through this once before, in 2001. "Run!" he yelled, as the trio joined the mass-Exodus of workers making their way to the nearest set of dry-dock stairs.

ELSEWHERE IN THE shipyard there were 18,000 other day-shift federal employees, contractors, and sailors going about their daily business. One of those was Captain Marie Darnell, the current Commanding Officer of WSNS and only the second female to hold that honor. The tall, slightly graying, blonde officer was fifty-one-years-old and possessed a stellar resume. The Navy had grown a lot regarding diversity over the course of her career, but like most senior positions in the military, this one was not a token spot. It was earned. With one hundred percent certainty, when the Navy planted a new CO in charge of a shipyard, that person had proven themselves many times over. Her integrity and intelligence were beyond reproach. Marie was proud of being promoted—not for pushing past glass ceilings but because she knew what it meant—"Big Navy" thought highly of her.

Like any organization of this size, the shipyard was "metrics" driven. *Metrics. Remember when we called them statistics?* Marie thought. She was sitting in her Tuesday morning metrics review meeting with her department heads, comprised of two other captains, a handful of junior and mid-level officers, and several of the senior civilians. At this level, a shipyard CO's ability to multitask was a must. Prior COs had set a precedence for scrolling through their smart phones during such meetings, occasionally chiming in with a question to prove they were listening. Marie didn't do that—it wasn't her style. Early in her career she learned that as a female she *always* had to make eye contact. She *always* had to be seen paying attention. She made it a point to notice people and to make sure they noticed her.

"Wait. Wait—" she said, cutting off Nick Prince, the civilian head of the production resources department. When the CO interrupted, a person knew to shut up—even a GS-15. "Explain that. Last week, your capacity for the machine shop for next summer was about two percent higher." Two percent didn't sound like much, but when a major organization was forecasting their own ability to provide critical support, two percent was huge—especially for a trade that took years to become proficient at.

This was the core of Marie's job. Somebody had to be the person the Navy could hold accountable if the shipyard couldn't fix their nuclear-powered carriers and submarines on time. The officers who promoted to Captain did so in part due to their ability to call malarky when they heard it. Marie refreshed her malarky-filter before meetings like this by reviewing the metrics from the week prior right before the meeting started. The former chemical engineer once worked for an oil company south of Houston before getting bored and going to Officer Candidate School. If there was one thing this strong Texan knew, it was bovine excrement.

The civilian senior leader being scrutinized started to explain the difference. "Sorry, Captain. I should have addressed that differently. What I meant was—"

He was interrupted by ceiling tiles dropping. It only took a second for the rest of the building to learn what the ceiling tiles knew—the earth was dancing. A subtle rumble was overlapped with the sound of a stack of chairs in the conference room closet slamming into the wall, as well as hardhats falling off hooks out in the hallway. Everyone instinctively crawled under the large, tan, solid wood conference table. Most were nervously mumbling to the people immediately to their left or right. Marie thought she even heard a couple of them laughing and joking. *Funny how some people react to danger,* she thought.

The laughing stopped after a few seconds. This conference room was in the middle of the seventh floor of an eight-story, 800-foot-long building, the largest office building in the shipyard. Only the machine, wood, and ship-fitting shops were bigger. The height of the building increased what the people were feeling by a factor of nearly twice what those on the ground felt. Those hiding under the table began clutching onto its legs just to hold it in place. *SLAM! THUD!* More tiles were falling. The lights flickered and then went out. The daylight coming through the windows was enough for Marie to see the looks on people's faces. They had morphed into concern. *I wonder what my expression is. CLANG!* The flagpole in the corner finally came off the desk it had been leaning against for the previous several seconds.

When the shaking stopped everyone paused and looked around before venturing out into the open. "Is anyone hurt?" Marie asked as she got up. Hearing nothing urgent in the replies, she darted across the hall to her office and grabbed her coat, hardhat, and safety glasses. Back out in the hall the senior leaders had started to file out the building. "Follow me," she ordered to Captain Trevor

Flowers, her Operations Department head and most senior subordinate.

The two captains made their way down the building's center stairwell, joining a flow of foot traffic as several hundred engineers and administrators began their descent to safety. Protocol was to congregate out on Monsoor Avenue, the extremely wide main thoroughfare that ran east to west through the shipyard. Monsoor Avenue separated Building 855 from the dry-docks, piers, and most of the production shops.

Once in the lobby, Marie found the lieutenant who was currently on watch as the Shipyard Duty Officer waiting just outside of the watch office. They ran to the gold, Chevy 2500 Quad-cab that served as the SDO's duty-rig, hopped in, and started driving west.

DR. STUART SCHWARTZ looked at his watch. Again. *Perhaps I've discovered a moment of time going backwards,* he thought. Judging by the looks on the other passengers' faces, they were having similar thoughts. Horizon Flight 64, the 8:50 A.M. daily-direct from SeaTac Airport to LAX, was running late. Like during most pre-flights, passengers were slowly creeping toward a silent gate agent as if being prodded by some invisible giant with an invisible broom. Like wild dogs, once people gained territory, they hated to give it up. When one passenger nudged themselves between another and the gate, the second person felt obliged to squeeze in by the trashcan. It was a small psychological jig that was danced in the minds of thousands of travelers every day. The doctor watched the procession with little amusement.

Stuart was returning home from year three of what was turning into an annual venture to his parents' retirement home in Sequim, Washington. The middle-aged doctor, one of the better plastic surgeons in Los Angeles, was near the front of the pack. He hadn't flown anything but first-class in almost twenty years. He enjoyed this annual trek to see his overbearing Jewish mother only slightly more than he enjoyed his annual prostate check. "I still cannot fathom why you moved all the way up here," he told them on every trip.

He understood the appeal—it was a lovely small city in the "rain shadow" of the Olympic Mountains. Where the areas to the south-east and west were doused in huge volumes of rain most of the year, Sequim averaged only seventeen inches per year. Situated on the Strait of Juan De Fuca, the sea level temperatures were mild enough that snow was almost never an issue. The California heat was usually the reason older Californians transplanted up here, and it was no different for his parents. Washington State was very progres-sive. They loved Californians here, even Jewish ones. *Still—it is differ-ent, in a Mayberry kind of way,* Stuart felt.

He looked at the girl near him, a pretty, petite Latina. *She doesn't look like a rich, daddy's girl. I wonder what she's doing up here in the front. Probably military.* The airlines had been doing that for several years, letting the soldiers board with the people who pay an un-Godly amount for tickets. Stuart didn't mind that. The army folks were always polite and didn't fart around. When it was time to move, they were ready. *People with kids, though. Ughh…*

"Ladies and gentlemen of Flight 64, thanks once again for your patience. The mechanics report that the minor issue is fixed, and the flight crew should open us up for boarding any minute now."

What a God-awful job, Stuart thought as the gate agent concluded her spiel. *I bet I could rhinoplasty her nose in fifteen minutes and double the amount of dates she gets.*

The low rumbling sounded much like a jet at first. People began to look at each other, wondering if a 737 was about to come bursting through the wall. Those near the windows were craning their necks, looking for the culprit. Out in the main passageway between the gates an old replica of "The Spirit of St. Louis" came crashing down, part of the "History of Aviation" display that SeaTac Airport was hosting that year. The rumbling and shaking were augmented by other sounds, such as the rattling of the various roll-up security gates as they shook in their holders above the store fronts.

A few people started to scream, which added to the confusion and chaos. The plane replica had landed on people. A few others had sprained ankles and bumped elbows. Stuart and the girl had both lunged to hold on to the load bearing column near them, as had a few other people. Some were trying to squeeze in under chairs. Parents were bunching up kids and turning themselves into human shields as pieces of tile and plaster fell in the gate areas. Almost instinctively, Stuart grabbed the girl's arm so they could help hold one another to the column. The jarring was making it hard to stay in one spot. Her counter grip told Stuart that she was okay with the plan.

When the rumbling stopped it was quiet for a second or two, except for a few distant wails echoing up the concourse. Then the screaming started.

2

Assessment.

SOMETIME IN THE minute of 9:17 A.M. a magnitude 7.1 intraplate earthquake released its pent-up energy at a medium depth of twenty-four miles below the Tacoma Faultline in the Southern Puget Sound. It lasted fifty-eight terrifying seconds. For nearly one minute the rain-soaked ground went through a process known as liquefaction, in which saturated soil shakes and everything on it sinks as if in quick-sand. Over the course of recent history, industrialized nations have made vast improvements in engineering infrastructure to withstand earthquakes. For thirty-plus years, new construction had been held to a much higher standard regarding structural engineering. Buildings and highways built since then had been designed to flex and sway in the shaking as much as possible. However, engineers reminded people that nothing was liquefaction proof. The deepest nuclear-bomb-proof bunker would still sink and break if the ground underneath it turned to mush. The Pacific Northwest just got clobbered straight on the nose. The brunt was in the south and central Puget Sound areas, but it was felt by everyone for a hundred miles in every direction.

PHIL AND DAKOTA went down to the pistol line to make sure his customers weren't hurt. The pair of older gentlemen weren't club members, but they were people Phil recognized as public patrons who came out two or three times per year to plink. They were using the pistol line under the watchful eye of Donald Kwiatkowsky, a double-retiree and the Lead Range Officer who normally worked Tuesdays and Fridays.

Phil left the office and walked north-east down a set of stairs. The pistol line was towards the left set-up in a south—north shooting direction. It was under a seventy-foot-long covered patio—enclosed for weather and noise control on three sides. Communication with the rest of the range relied on the use of two-way radios or walking down in person to talk. In the excitement of the moment, Phil had left his radio sitting on the office counter-top.

"You guys okay down here, Don?" Phil asked.

"I think so! We were all just saying that we're getting a little too old for roller coasters!"

The others were talking quickly, too, and concurring that they were fine. Phil could hear the excitement in their voices. With Dakota glued to his intact right leg, he ran back out towards the path that leads up to the office. He crossed over it to the eastward-pointing rifle line, which had a similar set-up to the pistol line. He walked the 130-foot-wide line, looking at the roof structure for damage and then climbed up the path at the far end that led back to the driveway end of the parking area. It was then that he noticed Tony's truck still idling in the lot. He hurried over.

"You okay?"

"Holy smokes…" was the only thing that the normally talkative Tony could muster.

"I'll take that as a yes," Phil said, laughing slightly.

"Um, yeah. Sorry, Phil." Tony climbed out of the truck. "I'm fine, thanks. Holy schnikies! Whoooo!!! That was my first big earthquake!" He started to laugh as loudly as he talked.

There he is. "Good to hear."

Phil continued his first scan of the three portable buildings—the office, the classroom, and the restroom. Nothing looked askew at first glance. He looked at the gate at the end of the driveway, which began at the Canal Vista Highway, the main artery to this part of the county. It was a sixteen-foot-wide, welded steel gate that swung up out of the way via chain-driven electric motor. The staff always left it in the up position during the day, but it was now lowered. *It must've reset itself.* "I'll get the gate for you."

"Hold up," Tony said, already walking to the roll-up doors on the driver's side of the truck. He grabbed six more jugs of water and set them on the ground. "Here."

Phil looked puzzled.

"Just in case," Tony explained.

Phil looked at the water, then back at Tony. *He's right. What am I doing? I have things to do.* "Thanks, man. I'll get that gate for you."

He used the manual-latch override since he wasn't sure if the power was even on at the gate. Phil motioned for Tony to stop as he approached the gate.

"Take care, Tony. If you run into any issues, come back out. I mean it. I live close by, so I'll be here sooner or later."

"Right on, Phil. Thanks, man. I'll be okay." Tony waved as he drove out and turned left, back towards Bartlett.

Phil was already sending texts. *I hope these make it through.* Phil knew that texting required a fraction of the bandwidth and power that voice calls used, and text messages were more likely to reach their intended recipient after a big disaster such as this.

He'd been a widower for five years. Caroline died after a valiant fight with pancreatic cancer that had lasted most of two years. These texts were to his adult children. He sent one to Payton first, because she's the girl and that's what dads did. He knew Crane would be fine. He'd always been a resourceful kid. Barring some anomaly like a building collapse, he knew that Crane could handle any challenge the day threw at him. Payton was single, pregnant and had a daughter—a trifecta of issues to deal with on a day like this. Texts sent, he began the process of worrying about his family while he cleaned off his glasses. First, he would finish a quick tour of the range. Then he would get home as soon as possible.

TWO-AND-A-HALF MINUTES after getting into the duty truck, Captains Marie Darnell, Trevor Flowers, and the duty officer were walking into the EOC, or the Emergency Operations Center. It was actually located on the adjoining Navy base in the old four-story officer's club and barracks. The old O-club had a fire in the early 1990s, and it had wiring issues ever since. In 2014, the Naval Base CO procured funding to tear down an old, unused supply center warehouse and build a new Officer's Barracks. That facility opened in 2017, allowing the shipyard time to gut and rebuild the old barracks into a new multi-purpose facility. The other floors housed the Apprentice and Employee Development Programs, but the entire fourth floor was turned into a state-of-the-art EOC. The building's height and position on top of a hill made it ideal for radio communications, both locally and with the bosses in the other Washington. It was also high enough to have a bird's-eye view of the shipyard from the roof.

There was only one other person there at the moment, that being the person on duty. The emergency planning department of the shipyard was staffed by a team of eight civilians. During nuclear refueling or defueling evolutions, which the shipyard was in the middle of performing on the submarine USS El Paso, the EOC was staffed around the clock. The duty was easy, mostly just being ready to monitor things and start the info-sharing processes if an unplanned event occurred. A small living area was provided, and the duty rotation gave the team a chance to earn a little overtime. Evolutions like this normally lasted about three months. The primary purpose was to contain emergencies related to the nuclear-power program, and natural disasters were often the trigger of the emergency during the practice drills. Those not on duty worked at their normal office inside the shipyard.

"Anything yet?" Marie asked, greeting the duty EMCO, or Emergency Coordinator.

"Just that there's been some sort of crane accident at Dry-dock A," he said worriedly. "Waiting for a report, ma'am, but I believe it was tied to the refueling crane."

This has the potential to be bad written all over it. "ETA on news?" *Screw you, Murphy...*

"Three minutes."

"Move along, EMCO. What else?" she asked.

"As you can see on the status board here, we still have power to most of the buildings, but the piers and dry-docks must have tripped themselves."

"Okay. Get me 'NavSurf' on the phone," she ordered the duty officer, referring to her boss in Washington D.C. It was the fast way to say "Naval Shipyard Repair Facilities," the designator for that branch of the Navy in charge of all the shipyards. Based out of Washington DC, NSRF was in charge of anything related to maintenance and repair of nuclear-powered vessels. "NavSurf" was the informal nickname for whichever admiral held that position, in this case Vice Admiral David Warburg.

While the duty officer was getting a secure line dialed up, she addressed the EMCO. "Send Group Text One." That was an order to every cellphone and email in the shipyard distribution system, announcing that all personnel were to perform an emergency "shelter-in-house" and muster. They would then send reports up their respective chains as quickly as possible. They were further directed to send partial reports within fifteen minutes, even if the musters weren't complete.

By the time the EMCO had complied with this request, several things were happening—the police and fire department radios were passing radio traffic that "wind-shield surveys" were commencing; various emergency managers and high-level department heads were strolling in; and both Captains' cellphones were starting to blow up with texts.

PAYTON WALKER'S first reaction to the earthquake had been to try calling Savannah's school. Savannah was only nine-years-old. *She needs her mom,* Payton told herself, knowing deep inside it was as much the opposite, if anything. On the first try the phone rang continuously with no answer. On the countless tries afterward—*twelve? thirteen?*— she only got the fast busy signal. Payton was starting to get pissed. She didn't need this.

Twenty weeks pregnant, Payton found herself single again, unexpectedly, about two weeks earlier. *Is un-engaged even a word?* She wasn't surprised. They'd been drifting apart for months. Brenden wasn't bad, he was just…indifferent. At first, he'd been open to the idea of adopting Savannah as his own, which was extremely endearing to Payton—*God knows Savannah's biological father has never tried to be a part of her life.* He didn't even want to live on the same side of the country. Brenden had taken a better paying job in Pierce County, installing fiber-optic cable along service routes, but the overtime and long commute meant less time together. *That's okay. Marriage is just a sham institution anyway. Brenden is decent, and he'll still try his best to be involved, like he should be.*

Payton inherited more of her mother's blonde hair and strong will than her brother did. Where Crane was easygoing and got along well with their dad, she and Phil had been in a frozen relationship for half of her life. It was really just the events in recent years that had started the "thaw." First her mother's illness and passing, followed by the shooting incident. Recently, it had become apparent since her break up with Brenden that her dad was trying to get the relationship going again.

Brrrrt… [Phil: "Olive, text me back. If this reaches you, and you can't reply, house first, then range. Let me know about Peaches. That's an order, love you."]

Wow. Olive. That had been Phil's nickname for Payton when she was a girl, based on her middle name, Olivia. Peaches was Savannah, of course. *He must be worried. I hate to admit it, but no matter how big of an ass he is, I know he'll always be there for me.*

Payton grabbed her phone and purse and made for the apartment door. *I'll reply later. Here's hoping I can get to that school.*

BY THE TIME Crane was out of the dry-dock, the jet-engine-loud evacuation alarm was wailing to the familiar "hi-low" siren that the employees and surrounding community heard tested twice per day, year-round. Only instead of the normal ten-second burst, it was continuing for one minute, then two. Finally, it turned off. *It's way more ominous when it runs that long,* Crane thought. The going had been slowed by the multitudes of people trying to evacuate all at once. Some people just couldn't run up eight dozen stairs as fast as others.

Crane had gotten a text from his dad around the time he arrived at the northeast corner of the area immediately outside the dry-dock. *We'll wait here for the foreman, just like during fire drills.* He looked at his phone.

[Phil: "Son, shoot me a quick word to say you're alright. If you have time, send more than that. You know where I'll be. Dad."] *Yep. The house or the range.*

[Crane: "*G2go. Will send more L8R*".]

The trio of shipwrights were now in the throng of things. Several hundred workers, sailors, and managers were already gathering en masse. There was no room for them in the designated area. They flooded every street and available space around all sides of Dry-dock F. Federal workers and contractors alike were scrambling, trying to work through each other and sort themselves into familiar groups. Sailors were responding in kind on the ship. Adding to the confusion was the fact that the two emergency diesel generators that weren't locked out for repairs and maintenance had somehow managed to turn themselves on. Diesel exhaust was billowing out of its designated chutes, a sight not often seen when a carrier was in dry-dock.

Across WSNS a very similar sight unfolded. Organized chaos was the best way to describe it, which was exactly how a member of the ship's crew had once described a normal day at sea to Crane. The sailors seemed to be the least bothered by any of it.

"C'mon," Billy said, dragging his junior co-workers towards the designated smoking area closest to their locker room. "Geoff'll know to find me here. He's never gonna find us in this mess."

Billy lit up a generic low-tar cigarette and jump started his lungs with a little cough on the first drag. Running full speed out of Dry-dock F—ninety-eight stairs—was something he hadn't done in a couple of decades.

Over the course of the next several minutes, many of the shipwrights from the two crews working on this project had arrived at the smoke-shack. They were fist-bumping and hi-fiving like they'd just won the Super Bowl. *Nervous energy,* Crane thought. Everybody was hyper and cracking jokes, telling anyone that would listen their version of "living through it," as if that person didn't just live through it, too. He was witnessing the after-effects of adrenaline. *Pretty soon, everyone'll be ready for a nap.*

"What next?" Crane asked Billy.

"Hrrumphh," Billy exhorted, suddenly disgusted by the recollection of what had happened last time. "If it's like 2001…you don't wanna know."

CARMEN MARTINEZ finally broke her grip from the well-dressed, short balding man who had grabbed her and helped her stay clutched to the column for one-minute of hell. Within a quick moment, people were starting to show the signs of panic and turmoil. The big TV that hung on the wall behind the gate agent had fallen off. *Someone is going to be pissed.*

Actual screams brought her attention back to the moment. Alarms were resonating, and the high ceilings in the terminal made the noise bounce around even worse. The power flickered, fighting for several seconds to stay on before finally giving up life. This triggered the emergency systems to activate, lighting up emergency exit signs and spot lights.

The screaming got louder as people began rushing…*the windows?* Carmen pushed her way to the front of the pack—one of the perks of being 5' 3" was maneuverability. She gasped in horror and forgot to breathe for several moments, not believing her eyes. *Oh, my God…*

Alaska 2340, the daily hopper from San Francisco, was two seconds from touching down when the earthquake struck. Naturally, the pilots didn't know something was wrong until too much speed had bled off for a fresh take-off to work. For several seconds the same confusion that struck most people that day had also stricken them. They couldn't figure out why the brakes weren't working. If they had lived through the crash, they might have learned that the massive buckling of the ground—while only causing minor cracks in the runway—had been throwing their plane up into the air. This happened thirty-nine times in just under a minute, which was more than enough time to lose a few thousand precious feet of runway. It had also blown out several tires. The high rate of speed, lack of tires, and lack of control from being jostled was too much for the pilots to handle. The tip of the right wing dug into the grass and runway lights, causing a domino effect of tragedy.

The first people to look out the windows had witnessed Flight 2340 cartwheeling off the end of the runway. Carmen caught the huge fireball spreading south. It was eerie, almost like watching it unfold with a mute button. The "Whoompf" and rumbling of the explosion finally began to reverberate through the terminal's windows about fifteen seconds after the earthquake stopped.

The public-address system boomed. "Attention all patrons and employees of SeaTac Airport! This is Assistant Chief Kim Royce of the Port of Seattle Fire Department! I'm declaring a natural disaster and Mass Casualty Incident! All flight operations are suspended! Everyone stay put and await further instructions!" Carmen could hear the stress in her voice.

The healthy and the walking-wounded we're starting to react to the cries and pleas for help from the injured. Carmen rushed over to the airplane replica, where a group of men and women were trying to pick it up and get to people. *This has to be a nightmare!*

TONY HAD CHANGED HIS PLANS. He was going back to the office instead of continuing his route. He was rolling his big Ford F-650 back down the Canal Vista Highway toward Bartlett while simultaneously trying to call in to work. The cell was just kind of hovering in no-man's land, continuously searching for signal. He glanced down at the truck's CB radio. *Frickin' CB radio. Who'd a thunk?* He wasn't sure what he was doing, messing with channels and a knob called "squelch" that just played annoyingly loud static. He doubted anyone from work was going to be on the thing anyway.

He decided to concentrate on the road and with good reason. Less than a mile south of the gun range was an S-curve. As he travelled through the second half, he had to hit the brakes. There was a big fir tree laying right across it. The tree had come off a high bank on the east side, running from left to right as Tony stared at it. He could see a couple of pick-ups and cars starting to build up on the other side of it. He switched on his flashers and got out.

"I don't suppose you have a lumberjack in your back pocket," he called out across the tree, smiling.

"Nope, no lumberjacks," the woman replied, playing along. She turned around. "Hey!" she hollered to the rig behind her. "Got a saw?" The woman must've heard a reply, because she turned back toward Tony and shook her head no.

Tony had been staring at the tree. He could smell the tree's pleasant odor strongly at this range. "You know…maybe we could just drag this thing with my truck? I think the truck's big enough."

"Oh, yeah. That'll work alright!" The comment came from a man standing next to Tony that he hadn't even seen come up to him.

"*Dad gummit!* Don't do that, brothuh!" Tony said, laughing. "You scared the hell outta me!"

The man laughed. "Oh—sorry. But, you're right. Come try to get some people behind us to back up while I cinch up my tow strap."

Tony followed the man back to his pick-up. Another vehicle was slowly coming to a stop at the obstruction. Tony went over to get the car to stop farther away while the stranger grabbed a tow strap from his cab. When the third car was stopped the man backed his truck up to give Tony's rig as much room as possible.

They went back to the front. Tony nosed forward and right to grab the tree as high up it as he could. He parked close into the branches. The man slowly stepped into the mess and wrapped a girth-hitch around the tree's trunk using the middle of the tow strap. He moved over to Tony's bumper with both ends and wrapped them both around the bumper and frame behind it, finally hooking the two ends together so the tow-strap was doubled up.

After the man moved away from the fallen fir, Tony slowly backed his rig, angling back to the northbound side of the road. He didn't get the tree completely off to the shoulder, but it was far enough. A small round of hoorays erupted from the other bystanders.

"Not bad for a Ford!" the man joked. He and Tony shook hands and everyone headed back for their vehicles.

Within a few minutes, people were able to start taking turns driving through the gap. *Man, that's nice,* Tony thought, smiling. *I love America—how people step up and help each other when the chips are down.* His thoughts returned to semi-worry as he thought of his wife and children. He decided he'd skip checking in at work and go see Sheila as the big truck lumbered toward the south end of the county.

3

Taking Action.

PHIL WAS HOME FINALLY, a feat only possible due to his proximity to the club—about two miles. It also helped that he typically kept a hodge-podge of tools riding around under the bed cover of his newer model gray pick-up. The truck was a byproduct of his settlement with the state after the shooting incident on the highway. The criminals were members of an outlaw motorcycle club that distributed meth and had just knocked off the headquarters of a small time rival that had tried to quietly steal territory. Due to the egregiousness of the incident, the State of Washington had used asset forfeiture laws to take every cent they could. Phil hired his attorney friend, a fellow shooter from Mason County named George Donovan, to help him get a settlement.

As Phil had turned left off of Canal Vista Highway and onto the dirt road that contained his and several neighbors' driveways, he almost ran into a tree that had fallen. He hit the brakes and got out. The tool-pile in the bed varied from month to month, usually influenced by the variety of improvements and repairs needed at the club. He found a battery-powered reciprocating saw, but the battery and blade were toast. *Ahh, the folding pruning saw. Why are you even in here? Field day, back in July. Okay. You'll do just fine.*

Phil had gotten the thing at one of the big-chain hardware stores for something like fourteen dollars, but it worked well. The folding saw had a short blade, but a person could need stitches in a hurry if they weren't careful where they placed their other hand. The little saw made quick work of the tree tops and select branches. *I'll bring the chainsaw down in a bit if my house is still standing.* Phil drove past the cleared obstacle and made it the full quarter-mile to his driveway without issue.

Phil lived north of the range on Medford Lane, a road that fed about fifteen properties. Most were about five acres in size. People out here in West Slaughter County tended to be more self-reliant than the more populated parts of the county. The windstorms that came rushing off the Pacific Ocean and around the Olympic Mountains typically pointed themselves up or down the Hood Canal. The canal was the other body of water that enveloped Slaughter County, turning it into a peninsula. It was a complex land mass that contained many sub-peninsulas and inlets of water around them. People out here lost power every year, at least partial days and at least a couple of times per winter. Even with some space between homes, Phil could always tell which neighbors owned generators within a few minutes of the power going out. Phil owned a dual-fuel generator that could run on both gasoline and propane, but he only lit it if the power was still out after one night.

Dakota and Phil hopped out of the truck into the driveway. Dakota went to sniff her normal area of the woods and investigate the chicken coop, part of her normal patrol procedure. The first thing Phil did was look at his well-house, a small enclosed structure about six feet by six feet and just barely tall enough to stand in. *Seems fine, might as well look inside.* The pressure tank and iron-filter were still standing, thanks to the strapping he'd wrapped around each of them and screwed to the studs of the little structure. The pressure tank and pipes usually kept Phil's house supplied with about thirty to forty gallons of water before he had to think about running the generator. The property's power lines were buried, which meant he wasn't worried about a tree taking them out.

The familiar vibration-ring of Phil's cellphone—he preferred the straight, old-school phone ring sound—surprised him. "HUH!" he actually said out loud to nobody but Dakota. "Hey, Fred."

"Hi, Phil, it's Fred!"

I know—I just said your name. "Ya' don't say. You caught me off guard, sir. How you doing? How's Phyllis?"

Fred O'Conner was the Lead Range Officer for Wednesdays and Saturdays. Like Don Kwiatkosky, Fred was a life member who had given thousands of hours of his time to the West Sound Sportsmen's Club. The Lead Range Officers were women and men who Phil trusted to make the right decisions when he wasn't there, and they generally ran the range lines and office, even when he was there. This freed him up to plan classes and work on projects. The number of subordinate range-safety officers—called ROs— on a given day varied from zero to ten. How many were there depended on factors like how busy those days of the week usually were, or if there were classes or events happening. The club membership was a strong and dedicated group.

"We're fine. All good here. Just kind of scary, that's all. So...I tried calling the office, but nobody answered. Are you guys alright?"

"Yeah, we're good. We had a couple of public shooters, but they left as soon as they could. Don and I both left after we did a quick scout of the property."

"Good, good...Hey, listen, do you think we'll be open tomorrow?"

"I don't see why not. Why? Do you want to take off? I'll be there—take care of Phyllis. It's okay."

"Yeah, I think I might. You know—my hip has been bothering me some, and the VA is taking their time. I just figured I might take another day off."

"Well, I appreciate the notice, Fred. Don't sweat it," Phil trailed off, pausing because he didn't know how to say the rest. He had to cut off Fred as he was about to start the normal good-bye sequence. "Listen, Fred—I'm not sure how to phrase this, but…you know…be ready. The aftershocks are never as bad, but they can seem that way because the damage will compound. You know, just call if you need anything. Better yet, text. I know you hate typing on phones, but you actually got pretty lucky getting this call through."

"Alright, Phil, I hear ya'. I'll talk to you in a few days. Bye."

"Later."

Phil went back to his checks. He did a full sweep outside the main house, feeding his chickens and inspecting his greenhouse along the way. His fall plantings were doing nicely. *Shop looks fine. Just some stuff to pick up.* He grabbed his chainsaw, bar oil, and mixed gas and placed them in the bed of the truck on the way back around the house. He finally opened the garage door—he wasn't surprised by what he saw. Most every item that used to live on a shelf now resided on the garage floor. Luckily that mostly meant messes along the walls. Crane's jeep looked fine. His son had spent a lot of his overtime money fixing up a midnight-blue, 1994 Jeep Wrangler. It was his baby. He kept it over here since he was renting a house in Bartlett with two high school friends and another shipyard worker. He and his roommates worked a lot, and he just didn't trust that it would be safe there.

Sitting in the back of the garage behind the Jeep was all of Phil's hunting and camping equipment. He'd been spending evenings going through it all. He had been "blanked" during the previous month's archery season and was looking forward to next week's rifle hunt. The freezer was getting empty. One benefit of being the Range Master at the most popular rifle-line in the county was meeting a lot of cool people, playing with a lot of neat "toys," and being invited on a lot of hunting trips.

Whereas a lot of people had built themselves "bug-out bags," Phil had built a bug-out "system," and his camping gear was at the core of it. His pack wasn't the typical, coyote-brown military-looking pack that so many people preferred in recent years. Rather, it was an ultra-lite backpacker's rig—an expensive one. When people balked at learning how much he spent on it, he'd always tell them it was worth every penny. He'd taped up one too many broken straps in the Marines, and he knew that he got what he paid for. He also knew that ounces equaled pounds which equaled pain. He had a set-up that allowed him to camp in a hammock. It kept him warm, dry, and off the ground. He could start fires a dozen ways, filter water, and even make coffee—life giving liquid gold.

His bug-out theory was that if he ever had to head for the Olympic Mountains—or better yet, Idaho—then that meant driving. And if he couldn't drive, then he'd better be realistic about what he was carrying. While in pretty decent shape, he had definitely packed on a few pounds since the shooting. *So many people build forty-pound packs without actually carrying them up and down hills.* The rest of his system was for vehicle travel, operating under the theory that he wouldn't be coming back home. It was stored in plastic boxes and brand-new, thirty-two-gallon cans. This made for durability and was rodent resistant. All of that gear was still out in the shop.

Phil went into the first floor of his house from the garage entrance. He did a quick sniff test for propane. *No weird smells means no leaks. Clock's dark. No power still.* Heading back into the garage, he went through the entire process to secure the breaker switches, start his generator, and get power going to the well-pump and select house circuits.

He went back inside and went upstairs. His house was a split-level entry with the upstairs acting as the main floor. He double-checked the kitchen and furnace areas for gas leaks and then went into the bathroom. He opened the vanity below the sink and grabbed a box. *Finally get to use this thing.* He opened the box and pulled out a lump of plastic that unfolded into a "Water Bob." It was a thirty-dollar plastic tank that lined the tub and held about a hundred gallons of water. It came with a cheap accordion pump to get the water back out. Lastly, Phil had a gravity-fed septic system, so he took the opportunity to take care of that business as well.

Good time to check the phone. He was starting to get a little worried about Payton. She still hadn't texted him back. *Maybe I'll get lucky…* He tried calling, but he only heard the familiar fast-busy. *Another text.* [Phil: "O, 2nd request for update. Don't make me come looking for you!"] Phil started thinking about getting stranded during after-shocks. *I think I'd better throw some more stuff into the truck.*

PAYTON HAD MANAGED to get to the school. She had to slow drive through a large pool of water in Sylvan. *Probably a broken waterline,* she thought. She and Savannah had an apartment on the west side of town, one of several units that sprang up in the 90s when the Navy bases started shipping lots of sailors to the area. Her path to her daughter's school took her under one of the Highway 8 over-passes and through two small neighborhoods. Everything looked fairly normal, all things considered. Signs that people had started clearing an occasional fallen tree were evident. In her short drive it seemed to her that power lines had fared well. She remembered all the road construction for several summers, something about how they're slowly burying the phone and fiber-optic lines.

During the drive she had gotten a text from her neighbor, Jennifer, who normally watched Savannah while Payton was working. She learned that Jennifer and her kids were heading over to her parents' house on Russell Island to check on them. She wouldn't be available to babysit. *Well, I guess Safeway will be short one swing-shift deli worker tonight…*

She was soon standing outside the front of the school with a growing group of parents. They could see the kids standing in groups out in the fenced-off field past the playground. "Why are you making our kids stand in the rain?" one mother asked loudly.

Good question, Payton thought.

More and more of the parents were starting to murmur similar thoughts. As new arrivals showed up the staffer who was keeping the group near the drop-off zone was becoming more boisterous. "Folks," she said, "please stay here. Principal Sellar will be over to update everyone as soon as she can."

I should just walk over and find my daughter, Payton thought. *What are they going to do—arrest me?*

Brrrt... *Great. Another text from dad.* She didn't even read it when she replied: [Payton: "Waiting outside the school. About to go postal. Everyone fine. Will call tonight when the power comes back on."] *That should quiet him.*

About that time three more staffers, including Principal Sellar, approached the group. They had come over from a pop-up canopy that been spread over the back of an S.U.V.

"Hi, everyone," the short round principal began. "Let me start by saying your children are fine. Everyone evacuated safely, and all were accounted for."

"But why—"

"Your children are standing in the field," the principal spoke over the vocal mother, "because our maintenance staff have reported that the sprinkler system is flowing out of its over-flow port. That means the system is down. We were trying to get the school district's engineer or the fire department to come out and check it, but multiple schools are reporting issues. The district head has initiated the emergency bus-schedule. I am releasing your children to you."

How very nice of you, Payton thought sarcastically.

Principal Sellar continued. "We need to have you sign your kids out just like any other day, so bear with us a few more minutes while we set that up under that canopy over there."

Payton waited her turn, and another twenty minutes went by before she could hug and kiss her daughter. They held each other's hands on the way back to the car, Payton carrying Savannah's multi-colored unicorn-adorned backpack in her other hand.

"Baby, Paw-paw said he's thinking about you. I'm not going to work tonight. If you get your homework done, maybe we can go get ice cream."

Tony Manners was crawling through traffic in Port View, making his way to Sheila's office. His wife was a medical assistant for a pediatrician in the south end of the county. Port View was the only city in this end of Slaughter County, with about 12,000 of the county's 270,000 residents living in it. Bartlett was the county's major city, but Port View was the county seat. The un-incorporated area all around Port View was quite populated as well. The south end of Slaughter County housed about forty-five percent of the total residents.

Traffic was crawling because just about every major intersection had a cop controlling the flow. While power had remained on in the central and north parts of Slaughter County, the south end was completely de-energized. Occasionally everything came to a crawl when an emergency vehicle went flying through. *This area already sucks for traffic,* Tony thought. *Now this.*

People complained about the traffic issues often, but they usually forgot to account for the geography. Being a peninsula with a lot of inlets and shore line, roads were often not "straight and square" like they were in more open communities. In fact, Tony had just driven through the one thoroughfare that connected the central and north areas of the county to the lower half of the peninsula. It went between Simpson Inlet and the Bartlett Watershed/Oro Mountain complex, and it was literally a choke point. People who lived south of that point had to deal with horrendous traffic almost daily.

He was finally driving east and almost there. His wife's office was near one of the bigger east to west thoroughfares in Port View. He arrived, and the big faithful Ford started creaking with the sounds of cooling off after he'd shut it down. He stretched a bit as he lumbered towards the office lobby. Tony was always more of an eater than he was an exerciser. He was a big man at 6' 2" and about 350 pounds. The only thing bigger than Tony's size was his heart. Almost everyone who met the friendly giant loved him immediately.

Born to a large and loving Christian family in Virginia, Tony had gone to boot camp shortly after high school and served eight years in the supply department, attaining the rank of First-Class Petty Officer. After he discharged, he worked as a sub-contractor at the shipyard for several small contracts, but he decided he'd had enough of the Navy. However, he'd married a local so now he was stuck in Slaughter County. He had worked over in King County at a warehouse for a few years, but four years earlier he took the water delivery job to be closer to his family.

Tony strolled in with his usual greeting, "What's up, ladies! Big Papa's in the house!" It was particularly funny because it always bothered Nick, the sole male receptionist. Tony didn't care. He got a casual "Hey, Tony" from a few of the other staff. His wife made a bee-line from behind the counter when she saw him. She looked worried. Instead of the usual smooch, Tony just got a quick hug.

"I've been trying to call the school and all I get is a busy signal," Sheila told her husband.

"Relax, babe. I'm sure the kids are fine. Schools are built tough!"

"They're on a field trip to Seattle today, remember?"

Awww, snap! "Alright, alright, now *calm down*, baby. I'm sure the girls are fine. I was able to drive here from Canal Vista. Everything's okay." He was doing his best to show that he believed it. He had to because he knew he would have to be the one that held it together.

There was a long pause. Her eyes drifted past his shoulder as she mulled his words over. "You'd better be right."

Tony knew that tone and was scared of it. "It'll be *fine*, baby. They're okay, I'm *sure* o' it." *I'd better escape while I can.* "I'm gonna run home real quick like, and then I'll call the school. When everything turns out to be fine, I'm goin' back to work. I drove right past 'em to come here."

His wife gave him a wary eye as she pecked him on the lips and headed back to the correct side of the reception counter. She stopped and turned. "You'd *better* be right," she repeated with extra emphasis as he headed out the door.

Whew. No kiddin', I'd better be right. Hell hath no fury... Tony fired the beast back up and made the normally five-minute drive to his house in twelve minutes. He backed in to his driveway, opened his garage door, and off-loaded sixteen five-gallon jugs of water. *But— just in case I'm not right,* he kept repeating in his mind.

THE SHIPYARD'S Emergency Operations Center was abuzz with multiple conversations, most of them urgent. Marie had called for a senior manager's meeting in the EOC's larger conference room, to begin at 0930. There were about sixty people crammed into a room meant for forty. Her chair at the head of the table was available and waiting. Everyone knew who sat there. She strode in, hanging her uniform coat on the back of the chair. Most days she wore the same camo-uniform every sailor wore. Some days she would go to meetings or retirement parties out in the community, and on those days she wore her working khaki uniform with the ribbon rack under the left side collar. She was wearing that uniform, which had an odd way of adding to the urgency of the meeting. She sat down.

"NERD, start your report with Dry-dock A, please." Nobody was giggling. No greetings. No time for that. She wanted to hear from specific people in a specific order.

The Nuclear Emergency Response Director, Jamison Thrall, stood up. "Captain, the crane accident at Dry-dock A did indeed involve the refueling team. They were in the process of raising a rod-cannister up after it had retrieved a spent fuel-rod when the earthquake hit. Those things weigh nearly four thousand pounds when loaded. It swung around like a giant weight and got caught on some of the ship's structure and piping near the hull-cut. It over-loaded the crane, which shut itself down following its own emer-gency procedures. Now we have a rod-container and crane stuck in an ominous position with unknown levels of damage to the rigging gear. This is unprecedented in even the most experienced team member's careers."

"What about the ship and the facilities, Mr. Thrall?"

"Ma'am, we're going to have to inspect the dock-setting before we do anything. We'll then need to measure list and trim and have the shipwrights take positional shots on the hull and the refueling complex. My guess is that things walked around a few inches."

"Okay. What about spills?"

"Ship's force reports some unplanned water in the bilge. Right now, an isolation perimeter has been set up topside of the dock by the shipyard workers, awaiting the dock inspections to clear the way to re-enter the ship.

"Mr. Thrall, do you have one of the encoded/encrypted radios?" the captain asked.

"Yes, ma'am."

"Good. Find me anytime you have new information. *Any* time. Understood?"

"Crystal clear, Captain."

"Dock Master," she said. "Give me some good news."

Glenn Harper, the shipyard's senior-manager of docks and piers, stood up. "Captain, I and my team have stopped by every dry-dock and personally directed the project managers to block off access to all dry-docks pending word from you or me." He let that sit for a second and then continued. "The pier-side ships and barges are still being inspected. So far, we're seeing that all the caissons have maintained a good seat-and-seal. Remember, E is already flooded and without caisson at this time." He was referring to Dry-dock E, which was open to the inlet for several months. It's caisson —essentially a ship designed to sink in a specific place and plug the dry-dock—was in a shipyard in Seattle being refurbished.

"And the pump wells, Mr. Harper?"

"I can speak to that, Captain." Standing up with her hand half-raised was Lisa Carpenter, the superintendent of Shop 66, the collection of trades that specialized in providing power, air, water, and most other temporary services to the projects and piers. "Ma'am, the pump-wells checked in via the radios and sound-powered back-up systems. They report a series of pressure spikes and drops that have slowly stabilized. All systems are operational. The transition to back-up power went as smoothly as we can expect. It will take a full day of testing and monitoring to be sure, but we're fairly confident there are no leaks in the dry-docks."

The average person looked at a dry-dock as nothing more complex than a concrete bowl with a metal plug. In reality, the dry-docks were built between seventy and a hundred and ten years earlier, mostly on fill material. There was a series of tunnels and pumps running below the shipyard that had to be continuously de-watered. This was imperative year-round anyway, but definitely in rainy season, which usually coincided with higher tides. If the pumps quit working, the docks would slowly fill with water, no matter how well the caisson sealed itself.

"Thank you, Lisa," Marie said. "I'm hearing from Public Works that the power-plant should be back up on normal power in an hour or two.

The meeting continued for another forty-five minutes. Marie took in every piece of information she could. Representatives from the security and fire departments were there, too. Damage to most buildings was superficial. The Navy had spent a ton of money upgrading facilities for several years; however, for a place this big, it took time. Two building managers were reporting severe damage, and at more than an hour into the event, not every person had been accounted for. *Lord, just let that be an administrative issue,* Marie thought. *No deaths.*

The local Slaughter County Department of Emergency Management was already asking for any news. They were extremely aware of the potential for hazardous things to drift from the shipyard into Bartlett in the form of a radioactive cloud. *Nobody wants another Fukushima, people, just give me a minute to gather some information...*

She had learned that the backup power plant out on the base had lit off two of the three boilers without incident. The third was out of service for maintenance, but it was being brought back online as quickly as possible. *As long as we don't lose our natural gas lines from Olympic Power Administration,* she worried to herself. She didn't want to resort to coal, as they only had a few weeks' supply of that stored.

She ordered her Public Information Officer to release a statement to the local press and civic leaders to the effect that while there was some damage, initial reports showed no issues, yada, yada, yada. Her final decision of this meeting was to slowly release noncritical shipyard and contractor personnel by zone, so as to not flood Bartlett with too much traffic. People were already starting to slip out anyway.

The meeting had finally broken, and people started to check status boards one final time before they went back down the hill to the shipyard. "EMCO," she beckoned into the open, not immediately seeing him through the crowd.

"Here, Ma'am," he said as he scurried over from just inside the Comms Area.

"Two things. First, send out a text and email instructing all building managers to implement the emergency power restriction plan. Secondly, have you heard from Captain Reese?" she asked, referring to the Commanding Officer of the attached Navy base.

"Yes, Ma'am, he says he can support. He'd like to talk it over with you in person, but he's already concurring."

"Good. Thank you. Call him back. Tell him to implement Phase One of the Emergency Sheltering Plan. Phase One only, at this time. Setting up the shelters would be a major event—no need to have him start until we're positive we need to. Tell him I'll be at his office in fifteen minutes."

John repeated the orders back to ensure he heard them correctly and then headed towards Comms to make it happen.

"Oh, EMCO, one last thing. Notify the Critical Personnel Distribution List that we're having a mandatory all-hands muster at 1130 hours in front of Building 855, right in the middle of Monsoor Avenue. Only critical watch-standers and the evaluation at Drydock A are exempt."

4

This Isn't Fun Anymore.

QUAKE + 2 HOURS.

THE LINE at the ATM was getting longer. *I hope there's still some cash left...* Dr. Stuart Schwartz usually carried a minimum of $600 on him. In his line of work, he went to dinners and parties a lot, usually hosted by an actor or singer who wanted his art performed on them. That's what he called it. *Art.* Cutting on people's noses and jawlines in a way that improved their looks without changing their sound was risky. Not just any meat cutter became skilled at it. After his share of a $1,000 dinner provided by a potential client, he usually covered the tip.

The power had come back on about twenty minutes into the event. Schwartz wasn't sure if it was the actual utility or just generators, and he didn't much care. *This airport won't be normal for a day or two at least.* He needed to get to Portland or Spokane—anywhere with a runway that flies planes to LAX.

He kept staring at his Mariner watch—bouncing up and down on the balls of his feet out of boredom, looking around. The wailing had slowed considerably. The authorities were performing triage by the book. Other than the obvious plane crash, Schwartz wasn't quite sure if anyone had perished, but there *had* been a couple of decent traumas in the replica wreckage by his gate. That one guy was definitely concussed, but all the idiots kept worrying about his mangled forearm. The whole scene was almost enough to pique his interest in real medicine again. *Almost.*

After twenty minutes, he was able to draw the maximum $600 from the machine. His money clip already had $280 in it. He hadn't reloaded for the trip up because it was Sequim, Washington, not New York or San Francisco. *Why the hell would I need all that cash where some redneck meth addict would just steal it anyway?*

He took his cash and stepped back to put it away. *Yep, that line goes at least a hundred feet farther back than where it was when I jumped into it. I'd better get moving.* His first thought was to get snacks and water and find someone who could sell him a bus ticket. Schwartz started to wander back out of Concourse B. *Look at all the people waiting to be told what to do. Don't they realize today is over? They're not letting anyone use those runways until at least tomorrow.* He was somewhat happy about their ignorance, though, because he would have a better chance at grabbing a hotel if it came to that. Schwartz stopped in an airport gift-shop and bought several bottles of water and a few bags of bland granola-type mix. It didn't escape him that many of the shelves were already running out of items.

As if on cue, the airport PA system sparked to life. "Attention SeaTac Patrons. This is the Public Information Officer. All flights are cancelled for the rest of today." This sparked a collective groan from several thousand people. "Please stay tuned to the local television and radio news reports for update, or you may contact your airline tomorrow morning at six AM Thank you for your patience and understanding."

Once the announcement was over, most people started to collect their carry-on items and move like a zombie hoard toward the entrance to the terminal. Several were voicing their complaints loudly. Nobody cared. They were all screwed. Schwartz did a slow two-step dance which he dubbed the "SeaTac Shuffle" for about a half hour. He eventually made his way up to the same car rental agency where he had checked in the late-model Lexus not five hours earlier. True to his suspicions, the system was down—*Ahhh, yes, the "system." That magical thing that breaks and screws us all*—and the rental agency wouldn't be renting anything until it was back up. Nobody could point out anyone who could sell him a bus ticket. *Do I chance an Uber to the bus terminal?* He deliberated his choices for several seconds. *Hotel it is.* He wandered out of SeaTac Airport, turning right onto International Blvd. under breaking clouds and a glimmer of hope that this would end soon.

CRANE NOTICED that the crowd was pretty big at the mustering-point but that not everybody was stopping there. An hour or so earlier, all shipwrights—and a few, other key trades—had been told by their supervisors and managers that they had two minutes to get into their locker rooms and grab their personal stuff. This had allowed most of them a chance to grab their lunches for a little energy break. When they learned of the "critical trades" muster coming at 1130, the rumors started, and like most rumors, there was a shred of truth at the core.

In his mind, Crane ran over some of the possibilities being tossed around. *Conscripted? Who uses THAT word anymore? Held back from leaving? Someone died? What's a critical trade? Inspections?* That last one made the most sense.

After the earthquake, Billy had told him that after the last big earthquake nearly twenty years earlier, they had made key trades stay behind. They had to inspect things like brows, barges, dry-docks, and dock-settings while everyone else got to leave. Judging by the fact that nine out of every ten people Crane saw were walking right past the gathering, Billy was spot-on. He was still surveying the passersby and making small talk with a rigger-diver buddy of his when the Shipyard Duty Officer's truck backed out of its parking spot under the parapet of Building 855 and slowly reversed towards the crowd. It happened so slowly that people were more curious than worried. The Chevy stopped about ten feet from the crowd, and the officer backing it up got out and just stood there waiting for someone. About two minutes later, Captain Darnell and several other leaders walked out of Building 855. She walked directly to the parked truck, dropped the tailgate, and climbed up, turning around to address the crowd. A junior officer who had followed her out of 855 handed her an electronic megaphone.

"Wow. What a day..." There was a low murmur from the crowd. They all knew what was about to be said. Workers who felt like they were about to get the shaft didn't generally put off a laughing, friendly vibe. "So, I'll get right to it. We got lucky. We've learned that this earthquake was somewhere in the 7.0 category, maybe higher. Power is out almost everywhere. The various utility companies say there are a variety of causes, mostly trees falling on lines. Some fires, too. Some dams have shut themselves down, apparently—a form of tripping-off for self-preservation. Reports that a plane crashed as it was landing. Locally we haven't heard of too many issues."

She continued. "The vast majority of reports mention minor damage—signs falling off buildings, things like that. The Hood Canal Bridge and the newer Tacoma-Narrows bridge are open. Roads are okay in most areas, but closer to the epicenter somewhere north of Tacoma there has been some road buckling. We've heard unverified rumors of a landslide in West Seattle. I emphasize 'unverified.' We've also heard that one of the legs of the Space Needle is showing serious structural damage. We've been rocked…rocked hard. There's no denying that. But it could have been worse.

"What I can't emphasize enough, though, is that rumors don't help anyone. Pass along information. Don't pass along scuttlebutt. That being said, I will lay to rest the rumors you've been hearing. I *do* need to keep you here, and I can't tell you for how long."

This caused an audible noise of irritation to rise from the crowd. *Billy called it,* Crane thought. He would've given the old graying ship-wright his due credit, but Billy had posted himself over near the closest smoking area. When the collective groan subsided, the Captain continued.

"Folks, I don't make this decision lightly. I want you to know that. I get it. It sucks, sitting here, watching other people walk by to go check on their families. Believe me… I'm a sailor. I understand your sacrifice." This statement eased the crowd's irritation a bit. "We have a real issue here, and I *need* you. I need your *help*. Your community—your country—needs you today." Dead silence from 1,600 people.

She's good, Cane thought. *She just punched us right in the patriotic gut.*

The captain continued. "We need some of you to go back into the docks and inspect settings and platforms. We need the portal cranes inspected. We need the piers inspected. We need the Hammerhead crane inspected. We need to verify shore power and industrial power is intact—that the ships have the correct services getting to critical systems." She paused for a moment to survey the workers. "I think you all get it. And I'm sorry. I hope to be able to send you home by the end of your regular shift, but we'll stay and get it done as long as it takes. Swing-shift was instructed via the automated reporting system to take care of their families and only come in to work if they have the means to get here safely.

"Here are some of our biggest concerns. For security reasons, there are some things I won't say out here in the open. But I will tell you that we have some concerns at Dry-dock A that are being moni-tored. Some of you are probably wondering why your work team is considered critical. It is because of your training. If you're not an engineer, or one of the rigging, scaffolding, and temp-service trades, then you're most likely here because we need your nuclear training qualifications. We need you to help us evaluate a situation."

Crane started to tune her out. *Once again, the grunts get screwed into staying while all the superfluous overhead get to leave. Figures. If they have a spill to clean up, why are they letting so many people go home? What about the rest of us? We have families to check on, too.*

Crane was worried. This place wasn't just a job, it was his career —this town was his home. *To Hell with earthquakes...* It wasn't supposed to be this way.

THUD. The cell phone landed with a small plop on the couch cushion. Tony had just tossed it like a frisbee, annoyed that his multiple attempts to call the school had gone nowhere. He picked the paper he found on the fridge back up. The twins had gone to the Seattle Center. There were several museums, the mono-rail...*What on Earth is the Museum of Pop Culture? Isn't that still called the Experience Music Project? Hell, I wanna go see that...* Tony shook it off.

He got up off the couch, picked his phone back up, and paced over to the kitchen to get a glass of water. He grabbed a cup, and out of habit tried to get water from the little spout on the refrigerator door. Nothing. *Fool—power's still out.* He filled his glass from the sink, wondering how long until that stopped working, too.

Brrrrt.... [Sheila: "On the way home. Hear anything yet?"]

[Tony: "Phones r still jacked. Itll b fine, baby".]

Yeppp...it'll be fine...

5

Tahoma's Hammer.

QUAKE + 3 HOURS.

PHIL HAD SPENT most of the last hour photographing everything he could. *Evidence, just in case,* he thought. Earthquake insurance in this area was next to impossible. He had it once, about a dozen years earlier, but they must've had some number crunchers re-do the math. His earthquake rider was dropped without warning. He remembered that after disasters, FEMA was sometimes able to help people apply for federal aid. That's what the photos were for.

He had received a number of texts from various club members and in return had been inquiring about the welfare of some of the more elderly members he was concerned about. It was a large organization, but the most active five percent were very close personally.

Phil decided he would throw some additional items into the truck and go check on a couple of families that lived nearby.

I should check on Hope, he decided. Hope Brazik was a widow and long-term supporter of the club. Her husband, Thom, had been a member for over forty years when he passed away from lung cancer two years earlier. Phil had always looked up to Thom and adored Hope. They'd been married fifty-two years. Being a widower to cancer himself, he felt a sense of duty to check on her as often as he could, usually about twice per month. *If Hope is doing okay, I'll go see the Fishers and do a last check of the range.*

Phil added some cans of stew and soup to one of the cloth grocery bags that had practically become mandatory in Washington State. *Anything soft,* he thought, thinking about what would be easiest on her. He went out to the truck and placed the bag on the passenger side front seat. Walking around the rear of the truck, he peeked in and paused. He stared at the bed-cover, in his mind trying to play out what else he had in there. He turned, went to the garage and picked up his camping and hunting gear. He threw the gear onto the rear bench in the cab, on top of the normal "get home bag" that he already kept in there. He then marched around the house to the shop, where he put more tooling into a well-worn, black and red "Porter Cable" bag. Trying to decide what issues he could possibly run into, Phil added a battery and blades for the reci-procating saw. He also tossed in some wire, "gorilla" tape, and a variety of small hand tools. Lastly, he added his shop's portable spotlight.

Before closing the shop, he also took his four-ton come-along off the wall and set it outside. He secured the roll-up door, picked up the tools, and headed to the truck while calling for Dakota to join him.

As he drove back down Medford Lane, he noticed that someone had already removed the rest of the tree from the roadway. He passed over a pile of woodchips and sawdust and turned right onto Canal Vista Highway. Just under eight-tenths of a mile south, he went through the round-a-bout and veered west instead of the usual south towards the club. Salal Road was one of the primary roads into the farthest western portion of the Slaughter Peninsula. He would need to drive the road's five-mile length and turn once more to get to Hope's place. Shortly after changing roads, Dakota started to whine.

About eight seconds later, Phil experienced what it must be like to be the blunt end of a jack-hammer. His head began to slam repeatedly into the ceiling of his cab. He performed a death-grip on the steering wheel, which seemed to have come alive, wobbling back and forth as if both front wheels had just come loose. He hit the brakes. Dakota and the bag of food crashed onto the passenger side floor. The bouncing intensified.

Phil barely saw "the wave." The road ahead of him literally was doing a wave, and it was coming straight for him. His thoughts weren't forming into words—there was no time. He just thought of Payton and Savannah. He decided later that it was a reflection of his desire to get past the strain in their relationship.

Trees swayed hard in the wave, too, as if bowing to some royal party that had just walked by. Some of them sprang back to life while others just kept going. When the asphalt wave hit Phil's truck, the front end lurched skyward and then dove into a valley of asphalt, all in the course of an eternal second. He had no control over the steering, and though he'd hit the brakes, the truck was still carrying its forward momentum. A second wave flipped the truck onto the shoulder of the wrong side of the road. It came to rest on its left side and continued to wobble, straddling the drainage ditch in a way that created a gap under Phil's door.

What felt like forever to Phil was actually three minutes and two seconds, and it made the first earthquake seem like a playground ride. The pause in the shaking only lasted long enough for him to open his eyes and look out his shattered driver's door window, as cans of soup and stew spilled out into the ditch below. Then the shaking started again.

MEGATHRUST. This is the result when two tectonic plates—in this case the Pacific plate and the Juan de Fuca plate—finally release their friction lock on each other. Their overlap had become known by scientists and civilians as the Cascadia Subduction Zone. Evidence had pointed to a M9.0 about three hundred and fifty years earlier, with a frequency of every 300 to 500 years. They were due.

Cascadia was a name that had come to symbolize the Pacific Northwest and was often associated with Washington State. In 2016, the federal and state governments conducted a region-wide exercise for three days, and they were glad they did. Agencies learned a lot about working with each other. Everyone learned just how devastated the entire region would be when the next subduction zone earthquake struck. *Not IF, but WHEN…* Perhaps the intraplate earthquake earlier that day was the final trigger to awaken the giant. Nobody would ever know, and it didn't really matter. The chicken didn't try to figure out the reasoning when its neck was being wrung off. It just knew it was about to die.

At just over six hundred miles long and fifty miles off the coast, the Cascadia Subduction Zone ran roughly parallel to the continent from Northern California to Northern Vancouver Island, Canada. It was 12:29 P.M. when the heated edges of the two plates had finally given in to each other. In terms of geology, continental shift is normally measured in centimeters per decade or even per century. This was the moment that 197-miles of the zone decided to drop roughly fifty-one inches, taking just over three minutes to do it. The epicenter was due west of Grays Harbor, Washington. Shockwaves of energy with nowhere to go echoed out in every direction. The pebble had just hit the placid pond.

Tsunamis are formed by the sudden crashing of water. When a shelf of land on the ocean floor drops, the water above does, too, causing the water on the "high side" of the fault to fall. A tsunami's speed is proportional to its depth. Deep ocean tsunamis have been known to travel five hundred miles-per-hour. The coastal region between the zone and Washington State was a relatively flat shelf of about two hundred meters in depth. Tsunamis start faster than they finish. As they near the shore and shallowing depths, the front of the wave slows down while the back doesn't.

The wave crest this day had three minutes to form—it was over a mile deep from front to back. As the front slowed, the back started to pile up similarly to how cars pile up in a bad freeway accident. Once it neared the shore the water on the coast started to pull off shore, feeding the front of the wave. With shallowing depth, the mile-deep wave grew in height.

Cascadia's wave started at a relatively slow ninety miles-per-hour, travelling the fifty-mile distance in just over a half hour. The four-foot wave started drawing water off the coast when it was about six miles out. The boats and ships in the fishing and tourist towns of Aberdeen, Westport, Hoquiam, and Ocean Shores that had not cast off their piers after the earlier earthquake started to stretch their mooring lines as they sank to the mud below. Lines parted and cleats broke off piers. People stopped what they were doing to gawk. The fishing crews and the tourists were the ones left watching. Many people were fleeing towards the nearest tall build-ings, while others just stopped to video. One enterprising couple who was on their twenty-fifth wedding anniversary put a good-bye video to their kids onto the Cloud.

When Cascadia's Tsunami reached the coast, it was twenty-eight feet tall and travelling about twenty-five miles-per-hour. The wall of water hit the cliffs on the Washington Coast north of Grays Harbor with the energy of 10,000 freight trains. The cliffs had already started to sluff from three minutes of shaking. Coastal towns and villages were consumed by water as terrified people held on to their loved ones. The religious prayed and confessed. So did many of the non-religious. High ground east of the cliffs remained relatively safe. Any home above 90-feet in elevation was relatively spared, at least in the areas where the cliff stayed intact. Ironically, it was their proximity to the coastal cliffs that saved them. Most of the energy from the wave hitting such a steep slope was absorbed. The rest was pushed proportionately north and south.

In the low lands, tsunami sirens had been sounding for several minutes, as if they were old air raid sirens in 1940 England. The giant wall was really the second of a one–two punch delivered by Cascadia. Many of the homes were better than sixty years old, far pre-dating modern construction requirements. Most of them had shaken right off their foundations in the opening moments. The wave only served to turn them into thousands of cubic yards of flot-sam. Those that had taken high ground in buildings taller than three stories—and there weren't many of those in the old logging and shipping towns—had managed to preserve their lives…if the building were new enough.

The harbor cities trailed off into a valley that led east towards the south end of Puget Sound. The north side of the highway was relatively high ground while the south plateaued. The wave marched up this corridor about twenty-four miles, destroying the town of Montesano in the process. The wall of cars on the highway leading out of the coastal cities did nothing to slow the wave. Most of those cars turned into two-ton coffins, stranded in fields and forests. Across the entire coast from Astoria to Vancouver Island, a similar story played out.

ACROSS WESTERN WASHINGTON and her neighbors to the north and south, the ground liquefied for three minutes. Even the newest buildings and highways, built with the best of modern engineering, were tested beyond their design limits. Waves of energy travelled west to east. People were frozen in place—literally. Fear aside, there was no way to walk or run and nowhere to go if they could. Every-thing was a target—no hallowed ground.

In multiple locations across Puget Sound, bluffs and high points of land sloughed off into the water, causing mini-tsunamis. These wave-energies met each other in the middle of the Sound in multiple locations, turning the water into a frothy brown and gray bath of turmoil. Any ships, boats, and ferries that were still out on the water after the earlier quake had suddenly found themselves in a tempest of rough seas. Many sank.

Roads buckled and turned into multi-layered asphalt shelves, especially where they were still the wettest, near the places that led to streams or other bodies of water. Many of the bridges collapsed. The older of two Tacoma Narrows Bridges—the famous "Galloping Gertie"—had lost most of its deck structure to the inlet below. It began to lean east, away from the other bridge.

In Seattle, the relatively modern sports arenas held up well, which was a stroke of luck. The streets of Seattle turned into streams of glass as the skyscrapers lost most of their windows. Paper rained on the city for days, as the wind and rain continued to drive it out of offices up high. The glass rivers were pocked with holes where the ground and streets gave away—Seattle was built on fill material after all. Watermains broke, flooding streets with water and sewage, an event played out in every town and city. Older buildings crumbled where they stood, turning into piles of rubble. This, in turn, started fires fueled by natural gas lines. Modern buildings had been built directly on top of older buildings. The famous Seattle "Underground" existed no longer as fill and building materials compacted in the shaking.

The famed Space Needle, once a marvel of modern engineering, let gravity have her as the northeast leg could no longer take the strain started by the first quake. People watching it fall described seeing it in slow motion, a phenomenon known as tachypsychia. The Needle was already starting to lean, bending rebar and spalling the concrete on the outside. As it started to go it looked like it was headed straight for the Museum of Pop Art. Gaining speed as it went, the Needle smashed through the monorail tracks to the south of the museum with the saucer coming to rest upright in the parking lot of the famed "Duck Ride" boats.

The once famous Alaska Way Viaduct no longer existed. It had been replaced with a two-mile-long tunnel—famous for taking almost two years too long to complete. The new tunnel turned into a watery tomb despite being billed as "the safest place in Seattle for earthquakes." The wet fill-earth around it jostled and gave way for three minutes leading to multiple cracks in the concrete tube. The dewatering pumps were already running at only fifty percent capacity to conserve back-up power. The tunnel—actually a series of tunnels wrapped up into one circular hole—finally split open, flooding the northbound lower deck first. The tunnel had just been re-opened to traffic, being the very first item that Seattle and State engineers checked on earlier in the day. They *had* to get people moving again.

At SeaTac Airport, the small cracks in the runways and taxiways had become major crevices. Like most of the roads and highways around Western Washington, the tarmac area around the terminals was pockmarked with collapses and sink holes. Boeing's runways suffered similar issues.

The shipping ports of Seattle, Tacoma, and Everett fared no better. The continuous shaking and churning of the waters had slammed vessels against the piers they were moored at, cracking hulls and flooding the ships. They sank right at their berths, many of them catching fire from fuel leaks.

Washington State was the nation's leading exporter of hydro-electric power to other states, most notably California. Washington residents got seventy percent of their power from nearly thirty dams, the largest of which were on the Snake and Colombia Rivers.

When Cascadia awoke the power distribution system was completely destroyed. Trees and mudslides had already started the damage after the first quake. Three minutes of ground liquefaction was more than the aging system could bear. Entire power stations sunk into the ground, ranging from inches to feet. High-voltage lines

on 300-foot-tall towers fell. Dams took structural damage, many of
them opting to release water through the spillways to save themselves. This panic-driven release flooded homes and towns for
dozens of miles downstream. The entire Pacific Northwest had just
re-entered the seventeenth century, electrically speaking.

TAHOMA. This was the most well-known Native name for the
volcano that Captain George Vancouver had named after Captain
Peter Rainer in the 1790's. At 14,410 feet, she could be seen from
almost any point of elevation in the western half of the state on a
cloudless summer day. One of only two North American volcanos
placed on the Decade List—a list of deadly must-watch volcanos—
she was quite beautiful, covered in large glaciers. As a stratovolcano,
these glaciers were what concerned scientists the most. Tahoma
could be capable of lava flows and debris flows, but it was the lahars
that posed the greatest threat.

Lahar was a word most people weren't familiar with. Glacial ice
would melt, sheering off trees and rock while mixing with earth.
The ensuing mudflows would stream down the mountain, flowing
like water, taking the path of least resistance.

Immediately following Cascadia, two more earthquakes were
triggered. The northern one struck along the middle of the Seattle
Faultline, a M7.0 that was fifteen miles deep and lasted forty-six
seconds. It was centered under the passage of Simpson Inlet
between Bartlett and Russell Island, a mere mile from the Washington State Naval Shipyard and Bartlett Ferry Dock. The other
quake was a M6.9, at a very shallow depth of six miles, lasting
eighty-eight seconds. Tahoma listened.

People within thirty miles of Tahoma knew something was
different with this quake. It just smelled differently, emitting a
noxious, metallic sulfur-like smell. The noise was different, too—
deep and penetrating. The homes and buildings they were hiding in

started to make horrible creaks and groans as if giving up the ghost in a massive fight to the death. Most of those older structures collapsed.

The top of Tahoma shot skyward, sending rocks ranging in size from pebbles to cars up to 80,000 feet into the sky. The western and northern faces started to dissolve into lahars of snow, ice, mud, tree, and stone. The lahars travelled down the steepest slopes, picking up speed as they went. Some of the towns' volcano alarms—those few that still worked—began to wail. If it weren't so tragic, it would have been comical. *No kidding, Sherlock*, everyone who heard the alarms thought, when the wind-up sirens started to whine. The lahars filled the river and stream valleys below, which acted as big funnels. Towns like Ashford, Eatonville, Carbonado, and Elbe were covered in mere minutes—covered as if they had never existed. Greenwater—gone. Orting—gone.

As the mud, trees, and rock crept quickly to the west and north, it continued to spread out of the river valleys. Lowland ports like Olympia and Tacoma were covered in up to four feet of mud. Highway I-5 was covered in a varying depth of mud from south of Yelm to Federal Way. Joint Base Lewis McChord and its priceless runways were covered in two feet of mud and another foot of ash, spared worse due to being on a slightly elevated plateau. Under that mud, the runways had been horribly cracked. At SeaTac Airport, the runways were split wide open—repairable, but only if the right equipment and material were brought in. It would have taken weeks in the best of times.

Farther north, the Seattle Faultline epicenter rocked the Central and North Sound areas with similar results. The southern end of Russell Island dissolved into the epicenter in a massive landslide never before seen in scale. The landslide and epicenter both combined to cause an eighteen-inch tsunami—massive for an inlet. The only thing that kept the tsunami from growing taller was the extreme depth of the inlets and Puget Sound. The shores were very steep. However, water began to pull away from piers and docks, which were starting to crumble from the violent shaking. The tsunami wasn't very tall, but it was wide and long. Feeding it caused large tidal swings.

Jet fuel is relatively stable, which normally makes it ideal for large-volume storage. It has a relatively small explosive limit range, which to the average person means nothing. To a fire-fighter, it means that the vapors have to be between .6% and 4.7% of the airspace they're in to be explosive. In general, if a person can smell the jet fuel, then it is too rich to explode, even with an open flame in the area. There is another property of fuels called the "auto-ignition" point. This is the temperature a fuel must reach in order to explode, even without the presence of an ignition source. For JP-8 jet fuel, that temperature is 410 degrees-Fahrenheit.

East of Port View in Slaughter County, the military housed their largest fuel storage facility in the continental U.S. at the Manford Fuel Depot. The 990-foot-long pier had split into two major pieces, ripping open several large-bore fuel pipes in the process. About midway down the pier was a small building used for a variety of maintenance tasks and—ironically— firefighting gear storage. The breaker panel began to spark as the pier ripped open from under the facility. A flammable materials storage locker flipped over, spilling several cans of gasoline staged to run the firefighting pumps. The sparking and spilt-gasoline eventually combined to catch the little structure on fire.

The little building's fire continued to grow, warming up the jet-fuel pipes just outside. Those very pipes that were spilling their fuel onto Puget Sound in another location. They were well over 1,200 degrees in temperature when the vapor level inside them dipped below 4.7% due to the fuel being absent.

The chain reaction was staggering…

As if the ecological disaster wasn't bad enough, the fire chased its way through the pipes to the transfer and pumping station at the head of the pier. It exploded in the first of over thirty fireballs that combined to look similar to the effects of a small, tactical nuclear weapon—sans the radiation.

The shipyard's 250-foot-tall Hammerhead Crane—the icon that often represents the entire peninsula in postcards and promotion videos—started to sink on its eastern pilings. At the Bartlett Ferry Dock, the tide suddenly lowered almost twenty feet as the water fed the mini-tsunami. The mooring lines that had been holding the ferries in place during terminal inspections stretched beyond their capability. The water rushed out to fill the void, caused by the splitting faultline and the variety of mudslides filling the Sound. The Captain of the ferry *Kaleetan* floored his engines, which are always running forward a bit to hold the ferry firmly to the pier. As the water rushed out, the aft end of the ferry sunk down into the muck below, forcing him to disengage his props.

As the water began to rush back in towards the ferry terminal, the *Kaleetan's* captain watched and waited. At about the time he thought his props were covered again he jammed the throttles into full-reverse. As the stern started to lift out of the muck, the propellers cavitated, shaking the end of the ship. Ultimately, the reverse thrust took enough strain off the front of the ship that the ship stabilized and rode out the ensuring wave action relatively unscathed.

The captain of the *Chimacum* had tried a different approach. He had ordered the crew to stage themselves with axes by the mooring lines until the terminals had been deemed safe again. When the second earthquake struck, he had his crew cut the lines and began to back off the terminal. He had managed to get about four hundred feet off the terminal, out over much deeper water, and his ship was still afloat.

What had seemed like a solid plan to the captain and crew of the *Chimacum* suddenly felt like a horrible idea. Even though he had her in reverse-thrust, the lumbering ship was no match for the rushing tide. Knowing things were about to end badly, the captain ordered for a hard-to-starboard steer, hoping to avoid colliding with the pilings and *Kaleetan* to the port. It worked. The port forward bow plowed through the piling packs farthest to the north, and the wave drove the big ferry into the smaller passenger-only ferry that was already taking her own beating on the next pier. Both vessels eventually broke loose of the carnage and began smashing into the smaller private vessels and piers to the north at the Bartlett Marina.

A similar tidal drop occurred at the Washington State Naval Shipyard, only to the lesser extent of twelve feet. Complicated by the fact that the area was already at low-tide, Navy-owned barges and vessels began to break free of their moorings. The shipyard employees had not yet fully inspected the outside of all the dry-dock's caissons and seating surfaces. If they had, they might not have let people back into the docks quite yet.

The dry-dock's caissons were essentially vessels designed to sink into very specific spots and act like bathtub stoppers. They sat in a groove, and even if every drop of water were removed from the outside, they would stay put—in theory. They were essentially sitting in a big notch, and their seating surface was what could be called a rubber gasket. The caissons were filled with many thousands of gallons of seawater, essentially turning them into giant weights. The first earthquake had churned up rocks, logs, and other debris that had slowly collected in the inlet throughout the years. Concrete and granite had broken off the almost 100-year-old quay walls outside a few of the caissons during the first quake.

When Cascadia fell and the ensuing intraplate earthquakes arose, the caissons were subjected to the same bouncing and shaking as everything else. The dry-docks were, too. Cracks and gouges had started to form. Caisson seats were broken, and water began to leak into the docks. Four-and-a-half total minutes of shaking might as well have been an eon as the churned-up rocks, logs, and broken pieces of granite and concrete found their way into some of the caisson seats.

A large merchant marine vessel—staged at WSNS for transporting army troops from Tacoma to a war zone—broke off its mooring at Pier 5. The big vessel was largely automated, running on a crew of barely twenty people. The vessel's master had not anticipated the second earthquake. Even with the backup diesels running for on-board power, there was no time to light boilers. Hoses and power cables snapped first, pulling out of their fittings and manifolds. Next to go were the mooring lines and bollards on the pier, which were not designed to contain a 60,000-ton vessel that had suddenly become dead weight. When the water came rushing back in, the vessel was aimed directly at the caisson of Dry-dock A. Every dry-dock was subject to incoming "torpedoes" made of boats, piers, rocks, and pieces of houses, but not so much as Dry-dock A's caisson. The structure managed to hold up well, all things considered. The big ship smashed into the west end of it, at about twenty-eight feet in height, causing interior frames to buckle and bulkheads to rip at the welds. The entire upper third of the west side of the caisson was open to the air. Inspectors in the dry-dock, operating under the rally speech by their Commanding Officer, had not been able to flee during the shaking.

Looks of sheer terror crossed their faces as they glanced up and saw daylight and a huge, listing ship where they shouldn't be. As the tide started to creep into the new seam, it looked like a small, trickling fountain for a moment. This quickly evolved into a massive gush. Approximately fifty people started scrambling for the dry-dock stairs, screaming to anyone that they could. People above the dock were watching in horror, screaming and waving at those below. It was useless, as anyone who rode out Cascadia and Tahoma in a dry-dock knew to leave as fast as humanly possible. Amazingly, nobody had been caught in the ensuing torrent. But the Navy's nuclear-powered nightmare had just taken a massive turn for the worse.

6

Shock.

BY THE TIME TAHOMA DROPPED ITS HAMMER ON THE NORTHWEST, the clouds had started to thin for the afternoon. There was something to be said about the magnitude of trillions of cubic yards of earth shooting more than twice as high as jets fly. It created its own weather. Particles ionized, causing lightning and thunder. The particulates were attracted to water vapor in the atmosphere, which aided in the formation of dark clouds. The sight was ominous, as the sheer volume of it was enough to be seen through and above the thinning overcast layer. The plume slowly decreased, and by the next morning it had dissipated into a smaller column of steam.

The autumn jet-stream over the Northwest travelled into lower British Columbia before turning south and crossing most of the United States in a south-easterly direction. It then banked left toward the middle-eastern seaboard somewhere over Georgia and South Carolina. Swipes of Tahoma ash were able to be sampled in the eastern states by the following afternoon. The ash took about two weeks to completely travel the globe.

That was only the beginning of the trickle-down effects to the rest of the nation and world. Within moments, power surges shot through the national electric grid. Rolling blackouts started occurring in the entire western half of America. The sudden loss of hydro-generated electricity affected California the most. Power wasn't the only utility affected.

Microsoft was deeply impacted by the devastation, as were their supporting cloud servers. Power and server cooling-water had become non-existent within hours. The world's leading creator of computer software quit issuing their hourly and daily security patches and software updates. Entire segments of cloud memory were suddenly inaccessible by individuals and corporations alike.

Amazon's Seattle HQ—literally several blocks of downtown Seattle—was reeling after sinking several feet into the soft fill the city was famously built-on. Fiber optic internet cables were crushed, which caused a domino effect of communications issues for the internet's largest retailer and the rest of America.

Death and destruction abounded. The hundreds of thousands who'd suffocated in the mud lahars was just a starting point. As bridges and overpasses collapsed, everybody was fair game—grandfathers, mothers, infants—nobody was safe. In areas where cars had begun to drive after the first earthquake, people drove right off the roads as they split open into crevasses. Signs and buildings collapsed, killing thousands instantly. Thousands more were trapped, condemned to die slowly of dehydration and trauma. Fires abounded as gas lines erupted. The hospitals that remained standing merely became large morgues as the critically wounded and sick started to die off. Over the next several days, everybody learned what *death* smells like. Nobody was exempt. It was everywhere.

Locally, the nefarious effects of the combined disasters weren't just limited to fallen buildings, bridges, and billboards—the sharpest of criminals were instantly aware of the golden opportunity. They began planning and cutting deals with each other for territory as they realized that there were people out there not ready to defend their goods and the cops would soon be out of the picture. Most people had scoffed at the modern preparedness movement—not ready to even walk home just a few miles let alone be ready to fight off armed attackers.

Tahoma may have hammered the Northwest, but her blow was delivered to the entire country in ways people had not yet realized.

TAHOMA'S HAMMER + 1 Minute.

PHIL CAME to with Dakota barking and trying to lick his face. She was actually on the ground under his driver's window, standing in the gap caused by his truck laying on its side at an off angle across the shoulder's ditch. Phil knew he'd probably only had a momentary "red-out" from taking a beating on his head. His truck had wedged itself in such a way that it just rode out the remainder of quake by rocking, not bouncing. He reached out through the broken window and rubbed Dakota's face. "It's okay. Shh-shhh..." *Calm down, girl.*

He braced his left arm against the cab's frame and tried the seatbelt's buckle. Click. He half expected his shift in body weight to rock the truck. *Nothing.* He shot a glance up at the passenger window, which looked intact. *No need to break it if it isn't broken yet,* he thought. The windshield was spiderwebbed. He rocked back and forth, finally deciding the truck was fairly stable. The airbags had deployed. He used his pocket knife to cut them out of the way. Out the driver's window he went, low crawling down the ditch until he came out near the rear quarter panel. He dragged himself over to the high side of the ditch and fell flat onto his back, sighing and closing his eyes for a moment. Dakota was still barking and pacing nervously around him. He threw his arm around her and pulled her to him. *Just another moment or two.*

It was eerily silent. No breeze…no birds… Phil slowly sat up, testing his head for steadiness. Another moment built the confidence that he could stand… slowly. *First—left knee to ground. Wait! Is the leg there? Yes. <Whew>. Right foot flat. Do a deep lunge-squat up, arms out for balance. Doing ok? Yup.*

He placed his hands on his head, doing a whole body check for bleeding. He found minor cuts on his left side scalp. *Wait—where's my glasses.* He looked around for a bit, deciding they must still be in the truck.

He checked Dakota—she seemed fine. It was this moment that he finally took in the scene around him. The truck lying in the ditch on its side almost seemed an afterthought. The asphalt was covered in cracks, some as wide as four inches, and there were trees down as far as he could look in any direction. The power lines on the other side of the road were down as were some of the poles that used to hold them. He looked west and saw the same all the way up to the curve he was steering towards five minutes earlier. He looked east. *Well…dang. This is going to take a while.*

He did a walk-around scan of the vehicle. Fuel isn't leaking… Then he noticed the left front wheel assembly at the bottom of the wreck. From this vantage point it appeared to have taken enough damage to be undrivable. *Damn it!* He stared at it for close to two minutes, thinking. *Have to at least try,* he thought sullenly.

Phil perked up a small bit when he remembered that he had tooling riding around in his bed. There were things that he may be able to rig himself back onto the road with. He pried open the cover on his bed and a bunch of stuff fell into the ditch. He spent the next several minutes rigging up his one tow strap, his come-along, some rope, and eventually the truck's jack. He utilized the standing trees as anchors and the fallen branches as dunnage to shore up the truck as he rigged it back onto all four tires.

After an hour of effort, he had the truck upright once again.

The left front wheel and tire assembly were leaning horribly outward and the fender was mangled around it. *The stupid thing'll fall off the instant I try to roll.* Phil stared at it dejectedly for a minute and decided he needed to quit moping.

He spent another thirty minutes cleaning up the variety of things that had fallen into the ditch and breaking down the tooling he'd set up. He performed a search for his glasses and found them in front of the brake pedal. One arm was completely broken. *Well, now...* He dug into his shooting bag in the back seat and pulled out his prescription shooting glasses. *These'll have to do until I find my back-ups at home...*

Phil packed up anything of value from the cab and put it under his locking bed cover. He put on his backpack and locked the bed-cover. He grabbed his chainsaw, pruning saw, and the ammo can that he kept in his truck to protect his emergency food from mice. *Sorry, Hope. You're going to have to wait a while,* he thought as he and Dakota started to hike to his nearest resource—the gun range.

FOR THE SECOND time that day, Crane Walker and Billy Soren sprinted out of Dry-dock F. This time it took them four minutes to even get started. They were paralyzed by the shaking, as if they'd just stepped onto the world's largest amusement ride. There was definitely water coming into the dock from the caisson. Crane turned to get Billy to catch up, but the fifty-seven-year-old smoker just waved him away, as if to say, "Go, I'll get there."

Like the other shipwrights and riggers who had been performing scaffold and dock inspections, Crane was sprinting north to report the flooding. The normal alarm panels for reporting fire or flooding issues were stationed down in the dry-dock and at strategic locations near the ship's topside accesses. Crane wasn't sure they'd be working anyhow. He ran at full-throttle until he found Max McPaul, one of the shipwright general foremen who had a radio. He was at the far north end of the area east of the dry-dock. As he approached the others, he could see terrified looks on their faces. Nobody was laughing this time.

"Floo…floo…" Crane gasped.

"Slow down, Walker," Max urged with his hands up, only making partial eye contact. He was staring southeast, dazed.

"Flooding! Flooding in the dock," Crane half-yelled, still scared out of his mind and panting for breath.

This snapped Max out of his daze. "What? What!! Where??" he demanded.

"West end of the caisson, up high, like forty feet up," Crane was able to compose himself enough to say. About this time Billy jogged up, wheezing.

As Max began to call it in, Billy tugged on Crane's coat sleeve, still out of breath.

"What! What?" he asked his mentor. Billy just pointed east with the one hand that wasn't bearing his bodyweight on a knee as he hunched over.

Crane's eyes traced Billy's arm down to his finger and kept going. To the due east he could see black smoke filling the sky—close, probably in the nearby city of Port View. Farther south he could just make out a vertical column of gray ash and dark clouds growing towards the heavens.

PAYTON AND SAVANNAH were both crying in the bathtub. They had managed to crawl into it during the shaking, hoping it would stop. Screaming had led to crying, as a pregnant mother tried to calm her daughter before they both died in Armageddon. Only the world didn't end. Their twenty-five-year-old apartment building was still standing. They were still alive.

It isn't supposed to be like this, Payton thought. *Why?*

"Ma...Mama," Savannah managed to choke out before sobbing and gasping took hold of her again.

"Shh -shhhh..." was the only thing Payton could think to say.

Five minutes earlier, they had been cruising through the backpacks Paw-paw had built for them at some distant point in the past. They had been laughing at the fact that there were still pull-up diapers and toddler clothes in Savannah's bag. Payton was half-mocking her dad for loading them up with flashlights, batteries, water filters, paracord, pocket knives, stainless steel water bottles, freeze-dried food, wipies, and all the other trinkets. They had been guessing to each other when the power might be coming back on so they could get pizza and ice cream.

What a difference five minutes could make on someone's sense of reality. They were now scared to death but still stuck in the normalcy bias that she would ride this out in her apartment.

She had also been worried about Brenden. He had sent just one text checking on her, shortly after the mild earthquake earlier in the day. They may have called off the wedding, but she knew he still cared about the baby growing in her. She knew better than to expect any communication from Savannah's father.

"Mama," Savannah started, still gasping as she spoke. "Wh-what are w-we gonna d-do?"

"Sweety, we're going to sit here calmly while Mama thinks." *What are we going to do? I just wish we could start the day over! Can't this all just stop!*

She knew what her one best option was, and she didn't like it. She finally announced, "If things aren't better tomorrow, we'll go see Paw-paw."

"P-promise everything will be alright?"

"Of course, sweety," Payton lied, knowing she couldn't keep it.

CAPTAIN MARIE DARNELL had been out touring her shipyard with her duty officer, conducting their own windshield survey. They had heard that the foundry had suffered a partial collapse. It was a historic building with very little use, so no casualties were expected. Next, she'd stopped close to Dry-dock A to get her own eyes on what was happening with the serious issue at the USS El Paso project. It looked almost normal, a facade of the problems she knew her workers were getting a full scope on at that moment. The crane was rotated and had a line lowered into the facility the shipyard had installed on top of the open reactor compartment. If she didn't know any better, she'd think there was nothing wrong over there.

She was almost at the radiological incident's mobile command post when Tahoma's Hammer struck. She and everyone in site had no choice but to live in the mercy of gravity as the asphalt all around them did the wave over and over again. Many of the underground steam-lines and service tunnels around the shipyard collapsed and caved in. There was an ominous roar that filled the air as earth, asphalt, concrete and brick lifted and sank over and over again. About two minutes into the event, the stuck crane's rigging finally broke, no longer able to take the constant stresses imposed by the crane itself being jostled by the ground and the stuck load that was being yanked by the shaking submarine. With a horribly loud whine, several hundred feet of cable began to runaway play itself into the submarine, which caused a crashing sound to emanate out through the open roof of the facility above the submarine. There was nothing anybody could do—nobody could even walk let alone prevent the new disastrous accident. It was pure fortune that the crane boom didn't snap-off.

Four minutes later Marie picked herself up off the road— bruised, scratched, and surveying the area around her. A fireball was rising to the east. *The fuel depot!* Her Navy instincts kicked in. *Don't get tunnel vision.* She started surveying in all directions. The portal crane... *Oh, no! The El Paso looks like it's listing! It must have jostled around in the setting!*

"Lieutenant, ask for a sit-rep," she ordered, eyes finding the big ship out of place just past the dry-dock she had been walking toward. She started to run, sprinting past the mobile command post and the radiological technicians trying to talk to her. Her eyes caught the buckled caisson.

"Get out of the dock!" she screamed at full voice.

She was waving wildly, not at anyone in particular but just because she had to do *something*. People who had been conducting the inspections she ordered were flying up the stairs. She ran part of the way down the eastern top-side of the dock, looking at the crumpled caisson and the rapid flooding. The southern end of the dry-dock was already a foot deep with seawater, and the leading edge of the water oozed north at a rate of one foot per second. Her senses began to get overloaded. She turned to look at the ship drifting lazily between Piers 5 and 6, its bow crumpled from the impact. It was trimming forward and rolling in the waves caused by the small tsunami that had smashed into the shipyard. Her eyes caught the Hammerhead Crane. Words escaped her as she saw it leaning, proudly holding on to the sky for the moment. She turned north again. There was her Shipyard Duty Officer, talking rapidly—and apparently loudly—holding the radio up to her. All she could hear was her heart thumping in her ears.

7

Decisions.

TAHOMA'S HAMMER + 10 MINUTES.

SANDY MCALLISTER HAD BEEN PREPARING for this moment for almost her entire career. The irony wasn't lost on her. At sixty-two, she was finally looking forward to retiring at the end of the year. She was headed to Arizona where her husband was already playing golf every day. She had been the Director of Emergency Management for Slaughter County for over fifteen years. That was enough. *Figures. I sure as hell won't be retiring in two months, will I?* she asked herself.

"Quiet, everyone," she commanded, as the excited stress of the event was showing itself in her staff. *We're up to bat. Let's act like professionals.* "Work your check-lists. Take a breath. Keep calm." The EOC had been rocked by the shaking, too, just like everywhere else.

Computer monitors had fallen and binders had shaken off of shelves.

Though no one had made the mistake of saying it in front of her for nearly five years, they called her "The Godfather." The short, graying grand-motherly figure secretly loved it, but she would never let *them* know that. She liked it because it meant they did what she said. She was in charge, and they knew it. A former insurance broker from California, her speech had a mild twang to it. She knew how to handle people and guide them to what she wanted. She had seen many county commissioners, mayors, and Navy leaders come and go. She had even helped bury a few secrets in her day. Sandy McAllister had influence.

The thing she loved the most about working in this county was its uniqueness. Like the county's hilly geography itself, the economic and political landscapes were something of an anomaly. The bases and shipyard here were key national assets. The Navy home-ported an aircraft carrier at the Bartlett site and a fleet of ballistic missile submarines at Submarine Base Bogdon in the north end of the county. There were also a few specialty "attack" submarines home-ported here. Federal "impact" funds to help offset the expense of the 30,000 sailors and their families were a vital piece of the county's budget every year. The shipyard's payroll alone was over one billion dollars per year. Yet despite that, the voters were usually progressive, which aligned with her California ideals.

"Gerry," Sandy called out to her number two. Geraldine Johnson was hovering over a subordinate's work station as Sandy approached.

"Ma'am," she replied as her boss approached. During informal meetings and day to day business, she was allowed to use Sandy's first name, the only staffer granted that courtesy. She was always smart enough for professionalism when it was required, though. "ARES says they are approximately forty-percent staffed throughout the county. They're doing a radio-repeater check right now." She continued her update. "Major Matsumoto has reported to the

Armory and is mustering the Guard as we speak. He will be over here at 1300 hours to provide more details in person."

The National Guard Armory and Slaughter County DEM's offices where literally a stone's throw from each other, as was the county's regular 9-1-1 dispatch center. Their complex was perched on top of a hill in West Bartlett, overlooking the main highway and the local car-sales mecca. This vantage gave their antennas a straight line of sight to every radio-repeater in the county, as well as access to the best fiber-optic network on the peninsula. Nearby was a large, city-owned softball and soccer park, perfect for setting up a FEMA shelter...or staging troops.

ARES—the local chapter of HAM radio operators dedicated to providing critical communications to their community—had their own radio shack directly connected to the Emergency Operations Center. Their local volunteer director was Dillard Hawkings, a retired Navy Radioman. He had reported to the EOC almost immediately after the first earthquake. His co-HAMs—all of them volunteer, amateur radio operators—had pre-designated fire stations, utility districts, and schools that they were to report to during drills and emergencies. This being a weekday and a real disaster, forty percent muster seemed like a pretty decent number. *Hopefully that will go up,* Sandy thought.

"Okay...good," Sandy said, already looking at the next twelve steps in her mental checklist. "Find out what the shipyard has to say."

DR. STUART SCHWARTZ was standing outside the SeaTac Holiday Inn Express, disbelieving his senses. Cars were strewn everywhere. Fast food restaurant signs had fallen. Something somewhere was making a loud hissing, like a steam-line had ruptured or something. At least two hotels had collapsed into piles of rubble. People were running back and forth, calling for help, screaming. *Where do they think they're going?* was all he could think to himself. *I must be asleep on the plane right now. That's the only explanation.* He glanced to the south, looking at the plume shooting skyward. It seemed to just keep growing. *Maybe it'll actually break through the blue-gray and hit space.*

He shook himself out of his daze and decided to wander back into the lobby of the fully-booked hotel, the fourth one he'd tried that day. He strode up to the counter. The lobby was in complete chaos. People were crying and panicky, some openly wailing. A few were hurt. The sole person working the counter was completely overwhelmed with strangers demanding help.

"Miss—" he tried saying a couple of times, realizing it was never going to work. He walked around the corner and tried the handle to the service desk door. It opened. He strode in, looking for a phone book.

"Sir!" the lady screeched.

He ignored her. Seeing the phone book under the overhang of the counter, he grabbed it and held it up to show her what he wanted. He turned to leave. As he closed the door, he could still hear her barking, something about *rude* and *police.* He walked over to the corner near the lobby's front sliding doors—now stuck open—and started flipping through pages. As he was searching through the R-section he felt a presence hovering. *Now, what?*

"You're him, aren't you?" It was the Hispanic girl from the airport. "The guy who grabbed my arm..."

It was strange seeing her again. "Yes," he said, quietly nodding. Politeness felt right with her after their shared experience. She looked brave and tough, but he could see the wall behind her eyes just waiting for a moment to break. He looked back down at the yellow pages, continuing his search—*rescue mission... rescue mission... I wonder if she even knows how to use the yellow pages.*

He found an ad for an international organization but sensed it was more of an office than a facility. He started looking for homeless shelters. *Grace Lutheran Church. I wonder if they'll have room for a Jewish doctor,* he laughed to himself. She was still standing there.

"What are you thinking of doing?" she asked, somewhat coyly. "Were you able to get a room or anything?"

"No." *Help her,* something in his mind whispered. *You need each other.* "I was thinking of finding a homeless shelter for the night." He stared at her for a long moment. "I'm walking south if you want to tag along."

Thus began an unlikely and uncomfortable alliance.

MARIE WALKED BACK into the Shipyard EOC at full stride. "Status," she ordered, taking five seconds to get to the 100-inch electronic status board. On its display was a fully-integrated shipyard map. The buildings, docks, and piers on the map were fixed, but the ships and other equipment designators were able to be moved with the drag of a finger.

There was a new member of the emergency planning department standing watch as EMCO. "Ma'am, things are still somewhat fluid"—the pun was not intended—"but here's what we know from east to west.

"Pier 7 is splitting apart and falling into the water. The decommissioned submarine tied to it is being partially submerged by lines that didn't break.

"There is a significant leak in the floor and walls of Dry-dock C. The reactor plant from the last submarine recycle project was already set down on the barge and being welded down. The team down there is trying to get some lines installed on the barge to hold it steady when she lifts off the dock floor. They're confident things will be under control within the hour.

"The Hammerhead crane on Pier 6 has a lean to it. We don't know how much yet.

"Dry-dock A is reporting serious flooding. Unknown casualties. The sub's commanding office is reporting a contamination spill and reactor damage from the crane cable and flooding in the engine room. It's coming in from the dock through an access cut we'd installed in the hull. They're also worried about coming off the blocks due to air trapped in some ballast tanks.

"Dry-dock B"—the docks were labeled in the order they were built, which was not strictly east to west—"only had a future setting under construction. Its caisson is leaking but no ship at risk.

"Dry-dock D has minor flooding at the very bottom of the caisson. The ship seems to have ridden the event out pretty well and has no hull-cuts to worry about flooding issues.

"As you know, Dry-dock E's caisson is in Seattle getting worked on, so the dock is already wet.

"Dry-dock F is reporting a significant leak, high up on the west end of the caisson. The carrier's shafts are still out, and the pieces are at the machine shop. The ship's commanding officer is already trying to have their damage control teams seal up the shaft alleys.

"The inactive fleet mooring and maintenance unit is reporting that the moorings held but that some ships are listing. They think the hulls took damage smashing into the piers.

"The fire department says the foundry has finished collapsing, and there is significant damage to several buildings and roads. One small bit of good news is that the pump-wells are reporting pressures have stabilized in most of the docks. They're keeping up with —or ahead of—flooding in Docks C, B, D and F. Dock E is a non-issue. Dry-dock A is their only immediate concern, with F running a close second."

"What about the tsunami itself? Flooding issues, other than the dry-docks," Marie inquired.

"It was relatively small, mainly comprised of the water that it had just sucked out. The energy wasn't nearly as big of an issue as the large sudden tidal retreat and return. For Bartlett, we're hearing radio chatter about boat ramps, parks, and a catastrophe with a ferry at the marina. Still no confirmation from the ferry terminal," the EMCO replied.

Throughout all of this there had been a steady course of radio traffic and multiple discussions amongst managers, plotting courses of action. A steady burst of excited radio chatter caught Marie's attention. "What's happening?" she asked the nearest group of senior leaders near the comms station.

"Captain, it sounds like at least two of the cranes have fallen over," responded Captain Flowers. The portal cranes—like the one involved at the Dry-dock A catastrophe—were 100-foot-tall, diesel-powered behemoths that travelled around the shipyard on tracks. They could carry anything from a pallet to a 100-ton piece of structure.

Marie turned back toward the status board. "Which ones?" *If those have fallen, we're in even bigger trouble than I thought,* she said to herself.

Tahoma's Hammer + 30 Minutes.

Piney Hills Elementary School east of Port View was about two-and-a-half miles from Tony Manner's home. He decided he probably hadn't ridden a bike since before the Navy. Bikes resembled exercise just a little too much. In fact, it wasn't his bike but a neighbor's. Traffic being what it was, Tony figured cutting through the neighborhood roads would be easier on a bike, particularly if he had to walk due to sinkholes or broken bridges. He and Sheila had already been debating a trip to the school for some answers when the hammer fell. The explosion from the east—presumably the fuel depot—sealed their decision. Sheila was now in full panic mode. The normally friendly Tony had to finally yell at her to stop yelling.

He decided on a course of action. *Giving her a task will help her cope.* While Tony's wife went to borrow a bike from the neighbors across the street, he changed into loose clothing and tossed some food, water, and a flashlight into a backpack.

Being a delivery driver did have one advantage—he knew the

roads as well as any firefighter or postal employee. Tony was awestruck by the devastation. He lost count of how many of the older homes looked like they had shaken apart at the seams. He'd seen several on fire. At one point, he almost rode straight into a section of road that had dropped off in a two-foot shelf because he was staring at the ash plume ascending in the southeast. Most of the car alarms had silenced themselves, but at first, they were sounding all over the neighborhood. So were the battery-dependent fire and evacuation alarms in various commercial buildings just a couple of blocks to the south.

Everywhere he looked he saw people in a daze. Some were quietly trying to assess their homes and install tarps on roofs. Others were stuffing everything they could into their cars. He could hear various intensities of people crying and wailing. Others like him were trying to transit on bike or foot from Point A to Point B.

When Tony got to his daughters' school, the remnants of people still there were mostly staff. The children had been released before the hammer fell. He rode straight up to a large canopy someone had set up between the parking lot and the main building. He made a snap-decision to use his size to get some results.

"I need to speak to whoever is in charge," he stated loudly. A few people looked up, but they all went about what they were doing. "Now!" This had the desired effect.

Mrs. Engle, the lead front office administrator, came scurrying over. A 4' 11" Filipina, she was having none of it. "No! No yelling!" she said, reserving the right to do that for herself. "We are all doing our best here!" Seeing the shocked look on his face, she softened her tone slightly. "Who are you." It was more of a statement than a question, made even more ominous by her Tagalog accent.

Tony's mother-in-law was Filipina, too, a common demographic in any Navy town. He knew politeness and respect were his new best friends. "I'm very sorry, Tita," he said, using the Filipina title for Aunt, often used as a respectful title for non-relatives. This caused her face to grimace less. "I know everyone's stressed. I am Talia and

Tasha Manner's father. I believe they were on a field trip today."
Tony's voice started to crack a little. "Do you know where my babies
are?"

Mrs. Engle's face shifted from annoyance to genuine concern.
"Mr. Manners, I am sorry—we don't have any news about the field
trip. We have FEMA people here trying to find out." She was referring to the volunteer radio operator that had reported to the school.
"If you please wait with the other parents, we'll let you know when
we hear something," she said, pointing to where Tony should sit.

Tony noticed a second large canopy behind the first. Under it
were folding chairs and about a dozen worried-looking parents. He
took his large frame over to the second canopy and plopped down in
a chair.

After about an hour he asked for an update, but Mrs. Engle had
none to give. That hour had given Tony time to think. He decided
his idea was worth risking the time to look into. He went over to the
bike, jumped on, and rode north, which took him towards the water
near the south shore of Simpson Inlet. It was downhill so he made
quick time, other than the expected obstacles. He did have to scale
one creek with the bike on his shoulder as he got closer to his desti-
nation. A bridge on the road that navigates the base of the hill had
collapsed.

He rode up to the home of his real estate agent and former softball buddy, Jason Chou. Jason owned a boat, and he lived really
close to a boat launch. He knocked on the front door.

"Tony!" Jason stated, confused why his client would be here,
especially on this day. Sticking his hand out for a shake, he followed
up with, "Did ya' break down or something?"

"Hey, Jason. Sorry, no..." He paused, accepting the hand shake.
"Listen, I'm just gonna come out an' ask. Can you take me to
Seattle?"

8

Rest for the Weary.

Tahoma's Hammer + 6 Hours.

Ash was definitely falling. At first Crane thought he was imagining things. He'd first noticed what looked like a mild snow falling, a dusting that was noticeable as it floated by the shipyard's street lights. The lamps put off a yellowish hue. Now that it was dark, the lights and the ash combined to give everything an otherworldly effect. It made him wonder if this might be what the shipyard would look in some sort of alternate universe. As the shipyard workers finished up a long tour of inspections, they were being directed to busses to take them to the adjoining base. By the time he got off his bus at the softball fields he could see footprints and tracks in the ash, especially in the grass.

This must be what if felt like after 9/11 or Pearl Harbor, he thought.

Crane was too young to remember 9/11. The day had been surreal.
His legs felt like they were walking through invisible goo, sluggish
and weak. The earthquakes combined with the volcano and miles
of walking around the shipyard had taken the wind out of everybody's sails. Everyone was demoralized by the destruction—cranes
had fallen, many buildings had suffered severe damage, dry-docks
were flooding, ships were damaged—it was too much for the
emotions to deal with.

After the first earthquake, the workers had all been rallied by the
commanding officer. After the hammer fell, they had another
muster in the same spot. *No rah-rah speech by the captain that time, huh?*
They asked for volunteers to stay. Not surprisingly, about two-thirds
of the already depleted workforce had opted to leave. Everyone
wanted—needed—to go check on their families. Many of those
who'd stayed after the second muster were single or divorced. Crane
had decided to stay because he wanted to make sure those with kids
left first. He had sent texts to his dad to keep him posted, but he had
received none in return. He was fairly certain the cell towers were
either destroyed or log-jammed.

He strode down what was turning into a path through the ash,
from the bus stop to the tent city that had popped up over the
course of the day. He was joined by about forty fellow "yard-birds"
of varying trades and engineering codes, including about a dozen of
his brother and sister shipwrights. They slogged through the ash like
zombies. The group was greeted by a Navy petty-officer with a clipboard and a radio as they approached the big gap between the two
tents on the nearest corner of the camp. The tents were the large
canvas type with multiple peaks, similar to what Crane saw when his
dad watched "M*A*S*H" reruns.

"Welcome," the sailor said as the group came within earshot.
She pointed at the ground in front of her feet. "Please stop here.
Form a single-file line. I'll need your name and badge number. Once
six of you have checked in, one of the runners will give you a quick
tour of the camp. They'll show you where you can find a bunk, take

a shower, and grab chow." *Chow,* Crane thought. *I could use some of that. I don't care if it is Navy food. I'm starving.*

Crane was in the second group from his busload to check in and make it past the sailor. He was joined by Joey Garcia, another ship-wright. He recognized three of the others as electricians. The last person was someone he didn't know. Another sailor was just returning from taking a group on its tour. *They must have several of these sailors doing this,* he thought.

"Please follow me, sirs and ma'am," the sailor said.

Sir! Look how filthy I am. Do I look like a sir to you? The sailor began walking the group in a big, counterclockwise loop through the tents, which were basically set in a pattern of two boxes, the bigger box of tents completely surrounding the smaller one. It filled the entire ballfield. In all, there were six back to back tents forming the inner box, a wide aisleway around them, and then about twenty tents in the outer box.

"You'll find that the perimeter section of tents is all berthing, with the exception of the two you walked through to get in here. Your berthing tent is about halfway up this back long side, labeled Golf-35…here." He pointed it out as they passed it. "Keep follow-ing, please. We'll be back in about three minutes." He pointed to the nearest three tents in the inner circle. "These three tents are the heads," the sailor said, using the Navy's term for a restroom and showering facility. "The eastern-most tent is the female head."

As they began to start the back-leg of the short tour, the group all walked up a small ramp, along a small deck, and back down a small ramp. The fixture covered a slew of hoses and cables that were running up the space in between the two three-tent rows forming the middle box. *Those must be for plumbing and power,* Crane realized. That's when he realized he was walking in the glow of several portable spotlights up on masts, and he could hear a bank of large generators off to the west. *They've thought this through just a bit, haven't they?*

"Why is this here?" Crane asked.

The sailor was puzzled by the simplicity of the question. "Sir? To give you all a place to rack for the night…"

"No," Crane pressed. "I mean, 'Why' is this 'Here'?" he asked, pressing his hands on an imaginary piano keyboard, pointing at the ground. "Who set this up?"

"Ohhh," the sailor caught on. "I'm just an E-3, sir. All I know is that every ship and shore command was ordered to send twenty percent of their crews to help set up and staff all of this. It was stored in some conex-containers out by the power plant."

Crane nodded, somewhat apologetically for causing the whole tour to stop for his question. They continued.

"These three tents are for chow," the sailor went on, pointing at the other side of the inner circle. They were starting to walk back towards the corner they'd entered through. "The center one is the mess-line, and the tents on either corner have tables and a scullery. Please provide your shipyard badge number when signing in to eat."

As they approached the original corner gap they'd entered through, the sailor provided one last piece of information. "The tent to the right of the entrance is sickbay. Please check in with the duty corpsman if you have any injuries that need looked at."

Crane looked over and was surprised to see a few yard-birds and sailors through the open flap.

"The tent on the left is the Admin Tent. Any odd issues—need to try to contact your families, things like that—you can get help with in there. Any questions?"

One of the electricians asked, "What is that camp over there?" He was pointing at the soccer field.

"Navy. This camp is civilian, that one is for sailors. Some of the barracks and ships have been deemed uninhabitable."

The group thanked the sailor and all started drifting off in their own directions. "Food?" Crane asked Joey.

"Like, yesterday," Joey stated in clear terms. He was hungry, too.

They stepped into the line of the center mess-tent. Inside the flap was a table with a Second-Class Petty-Officer sitting at it. "Badge," she said flatly, as if they'd all been doing this for weeks.

Joey and Crane both gave her their numbers and moved toward the chow line. They moved through it, getting plenty of rice, pork adobo, and mixed vegetables to fill their bellies. At the end of the line, they found large plastic urns on a cart. In them was the Navy's famous "bug juice," which was nothing more than Kool-Aid. There was also plain water. Crane drank two cups of those before he even bothered to move to the next tent to eat.

When he and Joey ducked into the western corner tent they heard a familiar voice. "WA-HOOoooo!" Crane knew Billy's familiar greeting anywhere. It was a lone moment of happiness in an otherwise horrible day. The duo made their way to two empty chairs at Billy's table. Tracy and several other familiar faces were there, and a round of hi-fives started up. Unlike the fist-bumps earlier in the day, this round had a lot less enthusiasm to it. It was more like they were saying to each other, "Glad to see I'm not the only idiot who stayed."

"I lost you after the second muster," Billy stated to Crane. "Where'd you wind up?"

"Back at F. Then the piers out here on the base. Then back into the 'yard, ultimately all the way back to the machine shop. I think they're trying to figure out how to get the shafts back to the carrier. I heard the welders and fitters are working on some emergent train track repairs in several spots. You?"

"East end," Billy started. "We checked out Dry-docks C and B. They're trying to keep people away from A. Not good, bro. I'm hearing stuff—bad rumo—and all I can say is that I'm glad I got pulled out of the nucs when I did." Billy was referring to having his radiation qualifications downgraded for medical reasons several years earlier. He paused for a few seconds, thinking. "We also watched the port-ops boats tryin' to wrangle that big ship before it sank. I guess it broke loose and smashed into the Dry-dock A caisson."

He continued. "Then they had us go and set up a transit to take an optical shot on the Hammerhead. It's leaning almost two degrees to the east. Supposed to shoot it again first thing in the morning to see if its moving." Billy sat quietly for a moment, staring at Crane's eyes, daring him to ask.

"And?" Crane finally took the bait.

"She's goin'. Maybe not tonight, maybe not tomorrow...but she's goin'." Billy could hardly believe his own ears. He'd been dealing with the world of plumb and square his whole career. If he said it was going to fall, it would.

This dampened the mood, reminding the tired workers why they were there. *This is a defining moment in history. We ain't playing here,* Crane remembered. One at a time, they all got up and found the scullery to drop off their trays and utensils.

Crane made his way to the "head" tent to take care of business and then to tent Golf-35. He walked in and looked around. Next to the entry flap was a shelf unit with several sets of Navy-issued blue coveralls. *For after the shower, I guess.* He strode over to a cot that looked like nobody had claimed it yet and plopped down. *Maybe I'll just check my eyelids for light leaks for a second.* The shower could wait until morning.

PHIL WALKER HAD SPENT two-and-a-half hours clearing trees on his way from his personal ground zero to the club property. He drained his chainsaw of fuel and bar oil. He made it stretch by using the pruning saw to limb the trunks first. He knew that somebody had to man up and get the clearing going.

By the time he and Dakota got to the range, he was tired and dehydrated. *I think I may need to camp here tonight. Need to drink water and get onto the crutches for a spell. I just hope other people are clearing the trees north of the round-about.* He could hear the roar of chainsaws rattling through the woods and hoped he wouldn't have to do all the clearing himself. He was worried about the state of the house, more for the sake if Payton and Savannah showed up. *One issue at a time...* He checked his phone. *Still no texts. Hmmm....*

He went to the nearest outdoor spigot and filled up his water bottle. Dakota had found her bowl on the front porch to the office and started guzzling. He made his way to the rifle line and dropped his pack on the closest shooting bench.

Phil decided another walk-around was in order. There was no natural gas to the property, and the only propane was the cage that contained several twenty and thirty-pound bottles. His concern was more about structural issues than explosive threats. Amazingly, the little office was intact. He was worried about the three 700-pound gun safes falling right through the floor. When they moved them into the building several years earlier, a couple of the range members had gone into the crawl space and built brick stacks under the joists where the safes would sit. Seeing the small building intact, Phil wondered if those heavy safes had somehow actually helped the building stay put, instead of sliding down the small slope that helped it overlook the shooting lines. *There are a lot of guns in those safes.* Phil started to think about range security for the night.

The classroom seemed fine, too, but the restroom trailer hadn't faired so well. It had been shaken right off its setting. *That's unfortunate,* Phil thought. *I need to sit down and talk to a guy about a horse...* He decided that a field privy hole would be the fastest and best solution for that issue. He grabbed the wipies from his bag and headed to the woods for a moment. He preferred to carry wipies over toilet paper because it was more effective, the package made them somewhat water-proof, and they could be used to clean cuts as well.

After the "horse had been purchased," Phil and Dakota strode down range to check on the well house. The gap between the pistol and rifle lines had a large wedge shape, which contained the first four of several action shooting bays. At the end of that line of bays was an area with a couple of forty-foot conex boxes, which contained work benches and storage racks. The area outside of those had an assortment of barricades, tire stacks, plastic barrels, and steel plate racks. The well house was in this area.

There was a road at that point that went left—north—to access four more of the action bays. It ultimately circled back and uphill to access the rest of the property. The front shooting-lines and bays were the most used, about twelve acres overall. The back buffer of the property was about sixty feet higher in elevation than the front parcel. The 250-yard-long rifle line ended in a berm the size of a cliff, carved into the base of the hill at the beginning of this buffer area. The club members called the back sixty acres "the field," since there was a fifteen-acre clearing up there. In summer, most of the field caught a lot of sunlight since the fir trees were so far away.

Phil opened the well house and looked in. He didn't notice anything greatly concerning. He was extremely thankful that they had installed a hand-pump as a backup on the shallow well many years earlier. *That'll save some generator fuel.* He walked the property, noting all the downed trees. Most of the stacks of tires and barricades in the prop-storage area were strewn about. *There will be a lot of clean up.* What he was really doing was watching the areas where they had buried PVC pipes from the well house over the years. He'd been slowly setting up a service grid to the rest of the range, installing water spigots and power outlets in strategic areas. *I'll have to run the well on generator power and walk around to spot leaks in the distribution piping.* The drizzle earlier in the morning meant he might be slowly watching for a day or two just to be sure. This made him look up. *What was the forecast? Another "pineapple express," I think.* He was referring to the massive rain storms that came up from the central Pacific and doused the region for weeks on end. *Great.*

They went back to the restroom trailer, which was clearly knocked off its foundation. Phil went to the isolation valve and secured it so he didn't flood the area when he got around to testing the water system. *I'll deal with that tomorrow.* It was dusk and almost dark. *Yep—camping here tonight.*

With Dakota on his heel, he went down to the rifle-line and

opened his pack. He pulled his cooking set from the pack and started warming some water. He then pulled a dehydrated meal out of the ammo can. He took the ultra-lite hammock and down quilts from his pack and set up his "hang" from two of the legs that support the cover over the line. *No need for a tarp, I guess.* The water was about done getting to a boil. He started his food on the rehydration process, and then he headed up to the office. On the porch, he reached into the steel thirty-two-gallon can he used to store Dakota's food and filled up her other bowl for her. Phil transitioned from prosthetic to crutches to give his stump and skin some breathing time.

Using the small flashlight that he always carried, he opened the correct safe and pulled out one of his AR pistols. He preferred those over short-barreled rifles for the legality of carrying them loaded with his Concealed Pistol License. *Might as well.* He always had a pistol on him, usually a Glock 19 or Smith & Wesson M&P 2.0, depending on which holster he felt like wearing that day. But an AR pistol was the same caliber as a rifle, and this one had a flashlight and red-dot site on it. He closed the safe and office and then went and closed the front gate. It was finally at full dark, which happened early in the fall in the Northwest. He went back down to the rifle line. *Not exactly the hunting trip I was hoping to be on next week,* he surmised. Phil ate and turned in early, Dakota perching on a piece of carpet that normally covers one of the concrete benches. Usually he slept like a log in the hammock, but not that night.

Now, what? Carmen thought, as she and Dr. Schwartz trekked south, near the west side of Highway 99. They were walking from the hotel row near SeaTac Airport to a church in Des Moines that had an outreach program listed in the yellow pages. Along the way, they were quickly discovering a lot about the damage caused by the quake—and a little about each other. *This'll make the third detour*

through a neighborhood. She was losing patience. It was supposed to be a four-mile walk. Zig-zagging around every sinkhole, downed power pole, and flattened bridge had effectively doubled that. They weren't the only ones headed south. There was a collective group, somewhat resembling cattle, headed towards... *wherever it is that cattle head to,* she thought.

She also noticed that the wheels on the doc's suitcase were starting to wobble and squeak. She was glad to be using her Navy-issued "sea-bag." *As bulky as it is, it beats dragging luggage around.* The mood was downright depressing. They could sense a high level of anxiety, and the events of the day still seemed too hard to believe. The "cattle" were crying, which added to the misery.

They had just entered another neighborhood off the main drag a few minutes earlier and made a left turn, headed south. Up ahead, the "cattle" were starting to pile up. There was probably a crowd of thirty-five or so people jammed up against two cars that had been parked in the form of a blockade. There was a gap of perhaps five feet between the two vehicles, one an older light-green Honda Civic, and the other red, Mazda pick-up truck. The neighborhood was an older one, but it didn't look particularly run down. *Not like in Huntington Park...* She was thinking about her hometown near Los Angeles and the fact that if this same neighborhood were located there, every house would have barred windows and doors.

The petite, twenty-year-old had joined the Navy two years earlier, in an attempt to break "the cycle." She was the oldest of six kids and helped her mother with the others. Her father was a career "banger" who she hardly ever spoke with. When she was ten, he started serving what turned out to be four years of a twelve-year-sentence. After that, not talking to him was easy. The Navy was safer than the Army, in her reasoning. She had no idea what a Culinary Specialist did, but she became one anyway. *Why did they have to create such a mouthful of words just to say "cook,"* she often wondered.

"Five," was all the guy on the low-rider bicycle said as they approached the choke point. "Each," he continued, realizing they were together.

"Yo, I ain't payin' you no five dollars just to walk down the street!" she stated, her inner-L.A. Latina emerging.

The three teens running the scam suddenly looked on edge. The one on the bike stood up. The bike had been deceiving. He still had one foot on each side of it and was every bit of 6'1", despite britches that sagged enough to show his boxer shorts. This made Schwartz's eyes widen just a bit. He gave Carmen a look that said, "Shut the hell up."

"Here, I got it," he said, reaching with his left hand into his coat pocket and pulling out a single twenty-dollar bill. He handed it to the teen holding the cash. He paused and stared at the kid for about five seconds, when it finally dawned on him that they weren't in the "make change" sort of business.

Carmen had a bit of a stare off with the one on the bike as she and Schwartz passed right through. After they had moved about a hundred feet past the choke point, she whispered to Schwartz, "You're lucky they didn't roll us. When we get away from everybody —and I mean everybody—you need to break your cash up."

"I'm not an idiot," he said smartly. "I only pulled out one bill." To demonstrate, he pulled a fat wad and jewel-laden money clip out of his right-side pants pocket.

"Put some in each shoe," she continued as if he hadn't spoken. She took a glance around and back to make sure they weren't being followed. "Put some more in each pocket. Hide that money clip. And hide that watch, dude," she chastised.

Schwartz stopped. "Doctor," he said smartly.

"Huh?"

"Not dude," he continued. "Doctor. You may call me doc, doctor, Dr. Schwartz, even plain-old Schwartz, if you must. But you may not call me dude." He started walking again, as if to show who leads the way.

"Whatever," she muttered, shaking her head. *Jack ass...*

They finished zigging and zagging through the neighborhood and came out on 24th Avenue. A local told them the church was only about a third of a mile farther south. During their four-mile turned-seven-mile walk, they had both been probing the other with questions, looking for "intel." While she was headed back to her ship in Slaughter County, he was trying to make his way back to the north end of the Olympic Peninsula. They both confirmed their own suspicions that they were from polar opposite walks of life. Most importantly, they both figured out that they annoyed each other to the ends of the Earth.

It was finally past sunset as they approached the church. They saw a collection of canopies and tents set up in the southwest corner of the parking lot. There was a soup-line. They got in line behind what was well over a hundred people. Like Schwartz, many of them were dragging suitcases along.

"Soup?" the middle-aged gentleman behind the table said as they stepped under the awning.

"Yes, thank you," Carmen said, speaking for both of them. Serving food to others for two years had taught her a lot about treating your food servers respectfully. "Is there a shelter or something around here?" she asked the man.

"Not normally. But today isn't a normal one, is it?" the man said with a small smile. "We've set up some cots in those tents over there. And the honey-buckets are over there, too. Good luck, friends." He'd handed them their soup and turned his attention to the next people in line.

Carmen and Schwartz had meandered over to the area with the cots. Most of them were claimed, mostly by people who didn't look particularly homeless. They wandered to the far back corner and sat side by side on one bunk, since they couldn't find two near each other. They sipped soup quietly. Schwartz reached into his laptop bag and pulled out two bottles of water. "Here." He handed a bottle to Carmen.

"Thanks." She paused for a moment. "And thanks for paying

the toll." She was being sincere. There were several more moments of silence while they watched the coming and going of travelers and what was probably local people who'd lost their homes.

It's getting full. He may be a prick, but we need to stay together. She broke the silence. "Maybe we should just share this cot tonight…"

Schwartz looked at it, and then at her, hesitant.

"Not at the same time. I mean take turns—but stay here… together," she explained.

Schwartz took a good look around and turned back to her. "Yeah…I think you're right. Listen, I need to go find the honey-bucket. Would you mind watching my stuff?"

"Sure. Be back in five so I can go, too." She watched the doc wander off, wondering how likely this alliance was to last. "And don't throw away your water bottle."

9

Just the Beginning.

TAHOMA'S HAMMER + 10 HOURS.

"WE'VE SET-UP complete isolation around Dry-dock A. No one can get within seventy yards of it without going through the control point at Monsoor Avenue. We got another crane to the dock and reset brows so that we could get people into the ship. Ship's force did the best they could to keep the spill contained. Several thousand pounds of cable fell into the ship—right into the open Reactor Compartment. There were multiple systems damaged, which obviously caused multiple coolant system spills." Director Thrall paused to make sure everyone in the room was paying close attention. "We've lost folks. Six people aren't accounted for. All of them were working in the El Paso." The NERD wore a serious look on his tired face, as did all the close to one hundred men and women in the EOC.

"Did the spill become airborne?" Marie asked.

"Negative readings so far, Ma'am," the director responded.

"Mr. Harper, what is the update on the docking aspect to all of this?" she asked calmly. *Did I eat today? I had a protein-bar... Was that today? What time is it? Stop. Listen,* she told herself as she snapped out of it.

"The ship is approximately six feet farther north on its setting than it was before the first earthquake. We were able to get an approximate figure on that by referencing the markings along the side of the dock. It's pretty obviously been moved around and reset at a bad angle across the setting and with a list to starboard. Due to the unknown radiological readings and issues we haven't gotten onto the ship yet. We're going to re-task some of our shipwrights who have the correct nuclear qualifications tomorrow. They'll need to get on top of the ship and set up some targets and take some readings before we can give you accurate measurements, Captain." The man sounded tired.

"Very well, Dock Master. What about the caisson? No dancing around it—just shoot straight."

"That's an easy one, Ma'am. We need to get the divers to gut that broken one out with the floating crane so we can bring the backup one over from Pier 4 and set it in place. I personally checked it just an hour ago. It seems to have weathered everything without damage." Broken was a soft word for the state of the dry-dock's caisson. It had been ripped open like a tuna can.

"So, the dock stays flooded until then? I need a solution, Mr. Harper, not another problem."

"We're tossing some ideas around, Captain. I'd appreciate another day to give you the options with pros and cons."

"Okay," the Captain said, moving the meeting along. "What about the other docks?"

"Well, the second most pressing flooding issue is F. Right now, the other docks are maintaining enough of a pump-out to not flood. C is flooding due to dry-dock basin damage, but the barge with the reactor compartment on it is stable and moored. The barge didn't sustain any damage because its setting was simply a series of two-inch thick lumber boards bolted to the dock floor—no setting to rock in or fall out of per se."

He continued. "D and F are both flooding at the caisson. We'll confirm our theory with the divers tomorrow, but we think the shaking jostled them out of having good seals, maybe even slip out of their notches. We also theorize that the shaking managed to toss debris into the sills. Rocks, logs, broken chunks of granite and concrete from the docks themselves—things like that. However, F's leak is very high up and a lot bigger than D's leak is." Harper didn't state the obvious—losing a carrier to a flooding dry-dock would be catastrophic, both in terms of physical damage and to national defense.

Marie paused to think. Everyone sat respectfully quiet, waiting for the next question. More than a few had caught the Captain's case of the yawns.

She shifted gears. "I understand our sheltering plan worked well?" She looked for a nod from the EMCO to confirm. "It's been the first long day in what will be a countless string of them. I suggest everyone go down to the ball fields and get some rest. I asked Captain Reese to make sure you senior leaders had two tents ready. I want you all staying together, ready to share information. As if today wasn't challenging enough, we need to be thinking about aftershocks, and I want you all to pretend that the Hammerhead just fell. What is our plan for that eventuality?"

"Lastly..." She paused and looked down for a minute, searching for words. There were clocks for a dozen different time zones on the wall. All anyone could hear were the second hands as they punched away time. "Keep in mind the people we lost today. Not just the El Paso—we have people missing. We think there may have been some facilities workers in the foundry. And from what I'm hearing about

Pierce County, it's highly likely we have staff who were on leave today who are now gone—forever. *Everyone* has lost *someone* today. I won't presume to tell you what to believe, but I suggest you all say a prayer to your higher power tonight."

Marie stood up, which told the room the meeting was over. The bulk of the senior-management core filed out and headed down the hill to the sheltering camp. About a dozen stayed behind, volunteering to take the first nightshift of what was now a beefed-up watch rotation.

Marie went to comms and found the duty technician. "Get me NavSurf on a secure channel. I'll be over by the status board." *If the pump-wells quit running, we're screwed.*

PAYTON AND SAVANNAH had decided to leave for her father's house in the morning. They had carefully re-packed all the items into the bags he'd made for them. The night air and drizzle had turned the apartment cold, so the girls had bundled up in pajamas and coats. Savannah was in a hand-me-down Hello Kitty winter coat, and Payton was wearing her big, tan, "inside-the-house" button-up sweater she used in lieu of a robe. Payton went through flashes of being too hot and too cold, a side benefit of pregnancy. The sweater could be opened to help regulate temp.

Lighting some candles, Payton had taken a hint from the bags and started preparing for the next day's journey. She filled up all the worn-out cloth Safeway shopping bags with every bit of food from her cupboards that would fit, including the staples and spices. Under protest, Savannah started taking the bags the one flight down and three spots over to their older gold Acura. As her daughter was doing that, Payton started filling water bottles—the pressure in the sink was definitely down to a trickle. *Everyone must be filling water bottles,* she thought. *Am I too late?*

Next were clothes. They each owned one suitcase, both of which were gifts from her mom. *Mom, I need you right now,* she thought. Savannah had returned.

"Baby, go empty your unicorn backpack and put some toys and coloring stuff in it," mother instructed daughter. She filled the suitcases. *Can't have too much underwear,* she thought, dedicating probably half of the available room to panties, bras, and socks. *We might be there…a week? We can stretch three sets of pants and shirts a week.* Toiletries, medicines, and toothbrushes followed.

They made a few more trips hauling the rest of the stuff to the car. She noticed various people inspecting the apartment complex. *Must still be safe,* she surmised. Payton wanted to leave early since showers were going to be out of the question. She knew her dad had a generator and a well. They went to bed somewhat earlier than normal, having filled their bellies on mac-&-cheese from the cupboard. The little camping stove her dad had put in her bag had already proven its worth.

Around 12:30 A.M.—*Wonder how much longer this thirteen percent phone-charge will get me*—they were awakened by a decent aftershock. They were sleeping together in Payton's bed and had made their way back to the bathtub to ride it out. As they were calming themselves down afterwards, they heard a series of explosions around town.

"Mama?" Savannah stuttered, a look of fear wrinkling her face.

"Shhh, baby, I know," Payton murmured quietly.

They tried going back to bed, but a while later they were woken to loud violent pounding on the apartment door. She could hear a man yelling out there, but the words were muffled.

She ran out and opened the door. The thought that someone dangerous could be there had not occurred to her. "What!" she yelled, having to step out to see who it was.

The only person was a firefighter decked out in their gear about three apartments down, pounding, yelling, and moving. When he heard her, he stopped and turned. "Mandatory evacuation! Five minutes! Let's go!"

"Wait! Why?" she yelled back.

"Mama?" Savannah was at the door.

She could hear the firefighter repeating that same instruction over and over as he moved along the complex. She realized she heard other firefighters and deputies repeating the process all over the complex just as she noticed the orange glow from the east. There were fires all over the place. *The gas lines must have blown up,* she thought. There were sheriff's cars and fire trucks all over the multitude of apartment complexes that covered the mile of hill-side.

"Baby. Grab your coat! Now. We gotta go," she instructed.

"But, I—"

"Now!" Payton screamed at her daughter, cutting her off. "We need to move!" She was trying to manage panic so that her daughter wouldn't freeze up. As far as she knew, the place could blow up at any second. Or the hill could come sliding down. It was only God's guess what else might happen. *We need to go.*

They grabbed their coats and water bottles and made their way down to the car. More and more of the apartments' residents were following suit, most of them in shorts or pajamas. Payton was dismayed by the three inches of ash, at first thinking it was warm snow. *No way*! was all she could think, at a loss for words. She managed to find the words "Get in!" as she yelled them at her daughter.

Buckled in and car started, she turned on the wipers. They were frozen. "Sit here," she commanded as she got back out. She used her arm as a giant squeegee, trying to get ash off the windshield. *That'll have to do.* She got back in and started to drive. There was an odd orange hue with fire glow and ash combining to look like the devastation out of some Bruce Willis movie. She made her way south, joining the throng of cars trying to flee the once-thriving Sylvan. *Got to get to Dad's* was her dominant thought followed closely by trying to scan all mirrors and windows for the variety of threats that might end their lives at that moment.

She slowly evacuated south and west as the proper roads

appeared. About two miles—thirty minutes—after the panic had started, they were starting to head up the main, westerly artery to the Canal Vista area. Strawberry Hill Road was a three-plus-mile-long road with a couple of steep valleys but a relatively straight westward shot to the Canal Vista Highway. Once there, it would only be two additional miles to Phil's. In normal times, she could be at there in less than ten minutes from this spot.

The car lurched as it choked a bit, heading up the first hill. *Now what,* she thought angrily. It was like God was messing with her. It lurched again. And again. *Dammit!*

She pulled in to a county-owned property, a three-building facility that housed the administrative and maintenance staffs for the fire and water departments. She parked as quickly as possible and got out to look. The car was caked in ash, made somewhat moist by the night drizzle. The front of the car was covered. *The grill,* she thought. She was no mechanic, but she was smart. *Either the radiator is getting too hot or the engine isn't getting air.*

She could see the terror on her daughter's face as she got back into the car. "Actually," she said, the next thought in her head trickling to her mouth. "Let's get in the backseat. We'll rest here until daylight." They got out and moved the various bags to the front seat and trunk. They nestled under blankets, huddling, with Payton wondering what else could possibly go wrong as her daughter drifted back off to sleep.

SLEEP. It wasn't the deep sleep that Phil normally had after a tiring day. *No.* This was lighter, more alert. Like when he was in the desert in Saudi Arabia and Kuwait in '90 & '91. *I didn't really sleep for months, back then, did I?* he thought. *Is this event like the war? Naw...well... maybe,* he concluded. As any frontline Marine, Soldier, Airman or Sailor knew, war was ninety-nine percent boredom while trying to maintain alertness and order. Things like work details and unit discipline served as a reminder of why you were there—to embrace the suck with your buddies. It certainly wasn't because of any desire to prop up a politician's will. *Embrace the Suck.*

After the midnight tremblor—he'd swung harmlessly in his hammock—he donned his leg and battle belt and performed a quick check of the front area. He typically wore this belt when shooting in competition, teaching, or taking classes. He would also wear it when the range was really busy. He'd quit tending to the admin stuff and help staff a shooting-line as a range officer. He had several soft magazine holsters on it, including a couple for AR mags. On the right side was a retention holster with a slight amount of drop to it. The drop made it hard to use his right-side pants pocket, but it was a desired feature for when he had his "plate carrier" on his torso. Other features were a pouch for dumping partially used magazines, a multi-tool, a small life-saving medical kit, a tourniquet, and a flashlight. He'd taped a red filter over the lens of this light to help preserve his night vision.

He'd removed the belt, leaving his Glock in the holster. He kept the leg on and was trying to catch some Z's again. His mind was having a hard time learning the new definition of what normal sounds should be. The ash and the drizzle muffled the bug, frog, and coyote noises normal for October. What he knew was out of place, though, was Dakota's growl. *She heard it, too.*

Phil slipped back out of the hammock and immediately crouched onto his left knee. *SLLS,* he told himself—warriors called it "sliss" or "seals." *Stop. Listen. Look. Smell.* Something they hammered into every Marine and Grunt as soon as they started infantry train-ing. It was a concerted effort to listen through his heartbeat. The highway shooting was the last time he'd gone through this. Training was the only way to prepare for it, but training hardly ever got someone's adrenaline flowing like their mind did when it perceived a threat. *Definitely a noise coming from the office.*

Dakota's growling was intensifying. Phil put a hand on her hackles and smoothed them for a second. He felt her tension release a bit under his hand. He reached directly behind him—below the hammock—finding the belt where he left it. He slipped it on. He stayed in the one-knee kneel as he side-slid over to the bench where he'd laid the AR pistol. He passed his left arm and head through the adjustable sling, adjusting its tension and positioning to a tighter spot. This AR pistol was shorter than a standard rifle, perfect for rounding corners in buildings and easier to shoulder with a tight sling.

"Heel," he quietly told Dakota. She stayed one pace behind him as he slowly crouch-walked to the corner of the rifle-line awning. He "sliced the pie" on the corner, taking micro-steps to the right while pivoting his aim and site left, as if on an axis. He slowly walked up the ten steps to the parking area. He scanned left and right, keeping his rifle and line of site in alignment by turning at his hips. He then turned towards the office door and knelt once more. *SLLS again.*

Thunk. *Here we go again,* he thought, dreading the possible outcome of killing again. What most people who'd never been in combat didn't realize was that when a good person kills, part of them dies, too. Some people took years learning to cope with and accept it. "Better them than me"—while true—was still a hard pill to swallow when they'd just ended a life. "Stay," he commanded Dakota at barely a whisper.

Heel-toe-heel-toe. His combat-glide not only reduced the bouncing of the gun's muzzle—it also enabled him to be quiet and feel for tripping hazards. It was something he'd spent a lot of time re-learning since receiving his new "bullet-proof" leg. The office door was closed. He slowly tried the knob. It started to turn. *Dang it!* He remembered leaving the door unlocked on his last security check. *Some security expert! Now some tweeker thinks he's hit the pay-dirt.* He listened one last time, trying to see if a particular noise might reveal a probable location. *Cash register or safes, probably.* He readied his left hand on the seven-and-a-half-inch handguard, feeling for the pressure pad that would active the attached flashlight the instant he wanted to.

Standing on the right of the doorframe—the knob side—he slowly turned the knob and felt the door budge. *These hinges squeak, better just rip the band-aid off.* Using his right hand, he flung the door open, engaged his pistol-grip, and pivoted around the corner. Pressure pad engaged, the room flooded with 500 lumens of bright light. *Finger off the trigger,* he told himself, keeping it indexed up on the lower receiver of the pistol.

"Show me your hands if you want to live," he said calmly. Before him was a kid. Not a child, but a young man of probably nineteen or twenty. Grungy clothes, shoulder-length hair, beanie, raincoat, and scruffy facial hair—he looked like he could have been one of Crane's friends. The burglar's back was turned towards Phil. *He never knew I was here. Totally oblivious that someone may be here. Dummie.*

"Please don't shoot," the burglar pled. His hands went over his head. Phil could see the yellow bulk of a battery-powered grinding tool in the kid's right hand.

"Are you armed?" Phil queried.

"N-no sir," came the nervous reply.

Scan. Phil had almost caught tunnel vision, even with his tactical experience. He kept the light and rifle trained on the threat and looked around the room, then back onto the porch of the office. "Are you alone? Is there anyone else here?"

"Just me. I swear."

Please don't piss on the carpet. "Alright. Do exactly as I say, and you will live."

Phil had the burglar put the tool onto the top of the safe he'd started grinding into and then place his hands on the back of his head. He had the kid walk backwards down the counter area, then come out from behind it, keeping the pistol and light trained on his head the entire time. He was holding the red-dot site at the top of the head, knowing that at this close range the offset would put a canal straight through the middle of the skull. He slowly backed out of the front door, guiding the kid backwards with his commands. He continued the process until they were in the parking lot. Dakota was audibly growling now.

"Please don't kill me," the kid begged, almost crying. "I was just—"

"Save it." Phil cut him off. "Lay on the ground. Spread your arms out ahead of you." More compliance. Phil knew one-man searches were the worst-case scenario—something his training had taught him to do only as a last resort. He'd been trained in a lot of this while in the weapons-security detachment at the submarine base while he was in the Corps. The kid seemed genuinely scared, but that is often when trapped animals are most dangerous.

Phil kept the burglar covered while retrieving a chair from the front porch. Once daylight hit, he would photograph him and any identification he could find. He knew to continue scanning for threats. Like turds, dirtbags often stuck together. He tried texting Fred. [Phil: "Get down here. Intruder."] Then he thought of another resource he should text. *Charlie. I need Charlie here.*

10

"Endeavor to Persevere." – Chief Dan George, in <u>The Outlaw Josie Wales</u>

TAHOMA'S HAMMER + 1 DAY.

HE HAD to keep an eye on the upside-down umbrella to make sure that not too much ash was getting into his rain-water collecting bucket. Slaughter County Sheriff Sergeant Charles Foxglove Reeves, forty, was thirsty. *Thirst. It takes a man about three days of true thirst to become dangerous.* Charlie remembered learning that in—*Psych 101, maybe?*—in college. He was jerry-rigging something to augment the office's supply of water.

A member of the Suquamish Tribe in the north end of Slaughter County, Charlie had lived there his entire life. The 6' 2" Native was a solid 225 pounds. After high school, he'd walked on as a freshman at the University of Washington, hoping to become a linebacker. Average speed and a knee injury kept him benched most of the year. He opted to continue his education at the local community college to ease the financial burden on his family. While in school he picked up a part-time job for security at the tribal casino. This let him network his way onto the tribe's police force.

His interest in law enforcement became resolute. He applied for a lateral job transfer to the sheriff's department at the age of twenty-five. He'd picked up his sergeant's stripes three years earlier. Charlie was humble, likeable, and tough. Police, troopers, and deputies from all departments respected him. When the tribal police force wasn't in agreement with the north-end Sheriff's precinct, Charlie would make the thirty-minute drive up to the "rez," and he usually managed to get things smoothed out pretty quickly.

Charlie was a family man, married to Melinda, a school teacher up in Peterson. That was the county's "big city in the north," a town of about ten thousand people. They had two kids, both in grade school. While they didn't actually live on the reservation, they were close enough to be there for family and friends when needed. Since the quakes, Charlie hadn't been able to get home. He managed to pass and receive some simple messages via the DEM radio volunteers, so he wasn't too worried—yet.

Charlie was going into his forty-first hour since his last real sleep, and he was starting to feel a bit punchy. He'd snuck in a one-hour nap sometime the night before, before the explosions started. When the local fire district mandated the evacuations at the apartment complexes, it was all-hands on-deck. The evacs were ordered due to a mudslide and hill collapse at the far north end of the complex. An entire apartment building slid into the one below. The fire department made a decision to get all residents off that hill.

With no real place to shelter them, they were advised to make their way to the schools to the east and northeast of town. Apparently, the Red Cross and a few smaller non-profits had established some refugee centers. Most people had family and friends in those parts of town and opted to go elsewhere if they could. Traffic was murder—impacted by the lack of lights, roads that had been blocked off due to damage, utility posts that had fallen, and wrecks. Now cars were breaking down due to the ash or getting stuck in the wet ash in places where it covered up holes and crevices caused by the quakes.

Charlie was normally the graveyard shift patrol sergeant for the central part of the county. He operated out of the precinct office in Sylvan, though he found himself making runs all over Central Slaughter County, backing up deputies. At that moment, his thirst was slowly building, and it was all he could think about. He and his graveyard crew were on a mandatory hold—nobody going home. Due to overpass collapses and other road obstructions, they were told to stay put. The big fire station at the north end of Sylvan had set up a small shelter and feeding station for first responders. It made sense to Charlie, since the local Emergency Communications Center was there. That's where he sent the other grave-yarders. He opted to try and crash at the office.

At the moment his thirst was his driving thought. He'd already guzzled four water bottles. He was starting to feel like he was taking more than his share, so he decided to try to improvise something. Earlier, he'd found an old umbrella in the lost-and-found box under the public counter. He was trying to take advantage of the rain. Needing a clean bucket, he ran down to the strip mall where the bakery was. Once daylight came, many of the business owners and managers were trying to get into town to see if their buildings still existed. Charlie was given an empty icing bucket by the grateful baker.

On the way back to the office he checked on the perimeters of the buildings that were burning. Those included a gas station, a decent sized strip mall, and the Burger King, all on the east side of the main drag. There was really nothing anyone could do but watch them burn. Perimeters of yellow caution tape were set up about a hundred yards around each of the burning structures.

Charlie was watching the rain hit his umbrella and drain into the bucket via the holes he'd sliced into it with his pocket knife.

"Yo, Charlie, get some sleep." It was Ken Bomeister, the day shift sergeant. He'd just come onto duty when the first quake struck.

"I will," Charlie said looking back to see Ken. He turned back to his contraption. "I want to see if this works. I think there's a filter in the disaster supplies in the storage closet."

Ken walked over and gave the umbrella a little nudge so he could look into the bucket. There was about four inches of water in there. "I'd say so," he said, shaking his head up and down. He was truly impressed by the ingenuity. The two sergeants looked at each other for a few seconds, both sighing a bit, knowing the other one knew what he was thinking—*I'm tired, and I'm ready for this to be over.*

"You heard anything new?" Charlie asked.

"Yeah, let's see," Ken looked off into space, searching his memory. "The north end radioed that a preliminary inspection of the Hood Canal Bridge reveals it may not be drivable. The collapsed bridge and overpass list on the dry-erase board had a few things added to it. It's going to take a while to get around by vehicle, what with the road buckling, holes, and such. What else…oh, your buddy—what's his name, from the overpass shooting—" Ken was searching Charlie for the name.

"Phil?"

"Phil! Yeah, the gun-range guy—he caught a guy breaking into his office last night."

"What?" Charlie wasn't sure if he'd heard it correctly—he was pretty tired.

"Yeah," Ken went on. "Lisa radioed it in a bit ago. She says Phil waved her down. She recorded the perp's info and let him go. If you ask me, dude's lucky to be alive."

"Yeah," Charlie agreed, staring at the bucket. The rain was

starting to speed up. He'd head out to see Phil and then try to get some sleep in the evening.

"MAMA, I NEED TO PEE," Savannah said.

Me, too. Payton had been wondering what they would do about that for some time. There were definitely fire and water-company trucks coming and going at the facility. Over the course of the night and into dusk, four other vehicles—a car, a SUV, and two pick-up trucks—had pulled in to the public parking lot like she had. Several others had managed to keep heading west, up and over the first crest. There were a few cars heading east towards Sylvan, too. She though she saw a bed sheet tied to the front of one. *Must be for keeping ash off the grill,* she decided.

"Let's go see if they'll let us into the building," she told her daughter. Payton was hoping that they had water and power in there. She heard a generator running somewhere on the backside of the facility, but she didn't see any lights. They made it to the door, leaving gray dusty footprints in the ash, now closer to five or six inches deep. *Locked. Dang it.* About fifteen minutes earlier, a small family from one of the other vehicles had trekked off to the woods for five minutes. *I guess I know what they were doing, now, don't I?*

"C'mon, Baby. We'll go water the bushes over there."

A few minutes later with business handled, Savannah was safely back in the car while Payton was looking at the grill. She was making a good front for her daughter, but in her mind she was freaking out. *Just how bad is it? What if Dad's not there? What if he's dead?! I think we may be out there more than a week...*

Snapping out of her funk, she decided against opening the hood. She didn't want the fine, powdery mess to slip in and make the problem worse. She looked over at a man at a pick-up truck who was using his hand to knock ash off the grill. "Did you have engine issues, too?" she hollered over.

"Yeah," he said, barely glancing over. "I'm hoping I can choke this thing to where we're headed." He continued to knock caked ash off the area in front of the radiator.

Payton started the process on her own vehicle. She noticed that the guy at the truck was knocking it off his hood, too. He eventually popped the hood and pulled his air filter out, giving it several gentle whaps against the tire to knock ash out of it. It was hard for her to tell if there was much coming off, but she thought there was at least some. She changed her mind about opening the hood and mimicked what she saw. This whole process took her close to a half-hour.

When she was close to being done with her car, the truck fired up and slowly pulled out of the facility, headed west. He had left tracks in the ash. Payton hoped those tracks would enable her to drive out, not sure if the car would handle like it does in the snow. "Wish us luck," she said, smiling at her daughter.

"Luck," the innocent fourth grader replied.

Payton fired up the Acura, which responded with a few coughs but stayed alive. She managed to pull out of the lot and head west, finding that slow was better. The rain had dampened the ash into a paste, so it was handling pretty well, like in the snow when it slushes as the temperature rises. Cresting the hill, she could see down the long valley and back up the next slope for almost two miles. Road shoulders in both directions were covered in trees that had been cut up and dragged off the road. The power lines that ran east to west on the south side were down, only occasionally drifting up where a pole had survived. There were cars that had been stranded and at least two that looked like a tree had landed on them. When she drove past one of them, the inside of the driver's window was caked in blood. She could see one set of headlights coming east.

Over the course of the next twenty minutes, they slowly made the trek to Phil's house. She was keeping an eye on her temperature gauge, which seemed to be doing okay. In one spot on the Canal Vista Highway the road had caved in on Savannah's side. Someone had thrown orange cones out as a warning. She slowly drifted to the oncoming side and went around the sinkhole.

"Wowww…" Savannah managed to say as they passed it.

Finally arriving at Medford Lane, Payton turned right and carried on towards her father's house. *More downed trees. At least there'll be plenty of firewood next year.* Seeing trees drug off to the side of the road was the new norm, and it made driving more hazardous, as she could no longer see where the other roads and driveways were.

They turned up Phil's driveway. *Dad's not even here,* she thought, not seeing his truck. She confirmed her hunch by looking for the generator and not seeing it. They got out, Savannah with her backpack, Payton with her purse. "Let me go first," she told her daughter, who was starting the familiar trot to the front door.

Payton may not have enjoyed the shooting sports and tactical training as much as her brother and father, but one couldn't be a member of the Walker family without some level of competence in personal security. She reached into her purse and pulled out the Walther PK-380, keeping it pointed at the ground in her right hand. *Dad would be disappointed it was in my purse,* she thought. *At least I have it.* She set her purse down on the front steps and took the key to her father's house out of the inner zipper-pocket with her left hand. Not perceiving a threat, she decided just to be ready for the unexpected. She instructed Savannah to stay outside until she came back to get her.

She made a slow methodical entry into the house, choosing to carefully clear the downstairs floor first. The thought that her dad may still be here had occurred to her. She kept the pistol pointed down with safety engaged the entire time. She repeated the process for the main upper floor. After convincing herself the house was empty, she went back out the front door and told Savannah to come in. She was quietly concerned. *I wonder what happened to him.*

TONY ARRIVED at the boat ramp to find that his former realtor had already put the nineteen-foot ski boat into the water and parked his truck and trailer. Tony had left his house before dark, knowing that the road he would normally take to get here was unpassable. He'd found the orange glow of the large fire from the east—*definitely the fuel depot,* he thought—oddly beautiful. He was somewhat worried that a large wildfire might be the result, hoping that the rain would keep things wet enough to contain it to the base.

"Hey," he greeted Jason. Tony immediately began pulling his payment from the back of his Toyota Tundra—six, five-gallon water jugs. He was keeping track in his head, wanting to make sure he squared with his boss when this was all over.

"Hey," Jason replied. He had an orange, hooded Helly-Hansen rain jacket on with matching pants. Tony was decked out in his XXXL safety-yellow raincoat provided by his company. Seeing no rain pants on his client, Jason said, "Man, you're going to get soaked. You sure you don't have rain pants?"

"It is what it is," the normally jovial Tony replied. After he moved the water jugs to the back of Jason's Chevy, he picked up his stuffed backpack. "We ready?"

"Yeah. Let's get going." Jason's face told Tony he didn't really want to do this. Tony understood that sentiment. He was just glad his friend was willing to help. They had negotiated a trip over with Jason agreeing to wait for two hours.

The pair shoved off, taking in the scene across the inlet. The rain clouds were probably a few thousand feet in elevation, plenty high enough to see the leaning Hammerhead crane over at the ship-yard. It was a couple miles, so observing smaller devastation would have required a pair of binoculars. They agreed the marina and ferry terminal looked messed up but couldn't tell how much. The mood was somber as they made their way northeast, starting the u-shape of the waterway that connected Simpson Inlet to Puget Sound.

Jason was maintaining one-third throttle when Tony suddenly said, "Brothuh, do you see somethin' up ahead?"

Jason dialed the throttle down to a slow cruise. The boat's trim went nose-heavy as his big client slowly climbed up and through the hinging panel in the windshield to get on the bow. "Tree," Tony stated. "Steer left—uh…port—a little bit," recalling his Navy terminology.

The duo cruised past a tree—not a log, but an entire tree, which was mostly submerged. They shot each other a concerned glance. Both men noted the wrinkles growing on the other's face. They both started scanning the shore. Jason saw it first. Something was different. He'd probably driven through this passage thirty times, usually in summer but also during fall salmon-fishing.

"The island looks different," he said, referring to the south end of Russell Island. They kept cruising. As they got to the north end of the passage and started turning toward the southeast, it became clear that the entire south-eastern end of the three-mile wide island had disappeared. The cliffs were new and the passage seemed…*wider.* Trees and debris dotted the waters in every direction, getting thicker as they continued. Then they saw her. A woman, probably in her sixties or seventies, was floating face down, bloated and pale-blue. She was ghastly.

"Holy Hell!" Other than funerals Tony had never seen a dead body. He fought the urge to gag. "Shouldn't we stop?"

"Look!" Jason called, pointing ahead of the craft. Another body had just popped into view. Then a third. There were so many trees and pieces of houses floating around, they knew there were probably a lot more bodies out there. What was missing were life preservers. "These are homes," Jason deduced. "Wow…These people weren't on a boat…" he said, staring at where the rest of the island was.

Both men were in a state of shock and disbelief. From this vantage they had a pretty good line of sight to the fuel depot. There were tug boats spraying water onto fuel tanks. The pier was completely aflame. The fire covered the entire hillside.

"Surely they know about these bodies by now," Jason said, nodding towards the other vessels. "I think this is bad. I mean —*really* bad..."

Tony nodded in agreement. *My babies. Don't you back out on our deal, now.* He was thinking through his options if Jason started to change his mind, and he didn't like where his mind was going. Fortunately, he didn't have to find out. Jason steered the craft east towards Seattle, keeping them at a troll. Tony's worry started to grow. *This is gonna take a while.*

SCHWARTZ FELT his patience was being tested. He wasn't really an angry person. He just found himself annoyed by all the stupid people. *Why are they telling themselves the same stories over and over?* He was standing in line at a new tent that had popped up over by the church's main entrance. They had opened the doors the night before to let people use the pews to sleep on. Some fool, *fools,* he corrected himself, had filled the building's toilets with waste, despite signs being posted to use the honey buckets outside. *I wonder how long until those over flow?* he asked himself. He had left Carmen back at the cot to guard both it and their stuff. He was in search of any information about roads, planes, or transport in general.

"Excuse me," he said, stepping in front of a church volunteer who was headed toward the shelter area. "Have you heard anything about the airport, or busses, or anything at all?"

"The airport?" the man said, incredulously. "You kidding?" He could see Schwartz was not. "Oh, yeah. Ummm—the airport is down—for good. Or at least for a long time. The control tower fell. The runways are broken. There was a crash."

"I know there was a crash," Schwartz said, annoyed that this guy thought he was an idiot. "I was there." He paused for a moment. "Sorry, it's been a long night. What about busses?"

"I haven't heard anything. Maybe the Red Cross coordinator knows something," he told Schwartz, pointing toward the tent by the church.

Schwartz headed over there and slowly nudged his way towards the front of the pack. He could finally make out what the lady was saying.

"...is destroyed. As if that wasn't bad enough, farther east on I-90, the ash is a few feet thick. So even for the bridges and overpasses that are intact, vehicle travel towards the east will take days to implement. My best guess for east by ground is weeks from now."

"What about ship, out to the ocean?" someone from the crowd called out.

"We're hearing that most of the major ports sustained a lot of damage, and many of the ships caught fire and sunk right at the piers. Sorry, I just don't know much about the seaports yet." She continued her original speech about ground travel. "The state's Emergency Management coordinators are supposed to be at Camp Murray near the Joint Bases in Tacoma. The bases were largely wiped out, and the command structure is still trying to establish itself down in Vancouver. Therefore, information is very slow. One thing we have heard, though, is that getting busses going in the cardinal directions is a priority."

"Everybody," she continued. "If you're just walking, up the route to the south is completely unpassable. Most of Tacoma is covered in mud all the way to the tide-flats. The communities south of—" She began to choke up. "South of—"

A woman next to her took over. "There's no easy way to say it. Entire towns are gone. Highways are covered." Her voice started to crack too, but she held it together as the tears began to stream down her face. "The death toll is expected to be in the hundreds of thousands...or higher."

Schwartz looked around. People were quiet, sullen. Many were silently crying, not caring who saw. *This is depressing*, he thought as he started to drift out of the crowd and back towards their cot.

"Anything?" Carmen asked when he returned. She stood up, preparing to take her chance to stretch and go relieve herself. She had their empty water bottles in her hands, ready to go find their next refills.

"Nothing good," Schwartz sighed, plopping onto the cot. "Maybe some busses… someday…" he trailed off.

"What do you want to do?" Carmen asked.

I don't know, was the silent reply as he looked up into her eyes.

11

More Decisions.

"When will they arrive?" Captain Marie Darnell asked the panel of Admirals and Generals filling her screen. She was back in her "war room," a conference room attached directly to her office in Building 855. Despite the ominous name, it wasn't that big. It wasn't really meant for big meetings but rather smaller ones with her very top staff or visiting dignitaries. What it did offer, however, was privacy and a secure platform for video calls. About fifteen minutes earlier, she'd received a message from her bosses in Washington, DC, instructing her to call from a secure position.

She'd just learned that a fleet bound for Washington State would be departing San Diego in a few days. They were loading supplies, equipment, helicopters, and Marines. Not just any Marines but the combat-hardened 3rd Battalion, 5th Marine Regiment. *Figures,* was her first thought. *Priorities, I guess.* She couldn't argue with the logic, as much as she tried. When the fleet was off the coast, much-needed supplies would be arriving by helicopter. *We all have our jobs to do, even the Marines.* She had received the military three-minute version of "we don't know" as the answer to her question.

After the call, Marie took the stairs back down to the lobby, where that day's duty-officer was waiting for her. They hopped into the Chevy quad-cab and started to head back towards the EOC. "Wait," she instructed. "Let's head over to the control station at Dry-dock A."

The officer turned around, and they were there in less than a minute. When they pulled up there was a line of shipyard workers getting a brief. She walked up and joined the crowd, trying not to interrupt with her presence.

"...so, remember to check your dosimeters *regularly,*" the tech giving the brief said, purposefully emphasizing the frequency. "*At least* once per minute." He was referring to devices they could look into and make a quick assessment of how much radiation exposure they were receiving.

Radiation. People not involved in the nuclear-power industry often confused that word with "contamination." In simple terms, radiation was simply energy. Even campfires radiated energy in the form of heat and light. "Ionizing" radiation was energy emitted from a radioactive particle. Contamination was most simply explained as being a physical particle of some type, and it happened to be radioactive. The ash that would fall onto a person's head and shoulders while sitting around that campfire would metaphorically be the contamination. Both types of radiation existed in everyday life, making things safer and more efficient. Watch dials, bananas, or a small part of smoke detectors were examples of ionizing radiation that a person might find in their home.

The trick, though, was keeping the contaminated stuff contained, which the Navy went to great lengths to ensure. Great lengths meant a lot of time and money spent training and drilling. But no matter how detailed the plan, Murphy would sit back waiting and looking for his chance, like the improbable imp he was. It was just plain bad luck that the first quake struck when it did. No matter the level of planning and training, that crane hook had to hold that cannister over the open reactor top long enough to gently lift that container from the compartment. During the fifty-eight seconds of the first earthquake, the heavy container had swung around on the rigging-gear, slamming into facilities that had been set up and getting stuck in some of the structure.

During the hammer, the container and hundreds of feet of rigging cable fell into the open reactor compartment. The damage under the uncleared mess would probably be extensive enough to warrant ending the submarine's life cycle, but they wouldn't know until they cleared it. Before the shipyard could assess the damage and recover the bodies of their fallen comrades, they would have to ascertain the extent of the nuclear contamination issues and develop a plan to contain and clean them. That meant getting in there and taking readings and samples.

The shipyard workers were getting briefed on what they could expect to find when they entered the ship or dry-dock. There was a lot of unknown, and if not for the crisis nature of this event they would have never been allowed to enter. The dock had remained flooded due to the split-open caisson. The dry-dock pump-wells would try to pump it out whenever the tide outside dropped below the visible splits, but the dock wasn't pumping out very quickly. The working theory was that there were other splits and openings down low on the caisson. Marie had denied permission for the divers to continue exploring outside the caisson until they could get some contamination readings from inside the dock.

The replacement crane had put a small boat owned by the ship-wrights into the north end of the dock. They were to drive the boat for the radiation technicians who would be taking samples in several spots. They weren't expecting to have to deal with a spill that left the ship's hull, but they still had to go out and verify that with tests.

Marie was listening to the brief from the back of the crowd when she noticed a nearby shipwright looking at her. People had a general idea of who was who based on their hardhat color. Shipwrights were also recognizable by the fifteen pounds of tools and fall protection gear they normally had with them.

"Didn't I just see you graduate the apprenticeship recently?" she asked the young, auburn-haired man.

"Yes, ma'am," Crane said. He turned back towards the speaker, somewhat sheepishly for having been caught staring.

Marie wanted to speak more with him, to tell him how proud she was of him. She wanted to finally be able to thank a civilian for their service, the way that clerks and waiters always said it to her. But she decided she shouldn't distract him. She turned back toward the waiting Lieutenant and truck and climbed in, heading for the EOC.

CRANE WAS USING the manila rope to pull the boat over to where the dry-dock stairs met the current waterline. At his feet were three personal floatation vests, a ten-horse small boat engine, a paddle, and a partially filled can of mixed-gas. Two of the radiation techs were coming down the stairs with a couple more following. All were carrying a fairly full plastic bag. Crane was just about to climb over the stair's handrail and step into the ten-foot Livingston when he heard "Stop!"

The closest tech, a man in his forties, was coming down the stairs with a younger female following. Each had a plastic bag. Like Crane, they were decked out in a full suit of yellow coveralls, booties, rubber gloves, and half-face respirators. They looked like *Minions* but without the farmer overalls. "You need to take a reading on your dosimeter first. Just call it out. Tomi here will record it."

"Sorry," Crane hollered through the respirator. "I'm just a poor dumb shipwright. Name's Crane," he said, changing the topic.

"Rick," the man stated.

"Rick, as soon as I'm in the boat, hand me that stuff, motor first," Crane instructed. "Let me get the engine running warming up before you climb in." Crane donned one of the floatation vests, read his dosimeter, called out his reading to Tomi, and climbed over the rail. He stabilized his balance and turned to receive the motor. Once he had it set, he set the clamps down on the transom to make sure it stayed put. Rick handed him the fuel and a wood paddle that was sitting there. Crane primed the engine and got it started on the first pull.

Rick and Tomi had put on their float vests and were waiting for Crane to give them the sign. He held the dock's stair rail, using his stance to hold the boat steady while they climbed in. Every one to two minutes, Rick and Crane would call out their readings to Tomi, while she recorded it on a clipboard with a pencil.

Crane drove them around the dock in a pre-arranged pattern so that Rick could take samples of water and make swipes on the hull of the sub. He would screw the lid tight, tape the lid's seam, write on the vial, and set it into a pre-labeled spot of a gridded case. *Very efficient*, Crane thought.

While they were near the broken caisson, Crane took photos. He was issued a camera for this task, something that wasn't normal. Cameras in the shipyard were tightly controlled. He looked around and started to have an idea about something they could do. *I need to get back to the woodshop first*, he thought. *If we have enough timbers, it might just work.*

"WHERE'S PAW-PAW?" Savannah asked, confused about why he wasn't there.

"He's at the gun-range, baby," her mother replied, hoping she was right. They had just taken sponge baths in the kitchen. The faucets weren't working, and Payton wasn't sure exactly how to start and hook up the generator. She opted to warm the water up on the stove, which ran on propane. *Watch him walk in,* she thought, knowing in her mind that a little embarrassment would be okay in exchange for knowing he was fine.

The little pump on the water-bob in the bathtub was easy enough to figure out. They decided to warm some water in Phil's big saucepot that he normally made his extremely average spaghetti sauce in. Payton had a second pot boiling since she was unsure if the tub water was safe to drink. *Better safe than sorry…*

The Walker ladies used some of the boiling water to make ramen noodles and took their washcloth baths while the noodles were cooling. Payton opened the curtain at the sliding glass door and was taken back by what she saw. Her dad's back porch was gone, laying in a heap about ten feet below. It was a fast lesson in the new-world—*don't let Savannah go anywhere without checking it out first.*

Once the un-boiled water was a bit cooler they washed their hair, using the sink to catch the rinse water. She figured the septic would work until it didn't. She knew it had always worked during power outages when she was a teenager.

Her phone was dead. She knew it was around 10:00 AM, thanks to the fact that her old-fashioned dad still believed in owning at least one battery-operated clock. *Should we go look for him?* She thought for a while longer. Finally, she got up and began filling grocery bags with cans of food that had spilled out onto the kitchen floor. "Grab your stuff. We're going to the gun range," she told her daughter. *Please be there.*

It was late morning and the rain was steady, casting the world in a dreary gray—drearier than normal. So far four range members had drifted in, two with spouses. Fred O'Conner—"Airhead Fred," Phil sometimes called him, due to the oddball things that floated out of his mouth—was the first to show. He hadn't received Phil's text plea for help. He just had a feeling, so he packed up his wife in their twenty-one-foot Jayco travel trailer and came to the range at first light.

When he showed up, Phil was guarding the thug in the dirt parking lot. "I kinda felt sorry for the kid," Fred told Phil a little later.

"Why?" Phil could only wonder what he was about to hear.

"It was like a chihuahua picking on a pit bull," Fred began, "and the pit bull making the chihuahua lay in the rainy mud for four hours."

"Oh, Airhead," Phil said, smiling. "I'm glad you're here, buddy."

"I still can't believe the deputy just let him go," Fred said.

"Yeah. Before you showed up, I took photos of him, his license, and every tattoo I could find without removing his pants." Phil shuddered a little upon saying that. "Turns out he's related to the Matthews, one of the patriarch families out here. I know several. Some are okay, others...not so much. I'm not too worried about it. They know better than to come after me. In fact, I think they'll probably tune him up a bit just for being stupid.

"Say, Fred..." Phil continued. "Think you can hold down the fort here and let me borrow your truck while I take off to find the girls? People keep strolling-in. At some point I just need to leave, probably within the next half hour or so."

"Sure, boss! Whatever you need."

"Thanks, bud." Phil's mind was travelling in about twelve directions. He needed to find Payton and Savannah, but he also needed to decide what was happening here. People were just coming out, as if they sensed the natural defensibility of the property. People like Jerry Horst, who had shown up with "toys." Jerry was a HAM radio guy. When Phil greeted Jerry at his truck, he noticed a generator and several car batteries and plastic boxes in the back. *While I'm home I need to get my generator, too*, Phil thought. Jerry laid out a whole plan for setting up antennas and power supplies, and the whole conversation made Phil's head start to spin. *The world needs, nerds, too,* he realized.

As people slowly trickled in, Phil realized he needed to make a decision. *I don't want to camp here forever,* he thought. *But...this is fairly defendable, and there's strength in numbers.* What he was hoping was that the board officers would all show up so he could take a quick vote on what to do. But there was no guarantee any of them would show up.

He had been assigning tasks to people. He had Craig Wageman digging several slit trenches in Bay 9 with the backhoe. That would help with potty needs for the day while he thought through the long-term plan. They could move a couple of the Costco-style tarp-shelters over the trenches to provide privacy. As people did their business, they could cover their waste with dirt from the trench. It wasn't ideal but neither was having people start to create "cat-holes" all over the property.

He had Fred go up to the field and surrounding area to inventory the materials up there. The place had become a collecting yard over the years, as members donated materials in lieu of working their required participation time. There was PVC, lumber, fencing, piping, even an old wood stove. It wasn't like going to the hardware store, but they could rough in some facilities. He planned on having someone hop in the zero-turn mower and give the field a trim. He wanted to use some PVC pipe and plastic sheeting to make a greenhouse for his "winter starts," which were still at home.

Phil was already worrying about fuel. They might be able to scrounge sixty to eighty gallons of gas, if they were lucky, plus some propane. He had another ten five-gallon jerry cans of gas at home. He found that those and the additives "Pri-G" or "Pri-D" were the best way to store small quantities of fuel. The club had about fifty gallons of diesel available for the tractor. Things were not looking so bright if the members wanted to turn this into a working camp.

"Phil," the radio crackled. On his hip was one of the range's little Retevis Model 777 radios. They transmitted in UHF, on about one-watt of power. They were good for the property and not much else. *Ugh, how'll we recharge these? One more thing to worry about...*

"Yeah?" he replied. It was Stephanie Webster, who was watching the office while her husband Tim took a better look at the broken septic trailer.

"You have a visitor. It's a deputy. Also, please check the hand-pump on the well-head. It doesn't seem to be working very well."

Great... "I'll be up in three." *I hope its Charlie.* Phil started the John Deere Gator and headed back to the front half of the property. He made it clear to everyone there that shooting was suspended, which ensured that people could move freely while performing work. He took the southern back route out of the field and moved across the rifle line from the right, crossing a road that paralleled it after the road started near the gate. He banked left up the road instead of crossing the line and then turned into the parking area. There was the familiar green medium-SUV the local deputies were using now.

"What's up, brother?" he greeted Charlie, giving him a quick "bro-hug." It was a sign of respect, especially considering the role Charlie had played in saving Phil's life.

"I heard you spared a poor innocent soul today," the giant, good-looking deputy said, smiling.

"Ah, yes, I thought you might find your way out here. So, you heard, huh? What took you so long, Sergeant?" Phil asked.

"Been a long two days. Plus, I'm not sure if you know this, but I moved to graveyard when Mike McLaffin retired about three weeks ago."

"Roger that. The next shootout needs to happen on graveyard. Got it," Phil cracked. Both men chuckled a bit before turning to a more serious tone.

"So, Phil," Charlie led in, "what are your plans for out here?"

"Well, I think I'm still thinking about that. As you can see, members have started drifting out here," Phil mentioned, pointing towards Tim over by the destroyed restroom building. "Let's take a ride while we're talking." Charlie looked at his car, hesitant to stray too far.

"We'll be in the Gator," Phil reminded him. "We won't go far."

"Okay," Charlie said, trusting Phil.

Phil turned the little cart around and started driving towards the southwest corner of the property. He thought about his friendship with the deputy. They'd known each other for years from competing in practical shooting competitions. They'd been students at some of the same classes over the years, and Charlie had even taken some of Phil's classes when he was feeling rusty. But it was the bridge thing that had sealed their bond. Phil snapped out of it when he got to the corner.

He climbed out of the gator, and his guest followed suit. "What do you see here?" Phil asked. They were looking at the corner of the property, where it met the shoulder of Canal Vista Highway and veered due east along the neighboring property's border.

"You mean besides a flimsy wire fence? I dunno. Trees. Huckleberry. The neighbor's mail-box, the highway, the house just down the road..."

"The southern approach," Phil explained. "We can build a fighting position right here in the brush under the trees and have a clear view of the highway all the way down to that curve. The range already has tons of sand and hundreds of bags. A little spray paint for the bags, maybe a tarp—and our lookouts would never be seen."

Charlie nodded. The two men got back into the gator, and Phil took him to the back field. They pulled up to Fred at the far end, about three hundred yards away.

"Hey, ya, fellas!" Fred exclaimed after shutting off the mower. Fred shot a lot of the shooting sports and knew full-well who Charlie was.

"Hey, Fred, whatcha up to?" Charlie asked.

Fred shot Phil a look and answered after getting a nod. "I'm mowing this area down to hay, and we're going to build a green-house up here—a big one. Like one of those big "high-tunnel" kinds...except the budget model."

Phil took over. "See that spigot over there?" Charlie looked where Phil was pointing and acknowledged. "Well, we've been installing those all over the place for years. We have water, so we'll grow food up here. Not just the greenhouse but a big garden, too. As I've shown you, we'll put in fighting positions. We'll let people park their trailers in the action bays, set up showers and latrines. Maybe a school of sorts to keep the kids busy. I just need to talk to the board, first. *If* they show up. But I may have to decide without them. People are here already."

They hopped back into the gator so that Fred could get back to work. They continued to discuss the potential for the property as Phil dropped Charlie off at his patrol vehicle.

"Hey, bud, I think I need to get back to town," Charlie said. "I'll swing by tonight, if things don't get crazy."

"Yeah, I'm going to head home. If Payton's not there, I'll be heading to town to find her," Phil replied. "Oh! My truck is just a bit down Salal Road and undriveable. I'll get to it in a day or two."

"Don't sweat it. There's hundreds of cars stuck all over the place."

The two men made their good-byes, and Phil watched Charlie turn right onto the highway and take off to the north. He turned around and started to head into the office when he heard another car approaching. His heart skipped a beat when he saw Payton's gold Acura pull in. *Two offspring down, one to go,* he thought, smiling for the first time that day.

12

Autopilot.

TAHOMA'S HAMMER + 1 DAY.

MAERSK. Cosco. NYK. Hanjin. All of the world's shipping companies reacted with real time satellite communications, redirecting their cargo ships bound for Portland, Tacoma, Seattle, Everett, and Vancouver. Suddenly San Francisco, Oakland, Long Beach, and San Diego all had to double their capacity for shipping traffic. That was only half of the problem. The trucks capable of handling the containers were still on the way to the destruction zone. Worse yet, many of them were trapped or straight up destroyed during the devastation. Once the shipping industry realized the lack of trucks was the new constraint, they started redirecting from the East Coast. They also started sending goods bound for the eastern side of the country through the Panama Canal.

The reverse flow of goods was equally affected. Items scheduled to leave the destroyed ports were now rerouted, if they were found at all. Commerce with Asia and the Far East suddenly slowed. Goods worth hundreds of millions of dollars slowed to a crawl in their travels, and so did the flow of money. Compounding this was the fact that hackers were already taking advantage of the issues emanating from the crisis. It wasn't just Amazon and Microsoft who were hit. Portland was home to Intel and other major chip manufacturers. While their roads were mostly usable, Portland and Vancouver were suffering from the power outages, too. Criminals that would use malware, trojans, and other malicious code to steal money and industrial property were already hard at work.

The US Federal Government had started to put all their FEMA plans into play on the day that the hammer struck. By Hammer + 1, they had already found a number of anticipated but unmitigated obstacles. Helicopters just didn't have the range to get supplies or assistance as far north and west as they needed to be. The air, sea, and land transport routes and ports were all out of commission, some permanently. It would take weeks to months to get runways and highways cleared and repaired. Additionally, power outages in every major city west of Denver had caused a slight panic in those states, which was made worse by the doom and gloom media reports. Supplies sat at FEMA storage sites and on runways untouched and unmoving. The famous photo of thousands of cases of water sitting on a Puerto Rican runway for months after the 2017 disaster was now a slight hiccup in comparison to the wasted resources throughout the US after Tahoma's Hammer fell.

THE PRINCESS CRUISE ship listed heavily to starboard, and there was a bright rainbow sheen surrounding it for several hundred feet. There were tugboats tending to floating containment booms, trying to keep the fuel from completely escaping. It was a losing battle fought throughout much of Puget Sound. *That'll kill all the fish,* Tony thought. *Not good,* which was neither the first nor last time he'd thought "not good" that day.

Jason's original course had been aimed at Seattle's Pier 66. As they got closer, the two men knew they would have to adjust course to the north. The devastation of Seattle had left them both silent, at a complete loss for words. Buildings looked like steel skeletons, barren of their glass. The entire city was in a haze from smoke, with many columns of it still floating through the top of the film. Large fires—towering infernos—were visible and unattended. Buildings were written off as strategic losses. Structures meant to stay on piers were now submerged. *Paul McCartney won't be fishin' out of the Edge-water Hotel, anymore,* Tony thought. They could see throngs of people and emergency vehicles around the waterfront. Seattle's most famous skyscape icon—the Space Needle—was conspicuously absent. Tony's heart was in his stomach.

"Take me north," he said from the little boat's bow. "We'll land up at that park." He hoped Jason couldn't see him shedding tears.

Jason complied without comment. He was still trolling, not sure of what navigational hazards they might find. They had lost count of the number of trees, bodies, and other debris they had brushed against on the trip over. After another twenty-five minutes at trolling speed they finally reached Olympic Sculpture Park. The footbridge that led over the railroad tracks to the top of the hill was lying in a pile of concrete.

"Dude," Jason murmured. "I know I said I'd wait, but this…" His voice trailed off, eyes glassy with shock as he looked at a city that seemed as if it had seen a WW2 bombing campaign. He wanted to get home, and his face showed it.

Tony had known this was coming. Deep inside he knew he had no right to be mad. He swallowed his disappointment, knowing his friend had already extended himself. "It's alright, man," the enormous man said in the softest way his bass voice could. "I get it." Tony stuck his hand out. "Be careful."

Jason took the big paw. "I'm sorry, Tony. I hope your girls are okay." He stopped short of saying anything else, knowing he couldn't say he was sorry enough times to make either of them feel better.

When Jason nodded, Tony gave the boat a shove off the corrosion control rocks that lined the shore at the park. The boat drifted backwards with slight propeller power. Tony watched Jason turn and start to troll back into the drizzle to the west. He gave his backpack a cinch and felt to make sure his pocketknife was still clipped to his pants pocket. *Lord…please* was all he could think as he started up the grassy slope of the park, headed towards the Seattle Center.

THE MAROON FORD F-350 with a white cab-over camper pulled into the range driveway, and instead of the immediate hard left turn into the main parking lot, made the straight east shot through the secondary gate. It travelled down the road next to the rifle line. Everyone knew Don Kwiatkowsky's truck. The retired mechanical engineer was the Tuesday/Friday lead range officer. When he left after the first earthquake the day before, he hadn't dreamt he'd be back looking to camp there just a day later. He made the curve where the road crosses the rifle line, just past the hundred-yard target holders. He stopped near the mid-range storage area when he saw Phil.

That makes nineteen assuming Teresa's with him, Phil thought. He'd been setting up his canvas tent in Bay 4. After his joyous reunion with his daughter and granddaughter—he and Payton had actually hugged for the first time since Caroline's funeral several years earlier—he and Fred took the Kubota and Fred's truck and towed Phil's broken Ram back to his house. Phil used the bucket to take some weight off the engine end while Fred towed the Ram back-end first. The wheel did eventually fall off. They stopped and threw it into the bucket. He brought back his generator and fuel, eight-man tent, cots, sleeping bags, camp-stove, propane, bigger water filters, and more food. Payton had told him about the back deck, but he didn't take the time to do a more thorough check of the house.

He wanted to get Crane's jeep, but since he had to drive the tractor back, he decided to wait. He hoped to come back the next day for a more detailed check of truck and house and to retrieve the more extensive gear and food storage he'd been building for several years.

"I guess I'm not the only one who thought this might be a good place to stay," Don greeted his old friend.

"Hmmm," Phil hummed. "Yeah, we're somewhere between fifteen and twenty strong, I think. Good to see you, bud," Phil said, walking over and shaking Don's extended hand.

Don asked about the tent. "I figured you'd bring your cargo trailer. You can put your cot in our cab-over, if you'd rather," Don offered.

"Payton and Savannah made it out," Phil explained. "Need something a little easier to move around in. Plus, the truck was damaged. Fred and I towed it home earlier."

Hearing her name, Savannah popped out of the mostly-erect tent with a tail wagging Dakota just behind her. Phil had noticed that Dakota had been "herding" Savannah all day long. He knew it was good for both of them. "Hi!" she exclaimed, waving.

The innocence of youth, Phil thought. *She has no idea how bad it is, thinks this is a vacation.* "Peaches, do you remember Mr. Don?"

"No," she said with the friendly honesty of a nine-year-old.

"Hi, Savannah," the always-friendly Don said, waving back. "Cool backpack! You and your mom okay?"

"Yeah…" The word said 'yeah' but the tone said 'duh.' She turned around so she could show off her backpack.

"Man, that is a lot of unicorns!" Don said excitedly.

Phil knew Don was an awesome grandpa. "Peaches, please go back to playing so Mr. Don and I can talk," Paw-paw politely commanded. She took the hint and called Dakota to join her as she went back to playing in the tent.

"Got anyplace specific I should park?" Don asked.

"Several others had been parking in the open area across from Bay 7 and 8," Phil answered. "But in thinking about aftershocks, I've been advising everyone to set up their camps in an action bay. That way the berms will keep trees off people. Hopefully! I advise you choose anything from Bay 1 to Bay 8 that has a space for you. We have a temporary latrine in Bay 9, and I have other plans for Bays 10 and 11. If things get tight, we'll just use the rifle line and the overflow parking area, too."

Don was one of the trustees and therefore part of the board. "Any other board members here besides the two of us?"

"Just Alice. And Bob, of course," Phil said. He was referring to the club's president, Alice Huddlesten and her husband. Bob was a Pipefitter General Foreman at the shipyard, two years shy of his planned retirement date. "We're kind of at the mercy of what the wind and rain blows in." This got Phil thinking. "Say, brother, how was the highway down from Peterson?"

"Pretty bad. We had to detour several times. We could see the exit ramp and overpass at Highway 803 was collapsed. They're rerouting traffic on the southbound side down one of the lanes on the northbound side. The roads were much more cracked and bumpy than they were when I went home yesterday. And there's downed trees and flipped over cars all along the way." Don's face showed the worry that emanated from his voice.

The two men fell silent for a moment before Don spoke up again. "Maybe you, Alice, and I should meet and figure out how all of this is gonna work."

"Yep. I think you're on to something," Phil nodded. "Go get yourselves settled. Swing by here on the way up to the office."

"Alrighty," the retired mechanical engineer told Phil. "See you in a bit."

Phil had been contemplating this very topic for quite a while.

The first thing we need is a watch rotation—we need to figure out who is on guard while everyone else is asleep... It hadn't slipped his mind that just a few hours earlier he had been detaining someone up in the parking lot.

PETERSON WAS the biggest incorporated city in the north end of Slaughter County. It was due south of a Native reservation and west of another one. Charlie Reeves was a member of the eastern-most tribe, known locally as Suquamish. They were the ancestral people of Chief Sealth, whom Seattle was named after. Charlie's father was full-blooded Native American, and his mother was a local artist. A Caucasian, she was born and reared in the northernmost community, Kiaka. Charlie did have several uncles, aunts, and cousins from his father's side, but his busy life as a cop meant he did not visit very often. He didn't participate in tribal activities as much as he would have liked. He was an only child, as his mother and brother had been killed by a drunk-driver when he was six-years-old. His father had never remarried, and he died from lung cancer five years earlier.

Charlie had convinced his lieutenant that he would be of better use if he could get home for some shut eye. In truth, most every cop had snuck home by then, especially those that had worked since midnight two nights earlier. It was already mid-afternoon, and the best he could hope for before he had to wake up was maybe six to seven hours of sleep.

Melinda Reeves taught seventh and eighth grade science. Since school was cancelled, Charlie knew she'd be able to make sure he woke up on time. They were both relieved to see each other when he walked through the front door.

"Mel, I'm home." He started with a louder than normal version of his usual greeting to ensure she knew it was him. She popped up off the couch and ran to her husband, leaving her crochet in a pile of yarn in front of her seat.

"Hey, Boo!" She hopped up, grabbing onto him with arms up high and legs around his waist. She planted a big wet kiss on her husband. "I was beginning to think they'd never let you come home!"

Charlie let out an oomph as he adjusted to her hanging from him. "They almost didn't. But I think the LT decided it was a good idea when I told the same joke a third time," he said, smiling. Melinda hopped back down and held his arm as they walked over to the couch. He plopped down heavier than normal. "Where's the kids?"

"Over at the Kalick's, playing."

"Oh, okay." Charlie wasn't worried. Like all cops, he got to know the people his kids played with. Terry was an electrician and a jack-of-all-trades who flipped beater cars for a profit whenever work was slow. He'd helped Charlie through a handful of home repair issues over the years. Their kids played together all the time. Charlie trusted Terry.

He noticed his wife making a beeline for the front door. "No—no—just leave them. I need to sleep anyway. By the way, if I fall asleep, please wake me up no later than ten." He changed the topic. "Have you all been getting enough to eat? Keeping warm?" *This is really the only piece of business I want to handle before I crash,* he didn't say out loud.

"Just who do you think you married, mister?" Melinda asked sarcastically. Melinda was a non-practicing member of the Latter-Day Saints, the grandparents of the American Preparedness movement. Even those who didn't attend church regularly always seemed to have food and supplies stuffed into every available space in the house. "We're good. The only thing I don't like is having to use our jugs of water to flush the toilet. In fact, I should make you something warm."

"Hold up a second," he said. "You *do* know that the sewer

systems won't work for much longer, right? I'm surprised they still have back up power for the pumps at this point." She gave him *the look*. It was the look that meant "don't wreck my reality." He continued. "Phil Walker is setting up a kind of 'safety-camp' out at West Sound Sportsmen's Club. I think you and the kids should consider staying there."

"No way. Why would we do that? We have everything we need here." There was the look again.

Because I'll be able to work days at a time a lot easier knowing you're safe. "No reason—just wanted to see what your thoughts were. Forget I mentioned it."

"Don't be silly," she said, getting up and heading to the kitchen.

She already had a kettle and a big sauce pot warming on the wood stove that was planted where the living room and kitchen met. She continued to talk about the kids and school while filling a smaller pot with stew and setting it into the sauce pot to warm up. She poured water from the kettle into a mug so she could make him his favorite hot beverage—white tea and pomegranate. She continued talking about the stories she'd heard of various events around the city and north end of the county. She talked on while making him several days' worth of food to take with him that evening. Melinda was the type of person who could talk to a stranger in the grocery store line for five minutes and walk out with their life story.

When his food was ready, she went back into the living room. Charlie was snoring, still wearing his boots and gun belt. She put a blue afghan on him and went back to her crochet.

13

Windows to the Soul.

TAHOMA'S HAMMER + 1 DAY.

WHY DIDN'T I bring a hat, Tony asked himself for the third time in forty minutes. He'd cinched down the hood on his quasi-rain-coat—more of a waterproof work coat—as best that he could. A bill over his eyes would've gone a long way in keeping his morale up, he'd figured out. The rain was the familiar steady sprinkle—more than drizzle and less than hard rain. It was beating down the ash into a pasty slop that made crawling over rubble and across sinkholes slow and tedious. He had planned on a quick ten-minute hike. It had been almost an hour since he'd left the boat, and he figured he still had at least that long to go.

Tony had turned north just a few steps into his journey, opting to go around the park and stick to square blocks as best he could.

He didn't remember exactly where the Seattle Center was—he knew that if he went mostly east and a little north he'd eventually run into it. He crossed the tracks a few hundred yards south of where a derailed cargo train was located. Some of it was laying on its side and crumpled in a zig-zag pattern. Everyone he saw over there was picking through as if they were salvaging goods. *Odd—not a person there working to resolve the accident.* His worry was getting harder to keep pushed to the back of his mind.

Tony had made decent time up Bay Street, but a collapse of most of 1st Ave. near Denny Way had forced him south through an alley. He utilized pallets and garbage bags to try and hop over the murky pool that had built up there, knowing that there may be sewage in it. When he reached a large enough looking road, he aimed north. All along the way people were asking him for help. He largely ignored them. Some looked like the typical, Seattle heroin addicts, a demographic that had grown tremendously in recent years. *Don't look 'em in the eyes,* he told himself. *Don't need no trouble.*

Some wanderers, though, looked like him—average folks who just needed a shower and a bite to eat. The farther he got into Seattle the more he realized the pack seemed to be migrating towards the south, undeterred by rivers of glass and pillars of smoke.

Broad Street. He saw a sign as he turned left. He'd made it less than two blocks east when what used to be the top of a building presented itself as the next obstacle. *Mannn...I wonder how many people died in this...* The top two-thirds of what used to be a fifteen-story building was resting comfortably against the building to its north, as if it had just snapped and slid off the lower third. The bottom of the break was still sitting about forty feet up from street level. There was a three-story pile of rubble, clothing, and household goods lying below the building. Tony could actually see daylight through gaps in the pile. He was tempted to navigate through it but decided against the idea, knowing a poorly-timed aftershock could finish the collapse. *No, sirreee...* He was pretty sure the combined stench of sewage and dead bodies would gag a buzzard.

He wanted to go north, but one of the buildings there was still actively on fire. Turning south he made his way to Clay Street and was able to get moving east again. Then he saw it. *Holy Hell...Dear God—No!* Tony stopped in his tracks as he was able to see across an open parking lot. He could see the bottom sixty-three feet of two of the Space Needle's legs. He snapped out of it and started running. As he got to the far side of the lot, he came up to a Seattle Fire ladder-truck and a pair of police officers on foot. They were trying to keep the area contained.

"Whoa!" one of the police officers commanded, hands up in Tony's direction.

He complied but said emphatically, "I need to get in there!"

"No way," the other police officer said. "What's going on?" He was trying to reason with the big man.

"I'm looking for my daughters! They were on a field trip." *Calm down, don't get yourself tased. One o' these guys is a brothuh, but he's still a cop.*

"Look, man," the first cop said firmly. "There's a Command Post over by the fountain—east of Key Arena. Check in there. They may know something. But you're *not* getting in here."

"Alright...which way is quickest?"

The first officer pointed west. "Take Denny to 2nd and turn right. Where are you from, anyway?" the officer asked, surprised Tony didn't know where "the Key" was.

"Slaughter County," Tony said through the side of his neck, already twenty-five feet down the road.

Eight minutes later he was joining a crowd of probably two thousand people being shepherded into a staging area by cones and yellow tape. He had scanned as best he could. The Needle seemed to have missed the main body of the museum. Its north-eastern leg was the first to go, crushing the famous monorail track like it was made out of papier-mâché. It landed just south of the museum. The saucer was still upright. It looked like a crashed spaceship. It was resting comfortably on top of the parking lot for the "duck boats." He felt an acorn of hope plant itself in his gut. He was scanning the crowd when he saw someone in Seattle Center uniform. "Excuse me."

"Yeah?" the tired looking person said, stopping to look him in the eyes.

"My daughters were here yesterday on a field trip. Do you know where they may be?" The acorn was nervously rolling around in his stomach.

"Sorry, dude." Tony felt himself deflate as the hope acorn disappeared. The employee continued. "I've heard everyone talking about the arenas, though. You ought to try there."

Tony looked over at Key Arena, his puzzled look giving away his thoughts.

"No...I mean the 'Clink' and 'T-Mobe.' I hear they have a big shelter set up down there." The twenty-something hipster was referring to Century Link and T-Mobile Fields, a few miles to the south.

"Oh." Tony said. *That makes sense. Actually, that makes a lotta sense. They're new buildings, lotsa' room...* "Thank you... I mean it. Thanks." Tony knew this guy was probably tired and dismayed. He hoped the sincerity of his thanks made it through. He looked south, wondering if he should eat and get some water before he started the long leg of this voyage.

CARMEN WAS STANDING in the line for some soup. *Soup is filling the void, but I would kill for some of Mama's homemade chorizo.* Carmen's family was actually Puerto Rican in heritage. It always annoyed her when people assumed she was Mexican. "I'm a Puerto Rican-American, Cabron!" she would always tell them. She was passing time by looking at the people. Their faces had replaced shock with annoyance. Everyone was getting a little short with their fuse. They were all filthy, and many of them were getting...*ripe.*

I'm going to scream if I have to smell one more dude's pits! Everyone had just weathered an aftershock a few minutes earlier, but that didn't stop the hungry from standing in line. She was performing the slow crawl, along with all the other dirty stinky peasants, when her subconscious alerted her to something. She scanned her head back a little bit. *There!*

"That's right, whore! I'm lookin' at *you*! You keep your eyes off my old-man! Got it?" At the second row of tables about thirty feet away were a couple of greasy people Carmen had never even seen before.

What the... "I don't even know who your old man is, Puneta." Carmen was trying to not yell. *I don't need this!* "Go back to your soup and mind your own business." Her eyes told the lady the truth —*back off!*

The woman stood up and started to walk towards Carmen. *I bet she reeks of booze. Bring it, you old cow,* Carmen thought, as she started to square up for the fight. Several of the people between the two stopped the woman. Her old man grabbed her by the arm and dragged her out of the tent. His eyes were saying sorry as he looked at Carmen. Everyone could still hear the woman's tirade for several seconds after she was gone.

Carmen shook it off. *Reminds me of LA,* she thought, missing home once more. *People are getting territorial...I think I need to talk Doc into leaving.*

AT LEAST I BROUGHT GLOVES. While wishing for a hat, Tony was taking the small victories where he could. He had eaten a sandwich and drank some water before departing the Seattle Center. He walked over to a tourist information station and picked up a couple of maps of Seattle. *Just in case one gets wet,* he thought. His trip up from the waterfront had taught him a lot about the value of maps. *Who the hell uses maps anymore?* That day he had grown very disappointed with himself for becoming so dependent on his phone. He had asked about thirty people what time it was before getting an answer from someone. It was early afternoon when he set out for the football stadium at the south end of the city.

His map had shown him that trying to run south on any of the avenues would get him close. He wound up crissing and crossing some of the same obstacles and around the same fires that he had earlier. He had travelled down 3rd for a while, scaling piles of skyscraper glass and a tipped over construction crane in the process. A large sewage spill and fire at apartments between Battery and Bell Streets had forced him west. He was figuring out to stay on the streets and avenues and avoid the alleys if at all possible. *That's where the sketchies are.*

Along the way he had twice seen people shooting up heroin. *That's what's in the open—I wonder what's happening where nobody can see.* That thought made him shore up his resolve. He would kill anyone hurting his babies. *What happens to this town when these people run out of drugs? Or when the cops quit coming to work?*

Tony had decided he would push through all night with just small breaks—not trying to find a place to sleep. *Just like that first day at boot camp.* No sleep.

THE LOOK in Vice Admiral David Warburg's eyes was one of confusion. "You did what?" he asked Captain Marie Darnell over the secure video-link.

Marie, Captain Flowers, and about fifteen of her senior leaders were in the conference room up at EOC. They were updating NavSurf on the status of the various crises at the shipyard. First and foremost on his mind was the status of the re-fueling gone awry. He needed to be able to predict the future. He was due to give the Chairman of the Joint Chiefs a personal update shortly. He didn't want to end his career as the Admiral who lost a submarine by destroying its reactor.

"I handed over control of the flooding dry-docks to Captain Flowers, sir. All except Dry-dock A. This will allow me to maintain one hundred percent control over the El Paso situation without distraction." She could see the shift in NavSurf's eyes. He understood. *He was ruling out that I might be overwhelmed—in over my head,* Marie told herself. *Now he'll trust my decision making fully.*

"I understand, Captain. Good call. Are there other surprises? How's the situation?" the Admiral asked.

"Contained, Sir. We've taken the readings and verified the spill is all inside the ship. Rad-levels are somewhat high—we're not sure if the fuel rods were damaged, particularly the one that was dropped in the container. We've started fabricating a containment for the open reactor top and have re-established the services to the ship... well, the most critical ones so far. We're dealing with some tidal flow issues, too."

"What's your 'Plan A' to deal with the flood?" the Admiral queried.

Marie shot a glance at the Shop 46 Wood-shop Superintendent, Tyrone Biggs, for a quick eye-to-eye confirmation before she proceeded. It was his shipwrights that had come up with the idea. Biggs nodded. "Sir, it's already in motion. The woodshop is taking all of the timbers they had purchased to make the shapes for next year's carrier dock-setting, and they're starting to build a coffer-dam." She let him digest it for a moment. They were going to build a big wood wall in the south end of the flooded dry-dock.

Admirals who got to his level, while political creatures, were inherently smart. He got it immediately. He started talking the reasoning out loud, not caring who was listening. "Pre-built off-site... Can be lifted in with a crane... Blocks most of the water while it's being sealed up... Alright, Captain, I see it. What else?"

"The divers are pre-setting stacks of blocks to land the pre-fab pieces in between. As the pieces are set, a second crane will suspend a bucket and allow the shipwrights and riggers to shore it up and tie it together. We'll have a third crane running the sections across the shipyard as the first two begin construction. We're working on this through the night, hoping to start installing sections tomorrow morning."

Marie continued. "Our Shop 66 pump-well operators are confident that the pumps will be able to keep up once they aren't fighting tide anymore. As far as the ship itself, we're establishing strict, high-level entry protocols."

"Alright." He was clearly unpleased. "Captain, I can't impress upon you enough that the Navy needs those assets operational. There are already things that our friends from other countries are putting into play." Marie could speak "admiral." That meant "perform miracles."

"Understood, sir. Captain Flowers will now update you on the flooding and courses of action in the other docks."

14

Adaptation.

It took two days. Two days after the hammer fell the legislature of the State of Idaho had found itself in "special session." It was a bi-partisan vote that passed at an astounding eighty-eight percent rate—a vote to suspend selling power to other states. Everyone knew that California was the intended victim of the legislation. *Every* state was suffering power outages, not just Washington. *Every* state's economy was threatened, not just the Cascadia states' economies.

The Idaho legislators decided to save themselves another trip to Boise. They voted to call up their own National Guard for "humanitarian" reasons. It was flu season, and those Washingtonians' immune systems would be weakened. Utah followed suit the very next day. Soon the other states did, too. The sharks were starting to smell the blood in the water.

Locally, disbelief was slowly turning to anger. The unprepared were scraping together their food and water supplies. People had already started to make a run on the grocery stores, which couldn't make any transactions due to the power being out. A smaller scale of shopping panic was hitting the hardware stores, too. The managers of these stores were already cutting deals with security "experts" willing to help guard the stores for trade in goods. The enterprising, low-level thieves were sneaking out to their neighbor's cars at night to siphon gas.

On the international front countries like Japan, England, and Australia were mobilizing planes full of supplies and relief work-ers…with no place for them to fly towards. "Just get them into the air—they'll figure it out," had become the motto. The rest of the major cities in the American West received tons of aid from the international relief effort—relief which they "held for inspection." The rolling blackouts were slowly becoming extended blackouts, and the mini-riots were growing. Wave two of the hammer's impact had begun, and the week wasn't over yet.

THE RAIN WAS HEAVIER when Tony finally reached Century Link Field. Dawn was finally starting to shine through the clouds, though shine was probably too strong of a word. The skyline was a dark gray—ominous and disheartening. He could see gray through some buildings in areas where all the windows had shaken out. The streets were easily eighteen inches deep in rain water, glass, and who knew what else. His feet had been numb since the evening before, and the skin on them itched like they were covered in fire ants. The former sailor had learned the hard way that thing which every grunt knew —when feet get wet, cotton kills.

There was a buzz. It was a hum that filled the air, coming from the direction of the two stadiums. Even at—*7:00 AM?*—he could hear the activity. *I bet nobody got much sleep last night.* The crowd of people got thicker as he approached the stadiums. *This could take all day.* It had suddenly dawned on him that half the city had come down here looking for help or—like him—family. The buzz was primarily people—talking, asking for directions, occasionally elated, or sobbing. Generators and halogen lights were providing the rest of the noise. The scene replayed itself countless times around the outside of both stadiums.

Tony could see the lightbars of various emergency vehicles. The moving light they cast danced off the jagged buildings, people, and rubble. The mood was surreal, and the lack of sleep hadn't helped. Tony couldn't think of the words to describe the disbelief he felt. He started to scan for anything that could be useful information. *There —looks like some sort of tent.* He started slowly meandering through the crowd towards "the Clink."

He was cautious to move carefully, not wanting to accidentally start a fight. He was a big man, but he had no delusions about being bulletproof. He would occasionally pause and nod as someone who looked like they were in a hurry pushed past him. After fifteen minutes, which felt like thirty, Tony was within voice distance of some sort of emergency management station. Some people wore blue windbreakers with KCDEM on the back while other had bright orange FEMA coats on. There were also people in uniform. *National Guard,* Tony assumed. He also saw Seattle police officers, though not enough for his liking. *I wonder how long they've been stuck at work?*

One of the people behind the table had the task of keeping the crowd flowing. "You," she barked. "What do you need?"

Straight and to the point, huh? "I'm looking for my daughters," Tony replied with the same level of intensity.

"This area is for checking in to the refugee center in the stadium. All names from both fields are sent to the main Command Post. If you want to locate someone, go there. You?" The lady had already discarded Tony and was asking the next person what they needed.

"Where to?" Tony asked, raising his shoulders.

The lady caught his look and pointed toward the south while listening to the next person.

Tony looked that way and decided he'd probably know it when he saw it. He began his slow, respectful procession once again.

The building between the two stadiums had a large awning on the west side. Under that were perhaps two hundred people who looked like they were part of the disaster response effort. There were floodlights and the roar of several generators. People at the tables had computers and other electronics tied together in some sort of wired network. As Tony approached, he saw a couple of long rows of tables with signs on them that read letters such as "A-B" and "C-D." He decided that must be by last name. He got into the line that covered his last name, "Manners."

After what was probably forty-five minutes he stepped up to the table.

"First-time checking-in?" the person asked.

"Yeah. Yes, sir. Actually, I'm lookin' for my daughters. Manners, Tasha and Talia." He couldn't hear the soft clacking of the keyboard over the generators and commotion.

"T-Mobile," the operator finally responded.

Tony started to turn.

"Wait," the operator commanded. Tony stopped. "What's your name and birthday?" Tony told him. More noiseless typing. Finally, "Give me your wrist." Tony stuck his big arm out towards the man.

The operator wrapped and snapped a plastic band around it and then scanned the barcode with a reader. Then he picked up a different wand and checked that the RFID chip in it worked. "Okay," he said looking in the direction he wanted Tony to go.

I guess I can go... "Thanks," he mumbled as he headed toward the southern stadium. *Tagged like sheep,* he thought, hopeful he would find his babies.

"WHADDYA THINK?" Phil asked Craig Wageman. They were in the crawlspace of Phil's house looking at the floor and foundation.

"See that settling? There?" Craig asked, pointing. "And over there, too. Yep, I bet she's cracked, alright."

Dang. Can anything just wind up good for once? "Hmmm…alright. Let's not waste time under here then. Staring at it won't change anything." The two men crawled back out through the access door in the laundry room floor.

"Thanks for lookin'," Phil said, as they wiped webs and dust off themselves. "And thanks for going with me to check on Hope." Phil was itching to get over there and check on her, a task he still hadn't done since he first set out to do it two days earlier. He'd worked out with Don for Hope to come stay with him in his travel trailer.

"No problem," said the drywall contractor. Like a lot of construction workers in Washington, Craig had started with framing and general remodels. He eventually started his own business, specializing in drywall. People hated doing drywall, so he almost always had work. When times got lean, he would do remodels for cash. The divorcee was an active range member who loved shooting "falling-plate" matches. His kids were all grown and lived in other states, so he came to the range to see what he could do to help. That very morning, he towed his little R-Pod trailer out with his work truck, intending to camp for a while. Phil decided he could use some help for his errands, and Craig was the perfect guy to tag along.

"So… now what?" he asked.

"Food and gear, my friend," Phil said, leading the way. They hooked up Phil's black fourteen-foot cargo trailer to Craig's truck and backed it up to the shop. A flock of angry chickens let Phil know he was needed. *Shoot!* He ran over, threw some feed into the grass, and let them out, studying the coop. "We need to piece together one of these back at the range," he mentioned to Craig.

"That should be easy enough, considering all the materials we have laying around up in the field," Craig replied. "I'll get something going when we get back."

And my winter starts, too, Phil thought, looking at his greenhouse. *We need to move those.* He watered the chickens and plants and collected eggs while Craig got started moving supplies.

He was impressed. "What made you buy all this food?" he asked Phil.

"Not *if,* but *when,*" Phil replied.

"Huh?"

"The earthquake. They've been saying for years 'not if, but when'—yet nobody listened. Well...almost nobody." Phil reflected on the fact that most of his closest friends and allies were "preppers," laughed at by regular society as tin hat wearing conspiracy theorists. *Now who's laughing?*

"Do you know what the odds were for our earthquake?" Phil asked Craig.

"Uhh, well, one-out-of-one, I guess. I mean, we had one, so...."

"Funny. No. Seriously, they said there was a twenty percent chance sometime in the next fifty years. That sounded like there was a lot of time, but fifty years is like a 'second,' geologically-speaking. Their statistic told me one thing—they had no idea. It could be any day. So, I decided to start preparing."

They were hauling out what was a few dozen five and six-gallon buckets full of things like powdered-milk, rice, beans, pasta, wheat, and oats. After that they moved over three hundred "#10" cans filled with freeze-dried and dehydrated vegetables, fruits, meats, and baking goods. Phil preferred the "Thrive" brand for those items. There were two dozen boxes of water kept in mylar bags and multiple fifty-five-gallon steel cans full of MREs and Mountain House meals.

Phil also picked up the rest of his "I'm Never Coming Home" boxes which had things like clothes, medicines, toiletries, rechargeable batteries, and other survival gear. He had plenty of firearms and ammo in his conexes at the range, so he decided to leave his home-based ammo there for the time being. He used steel bolt-together lockers that could be secured to floors or walls for locking guns and ammo up. They were made out of the same steel as a safe but without the fancy door. The easy assembly made them some-what portable when they needed to be. *I'll haul the guns and ammo out tomorrow.*

"C'mon, Craig," Phil said. *I've worked you hard enough.* "Let's go check on Hope."

"No KIDS," Schwartz replied to Carmen. "Just one gold-digging ex-wife, who my mother hates by the way."

Carmen nodded. *The jerk is divorced,* she smirked in her mind. *Go figure.* They were marching south. As much as possible they were staying within eye-sight of Highway 509, otherwise known as the Pacific Coast Highway, or PCH. The incident with the passage fee on the first day, along with the lady's outburst at the homeless shel-ter, had taught them how quickly people's moods can change. Carmen was a little mad at herself for letting her LA survival skills get rusty. *You've seen this. You know what to expect.*

The unlikely partners had started exchanging biographies, trying to glean what they could about the other's character. She verified he was a rich obnoxious jerk, and in exchange he learned she was escaping daddy issues. She wanted Stu to know her gangster father was in prison so he would take her street-sense seriously. Small talk made for time passage and helped the mind take a break from worrying for short bits. The worry always came back, though. It was raining, and life sucked. *I'd give my last $100 for my foul weather gear,* the sailor told herself. She had found some plastic grocery sacks in a dumpster a bit earlier. She'd transferred the stuff from her soaked duffle bag into the grocery sacks and placed the items back into the pack. She looked at Schwartz. "Aren't you getting cold, Doc?"

"Getting? Heh…try 'gotten.' I'm not exactly dressed for hiking, you know."

"Me, either." *Either? Neither? Whatever. Funny the stuff you think of when you're bored, tired, and hungry,* Carmen internalized.

This leg had been uneventful. They had continued to witness signs of devastation. People were tarping the roofs on the houses that still stood. They saw several burnt-up cars and an apartment building still smoldering. Trees and draping powerlines had become a regular obstacle no matter where they were. Try as they might, they couldn't see the blown volcano. The storm system was too low, and the mountain was now about 9,300 feet shorter than it used to be. *We look like hobos,* Carmen realized. Like almost everyone they saw, their clothes were now a version of brownish-gray, covered in what used to be earth. The puddles and ashy sluice piles that had formed in every street made sure that no clean item went untouched.

They arrived at the Safeway at the intersection of PCH and 272nd Street. They saw a couple of men near the front corner on the side of the building.

"Hold up," Schwartz said. They stopped to get a better look. It almost appeared as if the men were filling water bottles.

Carmen had an idea. "Watch my back," she ordered and headed toward the men. Schwartz trailed about five feet back.

"What's up, guys?" she said, trying to appear as cute as she could without being flirtatious.

They looked up but weren't surprised by her presence. They were rugged-looking but not ugly—kind of hot in a Daniel Boone sort of way. The one at the water spigot had "Garren" embroidered on the back of his ballcap. They had a pull-cart full of big jugs of water.

"Hey," the one that was farther away half mumbled. He looked at Carmen and back at Schwartz. He then did a quick scan of the parking lot—even behind himself. The closer man just kept filling the jug from a spigot, not letting a single drop hit the ground. When the guard turned to look the parking lot over, Carmen thought she detected the bottom of a holster poking out the bottom of his coat. *Don't freak out,* she told herself.

She looked at the spigot on the building. It looked different. "Could we possibly purchase or trade something for water?"

The first guy kept to his task while the second one came around his friend to address Carmen. "Is it just the two of you?" he asked bluntly.

Carmen had to make a snap decision. *Lie and risk upsetting them,* she told herself. *Tell the truth and risk getting robbed, or worse…* She grew up in a rough neighborhood, and she wasn't picking up the normal predatorial vibes. "Yes."

The man looked around his entire perimeter once more. The he addressed the other one. "Looks clear. I think they're alone."

The first guy turned a plus-shaped key and pulled it out of the wall, stuffing it into his coat pocket. He turned and faced Carmen and Schwartz. Carmen didn't realize how big he was while he was hunched over getting water. When he turned to face her, he grew to a powerful looking 6' 2". He was wearing a tan ballcap with an arched banner that said "Ranger." On the ends of the tabbed banner were "2d" and "Bn" symbols. They stood for "Second Battalion." His crow's feet, hair length, and salt-n-pepper-beard told Carmen he was probably a veteran not active-duty. She felt herself relax a bit.

He looked her and Schwartz over for a good ten seconds before saying anything. "Alright. Get your bottles out." He pulled the sill-cock-key back out of his pocket and inserted it back onto the recessed valve stem in the wall fitting. When Carmen had placed her bottle under the spigot he snorted and asked, "That's it?"

She was taken aback. *Is he upset? Why would he be upset?* She looked at Schwartz, speechless.

Schwartz chimed in, trying to sound pacifying. "Look, sir, we don't want any trouble, we're just thirsty. We don't have much to offer…"

"First off," the big one responded, "I was an NCO. Don't ever call me sir again. Secondly, I wasn't scoffing at you. Sorry if that's how it sounded. That's just not a lot of container." He paused for a second, looking back and forth at the odd couple. "Where are you two headed?"

Carmen took over the conversation, "Olympia." *Don't give away the truth,* which was a message she hoped Schwartz was receiving telepathically.

"Olympia," the big one repeated, looking at his friend. "Yeah. Okay. Olympia." He paused for a second. "Good luck," he said, as he turned around to fill his own jug again.

"Wait." *Dang it!* "Okay, look, we just don't know you guys. Alright?"

"Lady, if we wanted anything you had it would already be ours," the shorter one said. "But we get it. You can't be too careful. Go wait by the corner while we talk."

Carmen and Schwartz moved twenty feet down the sidewalk and heard a few low murmurs as the two consulted each other for half a minute. Soon the shorter one waved them back over.

"Tell you what," he said. "We know you two aren't your average scum-bags. We're willing to sell you a water filtering straw and four one-liter sports bottles, filled, for a fair price. Say... sixty bucks?"

"Sixty bucks!" Schwartz started.

"Deal. Pay him," Carmen ordered, cutting the doctor off before he could say anything stupid. *Chump change to your plastic surgeon butt.* "But..." she went on, "I want our little bottles filled, too."

"Agreed," said the shorter one.

"May I ask why," Schwartz started in as he pulled three twenties from his left pocket, "you're being so generous?" The tone was received.

"Mister," the big one said, "you may not realize this yet." There was a pause while the man looked Schwartz up and down. "But everything is a resource. Water bottles. This little tool. Your shoes." He pointed down at Schwartz's filthy expensive loafers. "If it has value, you can't expect it for free. Not anymore. Not in this world." The man topped off their bottles while the other guy pulled their newly-purchased sports bottles from the pull-cart.

Schwartz wisely kept his trap shut. Carmen took the bottles and precious water-filter. They started to leave, continuing their journey south.

"Listen," the big one said before they'd rounded the corner. "I don't know where you're headed. But you're going to want to upgrade your clothing. And find yourself some leaf-bags. You can turn them into a poncho or collect some rain to drink."

Sixty-dollar water bottles, an invaluable filter, and good advice, Carmen thought. *Sadly, I think that these guys are the only ones I've met so far who have a real clue about what's happening.*

15

"A wise man adapts himself to circumstances,
as water shapes itself to the vessel that contains it." – Chinese
Proverb

Tahoma's Hammer + 2 Days.

"Girls!" Tony called out to his daughters. They looked up from their place on the tarp their entire class was sitting on. They could hardly believe their eyes.

"Dad? Dad!" Talia yelled.

Tasha was the quieter one, but she beat her sister off the ground and into a full sprint. The almost thirteen-year-olds had been going stir crazy. The FEMA people were trying their level best given the circumstances. Groups of children that had come in together, mostly field trip classes like the girls and their classmates—were kept together. Larger groups like theirs had been given tarps on the grass to lay on, along with enough cots for half of the group's number. The famous retractable roof of T-Mobile Park had been closed for post season painting and maintenance when the disaster struck. The bleachers were filled with people, but children and the elderly were given priority over use of the field so they could lay down.

Despite a small level of organization on the part of the emergency planners, it had still taken Tony almost two hours to track down his girls. The concession stands were converted to soup kitchens where meals were handed out. Everyone had an RFID chip inside their wristband, which entitled them to three meals per day. Several rows of portable johns were set up east of the field under where the roof sat when it was open. Fencing had been set up around that area, from the field to the train tracks. Tony wondered how long the authorities could provide services before the generators were out of fuel.

"Dad, are we going home now?" Tasha asked, hopefulness in her voice.

"No, baby-girl, I'm afraid not. Pops is tired and hungry. After I've had a chance to rest, I'll start workin' on the plan for that."

Both girls grunted dejectedly. One of the parent chaperones that had been on the field trip came over at that moment.

"Girls, you okay?" she asked.

"Yes, Mrs. Reynolds!" Talia said excitedly. "This is our dad! He came here to find us!"

Mrs. Reynolds was impressed and secretly disappointed. Mr. Reynolds had apparently not made the same effort. "Wowww… really? That must have…how'd you get here so quickly?" The confusion was strong with this one.

"Private boat. And, no—he isn't waiting for me." Tony could sense where the question may have led. "That was…thirty-ish hours ago?" he said, not really sure anymore.

"Oh," she said. "Well, we can always use another parent. Say… um, how is it out there?"

"Not bad," Tony lied. He wasn't about to tell her the truth in front of his girls. Not until he found a way to let them know in his own way first. He shot the chatty parent a look. *I'll talk to you later...* She picked up what he was putting down—*quit asking in front of the kids.*

Mrs. Reynolds excused herself. Tony walked out to the restroom area with twins in tow. He wasn't very happy when he got out there. There was trash strewn everywhere, and some people looked like they were passed out, many leaning against the wall of the stadium under makeshift tents made of tarps and sheets of plastic. The entire area reeked of human waste. *How are they emptying these things?* Tony wondered.

He got his girls' attention. "From this moment on, neither of you come out here without me."

Talia started to protest, "But, Dad—"

"Talia. No. I know you're big girls. You're just gonna have to trust Pops on this one."

"Alright, Dad." It wasn't like Talia to stop arguing so quickly. She knew the look on his face was a serious one, and she decided to let it go.

When they had concluded business and gone to their right field tarp Tony took stock of his backpack. He was glad he had brought toilet paper and had the foresight to put it in a freezer bag. Now he was worried he hadn't brought enough of it. He pulled out his hand sanitizer, and everyone tended to their hands. He then pulled out a couple of bags of Doritos for his girls, which they devoured. It might have been his imagination, but he felt a slightly jealous vibe being put out by other people, both inside and outside of the girls' group. *We'd better keep an eye on this pack.*

"Girls, I haven't slept much in the last two nights. I'm gonna catch a little nap. When you think it's been two hours wake me up." Using his pack as a pillow, Tony lay back on the ground next to one of the cots and for the umpteenth time wished he'd brought a hat.

· · ·

Tahoma's Hammer + 3 Days.

When Schwartz and Carmen had made it down the Pacific Coast Highway to about 288th Street, they had to veer west into a neighborhood. A diesel fuel supplier there had caught fire, and the underground tanks were belching fire and a four-hundred-foot-high column of black sooty smoke. The roads there were a series of winding loops through the neighborhood, making it difficult to keep a sense of direction after a while. The grayness of the day made it seem as if the sun were everywhere—and nowhere. Shadows didn't exist due to the overcast. They finally meandered out onto Redondo Way, which went south and brought them to within a stone's throw of the PCH again. There, they noticed that a swap-meet of sorts had formed in Sacajawea Park near a middle school of the same name.

"We should go there and see what we can find," Schwartz suggested. "I'm famished." *And I need to find some better clothes.*

"Me, too." Carmen was hesitant but agreed to back up her partner. "I'm not a fan of crowds. But…" She finally gave in. "Let's stick together. We need to watch out for each other."

"I agree." *Seriously. I need you more than you know. And it doesn't hurt you that I have the money, does it?* "Let's go."

They wandered into the makeshift farmer's and flea market without knowing exactly what to expect. Down through the tables, tarps, and canopies they went, looking at mostly junk. People were trying to sell lamps, blenders—even video game consoles. Everybody had "Food Wanted" signs out, but nobody was selling any. A small percentage of tables had usable items such as blankets, tools, or clothing. Some people were selling their camping supplies. This caught Schwartz's eye. He speed-walked for one of those spots, passing several less-practical tables in the process.

"Got any ponchos or raincoats?" he immediately asked. He

didn't care about the dirty look he was getting from the two men already there. *I'm too wet to be civil,* he thought.

"No," replied the lady. Her male partner was handling the other customers. "But I do have an umbrella."

"Can I see it?" Schwartz asked. Carmen was looking on from a few feet behind him.

The lady caught Carmen staring and became slightly guarded. "No. But I'll open it and let you look." She popped it open. Other than one dead rib the fabric seemed to be doing its job.

"How much?" Schwartz asked.

"Twenty."

Twenty? "Forget it." Schwartz started to walk off.

"Wait!" the lady said. "Fifteen?"

"Ten. And I want three of those big trash bags I see in the back of your van there," he said pointing.

"Fifteen, and two bags," she countered.

"Deal. Now, do you have any lighters or camp stoves?"

"Lighter, yes—stove, no."

"Show me the lighter works." *I'm getting the hang of this haggling thing.*

"Ten," she said.

"Five. That makes it twenty for the lot."

"Deal," she concluded.

Schwartz pulled a lone twenty out. They traded the stuff for the cash at the exact same moment, never losing eye contact with each other. Carmen's eyebrows were raised, impressed. "I didn't know you had it in you, Doc," she said after they'd walked away.

"There's a lot about me you don't know." *Once again this little girl thinks I'm an idiot.*

"Whatever." Her eyes rolled. "Let's see if we can get you some better clothes and shoes."

They wandered into the parking lot closer to the school. There was a guy sitting in a lawn chair behind a box truck that was closed. "Whatcha lookin' for?" he asked.

"Whatcha got?" Schwartz countered.

The man sized up Schwartz. "For you? Prob'ly nothin'." That made Carmen chuckle.

Schwartz was not entertained. "Work pants. Wool socks. Work boots. Gloves. Rain coats. Food. Camp stoves. Those are the kind of things we're interested in finding."

"Well then, step right up, brotha! You come to the right truck!" The man got out of his chair, looking around like people who live in a world of distrust are prone to do. Satisfied he wasn't being ambushed, he unlocked the roll-up door and threw it upwards.

He scanned Schwartz's feet. "Size ten and a half?"

"Eight," Schwartz replied, still not amused with the man. Carmen was digging it.

Without missing a beat, "Yeah, well today you're a ten and a half." The man threw a pair of worn out Danner work boots at the doctor's feet. Schwartz was pretty sure they would leak water, but at least he'd finally have some traction and a little lift in the puddles.

"What about the other stuff?" He looked at his partner. "And for her... Do you have any kind of waterproof coat for either of us?"

"Depends," the dealer said, in his most serious tone yet. "Depends on what you might have that I want..." He left it hanging there for their imaginations as he smirked at Carmen. Her stomach did a flip-flop.

"Easy," the short doctor warned. "That's my daughter you're talking about." Carmen played along, not wanting her face to give anything away.

The man held his look for another two seconds then broke out into smile. "Easy, brotha! We' all just folk here, tryin' to do bizness!"

Schwartz reached into his right pocket, which caught the man's eyes. He shifted his weight, not knowing what to expect. Schwartz slowly and carefully pulled out his gold-plated, diamond-encrusted, money clip—empty of cash. "We're out of cash," he lied, "but you can be sure that the diamonds are real."

The junk-merchant's eyes lit up. He knew that in less than an hour this money clip would be buying him several days' worth of drugs.

"Welcome to my store, brotha! I'm sure we can hook you up!"

THE SLAUGHTER COUNTY SHERIFF'S DEPARTMENT, like many policing agencies across the state, had upgraded all deputies to mandatory twelve-hour shifts. Sergeant Charlie Reeves was working a midnight to noon rotation. In normal times things would wind down before dawn. But on the third day after the event, Charlie noticed a shift in paradigm that coincided with Maslow's famous Hierarchy of Needs. *Everyone is down in the bottom tiers.* He couldn't remember the names of the needs, but he knew things like food, water, shelter, and safety more or less covered the bottom of the triangle. *Except for the heroin and meth addicts—they seem the same.* Charlie was no fool, though. He knew they would eventually run out of drugs and become the biggest threats.

Theft reports were lower than normal, a fact he attributed to the piss poor communications. He knew the addicts were stealing anything they could get their hands on. He figured the "honest" were starting to steal, too, once they realized the grocery stores weren't reopening. What most stores were doing, however, was hiring armed security. They were trading small amounts of goods to have a handful of people visible at all hours. *I can see it already,* Charlie thought. *There will eventually be a mass run on these stores as people get thirsty and hungry. Someone will eventually get shot. A lot of someones,* he corrected himself. His and other departments weren't even going to investigate small scale thefts anymore. They just didn't have the people, time, or gas.

Each morning the makeshift shelter at the mall parking lot had grown about twice the size as the morning before. He'd heard it was the same throughout the county. Some people were finding other places to crash at night, but before dusk he witnessed a migration.

They're getting hungry…and impatient. He knew these morning feedings were only going to grow, both in size and intensity. *I wonder when FEMA will push us to start shepherding folks to their "cattle-pen" in Bartlett?*

One of Charlie's patrol deputies had radioed for some back up at the mall. A small fight had broken out in the north parking lot. Charlie had just pulled in from the north end of Sylvan Way, forced to take a longer route due to a large sinkhole due east of the mall property. He had been up in the Hilltop neighborhood to the north-east, so it took him about four minutes to show up. He knew from chatter that another deputy was about two minutes further out.

"Up yours, pig!" he heard as soon as he stepped out of his rig. His deputy, a fellow grave-yarder named Jesus "Zeus" Ocampo, was trying to keep two pairs of people from getting at each other. The small melee was surrounded by about three hundred people waiting for a Red Cross food line to open. He ran over and pushed his way into the middle.

"Stop!" he commanded, pushing his big frame into the foray to join Zeus. His deputy was bleeding from his forearm and had his taser drawn. Charlie wanted to try to de-escalate if he could.

"Everybody! Calm down!" One person from the closer pair tried to lunge past him. She had fire in her eyes. Charlie stuck his big arm out, and she tried to duck. He reached down across her abdomen and pushed her back to where she came from. "I said stop!" That got her to look him in the eyes.

"These jack-wads cut!" Her face was flush with anger. "We are sick and tired of being walked over by everyone! We didn't eat last night because of jerkwads like this!"

Charlie could hear the retorts coming from the pair on the other side of Zeus as well as the woman's male partner. Charlie stepped into the space that would allow him to get a hand on the chest of each of his parties. Woman or not, he needed physical control. Charlie started pushing, using the onlookers as a human funnel. The former linebacker had no problem getting about twenty feet between the two pairs.

About then day shift deputy Lisa Hornet joined the cause. "Lisa! Control her!" he barked. Lisa grabbed the woman's arm and used a technique to twist her arm behind her back, enacting what they jokingly called "painful compliance." It worked, and she pulled the screaming woman an additional ten feet back.

"What's going on here, Hoss?" Charlie asked the man. Giving people a friendly respectful nickname was sometimes a good way to get them to calm down.

"Those jerks cut! Just like my girlfriend said. So, we called 'em out on it. Ask anyone! It was them!" the man yelled over Charlie, stabbing his finger towards the other pair of men. The crowd wasn't helping any. He could hear jeers and cheers no matter who was yelling.

"How'd my deputy get cut?" Charlie said in a calm but demanding tone. He glanced back to make sure Zeus was still okay. That pair of men seemed a bit calmer. *I'll never know the truth, here, but those who lose control of their temper first lose the argument.*

"Uhh," the man started looking around him. *He's searching for the lie in his head.* Most cops were good lie detectors. "I guess one of them pulled a knife. I don't know!"

Charlie noticed Lisa had already taken the woman over to her patrol rig and started searching her. The woman had her hands on the fender of the car and was being patted down. He took the man over to his own rig and performed the same procedure. His findings were relatively normal—wallet, keys, small folding knife, dead cell phone. He opened the knife—it looked dry. *Why are people still carrying dead cell phones?*

"Stay," he ordered after cuffing the man. He walked over to Lisa's rig, keeping a close eye on his perp. He saw a boxcutter, empty cigarette pack, and lighter lying on the hood.

The county was still locking up people when there was evidence of assault. He checked with Zeus, who said he was pretty sure it was the woman who'd cut him. Zeus' suspects were somewhat calmer and more cooperative than his and Lisa's pair.

By that time the day shift sergeant had shown up. They consulted and agreed on the plan of action—record everyone's data, photograph them, book the woman, and give her and her boyfriend a ninety-day trespass from the property. *They can fight that in court if they want,* Charlie thought. *If we actually have court anymore…*

CAPTAIN MARIE DARNELL was watching the cranes work at Dry-dock A. One was still hooked up to the last section of wooden wall to be installed. It was just starting to make the switch from the tracks that run the length of Monsoor Avenue to the set that travels down the east side of the dry-dock. *The timber-design "cofferdam" is actually pretty stout,* she thought. The shipwrights had basically built a wall out of 120 forty-foot long timbers, which would stand upright. They were fortunate to have them in stock, she'd learned. They were purchased for pre-building the setting for the next year's carrier project. *Finally—a bit of luck.*

They had pre-built the giant wall in twenty-foot wide sections, using three timbers across them horizontally to bolt them all together like an enormous piece of fence. They had created a system of notches to tie them together laterally. They also planned to install additional horizontal timbers across the intersections once the dock had been pumped out.

At each end of each section they ran a timber at a forty-five-degree angle down to the drydock floor on the submarine side of the wall. The divers guided the crane into landing concrete blocks at the base of each angled timber. The blocks were normally used as the base of the settings the ships sat on. Each supporting stack had several of the big blocks, bringing each stack's total to about 100,000 pounds. The finishing touch was several ¾" steel cables bolted into the top of the cofferdam and running south towards the two topside corners, near where the broken caisson was seated.

Several big anchor points were drilled and installed into the concrete.

The temporary wood wall was assembled about forty feet away from the damaged caisson—just south of a set of dock drains. Marie didn't need this thing to be waterproof forever—she just wanted it to keep the dock empty enough to take care of critical tasks—like welding up the hull-cut that had allowed the El Paso's engine room to flood. She understood there was probably about two more days of work before they were ready to try pumping water.

Once they weren't fighting tide anymore, she would have the floating crane and divers start chunking out the old caisson. They estimated they could have it completely removed about a week after they started. Then they would clean out the sill and install the reserve caisson. *I just need you to last a week or two,* she mentally told the wooden-wall.

The next major issue was getting the plastic containment built and installed over the reactor so they could start controlling the clean-up and decontamination processes going. Then they would be able to start lifting the cable out to ascertain the extent of the damage to the vessel and the fuel. Her gaze was stuck on the wooden wall being constructed, but her mind was on a hundred other worries.

16

Zombies.

It's only been four days, Crane thought in amazement. He had finally been given a chance to go home. Slowly shipyard workers were trickling back in to work, knowing their community was at risk. The scaffold and woodshop trades, which normally ran a strength of close to 250 people, had been operating with less than fifty for the bulk of the crisis. As of that morning twenty-three more had come back. The Shop 46 Superintendent had solicited for names of shipwrights and millwrights who would be willing to continue to stay. He expected most would want to go home, and he couldn't allow that. His plan was to have a lottery of fifteen chances to leave for one day. As it turned out, every person volunteered to continue staying. He picked fifteen and ordered them to go home.

Crane decided that rather than going to his dad's house, he needed to get to his place in town and check on his stuff. He would try to make it out there in a few days. He rented a house with three friends, one of which also worked in the shipyard. The Slaughter Peninsula had several major waterways, not just the inlet by the shipyard. Crane couldn't take the bridge he normally took to get home because it had been blocked with jersey barriers due to major structural damage. He lived about four miles north of work, but he had to detour to a different, newer bridge, which made the trip more like eight miles.

He'd heard how bad things were from his peers that had trickled back to work, but he wasn't ready for what he saw. The old hospital had partially collapsed. *Lucky the hospital moved to Sylvan this year.* He saw burned cars and condos that had slipped down hills. When he crossed the bridge, he couldn't see the inlet below, but he pulled over into a parking lot on the far side. He was curious about the rumors. Crane felt tears in his eyes when he saw broken homes washed up on the shore below. *All those people...* It was a lot for a young man who had never lived anywhere else.

He looked across the lot at the small strip mall. The stores were darkened. Nobody was there—it looked like a ghost town. Windows had been shattered on the bakery. The pub on the connecting street had sheets of plywood secured over their windows. He hopped back into his blue Subaru and got moving again.

As he made his way home, he passed a school and two churches that all had what appeared to be homeless shelters set up in their lots. They looked crowded, and a fist fight was in progress at one of them. *Where are they getting the food to feed people?* he wondered. As he passed people who were walking, he could almost feel the stares. *Everyone's on edge now.* He was beginning to realize how lucky he had it on his little cot at the base.

When he arrived at the fifty-year-old rental, he only saw one vehicle. He'd hoped to see three. He got out, pulling his backpack and worn out, green Carhart coat with him. He approached the front door as if it were any other day when his eyes caught the door being swung open.

"Crane!" yelled Maya excitedly. She was the one female out of the four roomies. She ran down the porch and threw her arms around his neck. It caught him off guard a bit, and he had to half-step back to absorb the impact.

"Hey!" *I'm glad to see you, too, but it's only been four days.* "What's up? Where's David and Joe?"

David and Maya were dating. The three of them had been friends since high school. After college, David landed a job as a pharmaceutical sales rep. He worked out of Kent, over in King County, and he spent a lot of time on the road. He had been trying to talk Maya into moving over there, but she wasn't ready to be that far from her mom. The other roommate, Joe, was a machinery mechanic at the shipyard.

Maya's eyes began to well up with tears. Crane could see it was too late. "We haven't heard from him," she uttered, the words evoking a new round of crying.

"What?" *Oh, man.* He looked down at the ground, searching for words but only finding his worn-out steel-toed boots. He looked back at Maya. When he saw the water works starting, he reached out and pulled her in for another hug. *This way I don't have to see her crying.*

"What about Joe?" he asked over her shoulder.

She leaned back out of the hug and headed for the house. "He came home on the first day and just went back to work this morning. We went to the bread line yesterday, and he bumped into some other yard-birds. They told him they heard the shipyard was hurting for people from his shop to come back in."

Bread line? Crane followed her into the house. He noticed some of the siding had popped off and the front porch had cracks in it. "That explains why I hadn't seen him. I was wondering if he'd gotten home." Crane and Joe usually carpooled. He stopped inside the door and saw Maya's tuxedo cat, Oreo, looking regal and unbothered by Crane's presence. It was a lone second of normalcy in an abnormal time. "Maya... about David. I... I don't know what to say."

"Don't say anything," she said quietly, looking out the living room window for his car once again.

She'll have to learn to stop looking, Crane realized. "Alright," he said, copying her quietness. He went to his room. It wasn't exactly inspection ready when he last saw it, but it was definitely a mess now. He reached down and lifted his dresser off the floor, kicking clothes out of the way so it would sit flat. All the drawers were still out on the floor with contents spilled. He also noticed several cracks in the dry wall.

He scanned the room, and his eyes caught his two rifle cases. They had fallen out of the closet. *That could be a problem.* He immediately worried about them growing feet the next time the house was empty.

He weighed his options. He wanted to park on base, which meant that if he followed the rules, he couldn't keep his rifles in the car. But he also didn't want to leave them in the house when he went back to work. *No time to take them to Dad's.* He dragged a stool from the linen closet and placed it under the attic access in the hall. He popped it open long enough to put his rifles in the attic. *Better than doing nothing,* he thought.

He walked back out to the living room and picked up his backpack. He reached in and pulled out two, full military-issue MRE's.

"Hungry?" he asked his roommate.

Maya's eyes brightened a bit. "I haven't had one of these since my dad gave me one when I was like twelve," she said, smiling softly.

Crane perked up a bit. "How's your mom? I'm assuming your dad is still at sea."

"My mom and I were texting on the first day. She was going to stay put and watch the horses. Dad was still out on patrol. You know submariners—never say when they're coming home."

That's true, Crane thought. He'd never known of a sub-sailor to talk about ship's movement dates, especially the ones stationed in Slaughter County. *Especially that boat.* Maya's dad was a Master-Chief on a special submarine that went on extra-special missions.

Crane reminded her how to work the water activated heater for her meal. "Speaking of water, how are we set here?"

"Running low," she said matter-of-factly. "Neither Joe or I got home until late that day. I filled all our pots with tap water, but it was just a trickle. We have a couple of cases of bottled that we've been living on." She paused and looked directly at Crane. "Do you think they'll have the water back on soon?"

Crane choked a bit on a bite he'd just taken. After clearing his throat and taking a pull off his plastic water bottle he said, "Uhh—no, obviously not." He looked at her to see if she was joking. She wasn't. *Sometimes it isn't so obvious, obviously.* "Oh, uh, sorry. No. I think it could be a while. You'd probably better start thinking about what you're going to do."

"Wait for David, obviously!" she said, pissed and throwing Crane's word back at him.

Ouch. I deserved that. "Look, Maya—I'm sorry. I didn't mean it that way. We've known each other our whole lives. You know I'm not like that. But it is bad out there. I mean—*bad.* You and Joe had to stand in a bread line yesterday. A bread line! An entire end of Russell Island slid into the Sound! We've been dealing with some serious issues at work. The shipyard commanding officer told us that Pierce County was more or less destroyed..." He decided he'd better stop.

They both sat in silence, slowly eating "Menu 22—Asian Beef Strips."

After a fifteen-minute silence Crane stood up. "I'm going back tomorrow. I'm dead tired, so I'm hittin' the sack. Wake me if you need anything." He paused and turned as he was exiting the living room. "It's not going to be safe here much longer. You *need* to go home. Better yet—go to the range. Leave a note. David will know that's where you went." The tired, young government worker went and crashed onto his bed, not moving the pile of laundry in the way.

IT WAS ABOUT NOON, Phil knew. He'd forgotten to shake his "automatic" self-winding watch when he didn't wear it the day before. Now it was dead until he could find a clock to set it to. The day was back to the normal overcast—less rain and a lighter gray. There wasn't enough of a shadow for decent time estimation, but he knew roughly when sunrise was. *Close enough*, he figured. He knew there was a battery-operated clock buried somewhere in one of his conex boxes. He just hadn't made time to find it. His mind was still distracted by the bad news from the evening before.

The day before, he and Craig found that Hope had perished sometime since the catastrophes began. She was lying on the kitchen floor with a pot of water spilled next to her. He didn't see anything that indicated crime. He figured it was probably just her age and the shock of the events. They took the time to bury her in the backyard. Phil was worried about the state of her affairs, particularly valuables and firearms. He made a decision to take as much of it as he could with him that day. They recorded what they took and stored all of it in one of the conex boxes. When they'd gotten back to the range, he had Jerry pass the information about her passing to DEM.

Phil had spent the last hour going around and gathering everyone at the range for a meeting. They were up to forty-five people at the evening count the night before. He knew he had to get some control over things. Fred and Don had been fully briefed already. They were posted as guards at the front gate. There was a fairly reliable stream of vehicle and foot traffic coming up the Canal Vista Highway. It wasn't a solid stream, but the gaps between groups rarely exceeded a few minutes. Phil theorized that more people were converting to walking as they ran out of gas.

Everyone had gathered under the rifle line, sitting where they could. Phil had brought chairs down from the classroom. *This could go on a while.*

"Hi everyone. Thanks for bearing with me. We have a lot to discuss. If you have questions, hold them if you can. I want to keep the conversation on track if possible. We have too much to talk about to get distracted by war stories and rabbit holes. For starters, who knows what a watch bill is?"

Several hands went up, mostly from the veterans.

"It's basically a schedule. We need to start posting guards in key locations, and if we have the manpower, a roving team or two." Hands already started going up. "Folks, let me get through the spiel first, and most of your questions will get answered."

Dr. Stuart Schwartz's feet were raw. He couldn't decide which was worse—being wet constantly or the rubbing from the boots that were too big. *When this is over, I will never go outside again,* he promised himself. He had open sores on the back of his heels—sores that hurt with every step. *Definitely a four,* he thought. His pain level was slowly creeping upwards.

He and Carmen had backtracked to the northwest, having heard that the elementary school in that direction had a camp set up. When they got there, they realized they'd been misinformed. There were people camping there, but it was camp-at-your-own-risk, to say the least. *Like something out of Mad Max,* Schwartz thought when he saw the collection of tarps and tents streaming off the playground equipment. Campfires had been built in several spots.

They were both wearing trash bag ponchos, which helped repel rainwater much better than Schwartz would have guessed. *Back in L.A., I have a perfectly good, $700 overcoat sitting in my closet.* When the school hadn't turned out the way they thought it would, they decided to meander back out towards the Pacific Coast Highway.

They'd gotten turned around, and it took several minutes to figure that out. As evening arrived, they ultimately had to set up a hasty shelter in the several-acre greenbelt near a sewage treatment station. The homeless people that lived there year-round scowled at them. *That's far enough,* but nobody chased them off.

Carmen had suggested they make do on the rest of the junk food they had for the evening and figure out how to use their new penny-can stove in the morning. While they had been at the swap-meet, they were able to barter her iPhone for a small camp stove made out of a couple of soda cans. It operated on rubbing alcohol and put out small blue flames through a bunch of holes. As part of the deal they got a small, tin windscreen that could act as a pot holder, a sixteen-ounce jug of alcohol that was maybe a third full, and a cheap metal bowl that was probably from an old camping set. They had bartered for six boxes of Hamburger Helper with a different vendor in the parking lot. It had cost Schwartz $180. *One-hundred and eighty bucks for a week's worth of food,* he worried. *We're going to starve.* It had started to dawn on him that the cash was becoming less valuable with each passing day.

The next morning, they had used a precious amount of fuel to boil a precious amount of water. Schwartz figured they had started with five or six ounces of fuel and might get two more good boils out of what was left over. His face showed his concern.

"We're screwed, aren't we, Doc?" Carmen asked. She was looking at him through tired, teary eyes.

He looked up through the purple bags that enveloped his own eyes. "Yep." They were huddled under a shredded, fading blue tarp that leaked badly, something a homeless person had discarded. *Ya' think? We're living under a rag that the homeless don't want anymore.*

Carmen started to let the tears roll, but she was trying her level best to not sob. She didn't want to seem weak, especially this close to a homeless encampment.

Schwartz wasn't naturally affectionate. He supposed he should put his arm around her or something, but he didn't want her to get the wrong impression. He tried a different approach. "Call me Stu."

"W-what?" Genuine surprise.

"Call… me… Stu." He repeated slowly, trying to smile. "I think we're past formal titles by now. Don't you?" Another friendly smirk. Carmen smirked back. It had worked. *Can't have you breaking down on me,* he thought.

"Okay… Stu…" She smiled a little more. "Are you accidentally warming up to me?"

"Listen closely because it's a moment of weakness," he explained. "I need you. There—I said it. Happy? I may be a man of great pride, but I need my business partner to hold it together. If eating a little crow is what it takes…So be it."

She nodded. He couldn't tell if she appreciated the honesty, but he felt just a bit better for saying it. "I'd like you to stay here with our stuff. I'm going to go into that camp and see if any of those people will help us. Hopefully they're already used to being off their meds." *Or their other medications…*

"FOLKS, the performance by the feds has been less than stellar. We need to start talking about alternatives." Sandy McCallister was using her best Southern California old-lady charm to downplay her growing concern. She was well into a two-hour status meeting with the Slaughter County Unified Command, comprised of several high-level leaders. All the fire and police departments were represented, as well as the National Guard, public works, various mayors, county commissioners, and two mid-level officers representing the navy's two bases. "FEMA Region X says that the delays are a combination of facility damage on our end and unanticipated need everywhere else. Apparently, the air conditioning isn't working in A… Oh, the horror." Her feigned mock shock drew a few chuckles. *I know what I'll do… I just need ya'll to get there on your own.* "Thoughts?"

"Look," said Sylvan's Fire Chief, Don Dale. "Knowing we're all at various levels of supplies and staffing that aren't going to hold up, just cut to the chase, Director. What are you thinking?"

"I'm thinking about our people needing rest, Chief." He nodded. Most of them did. "I'm thinking about what we can do to get the community to feel safe. Secure."

"How about a voluntary curfew?" asked Brandi Farrly, the Bartlett Police Chief. This brought about a course of murmurs.

Sandy was observing facial expressions. She knew this was a mixed bag of nuts. People were always so concerned with liberty. Some of them were trying to hide their disgust while others were nodding in agreement.

"I'm not sure that would work," Sandy said, still playing both sides. "I mean—we're a veteran-heavy community. We love rights and small government... Right?" Everyone in here collected a tax-based paycheck. It was a catch-22, and she knew it.

"Of course," said the Police Chief. "We're not talking about violating rights. We're talking about protecting lives. Keeping the community safe. These people can't even walk down the street without keeping their phones in their faces." Another round of small talk. The Chief concluded, "Besides, it'd be voluntary."

"True," Sandy agreed. "But how effective would *that* be, really?" she countered. "I mean, if we're going to have a lockdown that pretty much tells the community 'You can't move around from this time to that time,' how effective would it be if it were voluntary?" More looks and nods.

"Are you proposing a mandatory curfew?" Fire Chief Dale said, tired of playing "20 Questions."

"I'm merely offering food for thought," Sandy said. "Perhaps a trial. Mayors? Maybe within city limits? What say you? Feel like letting your hard working first responders have a lil' break?"

It only took another five minutes after that pitch. Though not everyone was convinced the vote passed, and the 10:00 PM to 6:00 AM curfew was implemented the next night.

"ONE MORE TIME, Jerry. How does this work?" Phil asked. Jerry Horst was actually pretty good at explaining the HAM radio stuff. Phil just wanted to make sure he understood.

"Okay," Jerry said, starting at the top. "These are called GoTennas. That's a brand name." Jerry was holding up a small black pod with a bright orange handle. It was an inch wide, an inch deep, and about six inches long. "They operate in the 900 mega-hertz range, maybe a watt or two in power. If you've linked your phone to them and you have the app installed, you can use them as a local network, basically. They call it a 'mesh' network."

"Alright. I'm following," Phil said. "Keep going."

Jerry continued. "These have been around for several years, but they just started to catch on in the last few. They're not cheap, and people who aren't into radio or tech generally haven't seen the value of them. Except for hikers," Jerry remembered. "They've been using them for a while."

"So how many of these are out there?" Phil inquired.

"Well… last time I looked at the map on the app we had a few dozen people around this part of the county that had registered them. Some people will plant them up in a tree for better height. Those are called 'fixed', versus mobile."

"So, these last a long time?"

"Ahh, no. They last most of a day if you're lucky. But they are really low draw, amps speaking, so you can keep them operating for extended periods with a small solar panel," Jerry explained. "And they recharge pretty quickly."

"But if we don't have the app on our phone…" Phil tried to catch Jerry, who smiled and held up a thumb drive, baiting him into asking. "Okay, I'll bite. You're saying you could hook us up?"

"That's what I'm saying. All we need to do is be willing to run a generator. Get everyone's smart phones. I'll charge them and install the app with my laptop. Pretty soon, we'll be able to text across the range. Probably farther. You know—as long as we have fuel to keep batteries charged," Jerry concluded.

For this force multiplier, I will go siphon the fuel if I have to. "So, what took you so long to show me this, bud?" Phil could see this capability being able to give them an advantage in a tactical situation.

"I've been a little busy, Phil. So have you. I've been setting up the radios and antennas, setting up my solar system, and running the AmRRON net, too."

"Sorry," Phil apologized. "I didn't mean to imply anything. This is just going to really help us out, that's all. So, how is the net going anyway? Have you been getting much from the 'Channel-3' thing?"

"Some. If I had started the net years ago and promoted it better, I think there'd be more activity. I'm down to running the net every six hours. I get the same four or five HAMs checking in who are usually getting the same twenty-something Channel-3 check ins."

Jerry was referring to the AmRRON and Channel-3 Project, which was a network started several years earlier, originally in Idaho. HAM operators would run a radio-net on a pre-determined frequency and schedule, similar to the way that the bigger HAM clubs and ARES organizations. There were a few key differences between the two, though.

The biggest was in melding non-HAM radios into the mix. Jerry would direct the listening HAM operators to run a short sub-net on Channel-3 of the "un-licensed" bands, such as CB radio. Other bands included "FRS" and "MURS." They were the names of frequency bands that people could use low-power radios to operate on. This allowed people who weren't licensed HAMs to participate in the flow of information.

Jerry used the body's venous system as an example when teaching people. If the ARES groups were the arteries and other HAMs were the veins, then Channel-3 participants were the capillaries. This was how blood—in this case, information—got down into the smallest nooks and crannies—through the capillaries.

"What about the emergency management folks? Have they been cooperative?" Phil asked.

"For the most part. The repeaters are all down, so everything has to be done in simplex." Phil had just wandered into the other key difference between his net and the big nets. "Line-of-sight," he explained. "The AmRRON local net focuses on line-of-sight transmissions since that's more realistic for disaster scenarios. The big clubs practice that part of the time, but they're highly reliant on repeaters."

He continued, "Everybody's talking antenna to antenna, now, which means height and power are our friends. Ironically, now that I've set up here in the office, I'm thinking about moving everything up to the field. We have more elevation up there, and I have a lot of choices in which trees to string both vertical and horizontal antennas from. I could set up the HF rig there, which will allow us to communicate with other parts of the country. All I'd need is you to move one of the big canopies up there."

"Jerry, whatever you need, I'll support. Look, I need to go check on the observation posts. I'll get Fred moving a tent up there when I see him."

Phil left the office and found Dakota chasing a squirrel. They started making their way to the range's other little used driveway on the northwest corner of the property. He wanted to make sure his vision was understood.

At the meeting earlier, Phil had laid out a grand plan. For security, they would establish a vehicle trap on the primary driveway, using sandbags from the pistol line. Off to the side they would dig in a fighting position and line the top with sandbags. The tarped-over control point would be for anyone watching the main gate. Starting with the farthest four corners of the property they would build fighting positions—AKA foxholes—in the woods, camouflaged as much as possible.

Phil wanted to man these five points around the clock with two people at each location. That took ten people at a minimum. Many of the people were somewhat elderly and probably not capable of performing basic infantry duty. Phil announced they would start with the three positions along the highway and staff the back corners once they had adequate numbers of people. He planned on running everyone through some tactical training in a few days to remind them of the differences between real world shooting and sport shooting.

The classroom trailer had a kitchen on one end, so it would become the chow hall. He was worried about varmints and rodents, so he asked people in tents to do their cooking up there. He was still mulling over the plan for those who had brought only a few days' worth of food with them.

His office was on the far end of that trailer. He considered using that as a lockable pantry for food that people were willing to donate to the whole group. He asked for everyone's thought on food conservation. Some people were for the idea of pooling their meals together while others were not. Phil said he would discuss it further with the board members and range officers.

Phil announced he wanted to cap the broken septic system. It was too close to the highway and perimeter. While the canopies and slit trenches in Bay 9 were a temporary fix, he decided a more permanent fix would be to install a rotational barrel system in Bay 7. That bay was fully enclosed to allow for shooting in almost every direction. They would move the back-hoe in there to bury about forty barrels. The range had countless blue-poly barrels for using as barriers during shooting competitions. Most of them already had holes in them, too, which would aid in the leeching and composting processes. They would piece together two mobile shacks—one for each sex. As barrels filled with waste, they would move the shacks systematically. The barrels could then have sawdust and ash from the volcano added. Phil asked for anyone who had an idea about getting some lime to speak to him after the meeting.

Fuel was a big concern. He wanted everyone who was willing to risk it to venture back to their homes and siphon as much gas and diesel as they could. He knew some people had brought some already, and he made sure everyone knew that that they would track what people were donating. He also reminded them that their home heating oil could double as diesel for the tractor and some generators. Some of the more "prepper-minded" had brought small, mobile solar panels and battery-converter systems, like those made by Goal Zero. Phil reminded everyone that gear and supplies—like those back up power sources—were the property of the owners, not the range. He wanted to quash the communal thought that every piece of gear was everyone's property.

He directed that the enclosed room at the far end of the rifle line would become a small infirmary. With a little work, it could house medical equipment and two or three bunks. They would use plastic sheeting and tarps to block off the two rifle benches in that area, creating a rain and wind-resistant triage area.

He wanted to move his winter starts to their new makeshift greenhouse and encouraged others to do the same. If someone chose to plant their seeds and starts at the big field, it would become communal. If they planted it outside their tents and trailers, it was theirs. He also wanted to turn one of the action bays into a chicken coop and enclosed run. Again, he was willing to share and asked that others do the same if they brought chickens, goats, or rabbits.

He announced that they would vacate one of the conex-boxes of the targets and range supplies to turn it into a classroom for the kids. He asked for any coloring books, toys, textbooks, and like items that people could donate to be taken there. If they were ever attacked it would be an ideal spot in the middle of the property to guard the children.

He had concluded the meeting with a prayer. Phil wasn't a particularly religious man, but the shooting incident a few years earlier had made him quit avoiding the topic of what he truly believed. He had spent those years reading the Bible and praying once again. He wasn't there to force everyone to worship the way he did—atheist, Jews, Muslims, Buddhists—all would be welcomed.

But the large majority of the membership were Christians, and they wouldn't hide that fact in the name of *political correctness*. "Political Correctness died last Tuesday," he told the group.

Upon arriving at the northwest fighting position under construction, Phil told Payton with a wink, "I don't recall the last time I saw you doing manual labor!"

"Uggggh," was the disgruntled reply.

"But seriously, Olive. You're pregnant—go do something else. Take a break." Phil started to clamber down the hole, carbon-fiber leg first. The other member with a shovel, Buddy Chadwell, was smirking.

"Dad!" she yelled, annoyed at his presence. "I got it. I'm not due for four months." She rolled her eyes and pulled the shovel out of his reach.

Thirty going on fifteen, I see... "Alright, alright," Phil said, hands raised. "Don't say I didn't offer."

He climbed out of the hole and looked at their firing-lanes. Scanning up and down the road and through the brush at the base of the trees, he advised, "This brush here and here will need to go. Maybe this tree, too. I have an old truck canopy at home. We can place it over the hole, throw some roof tar on the seams, and cover it with brush. Then this hole might actually stay dry." He realized as he started walking away that he was really just talking to himself. *It seems like I do that a lot in the "zombie apocalypse".*

17

Waiting.

Tahoma's Hammer + 7 Days.

A LIFETIME of societal decay had taken about a week to occur. The guards that the stores had cut deals with were no match for mobs of hungry people. Grocery stores, pharmacies, and super-marts were the first to get overrun, followed by everything else. The more enterprising thieves were organizing themselves with pick-ups, quads, cargo trailers—anything to up the volume of their haul. High-dollar generators, tools, and materials were snatched from the clutches of less than enthused guards at Costcos, Lowe's, and Home Depots across all of Cascadia.

Police and National Guardsmen were starting to spend the night at fire stations just to protect their own supplies from nighttime theft raids. Gangs were starting to patrol at night, knowing full well that the cops would rather pretend nobody was violating curfew than get into a shootout when there was no back up coming. The gangs were lobbying for turf, scouting for both customers and competition. The inability of the government to enforce the curfew became more apparent with each passing night.

The elderly and sick were starting to die off. Nursing homes looked like zombie movie sets as staff quit coming to work. The mobile geriatric eventually wandered out of their facilities, and those with dementia were actually the fortunate ones. There was nothing fortunate about dying of dehydration and starvation, but at least they were living in happier times in their minds.

I DON'T KNOW if I can take this stench much longer, Carmen screamed inside her head. Fear, anxiety, and depression were becoming her biggest threats. She and Stu had planted themselves in the same small set of woods for—*What? Three days now?* Stu had come down with a case of flu and was laid up in his leaf bag, shivering. They were trying to ride it out just in case Carmen got sick, too. The weather, lack of nutrition, and overall exhaustion were taking a collective toll. Carmen wanted badly to get moving, but she didn't dare leave behind the one friend—*Friend?*—she had in the new world. *Partner. I'll settle for that word.* It'd been almost two days since the last major aftershock. The small tremblers were almost mundane at this point. Growing up in California, she knew they were still there, just smaller now.

The woods here, called Powell's by the local homeless residents, smelled like rotten eggs and bad body odor. The trees acted as the southerly wind's filter for the sewage treatment plant to the north. The heavy rain had come back. During Stu's puking and fever phase, Carmen had ventured out to find anything of value. She had removed a little cash from his suitcase, intent on buying food or upgrading their gear situation. She had tried building him a fire, but the woods were too wet, and she had no idea how to start fires.

Carmen started to realize that the safest time to go out and handle affairs was first thing at dawn. The criminals seemed to prefer to sleep then. She didn't like to be out much past mid-day. She'd told Stu that when they finally felt up to travelling again they ought to travel between midnight and late morning. Her logic was that the cover of darkness and late hours might expose them to the least number of opportunists.

During her venture out, she met an older homeless man who lived in Powell's year-round. He was probably close to seventy, she figured. A somewhat-sane and toothless black man, everyone at Powell's called him Blue Jay. She first bumped into Blue Jay at the parking lot for the church over by Sacajawea Middle School. The church members were giving away clothes and peanut butter and jelly sandwiches. She watched Blue Jay ask for and receive condiment packets—specifically ketchup, salt, and pepper. She wandered behind him near the clothing tables, finally mustering the will to ask him about it. She would later remember this as Lesson Number 1 in being homeless—ketchup soup. Blue Jay explained to her that he had survived countless days of his life on just those items. They were blended with hot water to make a basic red broth. "Look aroun' you," he'd told her in his raspy, Southern twang. "People don't see tha poten-shul o' things right in front o' 'em cuz o' their own pre-conceived notions."

She was able to find a decent enough backpack for Stu as well as some more clothes for both of them. She asked for and received the same ketchup soup supplies she'd seen Blue Jay take. She took as much as they would give.

Back in the woods later that day, Blue Jay broke through the brush and strode up to the downed log they'd been using to prop up their decayed tarp. "You two look sadder than a preacher's kid in a whor'-house," he mumbled. "Here." He threw a grocery sack down.

Stu continued to lay there suffering while Carmen picked up the bag and looked. There was a big roll of plastic. It was used and smeared with dried-paint but intact. Under that was a mylar blanket, a one-quart metal can, and a roll of toilet paper.

"Put tha TP into tha can and close it up. Next time you kin scrounge some fuel, put it in tha can, too. Al-cohol, not gas-o-line. It'll work a lot bettuh than that little stove you been usin'," he told them. "Once you got your area covered in plastic, stuff tha foil blanket an' some newspaper into your armpits, shoes, an' nether-regions. It'll keep you warm." He turned and wandered back towards the main camp.

"Thank you, Blue Jay," Carmen called out, getting only a soft grunt and a quick backwards wave as he continued the two-hundred-foot trek back through the forest. Two days had passed since then.

"I'm sorry I've held you up," Stu said apologetically.

"It's alright," Carmen said, shaking her head lightly.

"I've been thinking," Stu continued. "If Tacoma is truly unpass-able, maybe we should start going west. Find a marina and barter for a boat ride back up to Bartlett. Get you back to your base in a few days."

This got Carmen's hopes up. *Now that's what I'm talkin' about!* "You think it would be safe?"

"As opposed to what?" Stu coughed a bit as he chuckled. "Starv-ing? Dehydration? Sleeping with drug addicts? Getting murdered if we pass through the wrong neighborhood?" He paused for a minute. "I think we should at least try," he concluded.

"Okay," Carmen agreed. "Let's leave when we think it's about midnight."

"FIND the next target with your eyes then move the rifle," Phil instructed. "This will ensure your shot gets follow-through. Too many people copy what they see in movies and tv shows. You want that site-alignment back into place when you prep your trigger, but you will acquire targets faster if you lead with your eyes—especially when they're spread out like this."

He was out in Bay 11 running several groups through a condensed version of his tactical rifle classes. People normally paid two hundred dollars a day for Phil's classes, especially after he'd recovered from "the incident." He had a long list of classes he'd taken from reputable instructors nationwide as well as a decent ranking in shooting competitions several years earlier. Combined with his time spent in the USMC Security Forces, and he had a lot of experience to draw from.

Brrt... [Jerry: "Tim and Stephanie need to see you at the gate. There's someone who wants in. NE."]

This texting thing is awesome, Jerry! The "NE" was something that Phil demanded be added to the end of every text. It meant "Not Emergent." If NE was missing, the receiver was to assume he or she was needed immediately. Phil was pretty stoked about the GoTenna app as a whole. Not only could they text, but they could share mapping data with each other and do it all privately. The phone batteries also stayed charged a lot longer than the little range-radios, which meant less time running the generator. This was cutting down on radio chatter, which thrilled the tactician in Phil to no end. They still had some people using the little radios, but overall there was a fuel-savings happening.

"Be up in five," he shot back to Alice, who was in the office. He walked Don through the next set of drills for the group and then made a beeline for the front gate.

"Paw-paw!" he heard from his right. Payton and Savannah were returning from Bay 10, where the group had parked the newly-built chicken run. She was followed closely by Dakota, who was on a leash while they were conducting live-fire training.

"Hey, Peaches!" Phil said, scooping up his granddaughter and continuing his march. He looked at Payton.

"Only two eggs," she said, reading his mind.

"Yeah, well… they're just adjusting to their new surroundings."
Like the rest of us.

Phil set Savannah down near the front of the rifle line where she and her mother continued towards the chow hall.

"Olive," Phil called as their distance apart grew. "Payton!" he called out, getting her attention the second time. "Come find me when you get a chance." She nodded. He reached the gate area a few seconds later. "What's up, guys?" he asked Jay and Stephanie Webster, who were currently standing watch.

"Hi, Phil," Jay started. "This is Paige. She wants to know if we'll let her and her kids come in." There was a disheveled lady with two pre-teen children standing there.

"Please! Please!" she started to plead. "We'll work, we aren't dangerous. Please!"

Phil tried to reassure her. "Whoa, whoa. Calm down. Listen— are you a range member? Can you present a current membership card?"

"No. But I *am* a successful business-woman. I've owned and operated two drive-thru latte shops. Please! We won't eat much!"

Phil had been dreading this. He and the other range officers and board members were drafting a list of skills they should consider letting in if the opportunity arose. "Espresso entrepreneur" wasn't on there. They also hadn't run the idea through the entire club yet. He'd known this scenario was coming—and it would only get worse. *We need to finish that discussion—tonight.*

"I'm sorry. We're just trying to survive ourselves. We don't have anything to give. And we can't let you in." His heart hurt, but he couldn't save everyone at the expense of those who'd earned the right to be there.

"Please!" It was turning into begging, which really bothered him.

"I'm sorry, no." He was trying to sound sincere and apologetic.

The lady and her two children started to sob. She grabbed her kids and turned. She led them back to the edge of the driveway and then turned back around. "You!" she screamed at Phil at full-volume. "Whatever happens to us—it is your fault!"

Phil stood there with a lump in his throat, speechless. He let out an audible sigh after they had walked behind the berm-sized shoulder between the highway and the range parking area. It was then that he realized that if someone came from the woods across the highway just a few yards north of there, none of the three foxholes on the west side would catch it. *We'll have to address that.*

"You should've let them in," Stephanie said coldly.

"Steph…" Tim started but his wife cut him off.

"No! I knew you would think that way, Tim. But you," she said looking at Phil. "I expected better from you. With your wife's passing…and the leg! You should have compassion. And understanding!"

She's upset and clearly needs to calm down before I try to explain myself. "We'll have another meeting tonight so we can get *all* the facts out. To everyone. Once. One discussion," Phil stated, holding up his index finger. "Excuse me. I need to go find my daughter for a moment." Phil was pissed that she'd judged him so harshly. *Better leave before I say something I regret.*

He caught Payton as she was leaving the chow hall/former classroom. She had left Savannah there to help Teresa prepare some food for the group. They were going to make a few crusted-stews in Dutch ovens over the range's big firepit that evening. "Walk with me, honey," he told his daughter.

"What's wrong, Dad?" They were slowly strolling towards the foxhole she'd helped dig a few days earlier. Phil wanted to make sure he saw the lady pass by.

"Nothing specific. I'm just trying to get a read on how you and Peaches are doing. That's all."

"Okay, I guess," she lied. He knew. "It's just…hard to believe. A week ago, my biggest issue was paying rent and dealing with the break up. Now I don't even know—" Tears came out of nowhere, interrupting her speech.

You don't know if he's alive. I know, honey. I get it. "It's okay, Olive. Let it out." She wrapped her arms around herself. Phil pulled her in to hold her. They hadn't been close in many years, so she held her wrapped arms in place, sobbing into her dad's chest.

"Everyone here knows what to do except for me," she revealed. "I'm pregnant. I don't have much food to contribute. I have no place, Dad—no purpose." She was opening up a bit about how she felt.

"You're wrong, Payton. We all have *something* to contribute. Take it from me—some people have to be on the verge of death before they figure things out." *I know what I'm talking about.*

WE NEED to get out of here! Soon, Tony told himself. It had a been a week since it all began and five days since he had arrived at the T-Mobe. It felt like a lifetime ago. Sleep came in small restless doses. *At least the kids seem to be keeping their energy and spirits up.* He didn't like feeling this way. Even when he'd been out to sea for months in the Navy there always seemed to be something fun to joke about. People bonded in the misery of deployment, but this wasn't the same. *Despair. That's what I sense. If despair has a smell,* Tony decided, *it must be un-brushed teeth, armpits, sweaty socks, and farts.*

He was standing in line once again. *I woulda never guessed that the end of the world entailed so much standing in line.* This one wasn't for food, water, or access to an overflowing plastic toilet. This line was for information—or the lack of it as it usually turned out. He was performing his daily ritual of trying to learn when there might be a ferry running to get back to Bartlett. Every day before had produced the same result— "Sorry, sir. The state hasn't given us an update." *Why should today be any different?*

"Yes?" the county DEM employee asked.

"Has there been an update on when the ferry may be running?"

The person began the diatribe in their normal fashion and then caught herself as she flipped through the clipboard to the appropriate page. "The state still hasn't—hold up." She flipped back and forth for a moment.

I'm sure she's just as tired as the rest of us, Tony thought.

"*This* is new. Not much help probably but new. It says that most of the ferry docks were badly damaged, but they may have one here in Seattle operational within one week. There is one in Bartlett as well as two ferries that are operational. One of the ferries will be serving the northern run out of Everett. They will have to off-load stranded cars first. All sailings will be passenger only for the foreseeable future. It cautions people to keep in mind that fuel and power limitations will be limiting factors."

Tony soaked it in. "So…maybe someday, and then—maybe a limited number of runs…"

"Maybe a week. It's more than you knew two minutes ago," she said smugly.

"Thanks," Tony muttered as he walked off. *A week!* The thought depressed and angered him. *It's karma. I laughed at all those whack-jobs on "Doomsday Preppers," and now I'm paying for it.* He didn't really believe that, but like most people in dire situations he was trying bargaining on for size. He went for a stroll around the main level of T-Mobile Park trying to stretch a bit. He was on a mission. He'd started noticing things, and now he was focused on learning if it was his imagination or his instincts.

He first noticed it in the soup and bread line a few days earlier. People that were eating when he and the girls left their tarp were standing in line behind him minutes later. He wrote it off as mistaken identity. But then he noticed it again. He started watching more and more people. He didn't know what the scam was, but he was sure there was one. It wasn't in his nature to care one iota about people taking advantage of the system. Then he remembered that the system had a finite amount of food, and it was keeping his babies alive. His first instinct was to grab photos, but his phone was dead. He'd never invested in one of those twenty-dollar back-up batteries that people keep in their purses and backpacks. *Now I wish I had three or four of 'em.*

Another thing he noticed was that there was never a shortage of drugged out looking people by the plastic restrooms. *Where the hell are they getting their heroin?* He was certain there was sex-trafficking happening to pay for the drugs. That was the one currency that everyone possessed and the authorities couldn't confiscate. That one bothered him—a lot. He wouldn't hesitate to beat wholesale-ass if the wrong person tried talking to his girls.

Lastly and most disturbingly was the thing he saw just earlier that morning. He was near one of the gates, and he witnessed people being denied the chance to leave. *What, are we prisoners now?* That went against his intuition. *I served this country to ensure people would never be their country's subjects again.* He could only figure that they wanted to keep people penned up to slow the tide of lawlessness that was surely coming. He finished his lap and made his way back to his girls, feeling helpless.

18

"We must accept finite disappointment but never lose infinite hope."
- Rev. Martin Luther King, Jr.

Tahoma's Hammer + 9 Days.

Payton woke up because of back pain. *Cots suck,* she thought. *I miss my bed. I miss showers. I miss a lot of things.* Savannah was still sleeping. Her dad's cot was empty. *Of course. Always has to be out and on top of stuff, doesn't he?* She pulled off the thin, warm base-layer pieces Phil had provided. He had set aside some clothing for her and Crane years ago as part of the boxes he packed out of his shop. The undergarments were stretchy enough to compensate for the girth that came with both age and pregnancy. She slid on her favorite purple leggings. *Gonna have to wash these soon,* she thought, giving them the sniff test. *Ugh. Nothing like having to pee every two hours during the apocalypse,* she mused to herself. She put on more used clothing and a camo-colored military poncho—*what on Earth is flecktarn?* she wondered, looking at the weird pattern. She opted to let Savannah sleep, wondering if she was putting too much trust in the range's perimeter and guard network. She made her way to Bay 9 to take care of morning business.

Dawn was starting to break and there was only a mist. The rain had stopped an hour earlier. *Someone's kept the burn pit going,* she noticed. It was decently sized at just under seven feet across. Pre-Hammer, its purpose had been for disposing of natural vegetation every time they had a range clean up. Now it had become a source of heat, light, warmth, and trash disposal. There were mounds of firewood up at the field, and several members had moved some down near the pit. Somebody had used scrap metal to rig up two supports and a pipe across the pit. There was a kettle and a Dutch-oven hanging on the pipe. *Maybe we can build a clothesline here, too…*

She wandered past the bay where their tent was set up and continued up the path towards the office in search of her water bottle—and coffee. Several people had set up their propane camp stoves at the kitchen. *There's always old people up by now, and that means coffee is ready.* She got a wave from her dad as she passed the office. The candle in there cast a soft glow in the gray of pre-morning. There was a lantern lighting up the kitchen end of the chow hall.

"Mornin'," she mumbled as she strode into the small space.

"Oh! Hi!" It was Donna Gladstone, wife of one of the range officers, Vic. "You snuck up on me," she said, laughing. They were spry for their age, probably mid-seventies, Payton decided.

"Sorry. Just looking for some go juice. And a bite, maybe."

"Yes. I was, too. I thought I'd left a jar of cinnamon apple slices out. I can't seem to find it, though…"

"Hmmm…" Payton said, sounding more like Phil than she realized. "Haven't seen it." She poured herself a cup of the real stuff and walked out. *I'll have instant on cup two.*

Payton sat at one of the tables in the bigger room and stared out the window at the parking lot and roof to the pistol line. She was realizing that the events that had driven her out there were not going to resolve themselves anytime soon. Normal pregnancy thoughts about reveal parties and baby showers were starting to replace themselves with real worries. She couldn't help but think about things like having enough diapers or pre-natal vitamins. She was also continuously worried about what she would do out there if the event didn't wrap itself up. *What am I doing here? Laundry? Meals? It all sounds so boring.* Lastly, she was stressed about her baby brother. She hadn't heard from him and the thought that he might be dead was too much for her to bear.

She headed across the lot to the office and found her dad inside.

"Have you noticed things disappearing?" she asked her dad.

"Um... no?" Phil said half questioningly. "Why?"

"Donna can't find something in the kitchen. And yesterday I had to find batteries for a flashlight that had them the day before."

"Great..." Phil said. "Just what we need." The look on his face told Payton he wasn't pleased to hear that. He was continuing to look over the lists of people staying at the range.

"Whatcha doing?" she asked as she sipped her coffee.

"Just thinking about the watch-bill. Trying to see if we can get the back corners manned—maybe start a twenty-four-hour command post up at Jerry's HAM shack." He eyeballed her coffee, sniffing jealously. "Whatcha up to, honey? Where's Peaches?"

"Sleeping." *Duh...*

"What? You're kidding, right?"

Oh. My. God. "Why are you starting with me so early?!" Payton exclaimed.

"Lose the attitude, kiddo," Phil responded in his best dad voice. "Pardon the pun," he said while eyeballing her mojo, "but you need to wake up and smell the coffee. Crap's gone sideways!"

"I don't see what the big deal is! Your wannabe mall-ninjas are guarding us! She's fine!" *She's my daughter, old man. You raised yours—let me raise mine!*

Phil set down his papers and stood as close to his original 5' 11" that his false leg would allow. It always seemed that those closest to people knew exactly which buttons to push.

"It is a matter of time, Payton. The rule of law is dissolving. One day soon people out there are going to decide they want what's in here. It's no more complicated than that!" There was no hiding the emotion on Phil's face when his kids pulled his strings. He wasn't as upset with her decision as he was with her know-it-all attitude. "You'd better realize that you need a plan to guard her at *every moment!*" His voice was raising as his blood pressure went up. "Lose the sarcasm. Now!"

Payton slammed her coffee mug down on the glass display case. With fiery eyes she turned and stormed out.

THE RUT. That's what Crane had started calling his life. *Get up. Eat. Bus. Work. Eat. Work some more. Bus. Eat. Sleep. Repeat.* He was starting to lose his sense of humor. Everyone was. *I don't know how these sailors can do it for months on end.* He was sitting down in his old locker room near Dry-dock F, eating a partial MRE for lunch. The sailors at the camp were issuing them to the workers whenever they headed back into the shipyard. *I wonder how long until they start cutting these in half to make them last longer.*

He had been reunited with Billy and Tracy. *Just like "The Day,"* Crane thought. Previously Billy had been working at the east end of the shipyard, monitoring the leaning Hammerhead crane with a transit. The old tower had finally given up the fight the day before, crashing to the east. It was a loud death as tons of eighty-year-old concrete and re-bar twisted and broke, releasing the green steel skeleton. The giant crane only damaged its own pier as she went, landing in the water south of the next pier over. The stout turntable had miraculously withheld the force of the impact, and now the crane's boxy engine compartment stuck out of the water, pointing up and westward almost a hundred feet in the air. The boom rested near vertically, smashed into the bottom of the inlet. The proud behemoth that had once placed barrels into battleship turrets had now finished her own history, another victim of Tahoma's Hammer.

The trio were part of a fifteen-person scaffold team assigned to that dock, trying to save both it and the aircraft carrier inside. The shipyard was operating on back-up power provided by their own power plant out on the base. The boilers ran on both natural gas and coal. *There's irony,* Crane thought. *Using coal to save nuclear ships.* Nobody was saying how much coal they had, but Crane figured it wasn't much the way they were pushing to get things done. He was pretty sure the gas lines were all broken. He also knew they were up against the invisible wall called "time."

"Dude, I can't stop shivering," Billy said.

They had come up for a meal and to dry out. The day before they and several others had built a forty-eight-foot tall scaffold tower. It was to be placed at the worst of the leaks on the west end of the Dry-dock F caisson. That morning they and the crane-riggers set the tower into place directly in the gush of seawater. The shipyard had propane-powered shower trailers which were lukewarm at best. The trio had donned coveralls after their showers. The petite Tracy was even worse off. She was short and skinny, lacking the necessary body fat to maintain any warmth. Crane felt sorry for her.

"You two should hug it out. You know—to keep warm," Crane snickered.

"Uh—ewww!" Tracy said. "You know you're older than my dad, right?" she said to Billy, ensuring there were no false impressions on his part.

Crane and Billy started laughing. It turned into one of those moments where they all started laughing hysterically, feeding off each other. *If we're not laughing we're crying, I guess.* "What's next?" Crane asked Billy.

"Well, Geoff says we need to stand by and be ready to add,

raise, or lower levels at the welder's request. Personally, I don't think this is going to work."

"Why not?" Tracy asked.

"Heat," Billy guessed. People who worked in the shipyard for entire careers started to pick up key aspects of the trades around them. "How many times have either of you gone and built a rain cover for the welders?"

They were both dumbfounded by the simplicity of the question. "Countless," Crane said. "It's Washington State, for crying out loud."

"Yeah, well, that's not just cuz they're pansies. The steel needs to be dry and hot."

"Ok, but what about underwater welding?" Tracy countered.

"Look, I'm no welder," Billy stated. "But I do believe that underwater welding uses different processes, like gas-curtains and such. I don't know…maybe I'm wrong. I just got a feeling."

Yeah, Crane thought. *And just yesterday your last feeling came true in a crash of glory.*

"MEL, YOU HAVE TO TRUST ME," Charlie pled with his wife. "You don't know how bad it's getting. I do. The stores have been robbed blind. Honest people are stealing from each other."

"What about the curfew?" his wife asked earnestly.

"We can't enforce it. There's just not enough of us anymore." What he didn't say was that they were outnumbered by the gang patrols. Charlie was pleading with his wife to move out to Phil's camp.

"But I don't know those people," she said. "The only one I've met is Phil. You don't know most of them either," she reminded him.

"I've been out there a few times since it started. Phil has set up the real deal. And since when have *you* been afraid to talk to people?"

"Shouldn't we just go to one of the FEMA centers then?"

"The FEMA—" Charlie cut himself off as his voice started to raise. "Hon, the FEMA centers are crowded. We go there almost every night to break up fights. They have food, but they're jam packed, and they don't have much in the way of security."

"I thought the National Guard was protecting them?"

"The ones that showed up are." He knew something his wife didn't. The Guard had a less than sixty percent show up rate and had been seeing a slow increase in soldiers going AWOL. They'd go out on a task and never come back. "But they're overworked. Pretty soon we'll have to start backing them up. And *we're* overworked." *Some of the deputies have quit coming in, too,* he didn't add.

They sat in their living room, quietly debating because neither wanted to upset their kids. The kids were in their rooms listening to every word, duly aware that their police officer father was scared about something.

"Give me one good reason—besides our safety—that you want me and the kids to go stay at this gun range of yours."

Charlie had been prepped and waiting for this argument, but he pretended to think for a bit. "How about my safety..."

"Huh?" Melinda wasn't expecting that.

"Hon, it is a dangerous time. We've been seeing an increase in violence like we've never seen before. Every night we get stopped by people running out of their house. They've been tied up. Beaten. Robbed." He choked up thinking about it. *Raped,* he didn't add. "People are hungry and thirsty, which makes them desperate. People who've never stolen a thing are stealing." His closing argument in this court of debate was, "I can't do my job if I'm constantly thinking bad things are happening to you and the kids."

If that doesn't get her...

After an extended silence, "Alright. What do we need to do?" the middle school teacher conceded.

"How bad is it?" Sandy McCallister asked Major Adam Matsumoto. The Port Angeles resident normally managed a Home Depot. He had done his six-year active-duty obligation after college, separating from the Army nine years earlier. He'd worked for the national retailer most of the time since, taking the manager's job in that city's branch a year earlier. The Guard had allowed him to transfer to the unit in Bartlett from his original one in King County just four months earlier. He was the Commander of Charlie Company, 3rd Battalion, 191st Infantry Regiment, 61st Brigade Combat Team, known locally as "The Huntin' Cougars." Adam was *not* personally pleased with the company's moniker, likening it to many of the women that frequented the bars in the Navy town.

"Not good, ma'am. We're running at about fifty-five percent strength." The major had been on active duty long enough to remember to only answer the question asked and nothing more.

"And what is the Guard doing to fix that, Major? May I remind you that the police are over-taxed? Some of them go home and don't come back! The charities are running out of food, and the crowd down at the sports field is starting to get vocal."

"Well, ma'am. We have the best show up record in the battalion and second best in the regiment. Honestly, there is nothing *to* do. Regarding the unrest, I thought there was a curfew…"

"Ineffective." Sandy paused. "And your muster rate just isn't satisfactory, Major," she said, not wasting any of her charm on a reserve officer.

"No, ma'am. I can't disagree."

When people use double negatives, they're hiding something, Sandy thought. "Well I'm glad for that, Major," she said sarcastically. *This goofball really doesn't like me, does he?* "Major, you're going to need to lockdown your AWOL rate. I have some friends down at Camp Crandall that can help you if you need me to call them." Camp Crandall was what they were calling the state's replacement EOC down in Vancouver. She could tell by the look of anger that he was getting the message. "Have your superiors mentioned anything about *regular* troops?"

"You mean, as in active-duty, ma'am? No. I believe posse comitatus would interfere with that. Right?" He was referring to the law that made it illegal for the American armed forces to perform civil policing.

"Until it doesn't," Sandy said. "You see—if you all and the police and everyone else quits coming to work, things are just going to get worse. Aren't they?"

"I suppose so, Director McCallister." He was ice cold.

"Enlightening. Thank you for coming over, Major." *You're excused.*

The citizen-soldier picked himself up out of the cushioned chair in front of Sandy's desk and left. She gave him a five-second head start and then followed him out into the county's EOC. "Gerry? A moment," she ordered her Number Two.

"On the way, Director."

Geraldine closed the door behind herself as she entered *The Godfather's* lair.

"Just before the Major showed up, I was on a secure call from Camp Crandall. Things aren't well."

"How so, Director?"

Sandy was blunt. "The feds. They're not coming."

"Ma'am?" Gerry choked. "What does that mean, 'not coming?' They can't just... not come."

"Well, I guess it's a 'straw and camel's back' thing. The assistant state director said that FEMA Region X told them we're on our own. Something about blackouts, hackers, riots... Every darned city west of the Mississippi is in lockdown, not just us."

"The 'trickle-down' scenario..." Geraldine reasoned.

Very good, Gerry. Do you remember what comes next? "That's right," Sandy said, smiling softly. She was pleased that her protégée was catching on.

"When are we telling the County Unified Command?" Geraldine asked.

"Have the radio room set up a video-chat for an hour from now," Sandy said. "And see if Suzanne knows where those bio-chips are."

19

Baser Instincts.

Tahoma's Hammer + 10 Days.

There were sixteen official bridges, dams, and railroad crossings between Oregon and Washington, plus one ferry service. That's where Oregon started securing their border on the eve of the tenth day. The people migrating south were starting to bring their problems to The Union State, and they had enough of those already. Chief amongst those problems was an aggressive form of flu the horde was carrying, followed closely by dehydration, hunger, and crime.

Early on after the crisis began, Oregon and Idaho had activated their National Guard units. Both states had begun to prepare for a border sealing almost immediately. Oregon established control points on the south end of every Columbia River crossing, including the railroad crossing and four dams. They secured them all in the course of that one night. It took them about two days to secure the roughly one hundred miles of land border east of where the river turned north.

Not to be left holding the welfare bag, Idaho noticed what was occurring and began their own border securing operation by lunch on Day 10. Canada merely reinforced the international border crossings with local police and extra patrols by the RCMP. The leaders of the other states and provinces went onto their local news programs, vowing to continue humanitarian missions and shepherd people across the borders with speed and minimal red tape. What happened in reality was quite different.

Riots broke out—not only the I-5 and I-205 bridges between Portland and Vancouver, Washington, but also on the Portland side of the control points. People in black masks and red armbands had grown accustomed to getting their way by a feckless pair of city and state governments. They weren't used to the police fighting back, and they certainly weren't used to the modern riot control methods enacted by the Oregon National Guard. Non-lethal methods were enacted quickly. Every rifleman had riot control rounds in half of their magazines. Several of the Hummers had been retrofitted with new tech.

One model had a "microwave cannon," the ADS, which used an invisible beam to make people feel as if they were on fire. Soldiers jokingly called it "the heat ray." It caused no physical damage, but the pain level was intense and caused people to drop to the ground and try to "roll it out." The other model was fitted with the LRAD 2000X sound cannon, capable of transmitting voice commands or obnoxious noises up to 162 dB at a range of up to five miles. The sound waves caused extreme pain, and smaller versions of them were already in use by police departments around the country. These models were deployed in pairs all along the border.

The leftists were not prepared—physically, mentally, or emotion-ally—to hear no to their demands. Mass arrests were performed on the Oregon side of the border. People on the bridges had no direction to go except back into Washington.

Elsewhere along the highways leading to Eastern Washington, the ash was slowly washing away but not quickly enough. There just weren't enough state resources—equipment and people capable of plowing and removing it. In the shallower ash to the rain-prone west, it had turned into a pasty slurry that led to massive fish kill-offs in every stream and lake. To the drier east, though—where it was up to three feet thick, tapering to a few inches deep near the Idaho border—the smaller amounts of rain couldn't run off. The ash turned to a compact and almost concrete-like substance. Small municipalities tried to clear the roads as best as they could, but they ran out of fuel before they could work enough of the highways to make a difference. This, combined with the re-routing of semi-trucks to the ports in California, meant the influx of relief supplies and food that people were counting on would never come.

"WHAT THE…" Phil mumbled to Jerry.

"Precisely what I thought," Jerry said. "Sure sounds like no help is on the way."

Jerry had texted Phil to come up to the HAM shack near the new garden in the upper field. He wanted to give him this news in person—definitely not over the radio. Jerry had taken a little time to transpose several of his HAM radio messages—which were limited in size—onto one piece of paper.

From Slaughter County DEM — To all Slaughter County Unified Command ECCs — FEMA Region X update — Cease all relief operations to Rainier Impact Zone (RIZ) — Factor: incapacitated seaports — Factor: incapacitated airports — Factor: Incapacitated highways and rail — Factor: national and international relief goods stranded in staging cities — Factor: staging cities are negatively affected by power, cyber, and economic impacts from Rainer event — Factor: non-RIZ cities losing social control — Directive: all

non-RIZ cities affected by trickle-down impacts will prioritize distribution of
staged goods locally — Await further direction — Stop.

"I guess I shouldn't be surprised," Phil told his communication
expert. "But I am." *How many people have they condemned to death with*
this decision? His thought was too dark to say out loud. Phil felt the
hope for help draining from his soul. "Anything else?" he asked
glumly.

"Couple of things. For one, thanks for sending the new kid up.
He's a quick study. Believe it or not, there are a lot of kids who are
HAMs. Their minds are sponges for this stuff as long as you present
it in a cool way. Not bound by their own pre-conceptions."

He was referring to thirteen-year-old James Bryant who was one
of Don Kwiatkowsky's grandkids. Don and Teresa's daughter had
shown up with her husband, kids, and brother-in-law the evening
before. They were from the south end of Mason County, to the
southwest, and had left their home two days earlier. The vehicular
travel was slow going due to traffic jams, mudslides, and collapsed
bridges. They had started with a half-tank of gas and had run out
due to all the detours and idling. They had walked the final eighteen
miles.

As Phil was showing them the property, he noticed that James
had become enamored with the cool gear and maps in Jerry's
"Command Post"-style HAM shack they'd built out of one of the
plastic carports. He suggested that James stay and learn how it all
works, which his parents were fine with. Phil was hoping to get a few
people who knew what they were doing up here in a watch rotation.
Relying on only Jerry to do it all was a serious planning flaw.

"Secondly," Jerry continued, "I've been able to make contact
with the national AmRRON net out of Idaho. They're running a
special net just for Cascadia operators. If I'd had the time and
money to invest and train in digital equipment before all this, we
would actually be able to send them emails and photos, hold conference calls, and the like. Anyway, they're saying that our event has
had a cascading effect on the entire country. Power outages, entire

segments of the internet just gone, shipping—some real and serious blows to the nation's economy. There are even rumors that we should be aware of. Things like China calling in all the debt we owe, Russia getting mobilized militarily, Oregon and Idaho shutting down the borders to control a flu epidemic…"

"Hmmm…" Phil mumbled. "In case I haven't said it, lately— you're worth every penny, brother. I owe you an ice cream sundae or two someday."

"Just keep me fed and protected and we're square, my friend," Jerry replied as he went back to his gear.

Phil excused himself and began the walk back down to the front of the property. He took the south to west route so he could stop by and check on his chickens in Bay 10. The girls were starting to produce about an egg each per day, finally comfortable in their new digs. He bumped into Melinda Reeves and her kids, who were exiting the bay as he arrived.

"Hi, Melinda. Kids," he greeted them. "How are you all accli-mating?" Charlie had brought them out to stay the evening before. They were camping in their family tent in the small tent city building between the hundred-yard and hundred-fifty-yard markers on the rifle line.

"Hey," she replied. "Just fine. Everybody here is really nice. I got to meet the new family that showed up this morning. Their tents wound up next to ours. They seem nice. I guess she's a school teacher, too."

Phil had met Melinda a couple of years earlier, and he remem-bered thinking then about how this lady could have dragged conversation out of a corpse. "Really? I guess I hadn't learned that yet."

"One of the other ladies—Teresa, maybe?—mentioned you were thinking about setting up a classroom?"

"Yeah…well, classroom might be a bit strong. More like a kid-zone/library type thing. But, yes. I had a thought or two about it. Is that something you'd be interested in helping with?" he asked.

"Sure," Mel said. "But I don't know how effective it would be since we'd be mixing a lot of ages together."

"I'm not expecting SAT prep, Melinda. Just looking to keep the kids learning," he said with a smile. "You know—teaching about how to do stuff out here. Gardening, keeping them reading and writing. Let the youngster's color or whatever."

"Okay," she said. "I think this would be a great way for me to help contribute…as long as the others can help teach the life-skills. I'm not much of a gardener!"

"That's perfect, Melinda. Thanks."

Just then Savannah and Dakota came running up from the office area. "Paw-paw! Paw-paw! He's here! He's here!" She was screaming elatedly.

"Hey, Peaches! Who's here?" he asked, scooping up his excited granddaughter.

"Uncle Crane, silly!"

"Awesome!" Phil was hamming it up for her, though deep inside he was overjoyed. This news lifted him from the funk he'd been in since the HAM shack. This would be the first time he'd seen his son since it all began. He set Savannah down. "Show me the way, Sweety."

He gave the Reeves family a little wave as he was being dragged by the other hand towards the office. When he arrived, there was a small crowd gathered at the office's front porch. Most of the range members were in their mid-life or senior years, and they all felt that Crane was part of their family, too. Many of them had watched him grow up. There was excited chatter as people were peppering him and the other new arrival with questions.

Phil followed Savannah and her faithful canine companion up the stairs from the lines to the office, and the crowd parted a bit upon seeing him. Phil nudged his way in and gave his son a big hug. "Your sister's been worried about ya'."

"Hey, Pop," Crane replied. He knew his dad was deflecting.

They let go of the embrace, and Phil took a better look at his son. "I see the goatee has become a shaggy hunter's beard now!"

"You looked in a mirror lately?" his son retorted.

Both men had quit shaving when they realized it was not worth the use of precious water. In actuality, this was true with most people. The lack of electricity wasn't the only medieval aspect of their new lives as people were living through itchy chins and legs that were becoming natural again.

"Look who I brought with me," Crane told his dad, turning to drag in the newcomer.

"Reverend? Good to see you, Padre!" Phil told the man as he gave him a quick hug. A hand shake was just too impersonal for how he was feeling at the moment. Phil had met the Reverend Sherman Robertson many years earlier when he and his wife signed up for a few pistol classes. Reverend Robertson had inserted himself into Phil's life during both of his mid-life crises—when Caroline passed away from cancer and after Phil's near-death experience. Though in his late-seventies, the Reverend was still an active servant of God, moving to where the Spirit told him he was needed.

"Hey, ya, Phil! A little birdy told me to come see you."

"God?" Phil inquired.

"Uh—no. Crane." This caused a round of laughter. "Sorry to disappoint!"

Looking back to Crane, Phil asked, "So what took you so long, son?"

The smile on Crane's face dissolved. "Oh...you know. Work. It just felt like a good time to visit..."

Phil sensed the serious tone and didn't press the matter. "So, did you guys come out together?"

The Reverend hi-jacked the story. "Funniest thing. I was walking around the front of the church property picking up trash from the soup line when Crane darned near ran me over!"

Crane shook his head no behind the Reverend's back to down-play the story. "Yeah, I saw Reverend Robertson as I was getting ready to drive by, so I stopped in to see if he wanted to come out. We figured we'd make you feed us."

Phil was confused. "He's over in East Bartlett. Why would you have been driving by his church?"

"You haven't gotten out much, have you?" Reverend Robertson asked.

"I guess not," Phil said. "What am I missing here?"

Crane took back over. "Between bridges, sinkholes, landslides, downed trees, and everything else, there's not a lot of choices when travelling." He glanced around casually, seeing they still had a crowd. He wanted to tone down the scary talk a bit. "I know it's a bit early for lunch, but how 'bout that bite to eat?"

"Oh, shoot. Where's my manners? Follow me."

The small crowd broke apart as the trio crossed the parking lot to the chow hall/former classroom. As they stepped up onto the deck outside the single-wide trailer, Phil could see Payton pulling biscuits out of a small propane-powered oven/stove unit. One of Phil's canned clarified butters were out on the patio table. She stirred a pot on top of the stove.

"You guys grab a seat. We'll be in shortly." She was putting on a good show for her brother, but Phil knew she was still pissed about the previous day's argument.

They went into the trailer and sat down, chatting. A few minutes later Savannah brought in a plate of buttered biscuits followed by her mother carrying a pot of sausage gravy. "This is *well-peppered*," she said to her dad. It had always annoyed her that he insisted on peppering everything—*every*thing—before tasting it.

"Thanks!" the three men all said to the women.

"Reverend?" Phil said, asking without words if he would say a blessing.

"Oh! It's your spread, Phil. And your new home. You should." It was the type of friendly hint that only reverends and mothers could get away with.

Phil never said grace and was caught off guard. He nervously defaulted to one he remembered Gunny Sergeant Oplata saying at Thanksgiving 1990, out in the Saudi desert. "Rub-a-dub-dub. Thanks for the grub. Yea, God."

This caused Crane, Savannah, and the Reverend to burst out laughing. Payton was not amused. "Really, Dad?" she said, rolling her eyes in embarrassment.

"I learned it in the Corps," he defended himself. *Are we done being mad at each other?* "Just like peppering everything I eat without question." He reached for the salt and pepper shakers.

Payton let him keep the pepper, but she took the salt straight out of his hands. "Sodium," she scolded.

"You know, Olive, if you're not careful, you might just discover your role out here."

Crane looked back and forth between them trying to get a feel for the vibe. "Do I need to separate you two?"

The banter continued for almost two hours, long after the gravy pot had been wiped clean with the biscuits. Phil let his stump breathe, and Crane and the Reverend updated him on the true state of decay. He grew worried about their safety, encouraging both of them to be armed and vigilant. *Things will only get worse,* he told them. Crane reminded his dad that he was staying on base and told him where he'd hidden all his firearms. Phil promised to try and retrieve them, and Crane promised that when he eventually quit staying on-base that he would move out to the range.

The trio left the classroom and made their way toward Crane's car. This gave Phil the opportunity he needed to say what had been bothering him. "Son. I'm sure what's happening down there is important. Just remember—whatever it is isn't worth your life."

Crane's face wrinkled in disgust. "What? I can't believe I'm hearing this from you of all people."

"What..." Phil was dumbfounded by Crane's reaction.

"What would you have said to your dad if he'd said the same thing to you before going to the Gulf War? You'd be pissed!"

Phil hadn't thought about it that way. "Well, for starters—I was enlisted. It's not exactly the same thing—"

"But it is, Dad! It's *exactly* the same thing! I'm serving my country same as you did. I know you're disappointed that I never went into the Marines. I get it. But what I'm doing matters… More than people out in town will ever know!"

"I—I didn't think—"

"No. You didn't." Crane leaned in to give his dad a loving hug goodbye, knowing it would stifle the rest of the conversation. "And go easy on Payton. She's trying."

"Love you, son," Phil said, squeezing his boy. He wasn't used to Crane being so grown up.

A sad round of goodbyes played out with Crane promising to return as soon as he could. Phil watched the gate get manually lifted by the members on watch. Crane snaked his Subaru through the sandbag vehicle trap before disappearing to the south down the Canal Vista Highway. As the gate was lowered, he caught site of another pack of pedestrians coming into view from the same direction. *We still need to get an OP built across the highway,* he remembered. Like the positions at the property corners, that one would be concealed as best as it could be. If anyone were to attack the range from the woods to the west, he wanted them to have to sneak past that very post on their approach. He snapped himself back into the present and scurried down by the gate to observe the pack.

Like the gate guards, Phil was out in the open—seen by the passing group. The site was horrifying. Whereas the club's water well had made it possible for people there to keep themselves and their clothing relatively clean, this group represented a different dynamic. *Refugees,* he thought. *Holy moly! These people look like something out of the history books. Poland. Vietnam.*

There were nine people in this group. They were filthy—covered in grime and ash residue. Their skin was blotchy from dirt. Their energy was low and their morale even lower. Only one of them dared look at Phil and the others as they walked by—a woman wearing a torn, tattered, wet sweater that was probably green at one point. Her hair was wild and unkempt, and her face had open sores. *Tweeker. No doubt about it. Maybe all of them are by the looks of 'em.* At first glance, she looked humiliated. She held her glare defiantly on Phil's eyes as she continued the slow trek. *Anger*, Phil thought. *That's not humiliation—that's rage.*

"Whatcha doin', Paw-paw?" Savannah piped up. She startled her grandpa with her surprise appearance.

"Huh? Oh, um, just thinking. Peaches—do me a favor and go check for eggs." He wanted her out of sight. She took off, happy for the fun assignment.

He looked back up and could tell he'd just caught the woman's head turning away as the group continued north. The hairs on the back of Phil's neck stood up.

PUGET SOUND SAILING INSTITUTE, the sign said. Carmen and Stu had spent three nights slowly moving west until they hit water. The last leg of the trip had been walking south along Marine View Drive. Even at night they could tell there was a marina down below the greenbelt. When they got to the main entrance, it was still pitch-black—in the wee hours of pre-dawn. They drifted back into the woods and camped. Even after the sun had been poking through the gray and light rain for a couple of hours, they sat...observing.

The marina had several sunken vessels and broken piers. As they watched, they saw the slow signs of activity start up in late morning. The intact vessels—few that they were—seemed to have people living on them.

"Well?" Carmen asked her partner. "What do you think?" *Because my alarms are screaming.*

"Something's off," Stu said. "But what choice do we have?"

Carmen let that hang in the air for several seconds. "Yeah..." *Gotta ignore these vibes.* "True."

I just need to get back to my ship—then this nightmare will be over. "Let's roll."

The duo made their way out of the woods and down the driveway of the sailing school. When they were in the main parking lot, they noticed several industrial-sized structures acting as dry-storage. Under them were sailboats and cabin cruisers that had been shaken off their racks. They were laying over on each other like expensive giant dominos. There was one main pier to the left of the parking lot and another four past the dry-storage area. They went in that direction, searching for signs.

Their sixth senses were in overdrive as they passed the piers. Most of the vessels were broken and sunk. Some of the piers themselves had just dead ended where they had broken off in the quake. The people who were standing on the few intact vessels looked like they'd been partying for days. There was so much broken boat-material and earthquake debris washed up on the shoreline that it took Stu a long time to figure out what the smell was.

"What in the world is that stench?" Carmen asked.

"Death," Stu replied. He was absolute when he said it. As a resident after med school, he'd handled his share of drowning victims.

Carmen didn't know what to say. As they passed another pier littered with boat carcasses, they could see a small cabin cruiser with graffiti all over it about a hundred yards out. There was a woman cooking something on a small BBQ on the pier and a man standing on the boat's stern, glaring at them. "RRrrraaarrrgggghhhhh!" he screamed at them.

Carmen and Stu picked up their pace past the head of the pier, hoping to find a boat and people that seemed promising before too much longer. As they approached the next pier, they could see two men milling about somewhat soberly on a Chris-Craft that was about thirty-five-feet-long. The boat looked older but well-kept. It had weathered the destruction relatively well, though some of the paint and trim had been damaged by the slip. Carmen and Stu glanced at each other. *This is it,* she thought.

"You sure you're ready to part with that rich man's watch?"

"I can't eat a watch," Stu said, "or ride it across Puget Sound."

Carmen nodded. *Here goes nothing.*

Kah-Krowww! The roar of the single rifle shot reverberating throughout the T-Mobe was unmistakable. It was preceded by another of the day's fistfights—they had been breaking out, several per day, becoming more frequent and involving larger groups as each new day began. Only in this fight at least two pistols had been brandished.

Pop-Pop! Pop-Pop-Pop-Pop! One pistol reported back.

Kah-Kah-Kah-Kah-Kah-Kah-Kah-Kah-Krowww! The pistols were no match for the M-4s carried by the Washington National Guard.

Panic ensued. Screams were adding to the chaos and confusion as 120,000 panicked people with no place to run began running. A bear of a man named Anthony Wendell Manners scooped his tween twin daughters into the workspace of his large frame and herded his flock towards the center field wall, just to the right of a beer advertisement. His only thought was to be able to put his girls against something and crouch over them. The noise was coming from the left field gate area of the main concourse.

Police and Guard personnel were scurrying around trying to maintain some semblance of order. They were yelling at anyone in their immediate area to get on the ground. Few were listening. Tony had physics on his side as he pushed his way through people. He continually had to re-grip his girls from the impact of others. Most people just bounced off him, but he took a few good shots in the ribs and back before he got to the fence. "Get on your knees!" he commanded his girls. As they got up against the fence as low as they could, Tony made himself into a human shield. This was the first time one of the fights had resulted in gunfire, but Tony wasn't surprised. He knew this was an eventuality.

The T-Mobe PA system had been long dead, but Tony thought he could hear orders being barked through a megaphone in the direction from which the chaos started. *We need to get out of here!* Tony was angry. He didn't know how much longer he'd be able to contain his growing rage. He held it in check for the sake of his girls. They were all tired, hungry, and frustrated. The last update was that there would be extremely limited and valuable ferry service starting the next day. Damage was only one factor impacting it. Many of the ferry workers had quit coming to work to tend to their own families. And no state employees—ferry crews included—were getting paid because the state had mandated everybody take electronic paychecks almost twenty years earlier. The incentive to go out into society and produce was now much more primal—food, medicine, and water were tangible. Cash wasn't. Electronic money didn't matter anymore. *If you can't hold it, you don't actually own it,* Tony remembered someone saying once.

He wondered if this eruption of violence was related to the obvious gang members he'd been seeing in the stadium the last few days. The drugs were coming in from somewhere, and the stolen items from the thieving and sex-trades had to be going out some-how. What he couldn't figure out was how they were getting their weapons in with them. He decided it was probably a combination of bribes and threats, wondering to himself if he'd just seen too many movies. In his working career, though, he'd learned that the "KISS" method—the simplest explanation—was usually pretty close. *"How" don't much matter, does it? The bad guys an' the government have guns. I don't. That's the stinky reality.*

Tony had noticed three different groups of people that he thought were gang members, and they aligned with ethnicity. Having grown up somewhat poor, he knew a thug when he saw one. In essence, he saw traditional black and Hispanic gang members, but he also saw some obvious white biker types. He had no idea if they were collaborators or competitors. Tony was smart enough to realize that not all who were prepared for this new world were righteous and pious people. He just didn't expect them to be so...*out in the open. Nature hates a vacuum*, he remembered. *And right now, society is runnin' in a void.*

"DEAL," the man said. "Name's Trip. He's Shorty."

"I'm Stu," Stu told the big man. He and Carmen had just bartered his *Mariner* watch for a *boat ride* up to Slaughter County. *How ironic*, Stu thought. He was a little disappointed about losing the watch but not largely upset. *It's just a watch.* If Stu hadn't been so tired, sick, and hungry his instincts might have tipped him off to the fact there had been no haggling. The pair of men wore leather vests with patches on the back. The center patch was a silhouette of a zombie outlined by a moon. The rocker-patches above and below the centerpiece said "Risen Dead – Washington."

"Carmen," she said, introducing herself.

"You guys got lucky," Trip said. "We're runnin' late."

"Lucky us," Stu said. The lack of details on where they were about to go had not escaped Stu's attention. He decided not to ask. This was strictly a business relationship. *No need to open a door for them to learn too much in return. Still...some intel would be nice...*

"Nice boat, Trip. Chris Craft's aren't cheap, especially big ones like this. Looks like she faired okay through it all." Stu was probing just a bit.

"Oh, umm...thanks," the large, pony-tailed man said.

You look like you should be on a Harley, Stu was thinking, *not a wooden cabin-cruiser.* He had no idea how right he was.

"I inherited her from my dad," Trip lied.

"Your dad named his boat the 'Aqua-desiac'?" Stu asked skeptically. Carmen was trying her best to give her partner the 'just let it go' look.

"Heh! Yeah...he had an odd sense of humor!" The big man laughed loudly.

He's friendly enough, Stu thought. *Still...if these guys are criminals, we're as good as dead.* "So, is there anything we should do? Or just stay out of the way?"

The shorter one had wild wavy hair, a ring piercing the septum of his nose, and part of a tattoo covering his neck and throat. Stu couldn't tell what it was.

"Just sit tight," Shorty said. "You guys might be better off in the cabin," he suggested.

Carmen and Stu carefully made their way down into the dark hold. There were no lights on, but the drapes on the portholes were open. The place was trashed. Clothing, food wrappers, cigarette butts, and liquor bottles littered the entire cabin. The toilet in the head was backed up, and the entire space smelled like burnt plastic.

"Don't you dare leave me!" Carmen hissed at Stu.

"Me!" Stu asked shocked. "You're supposed to protect me, not the other way around!" he quipped. It didn't make either of them feel better.

They heard a dull rumble as the Chrysler Marine 426 found life. They could hear their "crew" moving about on deck. Within five minutes they were cast off the pier, and the vessel was slowly crawling out of the watery graveyard of hulls, trees, and debris.

Stu looked out the portside portholes as they drifted into Commencement Bay. He couldn't believe his eyes, so he headed back out on deck, Carmen right on his heels. The day was some-what clear. Their eyes stared at the empty steaming crater southeast of Tacoma. The giant known as Tahoma/Mt. Rainier was a mere third in height of her former self. The overpowering smell of mud and decay forced them to start scanning the shoreline. The bay was a giant mud-pool. If they had turned south towards the tide-flats, they would have become stuck and unmoving within a few minutes, Stu realized. Buildings and port cranes were toppled. Even having lived through it all, Carmen and Stu were still in disbelief. *At least our luck is finely changing,* Stu thought.

20

Turning Points.

TAHOMA'S HAMMER + 10 DAYS.

"THE TASK GROUP will be off the coast by 0400 the morning after next. Expect a series of sorties from the helicopters by 0800. Bear in mind they will primarily be setting down slung loads of supplies, but you should have at least two different LZs ready to receive some people we're sending up. The fuel trucks and troops will be off-loaded up in the north end of the county by the next day. You should have enough to keep your cranes and generators going for another month or so."

Washington State Naval Shipyard Commanding Officer Marie Darnell was in the secure conference room near her office in Building 855, along with Captain Flowers and Jamison Thrall. The big screen on the wall at the head of the table contained a different view than normal. Instead of her bosses in the other Washington, the screen contained most of USINDOPACOM's senior-staff. They were gathered around a large mahogany table somewhere near Pearl Harbor, HI.

"Two landing zones, sir. Understood." She was getting directions from an Air Force Major General Russell Driscoll, the Chief of Staff for the office that was responsible for the entirety of U.S. Military Operations from the West Coast to the Indian Ocean. "How many personnel, sir? Roads and vehicles are still somewhat dicey. And there is a…declining civility factor that will need to be considered as well."

"Understood, Captain. We're observing from above. We're aware of your populace issues. We'll only be sending some people to augment your Marines guarding the El Paso and a few engineer-types. The Marine Raiders and Delta Force will be landing directly at Bogdon at a time that…well, you don't need to know. The main landing force will arrive when the Task Group gets to the mouth of Hood Canal."

Observing from above? Marie felt sheepish about never considering that PACOM would be keeping an eye on things with satellites. But when talking about keeping the Navy's entire West Coast nuclear weapons arsenal secure, no measure was too drastic. If Slaughter County fell into the wrong hands, it would suddenly become the world's fourth-largest nuclear power, behind only the rest of the U.S., China, and Russia. "Yes, sir. I understand the gravity of the mission completely, General. And we appreciate the re-supply, sir."

"Just get it done, Captain. Things are in play internationally. The nation can't afford to lose that carrier." With that, the screen went blank.

The three senior leaders sat in silence for a few moments. Captain Flowers got a text and stared at his phone for a long time. He finally broke the silence. "Skipper, have you heard the latest estimates from the power plant?" In this small setting amongst this high-ranking team, titles became a bit relaxed.

"Not since yesterday, Trevor. Do you have something newer?" She saw the look on his face. *He's concerned.* "What?"

"Yesterday they said about seven to eight days. Today they lowered the estimate to four or five."

"What? Did they give a reason?" Marie was visibly livid. "And why didn't I get that text?" Running out of fuel before they got the carrier's shafts reinstalled was the catastrophe they were trying to avoid. Propellers and rudders could be put on with a crane and divers later. But a flooding dry-dock would fill the carrier's engineering spaces with seawater.

"Marie, I told them to go through me to keep things off your plate until you needed to hear them. I *just* got this information."

Marie sighed. She was tired—they all were. "You're right. So why the big reduction?"

"They say that as more people come back to work, more buildings that we had secured power and steam to are becoming energized."

"Well...darn. That makes *perfect* sense. Maybe we should take a thorough poll of who's here so we can start consolidating work areas..."

Director Thrall chimed in. "Maybe an email explaining the need to conserve energy?"

"Should we, though?" Trevor asked. "We normally don't release critical details to the workforce—don't want them to feel the 'schedule-pressure,' and all."

"While all logic backs up that statement," Marie said to Trevor, "I think that in this case, I agree with Jamison. For starters these are anything but normal times."

The other two nodded in agreement.

"And," she continued, "most of these people never left. They know the situation, and they're still here." She started to get a little emotional—she could feel it in her voice. "I'm so proud of this workforce. Proud beyond words. The rest have come back—not because they're hungry but because we need them. The cofferdam worked. The capping plan for the El Paso's reactor—well—that's still a mess, but we have people out there exposing themselves to the high radiation levels, knowing full well what the risks are." She stopped. They were getting it, and her voice was starting to crack a little.

After a full minute of silence, the Commanding Officer made her decision. "Tomorrow morning let's gather everyone out on Monsoor Avenue and update them. On *every*thing."

THE GOING HAD BEEN SLOW. Carmen and Stu had been keeping themselves up on the bow for the first hour or so to help spot for floating obstacles. They had seen their fair share of fish. Many were dead and some of the live ones were dining on human bodies. There were still fires dotting the shore in places. Shorty had started out suggesting they get down into the cabin—"for their own safety" —somewhat passive-aggressively. It eventually become an order. "Look, I got this. You two just stay out of my way," he barked.

As they made their way back down to the hold, Carmen caught Trip's eyes while he was at the helm. His face was calm, but his eyes were silent. *Dark—like there's no soul in there.* It made her nervous. It didn't help that they looked like they belonged to a gang. *Too many TV shows,* she thought. *He must be 6'4" and well over three hundred pounds. I don't think I'll be able to sleep on this boat...*

Stu had found a cribbage board and was attempting to explain the game to Carmen. She was playing, but she couldn't focus. "Keep an eye on the hatch," she said. "I noticed a scuttle back aft over the engine compartment. I'm going to sneak out and see where we are. Somethin's wrong, but I can't figure out what it is."

"Be careful," Stu warned. "We can't handle these guys."

Carmen put her hand on her partner's as if to say *I know.* She stood up and slowly crept forward, stopping next to the small set of stairs that led up to the bridge cabin. She could overhear low murmurs between the two men, though what was being said was unclear.

"…. Tomorrow… brother… stuff… fox… signal… guards… scape…" *Wait! Was that "scape" or escape?"*

She turned aft, showing Stu her worried look and slid back into the next area, which contained only a bunk and some storage spaces. In that room's aft bulkhead a scant six feet away, she opened a small interior hatch which led her into the engine space. There was a small hatch in the overhead of the old wooden boat located on the starboard side. It had two sets of hinges connecting the two boards that made up the roughly two-foot-square access. She flipped the first board back onto the second, and then she flipped them both back onto the topside deck. She slowly peeked forward. Not seeing anything, she slowly pulled herself up but crouched below the windows of the upper cabin.

There was still daylight, and she could see the expected—land in every direction… carnage… smoke. *The sun…* Though it was over-cast, the weather was mild enough that she could tell where it was. They were sailing in the direction of the sun. *If we're heading north it should be on our left in the late afternoon.*

Then she saw it. *Oh, no…* She scrambled back down the hatch and as quietly as she could she made her way back to the forward lower cabin.

"Well?" Stu started.

"Shhh!" she hushed him as she went to the forward end stairs and peeked up. Trip was still sitting there, steering. She went back to Stu, who was standing with a concerned look by that time.

"I saw the bridge!" she hissed as quietly as she could.

"Bridge…" Stu was confused. "What bridge?"

"*The* bridges!" she insisted. "The Tacoma-Narrows bridges. The old one is barely standing. We're sailing right for them!"

"That doesn't make sen—" THWUMP! Stu crumpled to the floor, and the space behind him was filled with a short sneering biker holding a hammer.

"WHAT DO YOU MEAN 'TOOTHLESS TIGER'?" the commissioner asked.

"Exactly that, Commissioner. The curfew has been unenforceable. There just isn't enough manpower. We have no idea how many thefts have gone unreported. Or murders." Sandy McCallister was once again leading a session of the Unified Command. "How many of you beefed up your security to get up here today?"

There were no shows of hands, but the men and women looking around the room—more importantly, the looks on their faces—gave Sandy her answer. "Violence isn't our only problem. We're about to face a serious death wave." This caused a murmur, particularly from the politicians.

"What exactly does that mean?" asked the mayor of Port View.

"It means that without power the critically injured and ill are in the process of perishing... if they haven't already. Refrigerated medicines, life support systems, people on breathing treatments, cardiac patients, strokes—these are the people we bought all those three-person grave liners for. Well, them and eventually the diabetics and asthmatics..." She was being blunt. She was too tired to be political anymore. "Tell me, Greg, when was the last time you checked in on the nursing homes in Port View? 'Cuz you sure aint gonna like what you see!" she said, reverting back to her grandmotherly slang to soften the blow.

The mayor just sat there staring back—the politician in him not wanting to say the wrong thing. *He knows I'm right,* Sandy thought.

"Folks, we all heard from Sheriff Raymond himself. How'd you say it, Ward? 'Negative values on supplies needed to care for detainees?' That sure sounds a whole lot like 'We can't feed the prisoners anymore' to me." She looked around for a few seconds. "Lucky for you, we have a solution. Gerry?"

Sandy's right-hand come over from her wall chair holding a new padded pelican case. She set it down on the table and unsnapped the lid, hinging it open. She pulled out a handle that looked similar to the type a grocery cashier might use. She held it over her own arm and it made an audible beep. She then showed it to the South Slaughter Fire Chief, the closest person at the table.

"Johnson, Geraldine," he read on the scanner, looking up in disbelief. It took about five seconds of staring at each other for the room to erupt. They were speaking over each other, most just in shock but a few vehemently opposed. Sandy couldn't have cared less about all of them. *There's only two men I need to make this fly.* She watched National Guard Major Matsumoto and Sheriff Raymond's faces. Both seemed to be considering the idea quietly.

"We call it catch and release. Not only can we release the lock-ups and find them later, we'll be able to chip anyone who was involved in any type of violent event. That way we can hold trial later on when things are normal again." *Things will never be normal again. You fools just need to believe they will be.*

"Pardon my ignorance, Director," said Don Dale, the Sylvan Fire Chief. "If we're ultimately going to have people flocking to the big FEMA camp at the sports park next door, why wouldn't you just feed the lock-ups from that supply? That way—they're still *locked up!*" The chief's snarkiness was not lost on anyone.

"Our supplies are for the law abiders, Don. Let the prisoner's families worry about feeding them. And in case you hadn't noticed, the camps are already becoming somewhat…restless." *Ignorance not forgiven. Idiot.* "Now—let's talk about what to do about guns, shall we?"

It was early evening and Payton and her father were walking north on Canal Vista Highway. They were almost to Medford Lane. They had been engaged in a dialogue along the way, taking advantage of the time to talk about the lunchtime visit from Crane. They eventually tried to thaw the chill from their earlier tension. All conversations eventually turned towards ways to improve the camp. Several days earlier Phil had made a big run to his house for ammo and the rest of his equipment. While not in the realm of possibility to completely move *all* his goods, he felt alright about what was left. The point of this trip was to talk, not grab stuff.

"Laundry," Payton said. "That's another thing. We're going to need more clothes because hand-washing is a fairly abusive method. And we need one of those washboard things of our own. I hate asking Teresa to borrow hers every other day." *And because I finally found something I can do for other people.* "I've been offering to hand-wash some of the older women's loads for them."

"Wellll…it might be a bit late to get one of those, Olive," her dad said. "We may have to figure out a way to make one. It seems like that's just the latest example of old technology that is suddenly in demand again. I would die of joy if someone showed up with an old-timey plow harness to use with those horses."

Phil had approved the stay of two non-range members—Crane's roommate Maya and her mom, Pam Jorgenson. They had arrived on horseback with a third horse in tow. Phil had known them since the kids were in elementary school together, and he vouched for their character. He knew that the horses and Pam's ranch knowledge would be invaluable. Nate Jorgenson had been deployed on his submarine, USS James L. Hunicutt, and nobody had heard from him since long before the disaster. Despite Nate's being a sailor, Phil had the utmost respect for the man. He considered sheltering the family an honor-bound duty.

Payton nodded in agreement. "Anyway, I have an idea for building a semi-circular clothes line around the firepit. We could back it with mylar blankets, too, to make it more efficient."

"That's actually a great idea, honey! I can see it already. You draw up your vision, and we'll see what we can piece together."

They made the left onto Medford Lane. As usual the conversation eventually turned sour when Phil made a comment that Payton took as a slight. "So, with all the good ideas you've come up with, it seems like you're finally able to say you're growing up some, huh?" Phil knew immediately he shouldn't have phrased a compliment like that.

"You know…I guess I should be surprised by how long it took you to actually go there. Why am I such a disappointment to you?" She didn't want him to speak—she just wanted to make him regret saying yet another judgmental thing.

They were on the final approach to Phil's driveway. Phil suddenly wished they'd brought Dakota along to help deflect some of the vibe. He was starting to think about the flavor of crow he wanted to eat when something caught his eyes. He could see through the trees as they approached the house that windows were broken out.

Phil unslung the rifle that had been riding on his back. He re-slung it to the front of his body and started his heel-toe procedure for walking and aiming. "Wait here," he ordered.

"No way," Payton countered, drawing her Walther off the hip holster that she'd started using.

This wasn't the time and place to argue, so he kept going. He got to the stairs at the bottom of the split-level entry, and he pointed to her to go post herself on the corner of the house. She could cover that approach and the front yard if somebody tried to enter the house after him.

"No!" she argued. "I'm coming in with you!"

"Damn it, Payton!" he hissed as quietly as he could. "Do what I say and cover the house! They may still be *in* there and have a watch *out* here!" He was tired of *everything* turning into a debate.

Her face was livid, but she turned and moved to the corner by the garage. After Phil saw Payton set herself, he made his slow entry. Four minutes later, Phil came back out onto the front porch. "Clear," he mumbled dejectedly. Payton holstered her pistol and followed him upstairs. The furniture had been tossed over. Pictures were off the wall. Stuff was strewn everywhere.

"Mom's painting! Now I'm *pissed*!" Payton said. Caroline had painted a family portrait when Payton was about fourteen. It lay on the floor with a book case on top of it, the contents resting on the painting. "What was the point of all this!"

"We'll never know, hon. It could be kids, could be druggies, could be people who know I might have guns and ammo." Phil knew one negative aspect of being a well-known gun guy was that his property was a target for opportunists. He walked over to the sliding glass door and peeked out. The shop's roll-up metal door had a huge gash in it, like someone had cut it open with a chainsaw. "I bet they took the air compressor…"

They headed back outside. His damaged truck looked the same. He popped open the bed-cover and looked in. "There's still some stuff in here. We'll drive the jeep back and take this stuff…" His voice trailed off as his face turned sour. He made a beeline for the garage, unlocked the door, and rolled it up. The jeep was still there.

They started to head around the house. "Dad, do you suppose—"

"Shhh!" Phil commanded. At first, Payton didn't notice it. Out in Canal Vista on any given day a person could hear their neighbors enjoying their natural rights in the form of gunfire.

Klack-Klack-Klack-Klack!

"That's an AK," Phil said seriously.

"So?"

"Not the gun, Olive. The direction. That's coming from the range!" He started speed-hobbling back towards the garage.

Just then the HAM radio that Jerry had given Phil for the extended range crackled to life. "Phil! This is Fred! Get back here. ASAP."

"What is it, Fred? We'll be coming back in Crane's jeep."

"I'm not saying on the radio. Is Payton with you?"

"I'm right here!" Phil had tossed the radio to his daughter so that he could concentrate on firing up the jeep. It was difficult for him to drive a stick-shift but not impossible. Rocks went flying as he punched the gas. He didn't even look for right of way as he turned out onto the highway.

Even with the round-about along the way they had managed to make it there in about two minutes. He hit the brakes and clutch and came sliding to a stop in the end of the driveway, throwing open the door as he stomped on the parking brake. *The vehicle trap,* Payton remembered. She was wondering why he stopped there.

There were several members milling about excitedly, many of them with their rifles and pistols drawn. Upon seeing that, Phil pulled his rifle out of the back. About then Fred came running up.

"What happened!" Phil demanded.

Fred was overwhelmed. "Don got hurt—Dakota! Oh, God! Phil, its—"

"Calm down, Fred." Phil was marching past Fred, the gate, and the vehicle trap to the small crowd in the middle of the parking lot. He could hear Dakota barely whimpering from inside a circle of people and see Don's family tending to him. He was laying on the ground, bleeding.

"Phil!" Fred hollered, catching up. His face matched the other thirty faces Phil could see—they were panic-stricken.

"Spit it out, Fred!" Phil said loudly.

Payton had caught up. "Where's Savannah?!" she demanded, her mother's intuition firing on all cylinders. *Where's my baby?*

Fred's face was crinkled in guilt and failure. "They got her! That's what I've been trying to say!" The old man started to gulp air between statements.

"What?" Payton screamed. "What, Fred?!"

"Two people took her. Came right over the berm that separates the parking lot from the highway. They shot Dakota with an arrow and just grabbed Savannah while she was playing in the parking lot. When Don ran up to fight them, he got clubbed in the head! Then they took off through the woods to the west. When he got up he returned fire, but they made it over the berm too fast. We can't find any blood trails!"

Just then Jerry came flying up the lower road from down-range in the gator. "Phil!" he called out.

"Not now!" Phil growled. He was heading toward his tactical gear, which was staged down on the rifle line.

"Now, Phil! This will help, I promise!" He was reaching into the back of the gator and unzipping a bag. Phil stopped and took a breath, looking over. He changed directions toward the gator.

Payton had beat her father over to the machine to see what Jerry was excited about. *Jerry, I could kiss you,* she thought when she saw it.

21

"The only thing necessary for the triumph of evil is for good men to do nothing."
— A quote, though disputed, often attributed to Irish Statesman Edmund Burke

TAHOMA'S HAMMER + 11 DAYS.

PHIL and the others were moving slowly. It was dark, and the brush was thick with salal and huckleberry, which made travelling through it loud and cumbersome. They'd taken off after dusk intent on making ground—they knew time was of the essence. The small group was led by Phil with three of Don's family members insisting they go, too. They were fueled by the horror of what could be happening to Savannah. Deep in his mind, Phil was irate with himself. *If I'd gotten the stupid OP built and manned, my granddaughter would be safe, my friend would be okay, and Dakota would be alive.* He was doing his best to keep his emotions pushed to the back of his mind. He needed to keep his senses tuned to the moment.

The other old man in this mini-squad was forty-four-year-old Eli Bryant, Don's son-in-law. Eli was an avid hunter and knew his way around the woods and preferred bows or hunting rifles to tactical rifles. Phil wasn't going to argue, knowing it would be much better for Eli to use what he was familiar with. Seeing the rest of the fire-power in the group, Eli chose his compound bow with a Smith & Wesson Model 69 Combat Magnum revolver chambered in .44 to back it up. He carried it in a leather holster-sling that kept the pistol secured squarely on his chest. Eli was just over six-feet tall, with thinning dark-brown hair and was barrel-chested. He worked in a lumber-mill and had the rough hands and beard to prove it.

Phil had appointed Eli's little brother as second-in-command for the mission. Josh Bryant, thirty-four, had served five years in the infantry as a good old-fashioned "11-Bravo" Infantryman, including deployments to Iraq in 2007 and 2009. In the years since he'd worked as a plumber and gone through not one but two messy divorces. Like Phil, he was using his personal AR-15. He'd borrowed one of Phil's surplus chest-rigs and battle belts. While not containing actual plates, the chest-rig allowed him to carry maga-zines up in his "work-space." He had pistol mags and rifle mags on his belt in addition to one of Phil's older trauma kits. His back-up gun was a Canik 9MM pistol that he kept tucked into an appendix holster.

The third and final Bryant man to join the crew was Eli's seven-teen-year-old son, Jeff. At 6' 2" tall, his senior year playing tight-end for the North Mason Bulldogs had come to an abrupt end thanks to Tahoma's Hammer. Phil had lent the young man one off his AR pistols to use. Don had worked with his grandson a handful of times, so Phil knew the kid was proficient in the Four Command-ments of Firearms Safety.

All three Bryant men were decked out in a combination of hunting clothes and jeans. Phil had changed into multicam pants and shirt to go under his plate carrier. He was even sporting a ballistic helmet with PVS-14 monocular night vision attached. It was hinged down as they moved. He wore it in front of his non-dominant left eye, reserving his shooting eye for his red-dot sight. Phil was on "point." It wasn't the normal spot for a squad's leader, but he was the only one with night vision.

The evening before, as the gray dusk set in and the evening winds started to pick up, Jerry had shown Phil his latest gimmick in a seemingly endless bag of tricks. *Force multipliers,* Phil called them to himself, named for the tactical advantage the items brought with them. In this case it was a $4,500, quad-bladed DJI drone with high-resolution camera attached. Jerry had a side business filming promotional videos and had brought the drone so it didn't get stolen. They had only gotten about seven minutes of flight time because the batteries weren't fully charged, but it was enough to help.

The drone's camera didn't show the perpetrators, but it did show some broken brush and muddy tracks just past the fifteen or so houses to the immediate west of the range. Jerry carefully lowered the rig over someone's backyard, and they discovered what was an old trail leading further west.

"That's it," Phil decided. "Unless they're in one of these imme-diate houses, that's where they went."

Over the years Phil had met most of the range's neighbors. All of them loved having the range there—they were all liberty-loving patriots who appreciated the value of the gun-range. Phil had never gotten a bad vibe from any of them. He decided the trail was worth investigating.

Jerry went to work. He recharged both sets of batteries for the drone as best as he could while digging up a few Baofeng ham radios and two of the GoTennas for the crew to take with them. This had allowed Phil the time he needed to calm down and think a little more rationally. They all had a quick snack, and Alice—the club's president—suggested they all say a prayer. They gathered around Don, who was asleep, resting. Phil's hunch was that at worst he had a nasty concussion. Alice asked Phil, "Do you want to say a few words?" They were down on the far end of the rifle-line at the makeshift infirmary.

"No, Ma'am. I might say some stuff that contradicts the act of asking God for help," came his honest reply. He'd already thrown out his one prayer for the day.

Alice nodded and bowed her head. "Dear, Lord. We ask You now for guidance and protection. Please protect Savannah, and watch over these men. Bring them all home safely, Father, but above all, let Your will be done. Amen." Short and simple. A chorus of "Amens" rolled out around the group.

Having travelled for several hours, Phil estimated it was now about 0400 hours—he was reluctant to turn on his phone and cast bright light. He still hadn't reset his self-winding watch. The original, slightly overgrown trail had ended, but the people—*animals*, Phil reminded himself—had not been careful to cover their tracks. Phil was aware that the muddy footsteps and broken branches could be deliberate. He knew that experienced soldiers would leave sign for their trekkers and double-back in a large circle to ambush them from behind. He was keeping a close eye on his compass to make sure that wasn't happening. His pace count was telling him they had probably gone about two miles, which seemed slow to untrained people, but it was actually pretty far, all things considered.

They had travelled across a large open clearing and a couple of roads maintained for the contract-logging crews that Washington occasionally hired to log state-owned land. They had started to ascend some, which told Phil they were somewhere near the eastern slopes of Mount Verde, the highest point in the county. He knew there were a few desolate roads in the area. Most of the houses were on large tracts of acreage. There were a lot of horse ranches and old-fashioned "country-folk" that lived out here, but there was also a real and persistent element of meth addicts who stayed in old travel trailers and single-wide mobile homes.

Phil held his hand up near his shoulder, palm open and facing forward. He then closed his fist. *Stop.* They all took a knee. He wanted to stop the patrol there and wait for dawn.

⟁

Ants, crawling. But they aren't biting. Odd. Wait. Where are they going? I didn't know ants made noise. <Tap-Tap-Tap> Noise is getting louder. Ants are gone now. Owww, do I have a headache? Wait—that's not ants. Is that…rain? Oooooo, definitely a headache. I feel weird… wobbly. What happened? Is that screaming? Rain getting louder. Back of head throbbing. Wait!—

Carmen!

"MMMrrmmpphhh!" *What the hell?*

Stu slowly regained consciousness and realized there was a rag stuffed into his throat and duct tape holding it to his head. *Can't. Hardly. Breathe!* "Crrrrmmmmmnnnfff!" he tried calling her name once again. Then it hit him. *That's her—screaming! Oh, God! Nooo!*

"Cccrrrrmmmmmnnnnnnnnnfffff!" he tried screaming as loud as he could through the rag. It was no good. The sounds he heard coming from the next room were sounds of horrible violation, pain, and suffering.

Stu started to swell with raw emotion—anger! Disbelief! Rage! Fear…Tears started streaming down his face, some of them soaking into the greasy red shop-rag.

He could hear it—hear it all. They were raping her, viciously. "ARRRRGGGHHHH!" was all he could scream through the rag. There was pounding. He thought he could hear her fighting. *Keep fighting! Keep fighting…ARRRGGHHH! She doesn't deserve this! God—you can go to hell!* Stu knew deep inside it wasn't God's fault, but he was feeling too primal and exposed to think rationally.

His pounding headache was a temporary memory, replaced by adrenaline, cortisol, and norepinephrine as his body reacted to fight or flight. *Where am I? The engine compartment. What's holding me?* He couldn't tell. His hands were bound behind his back. His feet were bound, too. He tried wiggling around and was able to see several wraps of duct tape around them. *I might be able to cut through that.* He kept wiggling, but his body had other ideas. The stress was too much. He started to throw up. *NO! Mustn't choke!* He tried his best to suppress it. His vomit hit the rag and started to choke him.

He was breathing wildly and rapidly through his nostrils, trying to suck in as much air as his panic-stricken body needed. *Must maintain control!* he screamed in his own mind. He swallowed hard, gulping his contents back down. Slowly he was able to control his breathing. *Think the worst is past. Stop choking!*

He could still hear it, though the screaming was milder now. It was decreasing and being replaced by sobs. *No! Keep fighting. No!* He started to bawl through his rag, his flushed face heating his tears of shame. *I've failed you! Carmen, I'm so sorry…I'm so sorry…* Former narcissist Dr. Stuart Schwartz, bound and gagged, cried uncontrollably— not for himself, but for the only friend he had in the new world.

Somewhere in a waterway west of Puget Sound, a small boat bobbed at anchorage as if nothing were wrong.

WITH A VERTICAL RANGE of well over two miles, the drone picked up enough altitude for Phil to take a good bearing on a few landmarks which helped him confirm their location. He'd found a thin spot in the trees, relying on the others to cover security around the entire perimeter while he sent the drone up. Jerry had reminded him that neither set of batteries was fully charged, so he had just a few minutes at best. He didn't send the device up to maximum altitude, but rather just high enough to look for signs.

When he started to detect it during its descent, he opted to keep altitude there and send it in a slow circular search pattern. He was able to confirm that there were only two properties within five hundred meters of his position. A quick flight and scan of the properties showed that they were well-kept. He could even see someone's laundry drying at one of them. He was starting to feel stressed—the trail would be completely cold soon.

About that time, the drone descended to two hundred feet above ground level and starting hovering directly over Phil, a feature meant to tell the operator that the batteries were about to die. Phil cautiously brought the expensive toy down. Now he was forced to make a tough choice—send it back up on the last battery or press west?

He recalled Josh for a consult. Upon hearing the results, Josh provided his input. "It's overcast but dry. It's morning and plenty of daylight left. We've had a little break. I say press on. When we think we're around more houses, send it back up. But don't waste time and battery gaining too much altitude. I'm sure Jerry would rather know Savannah is safe than worry about some scumbag shooting down his drone."

Phil nodded. "Thanks. When your loved ones are on the line, sometimes you start to question yourself. But that's what I was leaning towards, too."

The HAM radio Phil was carrying was mounted to a pouch on the left side of his plate carrier, just behind some magazine pouches. He used a plug-in mic on the front of the carrier for speaking on the radio. That was connected to his electronic ear protection with a small wire that he ran through the carrier's should strap. This enabled him to listen for radio transmissions without blaring the radio out into the open.

Phil keyed up the mic. "Brewery. This is Keg. Over."

After a few seconds, "Keg, Brewery. Go."

"We are approximately seven klicks past the pub crawl. Any update? Over."

"Keg, the Bouncers have been notified and came back behind the bar to see for themselves. They are also out looking for the drunks."

"Brewery, Keg copies. We have scouted the bar's roof and have decided to proceed another three to four klicks. Keg, out."

"Brewery copies all. Out."

Phil recalled the other two teammates, and they continued their slow progression west. They were trying to stay on old hiker or game trails—not just for speed but to keep down on the noise that stomping through the dense underbrush created.

After two more hours, he called for a quick break. The mini-squad created a perimeter and hunkered down for a snack. "Everyone okay on water?" Phil quietly asked. Each member had brought a pack with gear, food, and water. They all gave a thumbs up, knowing that talking as little as possible was important. Phil gave everyone a "stay put" signal and headed south to a thin spot in the trees. *Yeah. This should work.*

He went back to the others and called them in. "Alright. There's a spot over there. I think I've seen enough signs that we're near some more horse farms. Re-pack—we'll head over, set security, and I'll send the drone back up."

Everyone complied, and within ten minutes the drone was up about four hundred feet performing another circular sweep. Phil saw one property on the tablet screen and moved the drone to the south. The drone passed over two pastures and a road on the way to the grimy, run-down single-wide trailer. It had junk all over the place. It looked like a hurricane had decided to spit out all its contents there. *That's it.* Phil got his hopes up. *It has to be. Look at it.* He called over Josh and Eli. "Look."

Eli spoke first. "How on Earth can people live like that?"

"Yeah," Josh nodded, locking eyes with Phil. "*That's* our mission."

Spoken like a true Joe, Phil thought.

"Alright," Phil decided. The other two went back out to their hasty perimeter while Phil brought the drone back down and stowed it in his rucksack. He pulled out his compass and took a reading that correlated to the direction the drone had flown back from.

About an hour later they were at the near edge of the second clearing he'd seen. He set security and everyone SLLS'ed for a few minutes. Then he called them in. "Here's the plan. We're going to run a Gotenna up a tree here. Josh—you and Jeff will box around this clearing on the east. Eli, you and I will go west. Jeff—Josh'll plant you in the woods about twenty meters in from the edge of the property. You'll watch our backs. Got it?"

Jeff nodded. "I'll be your overwatch." This caught Phil off guard.

"Alright, I gotta ask. How the hell—"

"Video games," Jeff said cutting him off. This made Phil smirk.

"Well, alrighty then," he said smiling. "Josh, set up due east of the main structure, we'll stagger ourselves so that the three of us triangulate. In one hour, I'll send out the first text to make sure we're all set. Everyone text in clockwise rotation. These antennas only last a day, max, but we have a second one. Radios are a last resort. Hopefully we'll see something soon. Remember—do not engage unless you're in immediate lethal danger. If you're seen, this spot right here is our rally point. Questions?"

Everyone was amped despite not having slept the night before. Hearing no questions, Phil sent the Gotenna up into a tree with a piece of paracord and a rock. Then he sent everyone out on their assignments.

He planted Eli in the tree line to the northwest of the property. Eli was basically covering one end and the back of the mobile home. He made his way about sixty meters farther south, planting himself on the other end of the property. They were all staring at a run-down singlewide mobile home that was light blue in color and had moss covering the roof. There was filth and junk in every direction. He sent out the first group text.

[Phil: "At SW corner. No activity. Back deck small. Junk all over yard."]

[Brrrt—Eli: "NW corner. May see movement inside."]

[Brrrt—Jeff: "North overwatch is all clear."]

[Brrrt—Josh: "East secure. Front a real craphole. Entry will suck."]

[Phil: "If we plan an entry we'll use the back."]

After a few minutes Jeff texted again. [Brrrt— "Now what?"]

Phil replied. ["Waiting game. Need better intel. Try to stay awake."]

IT WAS GETTING DARK AGAIN. Between his headache, stress, and lack of food and water, Stu had no idea what time it was, let alone which day. The engine had fired up again at one point. He feigned moaning the first time they came to check on him. The second time he decided to fake a seizure when they started talking about using urine jugs to wake him up. It had worked. They walked back out of the engine space, laughing.

Stu knew that he'd actually passed out, too. *Probably concussed.* The boat was quiet. *Too quiet. Are we on a pier?* The thought of being tied to a pier was bittersweet. On the one hand it brought the hope of escape. On the other it could mean the bikers were done playing with their prey and ready to finish them off. He started scrambling with his hands, still bound with multiple wraps of duct tape behind his back.

He spent several hours rubbing the tape on a small jagged edge he felt on one of the multitude of hoses and manifolds surrounding the big diesel engine. The tape was slowly ripping and loosening, pulling skin and wrist hair with it. He no longer felt pain. His arms were numb from being pulled back for so long. He finally managed to break the tape. As soon as he wriggled one hand free he used that arm to sit up.

Whoa, he thought. *Slowly.* He had felt a head rush. *Even when we're free I won't be able to fight these guys.* He felt despair start to win over hope.

Once his head had settled a bit, he began rubbing his shoulders and arms, trying to get circulation back. After several minutes, he had freed his legs and finally felt somewhat mobile. He stood up and set an ear to the door. *Nothing.*

He slid the door open just a fraction of an inch, looking. Seeing nothing, he worked it open a little more. The process repeated itself until he realized the men weren't in the rear cabin. He stepped in. The scene of the crime was enough to make him start to cry again. His eyes moistened with the salty tears of guilt for failing his friend. There was blood—not enough to indicate danger. It was just enough to say *someone's been brutalized here.*

He moved forward to the galley area. It was too dark outside to see much from the portholes, but they were definitely tied up at a pier of some sort. He slowly crept to the stairs leading to the bridge cabin and listened, hearing nothing but waves and seagulls. *She's missing. I'm wounded. It's dark and somewhat rainy. No idea where we are. Now what do I do?*

22

Hippocratic Oath Breaker

Tahoma's Hammer + 12 Days.

The walk up the manicured lawn was eerie. There was very little moon above the clouds, which made it difficult to see. Stu had let his eyes adjust to the dark for a good half-hour—or at least that's what he told himself. In truth he was working up the nerve. The house and property around it were pitch black. *Too risky. Deal with the one most important problem, just like in surgery. Find her. Save her. For once in your life do something that matters.*

Though Stu could never imagine how horrible it must've been for Carmen, he *did* know that listening to it was the worst experience of his life. He felt void of almost any emotion that wasn't hate. The only feeling he had was one of no longer caring if he lived or died. His only sense of motivation to do anything at all was to find

Carmen. He had no delusions about what lay ahead. Unless he got lucky, the monsters would eat them both. *Luck…what the Hell is that? Luck is an illusion…* He had paused at the end of a brick wall that formed the edge of a large, exposed-aggregate patio, looking and listening. Still nothing.

Maybe they left? No. They're predators. They'll finish me off first.

The rain was starting again, stifling the breeze that had been blowing through the fir trees. He slowly walked over to the patio door, stopping just shy of stepping in front of it. His pulse pounded in his ears as he peeked in. Still nothing. The house was huge, with wings that branched off the main body, providing many rooms with patios and views of the water.

They could be watching me right now.

He didn't realize how calm he'd been until that moment. Now all he could hear was the blood in his ears. He pushed on the sliding door, half-expecting an alarm even though the power had been out for days. He looked around as he stepped in.

He froze, listening. He wanted to give his eyes more time.

If I accidentally bump something, I'm a dead-man!

He realized he was standing in some sort of breakfast nook just off a kitchen area. There was an arched doorway to the left. *Dining table over there.* He looked through another opening to the other side of the house. *Entry in there.* He walked that way.

Once he was near that portion of the house, he saw a grand set of stairs that stopped half-way up and turned around. He walked to the bottom of the stairs and stopped again, listening.

I wonder if they're sleeping…

He looked up the stairs and walked up to the half-way point. Now he was standing under a large skylight in the ceiling above and looking out over a sunken living room.

He suddenly gasped in a big breath of air—he was so tense that he'd forgotten to breathe for a long time. His body had jolted him back to it. He took two more cleansing breaths.

Are those… Yes, stuffed heads. The owner of this house is obviously a big-game hunter.

THUMP-THUMP. The blood in his ears was circulating the new air.

He went up the other half of the stairs, taking his time. He was in the zone, not much caring at this point if they discovered him. He was in a central hallway that led to multiple sub-halls and rooms. The floors were wood, and there was an expensive rug in the middle of it. It was at least fifty feet long. There were paintings of scenic mesas, Native Americans, and cowboys. The walls were decorated with a variety of hunting and trapping paraphernalia. He chose a direction and walked, continuing this process until he walked into what he figured was the master bedroom.

Here you are.

He was looking at the bodies of two well-to-do looking retirees. The man had been shot where he slept while the woman had just managed to fall out of bed before her own demise. She was lying on the floor. Both were covered in blood. Stu put the back of his hand on the man's hand.

Fairly cool. Probably been a few hours.

A thought evolved. *I bet a hunter has guns, huh?*

He started looking for those though he knew he may not be able to figure out how to use them. The house was still… dark… quiet… so he continued.

When he found his way to the wing at the far end, he walked in to what was a large room for entertaining. It had a billiard table— the nice kind with red felt. There was an extravagant bar adorned with many more hunting trophies. There were two, large leather couches with four matching chairs set up around a huge marble coffee table and centered on a 100-inch TV that adorned the wall.

Carmen was on one of the couches—naked and unconscious, covered in bruises, and bound in duct tape. Her face was swollen from being beaten. Stu turned his head and gasped. He tried to remain quiet. *I'm so sorry. I've failed you.* Once again his eyes turned salty and wet with emotion.

The last discovery was the most important one... There was a big pile of heroin and meth on the table with two stoned bikers passed out in recliners.

On the slow backwards walk out of the game room, Stu's heel had knocked an empty whiskey bottle across the floor and into a cabinet. *WWWHHHHAAAMMMM!* It was just one whiskey bottle, but it might as well have been an artillery shell.

Nothing.

They must be as high as kites... I don't believe it. They're dead to the world! Plain dumb lu... No. Shut Up. There's no such thing as luck.

Stu went to the owner's study and stared at an expensive collection of gun cases and cabinets. Most of them were locked, but the old man had apparently staged a few around the house. Stu had picked up several components—ammunition, pistols, rifles, magazines—and had no luck in figuring out how to use them. *I'm an LA doctor—I hate guns. Or at least... I used to.* It didn't much matter to Stu.

I have another idea. He headed for the kitchen.

THE DRUGS WEREN'T of the best quality this deep into the crisis. And the euphoria of a heroin-meth cocktail wasn't enough to keep the giant gang member asleep for his own death. Stu was pleased about that. Trip's bloodcurdling, deep-voiced screech was deafening in the still mansion. Stu had remembered a critical detail.

I'm a surgeon, and these two wolves have self-anaesthetized—hard! I don't need to know how to use a gun. Screw the Hippocratic Oath!

He had studied the knives in the kitchen. *No. This guy was a sportsman. I bet there's something much better on a wall somewhere.*

He found it in the library, which was where most of the mounted marlin and other fish had wound up. On the wall in a display cabinet was a collection. Stu picked out a very nice, Japanese filet knife. It had ribbon-looking Damascus steel.

I'll bet this thing has never even been used.

He had originally been thinking about the aorta, but he remembered it was much too protected.

THUMP-THUMP!

I get one shot with this huge beast. Can't afford to screw it up!

THUMP-THUMP!

He opted for the near-side carotid artery instead. He knew exactly wear to plunge and was able to side step most of the spray as he twisted, pulling the twelve-inch-long blade out of the big biker's neck with a slashing motion. The big man grabbed his throat on instinct as he sat upright, but it was too late. It was too dark and the drugs were too thick. Stu imagined that Trip had been able to recognize him as the curtains drew twelve seconds later. In all the excitement, Stu had forgotten about the flashlight he'd been holding.

Shorty hopped up when he heard his buddy screaming at the top of his lungs. The drug-induced stupor and the lack of lighting made it impossible for him to tell that his laces had been tied together as he tried to take a step. Just as he started to fall face first, Stu turned on the flashlight.

Shorty screamed in horror.

His drug-stupor had not been deep enough to disguise the bear trap in front of him as anything other than what it was. With almost karmic accuracy, Shorty fell precisely where Stu had wanted him to. He threw his hands up in a reflexive attempt to break his fall. The trap wasn't an overly complicated device. There was a device with a gear and crank that assisted with springing it open in a slow, controlled fashion. Stu had tested it with a shoe in the master bedroom. He was surprised by how anti-climatic it was.

Shorty's hands hit the trigger plate.

The trap released its jaws with about four hundred pounds of pressure. They clamped tight onto both arms with lightning speed, crunching bone and ripping arteries. The left arm popped off entirely right were the radius and ulna met the humerus, ripping open his flesh with an audible tear. Shorty's right arm remained stuck in the trap. The little man's screams started about six seconds before his partner's died off.

Stu would never forget the sound of both men's screams playing in harmony.

He held out for quite a bit longer, screaming and flopping and watching his arms shoot blood onto the wall and TV across from him for a good minute before the lights went out for the final time.

23

Things Will Never Be The Same.

Tahoma's Hammer + 12 Days.

Phil had not expected his first tweeker house raid to be so slow. With the exception of one event, there had been no activity all evening or night. *They must have water and a gravity-septic system...or else it is disgusting as hell in there.*

Around 7:00 PM, the back door opened and a mangy tan and white pit bull came out. It relieved itself, and then it must've gotten a whiff of Phil's scent. It started barking in his direction and started a slow-creeping investigation. Phil was about five meters back into the woods. He readied his coyote-brown AR-15, which was fitted with a custom sound-suppressor. While quite effective, they still put out more than a whisper, contrary to what TV shows led people to believe.

The dog passed the assortment of junk lining the property—things like a discarded washing machine, an old door-less refrigerator, a car that hadn't moved in years—and raised the barking to include throat growls. It was standing at the brush line. It knew Phil was there, and it was a matter of moments before it defended its territory with its teeth.

The dog let out a whelp as Eli's carbon-fiber arrow tipped with a broadhead pushed its way through the dog's heart and lungs at roughly two hundred miles-per-hour. The missile, designed to take down elk, passed through the canine and imbedded itself in the brush and dirt about ten feet to the dog's left. The shot surprised Phil, too. It took him a second or two to react.

Phil pulled the fixed-blade knife out of the holster on his battle belt and began to creep forward, keeping his frame lower than the junk between the dog and the house. He was thankful that his half-leg was amputated below the knee. It made crouching and such a little easier than the above-joint amputees he'd met at the VA hospital. It was a moot point. The yelping and whimpering stopped about three seconds later as the dog bled out. He re-sheathed the knife and pulled the animal into the woods, gently pushing it into some bushes and out of sight.

Now that's ironic. Who'd a thought we'd shoot their dog with an arrow. He felt a bit angry—not with Eli but with the jerks who'd let this dog start starving to death. Some of the sweetest dogs he'd ever met were pit bulls. *Rest in peace, girl. I don't take the fact that you were about to eat my face personally.*

He waited for the reaction from the house—and waited some more. *I bet these losers let this dog run around out here for hours without even checking on it.* Even if these people weren't the abductors, it sat well with him as an act of mercy that Eli put that dog out of its own misery.

[Brrrt—Josh: "???"]

[Brrrt—Eli: "Shot a dog that was about to eat Phil."]

[Phil: "Saved us from blowing our concealment. Thx."]

About an hour later, Phil texted for each person to get two hours of sleep starting with Jeff and working clockwise. He decided he'd throw the other Gotenna up into a tree at 0200 when he got up from his nap.

The rain came back, testing everyone's resolve. He felt fortunate to have these men with him, shouldering this burden. He gave a silent prayer, starting with his usual confession and ending with a plead to protect his granddaughter. *Please let this be them, Lord. I can't face Payton if it isn't.*

Around 8:00 AM, Jeff sent out an alert. [Brrrt—Jeff: "There's noise coming from up the driveway. What do I do?"] There was an attached "worried-face" emoji.

Phil half hoped Jeff wouldn't check the phone, but he wanted to get this message out before Eli responded. [Phil: "B still"]

Soon enough a green van slowly pulled up to the front of the property. *Is that a county van?* Phil asked himself. He couldn't believe his eyes. It was a county-owned corrections-department van. Phil always saw this van parked near where ever the local lock ups were cleaning trash on the side of the road. It stopped and idled long enough for the passenger in the front to get out and open the double side-doors. From his vantage he couldn't tell what was happening. Soon he heard the van slowly back up and turn down the long dirt road. A minute later it could no longer be heard. He still couldn't see who had gotten out but figured they must've gone inside. He waited for a sit-rep from Josh.

[Brrrt—Josh: "Sketchiest perv ever just went in. Greeted by sketchy female. She looked stoned. Yelling started almost immediately"]

Phil decided to save battery and not reply. About three minutes later the backdoor flung open, allowing the voices of two arguing adults to be heard. The new arrival stepped out onto the small, rotting three-by-four-foot landing outside the back door. *What a scumbag*, Phil thought instantly. He had filthy clothes on—*probably what he was arrested in.* He was a middle-aged white man, average height, thin build, with long and thinning light-brown and gray hair. His face was covered in stubble and showed the wrinkles that came early in life to people who partied all the time.

"...your fault if anything happens to that dog!" he yelled at the woman behind him as he stepped out. She hadn't come out enough for Phil to see her, and he couldn't clearly hear her retort.

"Damned-dog... Food... money... a-hole!"

"Angel!" the tweeker yelled into the woods. "Here, girl!" He waited a few seconds. "Angel!" He turned around and headed back into the house. Phil could hear yelling as he slammed the door behind him, and he could still hear it even after the door was closed. *They're starting to go at it. Probably a normal morning for them. So much for warm reunions.*

Two minutes later the door flew open once more as the man came out. "...more frickin' mouths to feed!" She followed him out.

Phil's heart thumped hard. *Her!* It was the woman who had stared him down as she passed by the range. She had followed the man out to continue the fight.

"Angel!" he yelled again.

"... got her for you, Harry! I know that's what you like. Help you git your nut, since you don't like *my* old worn-out parts anymore! A-hole! Take her back! See if I..." The woman had turned back in and Phil couldn't hear the rest. Just a few seconds later she reappeared.

What the... Phil pulled his small waterproof binoculars closer to his eyes and held it as steady as he could. *...Hell?* His hands started to shake with rage. He dropped the binoculars at the base of the bush he was behind and put his hands on his temples, sighing out a deep breath. *Lord, please...* He picked the binoculars back up and took another look. The old woman and thrown it at Harry in anger. Laying on the ground was a multi-colored backpack, covered in unicorns.

He picked up the cell and sent a text. [Phil: "Confirmation wait 1"] He needed to stop his hands from shaking. He could feel his face getting hot. He took another deep breath and picked the phone back up.

[Phil: "Josh. South route to my OP"]

[Phil: "Jeff. Stay put. Runners will go up the driveway. Do nothing to them unless threatened. Then shoot—2 in chest 1 in head"]

[Phil: "Eli. Stay put cover back. Switch 2 pistol after first arrow"

[Brrrt—Josh: "Copy eta 15"]

Josh was careful not to be seen. He would have preferred to take an entire half hour to make a maneuver around the south over to Phil's position, but he knew things were in play now that "Harry" was home.

When he arrived at the position, he dumped his pack next to Phil's. "What'd you see?"

"The backpack Savannah wears every waking hour." Phil looked the combat vet in the eyes. Josh was there, one hundred percent primed. *Thank you, God, for sending me this vet today.* "You good to go?"

"What's the plan?" Josh asked with a head nod, almost insulted by the question.

"On 'Go,' we're going to run in to the concealment of that fridge and washer. Quick scan, then glide in. We'll both stack on the handle side, since it's daylight—stay out of the door's windows. I'll breech for myself and take the path of least resistance. Cover the opposite zone. Standard two man sweep and maneuver. Clear?"

"ROE?" Josh was wanting to know what the rules of engagement were.

"No telling how they'll react. No way of knowing if they're armed. Low on drugs and off-their-meds crazy is bad enough. Watch the hands. Only shoot if you have to. I plan on getting the sheriffs out here."

"Roger that," Josh said.

The two combat vets slid to the edge of the brush in a crouched position and took a deep breath. "Go."

THE MEN'S screams had caused a severe screaming episode for Carmen, too. It wasn't until Stu had the sense to shine the flashlight on his own face that she stopped screaming and writhing on the couch. She switched to bawling hysterically.

"They're dead. They're gone." Stu kept repeating himself, trying to get her to understand that the threat was over. He removed the tape-gag from her head. "I'm going to get a blanket. I'll be right back. I *am* the *only* person here. There is no one else in the house alive." His heart was aching for what she must be going through.

Stu left and came back in a minute with a big quilt. He held the flashlight on his own face again so that she'd know it was him. "Carmen. I'm going to come over and help you." He could hear her huffing and puffing loudly—borderline hyper-ventilating.

He knelt on one knee next to her and covered her with the quilt. He realized she was still bound. "I'm going to uncover your hands so I can un-tie you." He got no reaction from her regarding the comment. She refused to look at him or speak. As gently as he could he removed her hand and foot bindings. She flinched every time he accidentally touched her.

"I'm going to move you to a different room. Okay?" Nothing in return from her. "We just need to get out of this room. I'll treat your injuries in a clean bedroom." Still no response. Stu kept the quilt between his arms and her naked body as he scooped her off the couch. She stayed curled in the fetal position as much as possible as he carried her into one of the guest bedrooms and laid her on a bed. He found a couple of candles in the study and used them to light Carmen's room.

"Carmen. I'm going to clean you up some. Your arms, legs, back...face. I won't touch anything I shouldn't. I need to see how bad your injuries are." She was still ignoring him. "I'm going to figure out how to warm some water. I will call out to you to let you know when I'm coming back in."

Once again Stu felt things inside himself he'd not experienced his whole adult life—sympathy, remorse, compassion, even love… *I'm so sorry, sweetie.* Something happened inside the doctor when he slayed the monsters. He didn't know it yet, but he'd been reborn. The weak and pathetic socialite had been destroyed—a process started when the hammer fell and finished when he learned the difference between killing and murder a few hours earlier. Doctor Stuart Schwartz was a new man.

THE UNITED STATES NAVY 3rd Fleet had thrown everything that was available into a pair of operations, and it wasn't as much as the average citizen would think. Thirty years of poor national policy and planning were hard to make up for. In the early 1990s, American bases and ships were on the chopping block called "BRAC", the nickname of the Congressional Committee for Base Realignment and Closure. We'd won the Cold War. President Reagan's six hundred-ship fleet was 20th Century thinking. We were ushering in an age of world peace—a "new world order," according to President George HW Bush.

The attacks of September 11th, 2001 triggered two decades of war and taxed the members of the military with deployment cycles that nearly matched those of World War II—but for five times as many years. The "we don't need ships" mindset was hard to shake in Washington DC once the idiots on both sides of the aisle were used to spending the money in other, more wasteful areas. In the last few years before Tahoma's Hammer, though, an outsider had seen the light. He was trying to "right the ship" with a rebuilt Navy. Few realized that it would take the same thirty years to rebuild that the state of readiness had taken to decay. The current public and private shipyards were trying to keep up with maintenance and equipment upgrade cycles. Those shipyards that built ships just didn't have the dry-docks, facilities, or skilled people to manufacture ships at the necessary rate.

The Joint USN/USMC Strike Group, "Task Force Truxtun," had scrounged up as many ships as they could to support two operations in the Rainier Impact Zone. The largest were twelve amphibious ships of various classes. Each was designed with its own function in mind for war, but for peace time operations they could all do the essentials—haul food, people, and equipment. The Task Force had taken several days to load those items and set sail. They conducted briefs and training on the way up, learning the key aspects of both operations just in case unplanned events forced mutual support.

"Operation SOS" was meant to do one thing—support the missions at the shipyard and, to a lesser degree, assist the community. Warding off the potential nuclear disaster and preventing the loss of an aircraft carrier to flooding were their sole objectives. But they knew that workers would work longer if they knew their loved ones were being cared for, so provide that care they did. They'd left the distribution headaches to the locals to handle.

There was only one possible thing that could trump those objectives and that was securing the arsenal and delivery systems that may or may not have been stored at the Bogdon Submarine Base. The security at Bogdon was ironclad, but it was never intended to run unsupplied for an indefinite amount of time. Within two minutes of the news that Cascadia had fallen, there were military officers dusting off the binders with the response to this contingency already spelled out in them. Thus, "Operation Citadel Rampart" was born. Forces and supplies, first by air and then by sea, were being sent to Bogdon to secure it and its equipment. They were to transport the nastiest of that weaponry by sea to other locations for safe keeping.

It was a Sunday morning, and the shipyard workers had been told the day before to expect it. Crane and his co-workers were enjoying a hot breakfast and late start at "Camp Yardbird" when they first heard them coming. The loud bass thumping was barely audible in the beginning. The reverberations off the hillsides and waters of the inlet increased as the fleet of rotor-winged aircraft approached, each bird carrying three very stuffed pallets of goods in a net hanging under it. In a scene that had replayed itself over every person the aircraft passed from the coast to Bartlett, the helicopters were assaulted from below with friendly waves and smiles. People just assumed it was over. *We're saved!* they thought, seeing that many helicopters.

One occasional helicopter was not unheard of since the hammer fell, but this was different. They were coming in waves, like something from *Apocalypse Now.* Many people tried to count them all, but it was impossible—the sorties were spread out with one- to two-minute gaps to allow the ones ahead to drop their loot and get out of the way.

THWUMP-WUMP-WUMP-WUMP-WUMP! The gray MH-60Ss approached the Navy base from the southwest. Almost every able-bodied person heard them and ran outside—drizzle or not—to see what the ruckus was. The workers at the Slaughter County EOC on the hill in West Bartlett had one of the best views due to the elevation. There were close to three hundred county employees, volunteers, and Guardsmen watching as the four helicopters in each leg would adjust from a diamond shape to a staggered column once they were over the waters of Simpson Inlet. From there they spaced themselves out by adjusting speed. By the time the birds were approaching the Navy base a mile farther east they looked like little seagulls.

Most of the helicopters would come in and hover over one of two parking lots to the south of the worker's camp, Crane noticed. He was impressed at their effectiveness—proud that these bad-ass Americans had dedicated themselves to being the best. People like Commander Rebekah Paddington, call-sign "Def-Woman," who effortlessly glided her lumbering aircraft in to a spot she'd never flown before, hovered, and set down a slung-load of supplies—

finally cutting loose and pulling away less than thirty seconds later. The continuous noise of rotor blades "thwumping" assaulted the ears in a good way.

By the time the fourth helicopter had lifted and flown north out of the way, the next sortie of four were gliding in for their turns.

Crane noticed that four helicopters had taken turns landing at the commissary and exchange parking lots. They had stayed there for several minutes dropping off people, most of them in uniform, before joining the "hel-exit" operation.

Crane had no idea how many helicopters had come-in—*forty? Fifty? I wouldn't be surprised if someone told me seventy-five*—but he was glad he got to see it. He had goose-bumps. *I wonder where they came from?* The re-supply mission lasted almost an entire hour. The flying armada of hope had lifted everyone's spirits in an unpredictable way.

STACKED on the backdoor's right side, Phil made a snap decision to try keeping their surprise element as long as possible. He knew it wouldn't last much longer in the single-wide mobile, but anything would help considering they had no idea how many people were in there. He turned the knob and pulled the door open just enough to look down a long hall to the left. It was dark with only daylight coming from the windows scattered throughout. It was a bit of luck that the backdoor opened into a long, slender hallway that fed the three bedrooms and one bathroom. He could hear voices at the far end, presumably in the kitchen or living room area.

He turned his head and whispered to Josh, "We're both going left. Cover the six." Josh nodded.

Phil slid his left arm back out through the sling, leaving the rifle draped only over his neck. He did this to provide extra slack, knowing he may have to re-shoulder to his left side in the tight hall-way. He pulled the door open knowing it was mere seconds before this was all over. He could feel his pulse and respirations going up, compensating for the blood pressure increase that happens when the body surges itself with adrenaline and cortisol. He stepped in, fighting the instinct to look right and trusting his partner to be there covering it before a dirtbag could get the drop on him. He immediately started up the hallway.

Josh didn't let Phil down. He was moving towards Phil's space the instant he saw a shift in Phil's weight. Josh had his barrel pointing up at high ready, pushing the flash-suppressor down and level as it passed the doorjamb. As Phil moved in, Josh was pivoting to the right, using his peripheral vision to scan the entire darkened space from left to right as he entered. Two doors were closed with the two at the far-right end of the hall were open. He could only see daylight creeping from those rooms, with no sign of movement. All of this took one second. Josh did a lightning fast head turn combined with shifting his eyes in order to know where Phil was. He knew he had about three small strides to walk backwards before he had to re-check.

Phil had walked the ten feet down to the left end of the hall, scanning the scene before him. He saw one unexpected male, a young adult with long blonde hair sitting on a barstool at the kitchen's small counter. He was eating peanut butter directly off a butter knife. Phil heard Harry and the female arguing down at the far end of the trailer. He couldn't see any others. He assessed all of this in a quick moment, barely slowing down. He entered the kitchen. As he cleared the hall's threshold—transitioning from old, nasty shag carpet to worn out vinyl—he spun to the right to check the corner, knowing his partner was too busy covering the rear and walking backwards. This took a half-second before he spun back to cover the nearest male.

At this moment they locked eyes. The young male could hardly believe his eyes. "What the—"

Wham! Too late. Phil was already on him. He landed a left across the young man's chin, keeping his right hand on the rifle's pistol grip. The skinny-tweeker flew off the stool, hitting the floor at the same instant that Phil had his rifle back to level and trained on the other two. "Hands in the air! Now!"

He repeated himself at full volume over their protests, which ramped up the confusion. Harry was bargaining, while the woman was barking in protest, dropping f-bombs like she was a B-52. Harry was scanning the room and out the window, instinctively looking for the rest of the SWAT team. "What the Hell, man! This is entrapment! You a-holes just let me out this morning!"

Phil changed his commands. "I'm not a cop! Get on the floor! Or die—I really don't care which!" Both meth-heads were still barking and not listening. Phil issued more commands. "Get on your knees! I'm here for the girl!"

The lightbulb came on over the woman's head. "You!" The look of disgusted resentment came back to her face.

"Yeah...me," Phil said coldly. "You got 'im?" Phil yelled back to Josh, checking on the status of the one he knocked over.

"Yep."

Phil moved forward to the pair, keeping his rifle trained on Harry, who was standing between a cheap wood coffee table and an old holey couch. The woman was closer, looking indignantly at Phil. He wasn't having any. "On your knees. Now!"

"No, you son of—"

Wham! It was the first time Phil had ever punched a woman. *At least I used my left hand,* he thought. He hadn't held up—he used full force born from hatred. She flew backwards into an easy chair and then thumped to the floor, knocked out cold. Harry made a shift in weight, and Phil immediately re-covered him with his rifle.

"Please do," Phil said. Seeing Harry had wised up, he said, "On your knees...hands on the back of your head. Or else." Phil clicked his safety off, causing Harry's eyes to widen.

Harry complied. He clicked the safety back on and drew his pistol from his belt-mounted holster while using his left hand to lower the rifle to that side of his body. Keeping his Glock in his right hand and on the far side of himself from Harry, he rounded the coffee table and grabbed the tweeker by the back of the head, shoving it down to the table with full force. Harry let out a whelp as his nose-cartilage broke loose and started shooting blood. From the kneeling position he began yelling protests again, claiming police brutality.

Phil ignored him, lifting his metal leg through the gap between Harry and the sofa so he could straddle him from behind. He bent his knees, putting his weight onto Harry's back and keeping his left hand on top of Harry's hands and head. He re-holstered the pistol and used his right hand to rip open a Velcro map-sleeve on the front of his plate carrier. He pulled out one of the two heavy-duty zip-ties that he kept pre-looped in that sleeve and secured the dirtbag's hands behind his back. He hauled Harry up and drug him around, shoving him onto the couch in a seated position. He stepped out of reach and did another check on the woman. Seeing only a marginal amount of movement from her, he crossed over the space to Josh, handing him a zip-tie.

"Cover 'em," he told his squad-mate.

Phil re-drew his pistol and went back to the other end of the hallway. He stopped at the first bedroom door and crouched, turning the knob and shoving the door inward. He slowly cut the angle on the doorway while covering the opening with his pistol. He was using a bent-elbow technique and keeping the sights of the tan Glock in his site-picture but focusing on the room.

"Savannah. It's Paw-paw." He expected to hear nothing. The room was stuffed with garbage, old magazines, rotting food —*Howcan people live this way?* Phil thought once again. He felt his blood getting hot. *I may just kill them if she's not here.* He went down to the other closed door and repeated the process. "Peaches. It's me."

All quiet for a few, heart-stopping seconds. "H-Hello?" a scared, tiny voice murmured.

"Honey, its Paw-paw!" Phil called. His voice was calm, but

inside he felt a sense of elation he'd never experienced before. *Thank you, God!* "It's okay. Come here."

She ran over to her grandfather and jumped into his open arms, bawling. She was sobbing so hard she was shaking. Phil could have held her for hours, but he was keenly aware of his partner's situation. "Peaches," he said picking her up as he stood. "I'm going to take you outside and Mr. Don's family is going to protect you for a minute while I come back in here."

"You okay?" he asked Josh as he got to the back-door.

"One hundred percent."

"Be right back." Phil waved over Eli when he got outside. He handed off his granddaughter and reassured her once more. He went back inside and cleared the last two rooms. Returning to the living room, he saw that Josh had zip-tied the younger man's hands. He then found a modem near the cable TV and pulled out a phone line with an angry yank. He went over to the moaning woman, flipped her over onto her front as roughly as he could, and tied her hands behind her back with the phone line.

He stood back upright and said to Harry, "Now. Let's find out why you were in jail and why you were let out. Oh—and don't give in *too* quickly. *Please.*"

24

Out of the Woods.

Across Washington and the rest of the Pacific Northwest prepper groups were finally starting to amass at their retreat locations. Those with the foresight and fortune to live there year-round were busy preparing for the arrival of their friends, family, and partners. Foxholes were being dug, extra firewood cut—a multitude of things that would make life for four or five families in tight quarters somewhat comfortable. The people had good reason to flee. Murders were on the rise, sometimes the result of theft gone bad and sometimes old grudges being settled. Entire rows of homes in some neighborhoods were evolving their small local squabbles into the blood feuds of the old days. And there was nobody to stop them.

There was a lot less driving in Cascadia, too. Gasoline was too valuable, and riding in a car or truck was a surefire way to put a target on your back. So was running a generator. People were quickly finding out that if they wanted power, they'd better have a protection plan in place. As the use of vehicles decreased, the amount of old-school travel technologies increased—mostly walking. Horses and bicycles were becoming more common, too, but like generators, horses caught the attention of those that wanted them. When people did drive, it wasn't like the old days. Windows were left down so that watchers could see that the vehicle was stuffed full of people and rifles. *If you want what's ours, you'd better be ready to pay admission...*

In Slaughter County the people were also growing quite vocal about the helicopters. The Navy had turned over quite a bit of goods to the big FEMA camp in Bartlett, but it wasn't nearly enough. Rumor had it that the shipyard workers were hoarding it for themselves. Years of watching the "anti-fascist" protest groups riot unchecked had taught society that the correct course of action was to complain about what was owed to them. There were rumors of a planned protest in Bartlett.

Across the pond in King and Snohomish Counties a rumor had spread that Boeing's Paine Field was open for business, which was by far untrue but grounded in a promising report of reasonable reparability. Hundreds of thousands of survivors from several counties had started making the pilgrimage toward the fleet of supply stuffed airplanes that were supposedly on the way. The thirst and hunger fueled riots that resulted when they learned the truth left many thousands dead.

"WHAT DA' Hell, man?" Harry yelled, his voice rising in fear. "Git away wit' that! No need to be hostile, bro!"

"I wanna see what's under that bandage," Phil said flatly. He had drawn his knife out of its kydex scabbard and was using it to

slice the bandage off Harry's right wrist. "That's an awfully conspic-
uous place. You didn't try slicing your wrists did you, Harry?"

Harry was bound to an old, yellow vinyl dining chair, tied up
with paracord on all four limbs. Josh was posted at the hallway's
intersection with the kitchen, keeping an eye on the room they had
dragged the other two into.

"Suck my nuts, soldier-boy! I ain't tellin' you *jack*!" Harry made
the intake suction sound of someone about to spit when Phil's left
hand reached out and grabbed his throat, squeezing.

"You'd better swallow that! I'm not the cops. I'm still trying to
decide if the coyotes get to dine on you tonight." Phil was bluffing,
but Harry didn't know that. He'd radioed Jerry at the Command
Post earlier, instructing him to use his HAM magic to let the sheriff's
office know they'd found Savannah. He had no intent of making her
wait any longer than necessary to go home, but…*might as well extract
some intel while I'm waiting for them to show up.*

After about ten seconds, Harry started to flush in the face and
tear up, so Phil let go of his larynx. Harry wisely chose to swallow
the loogey. Phil sliced off the rest of the bandage. "What the…"

Harry was silent, scowling about his predicament.

"What's this?" No response. Phil smashed the base of his left
hand into the right side of Harry's head. "What is this?!" He was
looking at a little incision, barely a quarter inch, not even long
enough to need a stitch. *He sure as Hell didn't try to slice his wrist…*

"I dunno," Harry mumbled, staring at the floor.

"What?" Phil had lowered his face to be level with his prisoner's.

"I don't know, man!" Harry yelled. "They were doin' it to all of
us. No explanation! No choice!" After twenty minutes, Harry'd had
enough. "They drug us by block, man. Out to temp-holding. Gave
us a shot and gave us our belongin's back! Said they were letting us
go. Who was *I* to argue?"

"Incoming," Phil heard on his and Josh's radios. Harry's face
was worried.

"What's goin' on, man?" asked Harry. Phil was walking toward

the back doorway. "Hey, c'mon, man, I been straight wit'ch you—"
he heard Harry pleading as he went outside.

The first thing he did was scan for Eli's post. There was the tarp
with Eli and Savannah sitting under it. Eli gave him a thumbs up.

"Roger, that." Phil replied into the radio. "Whatcha got?"

Jeff replied, "We got one… no, make that two Sheriff's
department vehicles… Wait. They've stopped. They're just sitting
there."

Phil could suddenly hear the squad car's speaker blaring, but he
was too far away and on the wrong side of the house to make out
what was being said. "Can you relay?" he asked Jeff.

"He said your name. And he said his name is Charlie."

"Roger that. Just sit there. I'm coming up."

With his rifle still slung around his neck, Phil put his hands on
the back of his head and walked around the junk and the house to
the front driveway. He finally made it to a point in the dirt road
where he could see the two sheriff's rigs about a hundred meters
away. He kept his hands on his head and made his unusual one-
plus-a-partial-leg maneuver to get onto his knees.

The two rigs began creeping up slowly. They parked, and
Charlie Reeves got out of the first one. A male deputy that Phil
didn't know got out of the other.

"Well, well," Charlie said. "Get up, man. You look ridiculous,"
he said, smiling.

Phil stood up and said, "Yeah, well, ridiculous beats getting shot.
Ask me how I know." The two friends fist-bumped, and Charlie
waved his partner up.

"Phil, Wayne. Wayne, Phil." The two men shook hands. "So,
you found Savannah here…"

"Yep." He could read the quizzing look his friend was giving
him. "She's around back, safe. With a friend."

"How many 'friends' do you have here?"

Charlie's all-deputy right now, isn't he? He looks tired. "Three. How do
you want me to play it?"

"Call them over." Charlie shot Wayne a look, telling him it was okay.

Phil keyed up his mic. "West and North perimeter—fall in, my position. Bring the package with you. Interior, you stay put." Even with the authorities involved, Phil didn't dare say anyone's name on the air. Anybody could be listening. "I'm leaving one in the hall, right at the back of the kitchen," Phil told Charlie. "Name's Josh. He's guarding three adults—one male and one female in a bedroom and one male in the kitchen. All are restrained."

"Alright," Charlie agreed. "Wayne, go check on Josh." Wayne took off while Phil radioed Josh to let him know he was getting a visitor.

"So, while we're alone, brother, let me ask you something," Phil said.

"Shoot."

"Why was this effin' pervert *chipped*..." He paused for emphasis on that word, "and released this morning?" Phil could feel his anger building. "There are girl's panties in there that *don't* belong to Savannah!"

"Phil, I get it. It's bad—"

"Darn tootin' it's bad," Phil said cutting his friend off.

Charlie put his hands up at chest height to diffuse Phil's emotion. "Look, we don't make policy decisions down here in the trenches. What I mean is, *it's bad*. Things right now are not good, and they're only gonna get worse. The county can't feed the inmates. There's no choice."

"No choice!" Phil was incredulous. "There's *always* a choice when it comes to sexual predators!"

"Phil, it is what it is. There's no changing it. I don't know what you want to hear, but I'm giving you the truth out of respect."

Eli, Savannah, and Jeff approached at this point, sensing that the conversation was a bit strained. "Hey," Eli said on behalf of the group. Savannah went right past Charlie and to her Paw-paw's legs.

"Hey, Savannah," Charlie said, squatting to let her look eye to eye with him. "Remember me? We met at your grandpa's last year, at a bar-b-que. Also, my kids are Charles Jr. and Kiersten. They live at the range with you, now."

She nodded. Everyone could tell she was just ready to get home, find her mama, and get some sleep.

"Good," Charlie continued. "Say, in just a little while, a lady deputy—dressed in the same uniform as me—will come by to talk to your mom. She may ask you some questions, too. Is that okay?"

"Y-yeah-h," she mumbled, nodding her head.

Charlie looked at Eli. "Why don't you all go wait by Deputy Luzon's car?"

Eli took the hint and shepherded Savannah and Jeff in that direction. Charlie started for the house, dodging piles of trash on the front porch as he walked. Phil followed him.

Wayne had Harry untied from the chair and was frisking him. Charlie saw the piles of paracord around the chair and shot Phil a scowl.

Don't judge me, friend, Phil shot back with his own look. *It wasn't your grandkid.*

"The other two?" Charlie asked.

"Down in the last bedroom," Josh answered.

Charlie gave Josh a once over as he passed him, heading to the back room to evaluate the situation fully. Phil could hear them both start to bark about assault and lawyers. Charlie was back in the kitchen in less than a minute. He instructed Wayne and Josh to sit tight and watch everyone, and then he gave Phil a nod to follow him back outside.

Back out in the yard, he broke it down to his friend. "Look. The reality is…I'm supposed to confiscate your guns."

The air between them suddenly became still. Phil's eyes locked on his friends as his mind began to race. *Ironic. This is the one man in the world I honestly owe my life to.* "Well, that's certainly interesting," he said slowly and purposefully. *Did it suddenly get hot out here?*

"Phil…it's me." Charlie scanned his friend's face. "I got your back on this. I just thought you should know. We've been ordered to collect all weaponry from any incident involving violence."

Phil let out a breath. "Yeah, well…if there had been violence—other than the kidnapping of my granddaughter—you'd have never been called."

Charlie sighed. "I get it. All I ask is that you think of the pickle that the cops and the government are in. Entire neighborhoods are setting up armed check points, for Pete's sake! The county is doing their best to get a grip on a deteriorating situation."

"I do, Charlie. Look, I owe you a debt I can never repay. But I need you to remember why I was lying there bleeding in the first place. I know *exactly* what you guys put on the line every day. All I ask in return is for the cops to remember who's on their side—who's using guns to guard their families while they're at work," Phil reminded him.

The two friends were at an impasse, each wondering where this path would lead them.

CARMEN MARTINEZ DIDN'T NOTICE the beauty of the mansion. She didn't notice the polished marble counters or the art or the expensive furniture. She didn't look out the windows and see the beautifully manicured lawns. She didn't notice that the marine layer had burnt through, revealing a blue sky, autumn morning—the kind they put on postcards—if just for a little while. She was still in a daze of shock and anger. She was only following Stu's voice prompts because the prior week and a half had felt like a lifetime and every person before Stu felt like a distant dream. His was the one voice she could trust.

Stu brought her into the breakfast nook and instructed her to sit. He had found some bottled water and canned goods and set them out for her. *I'm not hungry,* she told herself at the same moment she was gulping down two bottles of water. Thirst was a more primal pang—it couldn't be pushed to the back of the mind like hunger could. Stu had wandered off to continue the search for clothing and equipment. Carmen could hear knocking on the front door, though she wasn't really listening.

She sat there in her shocked stupor, listening to the pounding increase. *Is someone yelling? Who cares,* she scolded herself. The whole world could go screw itself. *Nothing matters anymore.*

Stu came flying back down the stairs with an armload of clothing. He glanced through the doorway to make sure she was still there and then went to the front door. "Yes?" he asked through the door.

"Oscar?" he heard. "You're not Oscar! Who is this? Open up!"

Stu looked through the peephole and saw a nicely dressed, retiree aged man with a full head of neatly groomed white hair. He couldn't see the man's hands. "Okay," he hollered through the door. He placed his foot behind the door near the opening side about two inches and shifted his stance so there was quite a bit of weight on it. He opened the door to his foot and peeked out the gap as best as he could.

"Who's in there?" the man demanded. "I saw your boat! I'm going to get someone!" He started to back away.

"Wait. Doctor! I'm a doctor. Name's Dr. Schwartz!" Stu opened the door far enough to prop his face out. He hoped that two weeks of facial hair hadn't yet damaged his appearance.

The man looked back. "Where's the Nelsons?" He looked like he was ready to square up and throw down, old school.

Stu opened the door enough to step out with his hands raised. "There was an incident..." He didn't know where to begin. "The homeowners are dead, and so are the animals that killed them."

The old man stared, disbelieving. "No. No, that isn't right. I just talked to Oscar last night." He was clearly pondering what Stu was saying. "Wait. Doctor?" He stared at Stu for a moment. "Just what is going on here?"

"My friend and I were abducted and...brutalized. We were tied up on the boat. I managed to escape. In the middle of the night, I was able to sneak in and...stop them. But...too late to help your friends...I'm sorry." Phil had put his hands down by then, not too worried about the man. The visitor's demeanor had slumped with the shock of the news.

The man said he was the Nelsons' neighbor and had come by to check on them when he saw the boat, particularly after Oscar had failed to show up for a daily community meeting that morning. At the neighbor's insistence, Stu let him in to see the situation for himself. The man was already shocked by the events, but he paled when he saw the manner in which the two criminals had perished. When he met Carmen, he could tell that by the swelling and bruises on her face that Stu's story was true. He didn't press her for conversation.

The old man was at a loss for what to do. Stu reminded him that he and Carmen were victims, too, and they needed some time to themselves to recover. He asked that the man give them a day to clean up before he told anyone. The neighbor mulled that over for a bit. In exchange, Stu explained, he would write a letter detailing everything and providing his contact information. He would even leave one of his business cards.

"Look—we're in a pinch," Stu said as the man was preparing to depart. "I don't know how to say this without sounding opportunistic, but—Oscar isn't going to be needing some of his clothes anymore..."

"True," the man said, nodding.

"Or...a few pieces of gear. Like, his camping stuff, some food, or...his car."

"No, no, no—clothes and gear are one thing. His car? No way!"

Stu thought for a minute. "Okay, tell me this. Where are we, exactly?"

The man was dumbfounded. "F-Fox Island," he stammered, not believing that Stu didn't know.

"Island?" Stu repeated. "Please tell me there's a bridge."

"There is, which we've set up a guard station on."

Stu saw the lightbulb come on for the man. The people on this island had been smugly sure that they were secure. The neighbor was looking out the window toward the boat on the pier. He was figuring out that islands and mansions were no guarantee of safety. "You'll have to pass through them to get off the island."

"How about a counter offer, then? Maybe you can give us a ride off the island, maybe even to Gig Harbor."

The old man was sullen, reality slowly sinking in. He had to tell his peers what was happening. "Here's the scoop," he said. "I'm going to report all of this, but I'll explain *everything* to the rest of the neighborhood and keep them out of here for the night. Tomorrow, I'll give you two a ride off the island. But I'm definitely not taking you all the way to Gig Harbor! The world has changed. I'm too old to risk my life for strangers."

THE FERRY WAS PACKED TIGHTLY with bodies, bicycles, and backpacks. There had been two successful runs the day before, and Talia and Tasha's class had been given spots on the day two runs. The ferry system was limited in capacity by only having one usable slip in each city—Seattle and Bartlett. Other limits included limited fuel and crew resources. The stated objective was to get people back to their families with the ulterior motive of hoping that those families would feed them.

Tony couldn't believe what he was seeing. The day was quite clear, and the shorelines on both sides of the passage into Simpson Inlet were dotted with seagulls. *There must be thousands*, Tony thought. *Dozens of thousands. Where'd they all come from?* The seagulls were feasting on the crabs that were feasting on the countless bloated bodies that had washed up on shore. They were hard to see in all the tree- and house-rubble that made the shoreline look like a wasteland. He'd been able to take a better look at Russell Island—he was in awe at the sheer volume of the landslide that had disappeared into the Sound.

Marine hazards were still a valid threat to the ferries. The usual fifty-five-minute run now took over two hours. When they got to the approach lane to the terminal in Bartlett, Tony couldn't believe his eyes. He was looking at a ferry and pier debris that had been pushed up onto the shore to the north. After the ferry turned to approach the slip from the south, he heard a commotion on the port side of the ship and decided to investigate. "Follow me, girls." The twins were never more than five feet away.

Ho-Ly crap... Tony couldn't believe his eyes. The stoic Hammerhead crane was tipped over, standing out of the water like a giant green robot that had been beaten in combat by a giant green lizard. People were gawking and whispering. Some were even quietly crying to themselves. The thought that the "indestructible" had been destroyed made them feel vulnerable.

After the ship tied up, the Manners family joined the pack of people slowly moving off like herded sheep. As they started to leave the confines of the ferry terminal, the pack split apart. *Look at all the trash.* He saw tarps and plywood over business windows. Garbage was collecting in the gutters and piling up on the sidewalks. There was a weird smell, too—a combination of body odor, human waste, and decay.

"Dad. How are we gonna get home?" Talia asked.

"Still workin' on that, baby girl," he said. "Just stay close." He looked for where the foot ferry to Port View used to launch from. The entire marina—not just that pier—was now obliterated. The only remnants were some of the old creosote pilings sticking out of the water at odd angles. On the sidewalk someone had spray painted a message on a big piece of plywood—"Foot Ferry @Fountain Park, 1 Qt. Per" *Fountain Park is just over there near the shipyard.* Tony led his daughters to it.

He found a large group of people waiting. At most everyone's feet were some form of backpack, cart, or luggage. Tony scanned the crowd and soon realized that everyone had a container, too. Several of them were gas cans.

"What's the deal here?" he asked someone on the edge of the crowd. He noticed that just talking to the man had made the multitude of people behind that person perk up.

"Back of the line!" he heard someone yell from afar. There were several more similar chants about no cutting.

"Need a quart of gas or diesel to catch the ferry. First come, first served," the man said.

"How often?" Tony asked.

"They're runnin' about three per day. They fill up really full before they leave."

"Thanks," Tony mumbled and led his daughters several feet away. He was worried that they might get something thrown at them if they stood there too long.

"How are we gonna find gas, Daddy?" Tasha asked.

"I don't know, Tash'," Tony said, staring at the crowd. "I don't know…"

25

"The difference between the difficult and the impossible
is that the impossible takes a little longer time." – Lady Aberdeen

Tahoma's Hammer + 12 Days.

"Look, man—I got my daughters here. It's all on the up and up."
Tony was bargaining hard, trying to get a guy with a large supply of
gas to trade him for jugs of water.

"Dude, I don't know where you been," the opportunist said,
"but possession is nine-tenths and what not. I don't know you. You
could be makin' this bull up."

The man had apparently stolen some gas and set up a quick
business selling to people desperate to take the small private ferry to
Port View. Tony knew the gas was stolen, and he didn't care.
"Look!" he demanded, pulling out a stack of business cards. "See?
I'm a delivery and sales rep! See? Tony Manners. It's like a thirty-

minute walk from the ferry once we're over there." He showed the matching name on his driver's license.

"Let's say this is legit," the man said. "You're over here, the gas is over here...the water..." He looked across the inlet hoping the obvious didn't have to be stated.

"Then your two trip fees are covered. Let's cut a deal, man. C'mon!" Tony was starting to convince the man. "Surely we can figure out a rate. How about five gallons of water?"

"Five!" the man repeated, insulted. "Dude, I was thinking like, twenty!"

"Hmmpph—you funny," Tony laughed. "We both know that you'll be siphoning gas a Hella lot longer than fresh water'll be around." Tony paused for a second. "Ten. Do you really think I'd show you where my daughters live if it wasn't legit?" Tony's serious face convinced the man.

"Aright, dude. But I need to bring a friend and a cart to help carry, which is two more tickets. Fifteen." The two traders stared at each other.

I wonder if this is how it'll always be from now on, Tony thought. "Deal."

They spent the next five hours in line, waiting. Tony's daughters had grilled him about the danger of letting this man know where they live.

"Don't worry, girls," he said calmly. "We won't be there very long."

"Good to see you up and about, Don," Phil said, yawning. Don had pretty much recovered from a mild concussion. It was late afternoon, and Phil was still groggy from the almost three-hour nap, which had felt like four minutes. He was moving around the office on his crutches and occasionally sipping on some instant coffee. *We're going to need to score some more java, soon,* Phil thought. *The apoca-*

lypse starts when that runs out. It still felt like the day the kidnapping-ordeal had all started, which was two afternoons earlier. "That is quite the family your daughter married into."

"Heh, thanks. Yep, Eli has always been a good man—never had to worry about him doing anything to hurt Alana or the kids. I don't know his brother too well, but he's a vet. He's had a couple of bad divorces, but he saw some action, so I take that into account."

"Yeah, well, he's earned *my* trust. Josh is solid—a real asset." Phil turned his attention to the others in the office. He'd called all four of the other officers or trustees who'd made it to the range for a small meeting. In addition to himself and Don that included Fred, Alice Huddlesten, and Jose "Joe" Santillan, the club's secretary. There were some concerning issues to discuss before he called for an all-residents meeting the following morning. He started with a recap of the entire operation to rescue Savannah, which took most of an hour. His coffee had grown cold before he could finish drinking it.

"The lesson I took from Charlie is this—we're on our own. It wasn't what he *intended* to relay, but it was the truth behind the facts. Charlie and I even had a bit of a...moment of friction, we'll call it —regarding this whole chipping and gun confiscation thing."

"Did you remind him our guns are protecting his wife and kids?" Joe snapped.

"I sure did. But I really didn't have to. He knows," Phil summed up.

"Where does that leave us?" Alice asked worriedly. "Are we not supposed to defend ourselves?"

"No, I wouldn't put it quite *that* way," Phil replied slowly. "But if we have to shoot anyone, we may find ourselves in a new pickle when the sheriffs show up. Deterrence is the key. We just need to be sure we know what we're doing. I mean—the guys at the front gate were swapping war stories the day the group that snagged Savannah walked by." He let them mull that over for a second. "We need to let everyone know how things are now. This isn't camping. This is serious business. People out there—right now—*are* planning and plotting on how they're going to come in here and take our stuff. Including our children," he added for effect. "If we deter well enough, we may be able to postpone any attacks until the authorities have changed their minds about armed citizenry."

"Alright," Fred said, "but most of us aren't spring chickens. We're not going to be patrolling and what not." He was a bit pessimistic about the direction of the conversation.

"I get that, Fred. I have ideas. It'll be clearer at tomorrow's meeting with everyone, but I know we can up the training—not just shooting. I'm talking about really teaching people how to stand watch. And we do have enough youthfulness here to get some patrols going."

Phil moved the meeting along. "Next—when the deputies dropped us off this morning, the first thing I did after we got Savannah settled was to find Jerry. Some of his AmRRON contacts happen to be connected to other preparedness groups, including some that have been focused on team-tactics for years. I've asked Jerry to set up a meeting between myself and the leaders of some of those groups."

"Why?" Fred asked naively.

"Airhead...I love you, brother," Phil wanted to start softly, "but you need to wake up. There are threats out there. Most of them are obvious. Some of them will appear as help at first, but in truth—we need to make contact with the allies out there and get our act together."

Phil continued. "Jerry is still setting that up, but I did get another piece of interesting news from him just before this meeting. Did you know that the shipyard got a fleet of helicopters today? Plus, Bogdon got some, too."

They were all surprised by the news. "Doing what?" Don asked.

"Supplies, I guess."

The group started to distract itself with several side conversations regarding this turn of events. *What does that mean? Where'd they come from?* The theories were interesting. Eventually Phil reigned them all in. "Guys, we have a few more things to discuss for tomorrow's meeting. Let's stay focused so we can eat."

"What else you got, boss?" Don asked.

"Quite a bit. The flu threat. Protocol for dealing with passersby. And rats."

"Two-legged, or four?" Joe joked.

Though not Joe's intent, the crack had reminded Phil of Dakota and made him sad and angry once again. "Both."

WHEN TONY and the girls got home it was a tearful and solemn moment. It wasn't just Sheila—several neighbors were there, too. When the neighbors had learned of her family's plight, they had tried to force Sheila to come stay with them. She kept finding herself back at her house hoping to find her family. Eventually a younger couple with no kids from two houses down had decided to come stay with her. Over the course of several days they had convinced another elderly woman from down the street to come stay there, too. In the course of all that, three jugs of water had been used. Tony didn't mind that Sheila had formed a group in his absence—it actually took a bit of stress off his mind. He was just glad there were three jugs of water left to pay off his debt.

The two "businessmen" waited somewhat patiently, but they were passively hinting that they needed to square up. Tony broke off the reunion after a couple of moments. *I want these cats out of here, anyway.* He made good on the water and did his best impression of a big angry club bouncer to make sure they didn't get other ideas. They loaded their jugs into their cart and left.

"Baby," he told Sheila, "let's get inside."

The women were all still holding each other as a group when they went into the house, barely breaking apart to get through the door. The first thing Tony noticed was the smell. It wasn't just body odor, it was stale and musty. He realized that the lack of power in a modern home made for a stagnant living situation. "Hey, ya'll. Do you all mind if we have us a private family reunion?" Tony hinted at everyone. They all took the hint and left for another house.

Tony and the twins took two hours telling their stories to their mother. In the middle of it, they had rifled through the pantry and cupboards to scrape together some food. Sheila had traded some quilts for a camping stove at a swap meet down at the nearest church. She'd only been cooking on it and eating once per day to save fuel. While they were eating and telling their tales, Tony worked up the proposal he wanted to make.

The conversation had finally made its way to figuring out the plan for the future. Sheila led it off. "There's talk around the neighborhood about how the churches and shelters are starting to shut down. People all over are stealing from each other. We heard there was a murder on Hidden Oak Drive the other night. They're worried, which worries me. Do you mind if the others keep staying over here?"

"Baby, I have a better idea. I need you to be open-minded while I'm sayin' it." She shot him *The Look*. "I'm serious."

"Okay… go on." He'd brought home the girls. She figured she owed him one, free stupid idea.

"One of my best clients…he has a gun range."

26

Stay the Course.

"Jerry! Someone let you out of the shack?" Phil asked, teasing his primary radio operator. Phil was heading from the office to the rifle line and had bumped into Jerry at the bottom of the stairs.

"Yeah. Even I want to get out and see something else every now and then. Turns out JR is a Tech—er, HAM speak for entry level technician. He never got past the 'Baofeng' phase, so I've been working with him some. Between him and the kid, I figured I could escape for the meeting. Plus—I got an interesting message I decided was too weird to tell you through the text app."

"Oh?" Phil's curiosity was piqued. "What's that?"

"Ships," Jerry said as if the one word explained itself.

"Ships," Phil repeated, trailing his voice. *And...*

"A lot of them. Up north. They showed up overnight, and they began unloading troops and stuff."

"What?" Phil couldn't quite decide if Jerry was screwing with him.

"Yeah, the amphibious-type. They're unloading Marines—fuel trucks and Hummers, mostly. They're up at the county park north of the Hood Canal Bridge. Some helicopters. Lots of activity. Hubbub on the radio is that they're moving into Bogdon like World War III broke out. You know—except for the actual gun fire and all."

Phil put two and two together. "That must be where the helos came from yesterday." His mind was slowly piecing it together. The base housed all the ballistic missile submarines for the US Pacific fleet. It only made sense that the Navy wanted to protect them and their weaponry. "Who sent you this intel?"

"One of the Channel 3 project non-HAMs relayed it up the net from their CB radio. Why?"

"Because that right there shows why we can't put a value on the nets, especially in how they work without repeaters," Phil said. "This is a hard peninsula to get onto by land or bridge, but water? Bad guys could sneak on from just about anywhere."

"I've always said that communications are the most ignored preparedness item. Fuel is our weak link, though. I have some solar and batteries—we'll never stop being able to listen. But without generators our ability to transmit will dwindle to a bare minimum."

"Thanks for the reminder. Grab yourself a chair, Jerry." Phil wandered out to the front of the crowd that had developed under the rifle line. While the multiple casual conversations were ongoing, he surveyed the motley crew. *Quite the ensemble. We're at what? Ninety? A hundred? May be time to think about where our cap will be.* "Folks. Folks…"

The conversations still took a minute to wind down. "Hey, everyone. Last night the remnants of the club board that are here got together and had an executive meeting. We had some good discussion on a lot of important topics. By now most of you have heard the rescue story. I won't re-hash that here, but I must tell you—we have some real threats out there."

It was surprisingly quiet with everyone paying full attention to what was being said.

"Let's start with the internal ones, though." This got quite a reaction as people began mumbling and looking at each other.

Phil was blunt. "Thievery won't be tolerated. Things have been walking away—things like batteries and food." The murmurs grew in volume. "Ask around. I'm not talking about an isolated event. Several of you have had similar stories. It's simple—if you get caught thieving, you're out. Gone. Period." The crowd went silent, but the air was tense. Phil chuckled a bit, "Now's your chance, folks. Get it out."

Stephanie Webster raised her hand. *Of course. Who else would have a problem?* Phil thought, remembering Stephanie's accusation that he lacked compassion that day at the gate. "Stephanie?"

"You can't just make up a rule like that! Not every situation is the same! Each case may not be so cut and dry."

This club isn't a democracy, lady. "One—each case will be evaluated for facts. Two—this is the real world. We're not going for DNA conviction. If the evidence, common sense, and guilty-acting behavior all point to the truth, then we'll believe the truth. Three— yes, I can. I'm the Executive Officer. The board voted to back this plan." This got quite a few murmurs and grimaces from others in the crowd.

"What I *can't* do," Phil continued, "is argue about this with you for the next fifteen minutes. So…stay or go. The choice is yours to make, but you're not turning this into a debate."

To Phil's surprise, Stephanie chose to clam up, but her opinion was worn clearly on her face. She wasn't happy.

Phil changed the topic. "Next—bartering. The board wants to form a decent-sized committee that will set rates of comparison for trading. We need some standards to weigh against. What is a gallon of fuel worth compared to cans of tuna, compared to batteries, compared to eggs. Get it? It will take sharing to make this place work, and we need to share in equal values. Get your name to Joe if you're interested. He'll chair the committee and we'll randomly pick eight volunteers to help him. The only stipulation is that there can be only one member per family or sub-group."

"Lastly, you'll notice that we've started beefing up security, which has forced us to start thinking about some of the consequences of that. We have to figure out things like where is the best fit for people or how do we feed everyone. Take Fred, for example—"

"Please! Take him!" yelled out Fred's wife, which caused the whole crowd to erupt in laughter.

Once the laughter trailed off, Phil continued. "It's nice to be loved, isn't it, bud?" Fred gave Phil a big thumbs up. "Like I was saying, if Fred stands two different watches in a day, then how is he supposed to be working a garden?" This got a few quiet side conversations started. "And—how do we react the next time this place is attacked? Who goes where? See where I'm headed with this?" Head nodding and a few low audible concurrences could be heard.

"So, in addition to staffing the gate and the foxholes on all four corners, we're also constructing a hidden observation post across the highway. They'll be bedded down, quietly keeping watch on the approach path taken by the kidnappers as well as being able to see key points well down the highway. This'll take some labor and quite a bit of training. Josh Bryant is our lead for this position. What he says, goes."

"I also need each of you to know and truly comprehend something—if we have to use firearms to defend ourselves, the authorities will come out and remove them." This caused a near-instantaneous uproar.

"Hey! Hey! Hold up!" he said. "This is a mine trap that can derail the whole meeting. Let me get through the talking points, and then you all can rant until the cows come home…. Please." They slowly quieted down to let him continue.

"Like I told the board—deterrence is the key. We need to be

seen guarding our corners, staffing our patrols, making sure that attacking us looks like a suicide run. That leads me to the next upgrade point. We'll eventually have two roving patrols—a two-person team inside the perimeter, and occasionally, a four-person team outside the perimeter."

A few hands started to go up. Phil scanned them. "Craig."

"How are we going to staff all this? I mean—this is going to take some effort. Ya' know?"

"Funny you should ask that, bud. I'll answer that by moving to the next topic. Everyone, tonight I'll be heading out for a meeting with the leaders of a few other groups." This got the murmurs going again. "The abduction made me realize that society is decaying right before our eyes. We are *behind the eight-ball.* The authorities are releasing criminals and not arresting people anymore. I know of several morally-convicted groups—real patriots. Liberty-loving people from all walks. You want a melting pot? This is them. I'm going to open this up for discussion, but I'll start by saying…I want to invite some of them to stay here."

"GOOD MORNING, EVERYONE," Marie said to her assembled shipyard-force from her usual tailgate perch. She was greeted with the expected low-volume jumbled-word that is formed when a few hundred people all say "morning" in return. "I know we just met two mornings ago, but I thought you all deserved to hear an update.

"Two hours ago, we were able to open our containment and pull the pile of cable and fuel-rod container out of the El Paso. We were able to recover the bodies of your fallen shipmates." She stopped for a moment to let that soak in a bit. "I want each of you to know… your…our shipmates are being treated with the utmost of care and respect." She could hear some gasps and sniffles coming from the workers.

"This is really just the first step in a long and challenging journey, everybody. We're beginning a thorough assessment of the damage to the ship. We're going to have to figure out just how bad it is, especially considering the refueling was only about eighty percent finished. We'll have to reset the ship into the proper position in the dock before we can commence any of that work, though. And we won't be doing that in the near future because we have a fuel issue that will be seriously affecting out pumps pretty soon." She had been glancing at a note card. She was suddenly inspired to try an unrehearsed speech, so she put the card into her pocket.

"My ex-husband was a big history buff," she said, moving on to her rally speech. "Every year around Christmas we'd watch *Band of Brothers*. I would always marvel at what those men did at the Battle of the Bulge. For those of you that don't know what that is, starting around Christmas of 1944, the 101st Airborne Division was completely surrounded by the Germans at Bastogne, Belgium. Low on ammo, lacking food, and without winter gear, they held out until supplies could be air-dropped. Men were wounded with no place to go. It was the worst of all scenarios for the European theater." She looked at the crowd, who were intently wondering where this was going.

"This is our Bastogne. Surrounded by threats...lack of resources...mission that can't fail... sacrifice..." Another pause. "Love. That's what drives us forward. That's what held those men together in 1944, and that's why you all are fighting today. Love..."

She transitioned to the end. "Sometime in two days our power plant will go dark. That's bad for a slew of reasons, but the worst is because we won't be able to keep the pump-wells running. You all know the importance of what I'm saying. You all can see that the team reinstalling shafts into the carrier isn't here. We can't afford to stop. The last pieces should be on the railcar and headed for Dry-dock F by this time tomorrow. This is all hands. Hard as we've tried, we just can't get that leak sealed up. The caisson weld-repairs didn't take, and the shipwrights have been fighting the weight of the water as they try various methods of plugging the leaks.

"All of you go back and double check your docks for the coming flood. Help the docking team as they start installing lines and tackle to hold the ships in place once they lift off the blocks. Then, triple check everything. Two days. That's our deadline, and it can't be moved."

"IT'S NOT GONNA HOLD!" Crane yelled to Billy.

"It will!" Billy promised. "At least, it will for a little while!" The pair were yelling due to the noise of the rushing water.

The two shipwrights were up on the scaffold at the continuous flood, in the dry-dock and next to the west end of the Dry-dock F caisson. The multiple welding attempts had failed just as Billy had said they would. The initial structural damage was too severe, and there was too much debris in the sill. The caisson was leaking all the way from a point over thirty feet high to the bottom plus across the bottom for half of the caisson's two-hundred-foot width. A large team of shipwrights and riggers were continuously pounding wedges into the gaps with sledge hammers. Crane, Billy, Tracy, Joey Garcia and several other shipwrights were on different levels of the scaffold. They were trying various methods to lock the wedges in from behind with other timbers and wedges, but the scaffold was just too light. It was already rocking from the force of the water, the bulk of which flowed through without actually hitting the framework. If they hadn't placed it just right when they built it, the water would have knocked it over instantly.

"We could stack base blocks here!" Crane suggested.

"The wedges would pop out before we could even get the first one set, let alone put a whole column in here!" Billy replied.

Crane knew his mentor was right. They had gathered the team all around them to try their idea before the actual pumps quit running. Everybody was soaked with seawater. It was just a matter of moments before they were numb and unable to feel their hands.

The battle had become almost one hundred percent mental. Crane looked the two hundred fifty feet to the north at the teams of riggers and machinists trying to land and install another piece of the carrier's shafts. There were four shafts that drove the 100,000-ton beast, and each one was made up of several pieces. The shipyard had simultaneously started installing the propellers and rudders, too, as shaft assemblies were completed. It was truly all-hands on deck.

"I'm doing the math, Billy! It's gonna be close!"

"I know, kid!"

"They're gonna lose that equipment. This dock'll be flooding as they finish!"

"I know, Crane!" Billy had run out of cigarettes days earlier.

"We're going to have to pound these wedges continuously when the pumps stop."

Billy said nothing.

PHIL WAS in the upper field checking on his makeshift greenhouse. Not his really, but *everyone's*. They had taken some of the surplus materials and built several of them. They drove two rows of rebar into the ground about ten feet apart and used long pieces of PVC pipe to make semi-hoop ribs, similar to an old, covered wagon. Covered in heavy-gauge transparent plastic, the little structures made for decent starter greenhouses. *We can try to make something bigger and more permanent come spring,* Phil thought.

The afternoon was typically gray with a medium rain. It was the same type of weather that made his kids cover their Halloween costumes with coats when they were much younger. He was enjoying a moment to himself for a change. It wouldn't last long as he was on his way up to check on the watch stations on the range's far corners. After the morning meeting, people had finally seen the light on the importance of them.

"Hey, brother."

The voice out of nowhere caught Phil off guard. He turned and was surprised to see Charlie, still in his dirty and increasingly funky uniform. He was sporting a bandage on his neck.

"Hey…" Phil said, not sure where they stood with each other after the last conversation. "You getting a little family time for a change?" He noticed Charlie had ditched the gun belt.

"Something like that. Mel and the kids seem to be adjusting. Says you got her running a school?"

"Well, more like a glorified daycare, I suppose. I'm just trying to keep the kids occupied, and, you know, her being a teacher and all…"

"Yeah, yeah. I get it. Sounds like a good plan." Charlie stopped and they looked at each other, each acknowledging the elephant in the field.

Charlie continued. "Beefing up security, huh?"

"Yup." *Where do your loyalties lie, Charlie?* "Just makes sense, what with the abduction and all. So, where'd the, uhh…" Phil drifted his question as he was pointing to Charlie's neck bandage.

"Just another day of trying to keep the crowds under control. The big FEMA camp down in Bartlett is starting to get a little, shall we say, agitated. They went down to the Navy base today to protest the fact that most of the supply drop has stayed inside the fences."

"Hmmm," Phil mumbled. *How soon 'til they march up the highway and try to steal from this greenhouse?* "And how are you guys dealing with that? Use of force, I mean."

"Same as I told you this morning. Pacify. De-escalate. Chip the violent ones. Confiscate weapons if one is involved in something."

We are definitely at a crossroads, now, aren't we, brother? No way anyone is chipping me—even you. "I can appreciate that you're in a hard spot, bud, but doesn't that kind of go against the law? I mean—Liberty didn't die just because the power went out."

"I hear you, Phil, but you just don't understand."

"Try me."

"Okay," Charlie said, not even knowing where to begin. "Did

you know that the cops and Guardsmen can no longer enter certain neighborhoods? We're starting to suffer barrages of rocks when we drive around. Just this morning, a pair of guardsmen keeping the peace at a shelter in Port View were attacked by the mob. We've had guys get shot at. Ambushed!" Charlie was starting to get agitated that his friend was making him justify all of this. "The sick and elderly are dying off en masse. People are hungry! And thirsty! Phil —people are super dangerous when they're thirsty!" Charlie's face was starting to show his agitation.

Phil wasn't holding it back anymore. "Precisely why you shouldn't be taking people's guns, Charlie! I mean, you're a Native American! You of all people should appreciate the frickin' irony here!"

The two friends were about a foot apart from each other with eyes on fire and nostrils widening. They went silent, and the bigger deputy stared down Phil like he was a suspect. It was fortunate for the range members that none of them were there to see the argument. Charlie slowly took a step back. Unlike his daily encounters on the job, this one was much more personal.

"Phil, this is still America." He was trying to scale back his voice. "We still have a functioning government. People still need to respect the authorities—and their decisions—as we try to get a horrible situation under control."

Phil was trying to calm himself, too, but he was too amped up for the debate. "You're right, this is still America! This is *exactly* the kind of scenario that the 2nd Amendment was written for. Don't forget—self-defense is a *natural* right...not one granted by government. Politicians and police still need to remember who they work for. Tell me this—if law abiders having guns is such a bad thing, then why the Hell is your family still here?"

With anger and pain in his eyes Charlie took another two steps backwards, shaking his head as he turned around to storm off. "I don't know, *brother*!" he yelled. "But I can fix that right now!"

27

Phoenix.

Tahoma's Hammer + 13 Days.

"You guys need any more chili?" Payton asked Josh and his trainees.

"I do!" Savannah chimed in, not caring who the intended audience of the question had been. It was dinner time and inserting herself next to Josh at the table for this meal was the first sign of normalcy she'd shown since getting back. Since the return the morning before, Savannah had either been sleeping or attached to her mother. It hadn't escaped Payton's attention that her daughter was parking herself next to one of her rescuers.

"No kidding, silly. You have a hollow leg! I was talking to the grownups."

All four of Josh's trainees said yes while he quietly held his bowl up. Payton thought she caught a bit of smile when their eyes met, and she returned it. *He's kinda cute under that beard,* she thought, wondering if her opinion was swayed by the fact that he'd risked his life to save her daughter.

She refilled bowls while continuing the small talk. She was offering anyone who was doing physical guard training a helping of seconds. She wandered back into the kitchen end of the trailer, not realizing that Fred had snuck in unnoticed. "Hey!" she scolded the man she'd known since she was a child. Fred had literally been caught with his hand in the cookie jar.

"Sheeze, Payton, you scared me!"

"There's nothing in there, Fred! Just like the last three times you checked. The cookie-fairies have *not* come by." She could tell the old man was feeling a bit trapped, so she softened her tone. "Have an apple."

Phil had an apple tree at his house. Payton wasn't sure what kind they were, but they were sweet and crisp like Fujis or Braeburns. The tree filled up with apples every fall, and she had assigned several of the members to arm themselves and go retrieve them earlier that day. *No food source can be wasted.*

"Alright," Fred said dejectedly, more like a seven-year-old than a seventy-year-old. He took an apple and started to leave.

"My kitchen," Payton reminded him—half playfully and half not.

In reality, she was coordinating with several of the other women, most of them the middle- and upper-aged. They were working well together and had learned which men to keep at arm's length. Payton realized that collectively they could make their food go further by talking out their plans with each other, sometimes combining their canned goods and adding water or broth to make it stretch. Often, she would go tend to the Dutch-ovens cooking over the range's firepit to allow the older women to remain sheltered in the small building.

Payton wiped up the counters and looked out at the four men

and one woman eating around her daughter. *What the hell happened to the world. Has it only been two weeks?* Her thoughts drifted back to wondering what had happened to Brenden as she placed her hands on her growing baby-bump. She remembered that she was about to run out of pre-natal vitamins and started to think about things like wipies and formula—and the fact that she had no doctor.

"I said thanks," Josh said, who was now standing in front of her with a bowl and spoon.

"Oh!" she said, smiling in embarrassment at being caught lost in thought.

"The usual place?" he asked, wondering if she wanted them to put their dishes in the large, black plastic tub outside.

"Yeah."

They all started to file out, donning gear and getting rifles off the of the rack that had been staged on the deck.

"Bye!" Savannah yelled from the deck as the group headed down to the parking area and out of sight.

Josh turned back and waved at both of them. Payton went inside and started collecting the rest of the dishes that needed washing, not realizing she was smiling.

PHIL HAD TAKEN Crane's jeep, resisting the urge to ask the Jorgenson's if he could borrow their horses. They had to go too far, and he couldn't guarantee the animals' security. Besides, they would have been one short. He had brought Eli and Jeff along, leaving Josh at the range specifically to be in charge of security. He rounded out the foursome with Buddy Chadwell, the man who'd been digging the foxhole with Payton that day. He was driving and Phil was riding shotgun. Driving a stick-shift was a real chore for Phil due to the prosthetic.

Jerry had arranged a location for Phil to meet the leaders of a few other prepper groups, including one led by his lawyer friend from the next county. The meeting spot was somewhat in the middle for all. It was at the parking area for an off-road vehicle park, part of the state forest in the next county. The area was heavily forested, and though the downed trees had been cleared, the trip had been made more difficult by broken roads and fallen bridges. Jerry had been able to use his radio contacts to ascertain a somewhat accurate portrait of the travel route, but what should've taken twenty-five minutes by vehicle now took over three hours. The going was even slower because Phil insisted they drive slowly and even stop to check things out when they approached what he thought could be an ambush spot.

They finally arrived long after sunset, and there were four armed men decked out in various levels of camouflage guarding the entrance to the park's parking area. Buddy slowly approached and stopped, turning off the headlights and the engine. *I wonder how many we're not seeing,* Phil asked himself. He slowly opened the door to the jeep and stuck his hands up above it. His rifle's sling yanked on his neck as he stepped out onto the ground good leg first. He stepped out from behind the door. It was dark out, and he had lost sight of the men under the three flashlights now shining on him. *If this ain't them we're in deep kimchee.*

"Password," a voice commanded from the dark.

"Denver," he called out.

"Omelet," he heard in return. Everyone knew that the password wasn't a certain guarantee due to the fact that it had been established via HAM radio. It did add a certain sense of relief, though. The flashlights turned off. "Proceed," he heard.

Phil started to walk while Buddy fired up the jeep and turned on the parking lights, creeping it through the check point. He drove the two hundred feet down to the congregation of trucks and SUVs that had amassed in the dark forest. As Phil approached, he could make out a few chemical glowsticks on the ground in a semicircle. There was an eerie, multi-colored glow emanating from everyone. Three men sat in folding chairs and a few others forming a standing ring around them. As Phil passed his crew's jeep, he gave them instructions on how to disperse themselves to help guard the perimeter. He headed towards the empty chair in the inner circle.

"Is that a bulletproof leg?" he heard a familiar voice call out from the dark.

"Sure is. Whaddya call a thousand lawyers at the bottom of the ocean?" Phil returned.

"A good start!" came the reply. Phil's friend stood up and came over. He was about 6' 2" and like Phil, in his mid-fifties. He had graying temples on black hair. They gave each other a bro-hug. In the light of the glowsticks he could see his buddy's smirking grin. "I have to admit—I was surprised the hear from your radio guy. Pleasantly, of course—but surprised."

"Good to see you, Gary! I'm glad you all were able to take the call and make it out tonight." Gary was actually George Donovan, attorney-at-law from Mason County. He had written a successful series of prepper novels under the pen name "Gary Stonefence." That had unofficially become his real name for most people.

Gary walked back over to his fold-up chair and plopped down. "Phil, I'd like to introduce you to Lonnie Everly and 'Skinny' Kenny O'Brian." Phil wobbled over and shook each of their hands to the usual round of informal "how ya' doin's."

Gary continued. "Lon's from your side of the county line while Skinny lives here in Mason, not too far from me."

"So, you're the famous Phil Walker, huh?" Skinny said. Skinny was about sixty-years-old and was easily one of the biggest men Phil had ever laid eyes on. *Funny nickname.* Skinny didn't get out of his custom, oversized chair, but Phil figured him to be at least 6' 8" and over four hundred pounds. *His beard alone weighs ten-pounds,* Phil decided.

"Not so sure about famous. But I am the idiot who almost got himself killed on the highway, yes!" This got a round of chuckles from all of them.

They made small talk for about three or four more minutes before Gary got things going. "What's on your mind, Phil?"

"Bear with me, fellas. This is going to take a while." Phil went into the full version of the abduction of Savannah, including his recovery operation, use of the GoTennas, the drone, and most importantly—the county's curfew, chipping, and gun confiscation orders. "Our 'mini-squad' did okay considering we'd never trained together. I would've liked another four guys on that op, though."

Phil concluded his story. "It's a matter of time before they start trying a door-to-door gun-grab, I think..." He let out a big sigh and took a long drink of water while the council of men mulled over everything they'd just heard.

Gary sat silently while Skinny was the first to speak. "Don't let my calm demeanor, fool ya', Phil. That there pissed me right the Hell off. I'm tryin' my level best not to come unglued."

Lon was livid. "What in the world? I can't fathom this in America! My own county nonetheless!"

"Except we saw it after Hurricane Katrina," Skinny reminded him. "We saw people in Boston getting forced out of their homes by SWAT teams after the bombing thing. Not surprisin', really."

Phil agreed. "Just disappointing. Especially because the man who saved my life can't seem to figure out where he lies."

Gary was finally ready to chime in. "You all have heard me talk on podcasts about all the soldiers, spec-ops guys, and cops I talked to when I was writing the books." They all acknowledged that. "We're at the beginning of this thing, really...ya' know? Give it time. The Guard...the cops...they all need to come to grips in their own terms. I still believe in them—as Americans. They'll come around when the rubber meets the road. Many of them, anyway."

"I hope you're right," Phil said. "But I'm not as sure as you are. I think we need to be prepared for the other scenario—what if they don't."

"Just what is it you're thinkin'?" Lon asked.

"Well—for starters, we all know from books like Gary's that evil people will eventually band together and start taking from anyone who can't stop them." This got a round of agreement. "And we may need to be ready to *peacefully* resist our officials, which will only happen if we're united in numbers and tactics. Therefore, I think we—and others like us—need to be ready to work together. I know that the men out here tonight represent only a small sampling of the patriot network. We need to have mutual assistance plans in place —'no kidding, for-real' action plans." More agreement. "Lastly, if any of you have outgrown your areas or discovered issues with them, I want to extend the invite to come to the range. In full disclosure, while space is abundant, my able-bodied manpower is a bit lacking."

Skinny went first. "Me and mine are good wher'n we are, but I agree with everythin' you're sayin'."

"I'd like to come check out what you got," Lon said. He was blonde and probably in his late thirties or early forties, Phil thought. "My group is eight families strong, with several youth and adults trained up. We have plenty of food. What we're lacking, though, is a source of water and a defensible perimeter. We're all on less than three acres in West Slaughter, in amongst a bunch of other smaller parcels. I think we could mutually benefit each other." Phil nodded.

Gary spoke next. "Like Skinny, my *team* is set and secure out here on the north shore of Hood Canal. But I'm down with the idea that we need to start organizing. Let me talk in more detail to some other groups. I'll bring the leaders up to you when we can arrange it."

"Sounds good," Phil said. "Sooner is better. One last thing to put some serious thought into. Controlling the narrative."

"Meaning what?" Skinny asked genuinely.

"Meaning we need to take back the language. This is something the conservatives and patriots have sucked at for most of my life. The leftists and media have hi-jacked legitimate words like 'compassion' for themselves. And a very small percentage of idiots have made it easy for them to demonize other legitimate words—like 'constitution' or 'militia'."

"Where do you suggest we start?" Gary asked coolly.

"I can think of one word that nobody has demonized yet. One word that implies Constitutional legitimacy. This phrase kind of applies to the entire 'unity of effort' we're describing here—that word is 'posse'. We start by promoting that—the Slaughter Peninsula Posse."

"The SPP," Skinny said. "It has a certain ring to it," he agreed. There was general agreement around the group.

So, it begins, Phil thought.

28

No Greater Love.

Tahoma's Hammer + 14 Days.

The current rain system had picked up in intensity, making things like standing watch challenging, especially at night. *Hind-sight is 20-20,* Phil had thought days earlier. If he could go back in time and prepare one item for the range with the foresight that all of this would happen, he would've built proper fighting positions with good weather protection, cover, and concealment. The day's deluge started out heavy and got worse from there. At around ten in the morning, a scant five hours after Phil had managed to get to sleep, Payton came by the tent to get him up.

"Dad...Dad."

"What? What..." he said throwing his stump and leg off the

edge of the cot. "Brrr…" *Need to think about moving into the cargo trailer and insulating the walls.* "What, honey?"

"Someone's at the gate. Says he knows you. Tony something."

Tony… Tony… "I know a few Tonys, Olive," he said, pulling on his leg and his pants.

"Big black guy. Built like a semi."

"Oh, Tony! Why didn't you say so?" Phil missed the eyeroll as Payton left. He finished getting dressed and went out to the latrine bay to take care of business. A few minutes later he was at the front gate. There in a bright yellow safety coat was Tony the water guy. At just over two weeks old, the ordeal often felt like ages to Phil, but at that moment his mind went right back to the first earthquake.

"Let them in!" Phil ordered the gate guards. The gate was opened and then set back down after the Manner's family strolled through. He grabbed the big handshake that was waiting for him. "Hey, bud! I take it this is the family?" *They look like they've been through the ringer.*

"Hey, bro, good to see ya'. Yes, this is my better half an' my baby girls!"

Phil was still a bit sleepy and shocked to see them. "Well—come-in! We'll go to the chow hall and get out of this mess." He led them to the far end of the parking lot and into the single-wide trailer. Everyone went through the Washington state ritual of shaking off rain gear and hats and draping them over the backs of chairs.

"I'm taking it things aren't too good, Tony…" Phil invited, after a round of proper introductions had been made.

"No, brothuh, they aren't. If you got the time, I'd like to tell you our tale."

Phil listened to his friend patiently for close to an hour and a half, mesmerized by the descriptions of Seattle's damage, the events of T-Mobile Field, and the bartering system down in Bartlett. It concluded with Tony describing that they had made it about two miles from home the day before, but they had run out of gas due to it being stolen. "Phil, we got no place to go, man. I don't ask lightly, but here I am. We need your help."

Phil was shocked that Tony thought it was some sort of application process. It caught him off guard. "What? Yeah! No question. Of course you guys can stay here." There was a sigh of relief from both Tony and Sheila. "I do have to ask, though, do you guys have anything to feed yourselves with?"

The dejected look returned. "Just what's in our bags." Tony said.

"It's okay. I can cover you guys for quite a while from my own supplies. But there is an expectation that everyone pulls their weight around here. You know—guard duty and the like. Even you," he said to the twins. "And as this thing rolls on, we'll probably be more reliant on things like gardening, bartering for meat, or procuring fuel—all things you guys can help with."

They continued to chat for a while longer with Phil telling Tony that he would talk to a few of the retirees who had bigger travel trailers about sheltering them. "Get your gear back on. I'll show you all around."

TAHOMA'S HAMMER + 15 Days.

TODAY, Marie thought. *We run out of juice today.* She had a feeling of foreboding deep in the pit of her stomach. She was standing in the dry-dock, watching one team of workers scrambling to get the last piece of shaft into its proper place—bolted to the piece ahead of it and within the confines of its strut. Up forward on that same shaft, a different team was finishing the bolting sequence of the seals with four-foot-long wrenches, something not unlike bolting a car's lug-nuts but with more technical precision and on a much grander scale. Those seals had to be done perfectly or they wouldn't keep the ocean out of the ship.

There were a couple of small fiberglass boats staged in the dock ready to take on the last dozen or so workers if it really came down to it. The cranes had stopped installing the propellers and rudders and shifted to pulling out various pieces of large equipment. Marie knew that the floating crane and divers could handle the props later, but she couldn't replace the equipment. Not in the new world. She glanced south toward the caisson, spying about forty shipwrights and riggers. Their sledgehammers and wedges were staged on top of spare blocks, waiting to be slammed into the deluge once the pumps stopped running. The men and women were waiting for their moment, some sitting on blocks... others leaning against the dry-dock wall. She made her way to the stairs at the southwest corner of the dock and began the long ascent to the topside.

IT WAS DARK AND RAINY, which meant normal. In Cascadia, it was always fully past dusk by early evening in autumn and winter. People were settling into their tents and trailers after eating. Phil, Payton, and Savannah were settling into eating bowls of soup coupled with small-talk in the club's office when the duress signal whispered through the radios like the voice of a ghost—"Dakota, Dakota, Dakota." Phil had honored his dog's memory by turning her name into the code word for their brand-new observation post, buried close to one hundred meters into the woods on the far side of the highway. That word was meant only for letting the range know that a threat was approaching from the west.

Phil was the first to react, hopping out of the chair with his rifle. "Grab her and get to the school box!" Phil commanded as he poured himself out of the small trailer as quickly as he could. He rounded the corner off the deck to go down to bench "one" on the rifle line. That's where he kept his Minuteman Kit. When he got to it, he picked up a pre-staged disposable air horn—like the kind used at ball games—and gave three two-second blasts. He then threw on his battle belt, not worrying about aligning the Velcro hooks with the inner belt he used to hold up his pants. He had staged his plate carrier loosely intact so that he could don it by holding it over his head and dropping it down his arms. Next came the bump-helmet. He was buckling it as he sprinted down the rifle line. He opted to approach the gate from the far side of the line versus going up to the parking lot via either set of stairs.

"LET'S GO!" Billy yelled to all of the shipwrights and riggers. The dry-dock's lights had gone out, leaving only the big spotlights topside of the dock, powered by portable generators. The background noise of the de-flooding pumps was conspicuously absent, making the rushing saltwater seem louder and more ominous. "Yardbirds" began to scramble to their positions, taking the big wedges and hammers and slamming them into the flooding gap. Fall-protection-clad shipwrights scrambled up the ringed-legs of the scaffold like chimpanzees, the prefabricated stairs having been removed to lessen the surface area for the rushing water to slam into.

From the top, Marie looked down at the team members sloshing through the water to their critical jobs. *I'm so proud to call you my team!* she thought. Next to her, the dock master was issuing frantic orders into the radio, as almost two-hundred shipyard workers were scrambling to staff the ten mooring lines tethering each side of the behemoth ship to the topside cleats.

She spied the water's edge as it moved past the now-filled pump intakes in the dry-dock's floor. She couldn't contain the nerves on her face as it filled with frantic worry, watching the machinist and riggers rushing to correctly finish the shaft-sealing process. She could hear the rhythmic cracking of hammers on wood, which caused her once again to look south. She watched the forty shipwrights and riggers pounding giant four-foot-long wedges into the gaps, over and over again. Each one would pound a wedge and move to the next, continuously beating on the same three or four wedges in their area. Each wedge would work itself loose from the force of the inlet behind it. They were all soaked to the bone. Rain gear didn't matter on a job like this. Moving in it just tired a person out. Some of them had actually taken it off.

The shipwrights up on the scaffold were taking the worst of it. In addition to the stairs, they had removed most of the plank and guardrails to lessen the amount of shaking the scaffold suffered from the pounding water. *Yet there they are, in fall gear, swinging those big hammers over and over again...* Marie began to feel a pit of despair grow in her stomach.

PHIL HEARD Jerry repeating the code word from his perch up on the hill, just in case anyone hadn't heard it the first time. *The protocol is working,* Phil thought. "Ben Franklin," he said as he approached the main gate watches, another part of their new protocol. They would establish a new word after every incident, or once a week. He flipped down the night-vision monocular on his helmet and scanned the parking lot berm for intruders. "You guys see anything?" he asked Vic and Donna Gladstone.

"Nothing," Vic whispered.

His PVS-14 allowed him to clearly see other range members reacting. He saw one or two people at the far end of the parking area running north to reinforce the northwest fighting position. He could also see that Payton, Savannah, and several of the older members—children, men, and women—were heading east from the chow hall to the kid's school-room conex box.

He heard footsteps from behind and looked back, seeing all three Bryant men running across the rifle line. Eli and Jeff were running to back up the southwest corner, and Josh was coming up to the gate.

"Keep behind the sandbags," he told Vic and Donna. Josh, on

me," Phil ordered and started to move around the gate's bearing post and electric motor housing to head back toward the office and chow hall. That's when he heard the first shot. KA-KROWWW! *The north west corner!* He hit the dirt *flat*, as he was already about ten feet out in the open.

"Contact northwest," he heard Fred yell into the radio.

C'mon! C'mon! He was waiting impatiently for the newly-formed Quick Reaction Force to mobilize itself in Bay 1. They were supposed to call out on the radio when at least four of them were geared up and ready. BOOM! *Southwest! Sounds like a hunting rifle. Organized attack on both corners!* Phil started to worry about the wide-open east perimeter on the far side of the property. Past that were several thousand acres with an intermittent house here and there.

"Contact southwest!" someone else keyed up.

"QRF ready with six," he heard Craig Wageman say. About then the sounds of firefights were starting to pick up speed at both western corners of the property.

'Bout dang time. "QRF, form two squads and back up the west corners. Go. All hands, there are two friendlies in the parking area. Make sure you ID your targets!" Phil got back to his knees. "Moving," he told Josh.

"Move," came the experienced acknowledgment.

Phil kept his body, head, and rifle scanning the west, his body turned like a tank-turret as he slowly walked north toward the far corner of the office trailer. He parked himself on his left knee while continuing to scan the Canal Vista highway berm. He gave a quick scan to Josh, just in case he couldn't tell that Phil was set. Josh wasn't moving. *No night vision,* Phil remembered. Phil knew that several of the members had a night-vision scope on at least one rifle. *Need to make sure some of those get lent to the Josh and the QRF from now on.* He pulled the red-filtered flashlight off his battle belt and sent two quick strobes toward his battle buddy. Josh started the low crouching walk to Phil.

The firefight sounds were picking up on both corners. Phil

dropped the flashlight into his dump pouch and started re-scanning the highway-berm. The night-vision made positive ID a cinch. Before him were two men, one of whom he'd arrested in that very parking lot two weeks earlier. They had low crawled through the salal and fir trees at the top of the berm and were now rolling down the ten-foot embankment to the parking lot.

"Contact west!" he yelled at the top of his lungs.

He lit up the target to the right at the exact same moment that Josh's rifle-mounted flashlight came on, illuminating the other target as he was destroyed. Phil closed his left eye to preserve his night vision as he rhythmically pumped five shots into his target, flipping his safety back on instinctively when he was done. He kept the rifle trained up and re-opened his left eye, scanning the berm once more. Both contacts were still and quiet. Dead quiet. He continued to look around for new threats.

The sounds of the firefight slowed dramatically. *They must be retreating.* "Medic!" he heard a panicked voice through the radio. He couldn't tell whose. "We need medical to the northwest!"

He heard Alice acknowledge. She was a retired geriatric nurse, and though most of her experience was not related to trauma, she was still the most qualified.

"On me," he told Josh, and made his way to the flagpole at the top of the stairs by the office. When Alice had reached them from the safety of the conex boxes at mid-property, Phil was waiting to escort her. "Stay behind us," he ordered.

Phil ran ahead and planted himself past the deck and chow hall across the parking lot. He "sliced the pie" around the corner and walked back for several seconds, calling clear when he came back out. Josh and Alice followed suit while he covered their rear. He fell back in directly behind Alice. They could hear moaning and gasping as they approached the dug in position. They passed the three members of the QRF who were covering the west and north directions from the safety of trees.

As Alice dropped into the hole, Phil and Josh took cover behind trees. He wanted to scan the entire area with his night-vision. He could tell by the activity in the hole that they were working on Fred. The firefight on this corner had come to a stop. *Can't lose focus.* "Moving," he whispered quietly.

"Move," Josh ordered.

Phil moved toward a tree just a few meters from the shoulder of the highway. He was continuously scanning left and right on both sides of the road. He could see at least three bodies nearby. *Probably more down south, too.* He knelt and listened for two solid minutes, hearing Alice and Fred's two battle buddies—Joe and another person he couldn't remember—working on Fred.

He finally fell back, fairly certain they had just repelled an over-confident attacker. He took cover behind the tree next to Josh and said into his radio, "Southwest, what's your LACE report?"

"Our what?" came the puzzled reply.

Need to conduct training! Phil scolded himself. "Ammo and casualties. Status?"

"Oh, good on both."

"Roger that. Send your QRF unit up the south road and have them patrol the east border. All stations, friendlies moving through the parking lot to the infirmary shortly. Hold your fire." Phil then hopped down into the fighting position. "What we got, Alice?" He was worried about his friend.

"It's dark, Phil." She was trying to work by the light of a chem-lite. It emitted yellowish-green light, and it was easy to see that they had cut Fred's shirt open right up the middle. He had an entry wound with a steady flow of blood coming out the area between his heart and left clavicle. "We need to get him inside so I can see if this is a pneumothorax and start an IV. I'm sorry, Phil! I'm just not a doctor!"

Litters! Why the hell didn't you think about those before now! "Alright."

Phil unslung his rifle and handed it to Joe. He hopped out of the hole and sprint-wobbled as best as he could to the chow hall seventy meters away. He went inside, thankful someone had left a candle burning when they evacuated. He shoved the plates and cups off the nearest folding table and threw it onto its side. He folded in the legs and hightailed it back to the hole. He shoved the table down to Joe, who with the assistance of Alice and the other man managed to get Fred onto it. They lifted the table up, and Phil took feet end to drag it away enough for them to climb out. The three men picked up the table with Alice and Josh trailing, making their way to the infirmary at the far end of the rifle line.

Once they got inside, Alice went to work by the light of a LED lantern and a flashlight that had been pre-hung over the cot. Phil turned around, and Sheila and Tony Manners were running up. "I'm a medical assistant. How can I help?"

"Gunshot to the chest. Get in there!" Phil said, pointing toward the room.

"Brothuh, that's the last time I sit that out," Tony said. "I may've been a Navy supply guy, but I can still man a foxhole." He looked around and could see the old man's blood, even in the dark. "The thought that he may die protecting my babies…"

"I know," Phil said putting his hand on the big man's shoulder for a moment before walking away.

CRANE LOOKED BACK for a quick glance. "We're losing it!" he yelled down to Billy.

The water was at least two feet deep down at the bottom of the scaffold. The riggers and shipwrights down there were still trying to hammer, but the water was outpacing them. They were having to plow the maul through the water just to hit where they thought the ends of the wedges were. He could tell that the leading edge of the flood had finally reached where the shaft-seal team was finishing their complex torque pattern. They were torquing sixty-four giant nuts over and over again, to specific values and in a specific pattern, all while testing the seals for quality. It was slow going.

The caisson team was just trying to buy them time. "It's no use!" someone down below yelled.

The tired workers down below were out of steam and options. As the water grew higher than the wedges, the wood's natural buoyancy took over. First one popped. Then another. Soon there were four-foot long wedges floating everywhere, bouncing along as the rapid current took them north. The small boats three-hundred to the north near the shaft workers were starting to jostle as the water crept under them. The thirty workers who had been fighting the flood at the bottom of the caisson started making their way to the dock's stairs.

"C'mon!" one of them yelled up at the shipwrights. "Time to go!"

Crane looked down at Billy, Tracy, and the others. They were all looking up and down the incomplete scaffold at each other—wet and aching from swinging the big hammers. *This started with the hammer,* Crane thought. *It's how it ends, too.* He started swinging again. *Boom! Boom!* Billy started swinging again, too. Then Tracy. "Every second counts!" Crane yelled from the top. In all, there were still five shipwrights out there fighting to the end.

As the water continued north, emergency generators and floodlights were added by other teams at the top of the dry-dock. There was a crowd of shipyard workers watching. The high-rankers were out there, too. The shipyard's Commanding Officer was at the top of the dry-dock stairs, giving men and women blankets and thanking them profusely. She wasn't trying to hide the tears anymore. Nobody was.

Still, it continued. *Boom! Boom! Boom!* Five mauls swinging into one-foot wide wedge-backs. It continued several more minutes. More wedges popped out, which sped up the flooding. Soon the flood had reached the north end of the 1,200-foot-long dock. The only place for it to go now was up. The small boats were lightly bouncing against the scaffold to which they were tied, the same one that the shaft-seal crew was working from. The water was approaching the deck-level of that scaffold—about thirteen feet off the ground. At the caisson scaffold it was closer to sixteen feet deep.

The scaffold was bouncing around pretty well now. The lowest two shipwrights had peeled off the scaffold and started swimming for the dry-dock stairs in the cold October flood. They were tired, sore, and hypothermic. Both of them stopped swimming and started treading. Soon they stopped doing that.

"Swim! Swim!" people were yelling from above. A worker driving one of the small boats untied it and fired up the gasoline engine. He sped over and tried to pull the first one into the boat, but he was almost completely dead weight. The small boat capsized. Marie started to run down the stairs. "Captain, no!" It was Captain Flowers. He shot her a look as he passed her at the top of the stairs.

"This better not be because I'm a woman, Trevor!"

"You're too valuable, Marie! We need you." He pointed at the crowd. "They need you!" He nudged past her along with several other people, running down the stairs to see if they could help. A few of the workers at the creeping waterline on the stairs had braved the water, swimming out to assist.

Back at the scaffold more wedges had popped out. Tracy had dropped her maul, too tired and cold to grip it anymore. She slipped off the pipe she was standing on, hitting her head on one of the hard metal rings built into the legs. She got knocked out and her safety harness held her suspended in the rising water. Billy looked down and saw what was happening. He unhooked and started to climb down, stopping halfway to try to unhook her harness. She weighed too much for the tired old man, so he opened his pocket knife and began to saw at her lanyard. Just then a wedge shot out and crashed squarely into Billy's head, sending him flying untethered into the water swallowing the scaffold. Like Tracy, he'd been knocked out. He was dragged under by the swirling vortex that resulted from the rushing water. People up topside gasped in horror. They were screaming—trying to get Crane's attention.

Back at the shaft seal the mechanics were standing on the scaffold in knee-deep water when they finally finished the torquing evolution. They scrambled over to the lone small boat and climbed in. They made their way over toward the stairs where the shivering rescue swimmers had finished pulling the two shipwrights and small boat operator out of the water. They were pointing drastically at the caisson, trying to get the second boat operator to go find Billy and Tracy.

Crane had dropped his hammer, looking down to see that Billy was gone and Tracy was completely submerged. With numb and frozen hands, he climbed down the scaffold-leg's connecting rings into the water and took a deep breath. *S-so c-c-c-col-d i-it b-b-bu-rns...* *So cold, it burns,* he thought. He unhooked Tracy's lanyard, but it was too late. She was almost peaceful as she sank away from his weakened grasp. Crane's last thought was about his father, sister, and niece, as the swirling torrent slammed him into a scaffold leg and shot him submerged down the dry-dock. He was so cold and tired... so so tired...

29

Rubicon.

TAHOMA'S HAMMER + 16 DAYS.

WHEN IS THIS HORRIBLE "PINEAPPLE EXPRESS" going to end? Charlie asked himself as he ran into the county's primary EOC in Bartlett. There was a straight deluge coming down, as if someone had set off a firehose that covered half the state. His feet, socks, boots, and pants were soaked as he stepped into the building. The bulletproof glass door closed behind him, drowning out the sound of generators and rain.

Charlie had driven through not one but two check points to get into the parking lot. "Someone stole some of Peterson's squad cars," the second gate's guardsman had told him. *Some? Well, that sucks,* Charlie realized. *Now the criminals will be disguised.*

He'd been sent down by the Sylvan precinct watch commander

to represent the central county branch of the sheriff's department. Every police agency in the county had sent several representatives to this meeting, including the Navy bases and Tribal departments. There were also military officers attending. Not just the National Guard but Navy and Marine officers, too. *Something's going on...*

The entry into the big center was steamy from all the peace officers filing into it. There was an abundance of wet wool clothing, rain coats, and body heat, which made the foyer feel muggy. He recognized many of them, even the ones from other departments. Everyone was giving each other the standard *what's up* eyebrow raise. The women and men filed into a crowded conference room. *Even more humid in here,* Charlie complained in his own mind. *No ventilation.*

The room was abuzz with a few dozen conversations. Charlie scanned around himself, listening. Some people were just catching up, but most were either telling war stories from the last two-and-a-half weeks or theorizing about why they were there. Charlie had a feeling that it had to do with the escalating violence and the plan to deal with it. There had been both documented and rumored shoot outs happening all over, including one out in the west end of the county—his zone—just the evening before. The radio chatter was particularly guarded about whatever had happened. He made a stop out at the range earlier in the morning, but other than mud and dirt askew he found nothing out of place. *Mud and brush were askew everywhere,* he'd told himself. *If anything happened here it was cleaned up.* The only thing more out of place was Phil's icy-cold reception and one- and two-word answers—"Nope." "No." "Sure." "Will do." "Nothing."

There had been an escalating turf war in the eastern neighborhoods of Bartlett that had resulted in a free-for-all shootout between two gangs the night before, too. Charlie had heard there had been several members from both groups—Hispanic cartels and white bikers—killed or wounded. He figured they'd hear more in a bit.

"Team, we are going to get started," said Sandy McCallister in her slight, Southern Californian drawl. "We'll start with an update from the Shipyard's Public Information Officer, Lt. Commander Hutchins." A mid-thirties male officer in green camouflage came up to the podium.

"Good morning. The Shipyard Commanding Officer would like to update everyone on the issues we've been contending with, particularly because of the level of activity outside our fences for the last several days. We understand that the community has a certain... disappointment...in the misunderstanding of the mission to resupply ourselves. Several days ago, we were able to successfully contain an emergent condition with the refueling operation that was in process on a submarine when the disasters struck." This caused a murmur that forced him to pause.

"What does that mean?" he heard a voice from the audience say.

"It means that you can disregard rumors you've been hearing regarding nuclear power. Things like 'melt down' and 'radioactive cloud' are vastly blown out of proportion. We've been continuously conducting testing and sampling of the shipyard and the community to ensure that everyone is safe." There was a low skeptical hum coming from the police, politicians, and community leaders packed into the room. "Let me put it into terms you'll understand. Reactors that aren't operational don't melt down. Reactors being refueled aren't operational." He was obviously a bit on edge.

"Last night the Navy base's power generating station ran out of coal, which was our back-up fuel. We've been operating on coal because the natural gas lines feeding the region were broken during the events. We're now operating exclusively on emergency generators just like all of you. Our biggest issue is that the dry-dock pumps have stopped working, which allowed the dry-docks to flood overnight.

"We met a critical deadline on the USS Halsey in Dry-dock F." He paused for a minute to stare at his notes. The room could tell he was delaying to hold back some emotion. His voice gave the slightest of cracks as he continued. "Both operations have resulted in casualties." An audible gasp could be heard from several of the audience. "Nine people gave their lives to the community and the nation in service to the Navy. We also have identified several casualties from structural and crane collapses on the day of the events. The ship-yard has tried every method at its disposal to notify next of kin, but we need your help. A list of names and home addresses will be posted in the foyer. Copies are limited due to the power issues. I will not be taking questions. Thank you."

With that, the officer left the podium and the room. Charlie could tell the man was upset about having to make the announce-ment. He watched Director McCallister step back up to the front. She introduced a pair of other officers, who explained the combined Navy-Marine mission to extract national assets from the Bogdon Submarine Base. They explained that most of the task force had departed, leaving behind two supply ships and two destroyers, as well as a few of the amphibious ships and one littoral combat ship. The operation would take months or years and would surge in size as needed. A battalion of Marines was being left to beef up the security. It was made clear to the community that their sole mission was to protect their base and assets at any cost.

Director McCallister and several police leaders—including Charlie's own sheriff—then gave a detailed brief regarding the esca-lating violence across the whole peninsula. There was still no posi-tive word from the feds on when they would be able to ship in assistance. It seemed that the state's infrastructural damage was far worse than anyone had guessed, and the economic impact caused by the loss of electricity and cyber-capability had affected the country more deeply than anyone had thought possible.

They were indeed updated on the shooting incidents. They not only learned about the shootout in Bartlett, but also about several incidents throughout the county that had been chalked up to less organized crime—theft, revenge, and grudge murders.

Charlie noted that the thing the Director most worried about wasn't the violent hungry populace or the rising criminal enterprises

—it was the banding of people together to provide for themselves. He had been trying to stay awake and passively been listening for the half-hour that they'd rambled on, but their conclusion had snapped him out of it.

"... last thought to ponder," Director McCallister said. "The people will never be able to provide critical services for themselves. A few will, of course, but not on the scale needed. The people *need* *us*. They *don't need* a few vigilante groups running around with guns taking the law into their own hands. Their *perceived* Constitutional rights don't *trump* your *actual* right to be safe doing your jobs. That is all."

The room broke up and took its time filing out into the foyer as officers and Guardsmen stopped to check the list. Some of them made notes in their pads. Several minutes later Charlie was running his finger down it, not expecting to find what he found. He read it again. And again. "Walker, Crane, 6002 Doug Fir Dr., Bartlett, Emergency POC: Walker, Phillip."

STU AND CARMEN strode into the entry driveway at the Chapel Hill Presbyterian Church near the city of Gig Harbor. They'd been following the crowd, literally. They were both decked out in hunter-camo, waterproof rain gear, and durable, name-brand clothing. The homeowner's feet were bigger than Stu's, so he still contended with the rubbing issue, but calluses were starting to build. Sometimes the rubbing didn't hurt. They were also both sporting waterproof back-packs stuffed with camping equipment and canned goods. Stu hadn't felt a tinge of guilt about taking the stuff. *It can rain as hard as it wants as long as I have this hooded coat.*

Stu had even strapped on one of the former owner's hunting knives, a full-tang survival knife with leather scabbard. He didn't attach the leg-strap but rather, he had the rain pants pulled up between the scabbard and his pants for easier access. Carmen was armed, too, carrying a Ruger pistol chambered in .22 LR. She had remembered enough about pistol day at Navy bootcamp to know how to load the magazines, work the safety, and rack the slide.

They made their way past the church building to the large parking lot to the south. The heavy rain was pounding on the tents and canopies mercilessly. One of the enclosed canopies sounded horrible, as there were several people coughing relentlessly inside it. *Must be a quarantine of some sort...*

It's true, Stu thought in disbelief as he saw the big bus. There was a crowd of people braving the rain. They walked up to someone near the back of the pack. "Does this go north?"

"Not sure," said the woman. "I hear they run a few to Tacoma and a few to Bartlett every day."

"Where do they get the fuel?"

"Who cares?"

You're no help. Stu wandered forward until he found a sign to read near the front of the crowd. "Bartlett: 10:30, 2:30, 6:30, no fee," he read on one of them. *Courtesy of Mar de Paz Services,* he read at the bottom. *Peaceful Sea?* he asked himself, dusting off the junior high Spanish in his mind.

"We may get you to your ship, yet," he told Carmen. Her eyes were near-dead, but Stu thought he could see a small amount of life in them somewhere.

THE RAIN and softened ground were bittersweet. While it made digging the holes easy, the old Kubota was slipping around quite a bit, losing traction in the muck. *Can't afford the wasted diesel,* Phil thought as he finished pushing dirt back into the mass grave. He knew they'd all crossed a metaphorical line the night before. The old days were gone. *"Shoot and shovel" is how you handle these investigations now...*

The night of and morning after the attack had been a flurry of activity. They moved bodies and picked up the brass, letting the heavy rain wash away the blood. Despite the forewarning of a gun grab, some of the range members were making small waves about the clean-up. *They're not ready to face reality,* Phil worried. *That's the thing —it's still reality even if most of you don't recognize it. The truth doesn't care about your feelings.*

He'd afforded the bulk of the range members a partial truth— burying the attackers was the proper and humane thing to do. *Law enforcement is overtaxed,* he told them. *The coroner's office is shut down. We'll tell the authorities when things are normal again.* None of that was false, but he was trying to find a way to keep the sheriff's office from knowing about the shootout. Phil knew that his best defense regarding how this was handled was "sin of omission"—not lying but also not telling all the details. All personal items found on the attackers were being kept in one of Phil's personal ammo lockers in a conex box. As far as he was concerned, they were gone from the face of the earth. *We will have a much bigger problem if the National Guard comes out here, which will happen when the truth gets out. Not If, but When…*

He had just covered the mass grave which contained the bodies of six men and a woman, along with their firearms and all spent ammunition casings that could be found. He shouldn't have been surprised when two of the attackers turned out to be Harry and his girlfriend. He had no idea how they were connected to the kid from the range break in, and he didn't care.

He was up in the big field at the top of the hill, just a scant hundred or so meters from the closest of the temporary green- houses. He drove the tractor over the earth a few times to pack it, careful not to refill the nearby solo grave that they would all be standing around in a few hours. He was extremely angry, not having yet brought himself to full emotion over the loss of Fred O'Conner. He felt horribly for Phyllis, who had not come out of their little travel trailer to face the world just yet. *I wonder if I should dig a few more of these…*

As he was turning his head to back up, his eyes caught Jerry standing at the door to his Command Post canopy at the far end of the four-hundred-meter-long field. He was swinging his arms wildly, trying to get Phil's attention. Phil shut down the tractor and looked at his cell phone. There was a text waiting from Jerry, telling Phil to come over and keep quiet about it. Phil slowly controlled his descent off the orange machine and made the muddy hike over to Jerry, stepping into the tent.

"What can I do for you, bud?" The rain was pounding loudly on the canopy.

"I thought you should hear the update on the ships up north. Most of them left last night. There's maybe six or seven still out in the Hood Canal, some anchored and some moving around."

"Okay. Why do I get the feeling you have more?" Phil could tell that Jerry was perplexed about something.

"I do. Might mean nothing, but it's just…weird. My contact way up at the north end said he saw a cruise ship."

"A cru…really?" Phil said, not even finishing his rhetorical question. "Like—one of those giant ones, with water-slides and stuff?"

"No. A smaller one. Older. He said it looked like it had been parked somewhere for the last ten years and they just decided to start using it again. But definitely a cruise ship. White. Lots of portholes. No military features at all."

"Hmmm. Okay. There's no such thing as bad intel, I guess. Thanks, Jerry."

Just then, the little range radios chirped up. "Phil, need you at the office!" It sounded serious.

"Okay, Alice, I'll be there in a few. What's up?"

"It's Charlie."

*Twice in one morning. He knows something. Here we go…*Suddenly Fred's funeral wasn't the foremost thing on Phil's mind. He took ten minutes to walk down. They had all been walking to save fuel, anyway, only using the gator in emergencies. He saw Charlie's squad car when he got to the parking lot. *Just one car…maybe he just wants to probe some first…*

When he stepped inside the office, Charlie turned to face him. He had a look on his face that Phil hadn't seen since the day he was cinching a tourniquet just below Phil's left knee. *Oh, no! Something's happened to Mel...or the kids.* "Brother. What is it?" There were some things grudges could be put on hold for.

"I was at a meeting this morning..." Charlie was at a loss, his face starting to crinkle. He just slowly shook his head. It started to hang as he looked at his feet, searching for words. "It's Crane."

What the Hell does that mean? "What do you mean?" Charlie just stood there, eyes glassing over with tears. "Say it, Charlie. What are you talking about?!"

Alice had gasped and forgotten to exhale, hands over her mouth. She started to cry. She knew.

Charlie still couldn't find the words. All he could do was stammer. He started to cry. Phil felt his head get hot, blood pumping into his ears at full volume. "No." He shook his head. Charlie moved over to him. "No." The tears started flowing as he shook his head. Charlie pulled his friend in for a bear hug, wrapping his hand around the back of Phil's head. "No!"

Phil was trapped—not from the big deputy's grip—but from life and death. There was no escaping the moment. He had finally found his breaking point. Not with Caroline's slow painful death, or the rehab from losing a limb. Not from the world shaking itself sideways, nor with the near-loss of his granddaughter, or last night's loss of a dear friend. Then...at that moment...he had found his personal definition of Hell.

"My boyyyy!" he cried through the grief, remembering the tension the last time his son had visited. He screamed with rage and raw emotion into Charlie's shoulder.

30

"But as for me, afflicted and in pain—may your salvation, God,
protect me."
Psalms 69:29

Tahoma's Hammer + 16 Days.

It had taken most of the day to initiate the operation to recover
the bodies from the dry-dock. Marie was still standing out there. She
had taken the required time to go get onto secure video-calls and
inform the various admirals and generals of their success. *Success.
What a word, just like "mission accomplished,"* she thought. She was a
professional. She knew that in the great scheme of defending America, being prepared to deal with ordering people to their deaths
came with the job. It just wasn't something that officers in her
particular career path normally dealt with. But they were at war,
and she knew it. There may not have been a foreign navy bearing

down on the nation's shores—yet—but they had to be ready for anything. And they didn't have much time to get there.

Other than those duties and a nap in the duty officer's truck, she had been out there—guarding the dock with her presence. *I owe them that.* Once the seawater had reached the point of covering certain intake valves, the ship's crew started the reactor. This was a several hour process, and there was a period of tidal swings in which they needed to stabilize the floating vessel as it went up and down. Her staff had informed her they were finally able to allow others to enter the dock. She had thought about going on the small boat herself but realized that she would be a detriment. *Let the professionals do their jobs.*

They had found Billy and Tracy easily enough, their bodies near the surface. The diver-riggers had to swim for a while to find Crane, though. They finally did. He was wedged under the scaffold that had been supporting the shafting work. One of the shipyard's cranes had lowered a large metal box into the dock. It was white and had folding doors on the end. The divers opened the doors and signaled the operator to lower the bucket about a half-foot into the water. They gingerly slid the three shipwrights into the box and closed the doors. Up on the pier the rigger in charge of the crane signaled the operator to bring the hook up. She eventually added the "boom-over" signal to swing the temporary sarcophagus over to the topside.

Once the four-foot by eight-foot box was sitting on the ground, a procession of shipyard workers and sailors formed up a pair of columns leading up to the doors of the box. Two riggers entered the box. One at a time they secured their fallen comrades onto a body board provided by the shipyard's fire department. Each board was passed out through a tunnel of salutes from sailors and hardhats held over hearts by the yardbirds. As the board approached each person, they would gingerly take their turn handing it down the line. People had been flocking from around the shipyard and base to get into the columns. The tunnel ended at the far end of the dock, their bodies passing the entire 1,092-foot length of the war fighting vessel they'd sacrificed themselves to save. Over 1,200 people helped pass the trio, most of them sniffling and crying as they did.

The shipwrights were placed into the back of a newer box-truck. An escort of police and fire vehicles led and trailed the box-truck across the shipyard with lights flashing and sirens off. Marie, in the Duty Officer's truck, led the procession up to the shipyard's infirmary, where the deceased would be cleaned before being transported to join the others in the new cemetery. The severe power constraints forced Marie to make the decision to bury them instead of holding them for family.

She had decided that the lawn of the EOC building on the hill was an appropriate spot. The symbolism was thick. The cemetery would serve future generations using the first three floors for training and career development. It would remind them that those before them had set the bar high. It would serve the fourth floor as a reminder to always be ready to save lives even if it meant demanding the impossible. Once cleaned, the three shipwrights joined the six people who'd sacrificed themselves to cap the El Paso's reactor, as well as those who had been killed during the hammer's initial awakening.

TAHOMA'S HAMMER + 17 Days.

CARMEN AND STU weaved their way in and out of screaming protesters. There were between three and five hundred, Carmen estimated. They'd managed to catch that day's first bus to Bartlett, having gotten into the line too late the day before. It was odd to Carmen, because the bus travelled with an armed escort vehicle trailing behind it. The silver coach had dropped them off at the regional transit depot just a few blocks from the gate she needed to go through. *I need to dump the gun,* she'd realized when they stepped off the bus. She handed it to Stu as soon as she found a spot off the sidewalk to step into.

Barely ten minutes later they were trying to blend in with the protesters without actually protesting. Carmen had her military identification firmly in the grasp of her hand, which was buried into her coat pocket.

There was a line of camouflaged personnel in tactical gear with rifles slung around their torsos. They had formed a human shield behind some wooden barricades, way out near the main intersection. Between them and the actual gate were two different vehicle trap/barricades. One was the hydraulic kind, installed back at the beginning of the "War on Terror." The other was a temporary set up. It was constructed out of water-filled plastic barriers.

As they neared the front edge of the yelling protesters, she could see that these weren't base-police or sailors. *Marines...where'd they come from?* She turned to face Stu, quietly. They just traded looks for a bit, both of them letting the corners of their mouths curl up a bit. The silence had become normal. Carmen didn't speak unless absolutely necessary anymore.

"Good luck, Carmen," Stu said. "I'll...I failed you. I'm sorry. If I could go back in time and change things...change how I treated you...and others..." He was at a loss for words. "I'll never forget you."

He started to turn around when Carmen reached out and grabbed him around the neck, pulling herself in for a hug. Neither of them was crying, but it was truly a heart-felt moment.

She pulled a piece of paper out of her pocket and put it into his. He looked perplexed. "In case email or snail-mail gets up and running," she explained. She waited for a moment, searching for the right thing to say. "You would've made a terrible dad, Stuart," she said smiling slightly and causing him to chuckle. "But you're still the closest thing I've ever had to one. You didn't fail... Neither of us would be here without the other."

She gave him one more hug and then let go, turning around to push through the front row. As she did, she pulled out her ID card, which prompted a Marine to break ranks and reach over the barrier. He scrutinized both sides closely and then he let her pass through to head towards the main choke point.

Doctor Stuart Schwartz watched his only friend walk away until she disappeared into the next line of people. He'd decided he wanted to find a boat to get him across Hood Canal. He wasn't sure if the floating bridge was intact. He tightened his shoulder straps and rain hood and started trying to find a route northwest out of town.

"WELCOME, MAJOR. COME ON IN!" Sandy was using her charms on Major Matsumoto. She knew they both thought the other was an idiot, and she didn't care. "Have a seat, Adam."

"I'm good, Director. I can't stay long." He refused to play along when he could. "What's on your mind?"

"The safety of you and your men, Adam...I need to know what you're prepared to do about it."

TAHOMA'S HAMMER + 18 Days.

STUART HAD CAMPED outside of Bartlett the night before, somewhere in the woods west of Trout Lake. He'd attempted to find a route through the woods to the west, but when he got to the peak of a hill all he saw were a lot more hills. *Farther than I realized.* He opted to take the main thoroughfare to the north, which eventually forced him to walk up a winding and steep road. *At least the onslaught of rain has broken some,* he thought, appreciating the light blue poking through the clouds in some places. *Canal Vista highway...must be on the right path.*

He'd spent close to two hours slowly hiking up the hilly road, never once being passed by a vehicle. He'd seen a few other pedestrians, but people were learning to keep a wary eye on one another when travelling. He finally crested the hill and made his way through a few soft curves, passing the occasional boarded up or abandoned house. The sun finally burnt through the clouds, turning the day beautiful in the low angled fall sun of the northwest. He rounded a curve and saw a good flat straightaway probably a mile or so long.

As he travelled it, the only breaks in the shoulder were a couple of driveways. Then he saw a large, wood business sign—*West Sound Sportsmen's Club, Est. 1911*. Next to it was an American Flag in an angled holder. As he approached, he saw a stack of sandbags with a tarp suspended over them. To its left was a metal gate with more sandbags stacked up behind it, leading toward some trailers and a proper flagpole. To the right was another gate that led down a road into the property itself. He stopped and stared for a bit, finally seeing movement under the slight gap between the tarp and the outer sandbag stack. *I bet these guys could teach me how to use this gun...*

"State your business," he heard a deep and loud voice command him.

"Just passing by. Looking for a place to rest and plan my way north." He could sense these people were serious. "I'm alone." He had a vibe... almost an intuition... telling him not to worry.

"We know," he heard. "Wait one."

Stu waited for about twenty seconds before a man and woman stepped out from under the brown tarp. "Come on over," the man said. "But keep your hands visible."

Stu pushed his hands into the air slowly and walked over to the man, a very large black man who was probably in his late thirties. "Seriously," Stu said. "I'm just a guy who doesn't want any trouble. Had enough of that."

"Gotcha," the big man replied. "Name's Tony. The boss'll be along shortly. What'd you do for a livin'?"

"Well...*now*...I just try to survive," Stu joked. That elicited a small smile from Tony. "But, in the days that were, I was a surgeon. Schwartz—Stuart Schwartz. My friends call me Stu." *Friend*, he thought. He stuck his hand out, and the big man shook it.

The statement elicited a wide-eyed reaction from Tony. "Really..." he said, saying it more than asking it.

Stu could see a man with graying, light auburn hair wobble up to the gate with a slight limp. He was wearing military style clothing and had a rifle slung on his back. When he got close enough, Stu could see a mostly-white beard and dark bags around the man's eyes.

"What'cha got?" the man asked his gate-guard. He was obviously not in the mood for small talk.

"Phil, I'd like to introduce you to Stu," Tony said dramatically. "*Doctor* Stuart Schwartz."

The End.

EPILOGUE

TAHOMA'S HAMMER + 18 DAYS.

REYNALDO HERNANDEZ still couldn't believe it. Just two days earlier they'd pulled it off, and here they were doing it again. *El Jefe will surely appreciate my forward thinking,* he thought. He'd had this in the works for years. He'd first thought about it during his years in the FES—Fuerzas Especiales—Mexico's version of the naval special forces. They'd been performing counter-terror training on one of these old cruise ships for a few days.

After he was discharged, he travelled to Alang, India, to conduct research. Alang was one of the final destinations for the world's old cruise ships. Once they'd been deemed too costly to operate, the ships went there to be recycled. His new employer—who had a way of "persuading" former FES to join his ranks—had listened to Rey's proposal with keen interest.

"But how will this make me money, Reynaldo?" he kept asking.

"Jefe, I cannot promise you that it ever will. But I do know this

—it will never be a waste of money. And that is a very different thing."

This had become Reynaldo's pet project over the twelve years since that conversation. He had been given a budget and a team to help pursue the business enterprise. He'd been given the go-ahead to purchase and outfit one ship. Over the course of time, his bosses had found value in his operation time and time again. They never used it for smuggling. No…Reynaldo's ship had become much too valuable. It travelled the Costa Pacifico providing food, medicine— even doctors—to the locals. *Winning hearts and minds,* he remembered his American Special Forces trainers calling it. It had provided ten times the value in intelligence and commitment from villagers on both continents. Now it was *Flota Reynaldo*—Rey's Fleet. He had three ships—not just one.

When Tahoma's Hammer fell, Reynaldo knew this was the opportunity of a lifetime. He had been planning for something for years—anything. He always thought it would be a North Korean nuclear device orbiting over the American mid-West that would be his moment to shine. Never in his wildest dreams did he imagine that God Himself would provide the moment to pounce.

Two days earlier, his local branch of the Mendoza Cartel had secured the Alcoa refinery at gunpoint. It was just a few scant miles south of the Canadian border on the north end of Puget Sound. While it wasn't ideal to start that far away from Seattle, it worked for several reasons. Primarily, the pier had suffered no damage from the catastrophes due to its northern location. It also afforded privacy, fuel, and equipment. They had even conscripted the local workers —*liberated,* the true believer corrected himself. The evolution had gone without hitch, unloading two hundred of the cartel's most dedicated soldiers along with months' worth of weapons, drugs, and food. Rey had been preparing for this day in a way that would have made Cortez proud.

He smiled to himself as he watched *Santa Maria* being unloaded.

Pinta had left that morning, and *La Nina* was due in two days. It was time for the New World to be born.

I COULD USE YOUR HELP...

Three things.

One. *Please go leave an honest review* at your purchase platform, whether my website or Amazon or any of the other retailers. And if you truly enjoyed it, tell a friend (or six!)

Two. <u>Need the next book in this series? Or the next series?!</u> Please check out my website at authoraustinchambers.com. I direct sell most books and audiobooks there, the exceptions being any e-books that are currently enrolled in the Kindle Select program.

Three. Please consider joining my newsletter on my website. Starting May of 2023, I'll be providing a Free e-copy of <u>Tahoma's Hammer</u> to anyone that signs up for it. It is the best way for me to keep you up-to-date on my coming works, cover reveals, and what inspires me to write disaster and war thrillers. Thank you.

ABOUT THE AUTHOR

Navy veteran Austin Chambers spends his days concocting ways to drive his kids and grandkids crazy with new and untested "dad jokes." After multiple novels, he's finally getting comfortable with the thought of pursuing writing full-time. The former DOD Ship-yard manager and his family live near the Hood Canal of Western Washington and long for the day that God needs them to move somewhere warmer and drier. Until then, they garden and enjoy the few sunny days outside watching Combat Kitty kill moles and squirrels.

Made in United States
Troutdale, OR
07/13/2024

21203035R00217